WELCOME TO COTTONMOUTH

PRAISE FOR *WELCOME TO COTTONMOUTH*

"Jay S. Bell has arrived with a thriller
that is firing on all cylinders!"

—JOSHUA HOOD,

bestselling author of *The Guardian*
and Robert Ludlum's Treadstone series

"A fantastically original idea executed
with the style and skill of a veteran wordsmith.
If *Welcome to Cottonmouth* isn't on your must-read list,
then you need to fix that problem right now."

—VICTOR GISCHLER,

award-winning author of *Gun Monkeys*

"The kind of thriller you dive into when you're
looking for a killer weekend read: something hardcore and
enthralling with an old-school approach to kick-assery...
Welcome To Cottonmouth is a thriller's thriller."

—THE BEST THRILLER BOOKS

"Bell spins a tale of wild imagination...His dialogue's clever,
the action's spot on, his heroes and villains are snarky
and memorable, and the author has a way with suspense
and words. It's a fun and fabulous gunfire ride,
not to be missed."

—STEVEN HARTOV,

New York Times bestselling author of *The Last of the Seven*

"In his gripping new novel featuring former spies and unresolved conflicts in a town shrouded in deadly secrets, Jay S. Bell delivers a memorable Texas twist to the espionage genre that will have readers eagerly craving more."

—JEROME PREISLER,

New York Times bestselling author

JAY S. BELL

Published in 2025 by Blackstone Publishing
Cover and book design by Sarah Riedlinger

Printed in the United States of America

First edition: 2025
ISBN 979-8-8748-8193-1
Fiction / Thrillers / Suspense

Version 1

Blackstone Publishing
31 Mistletoe Rd.
Ashland, OR 97520

www.BlackstonePublishing.com

PROLOGUE

Mahoney inhaled the yeasty smell of spilled beer, mixed with the occasional iron whiff of drying blood. Only the flutter of the cards in his hands and the fuzzy squawk from cop radios broke through the cocoon of silence he wore like a blanket.

Crimson tracks outlined his knuckles and fingernails. Though he had wiped off the blood before picking up the deck, residual stickiness made handling the cards tricky. He played it safe, running nothing but a simple shuffle.

Nothing fancy.

Nothing cute.

Cut the stack in half, fan the edges together, bridge them into one pile, tamp everything together, then do it all over again. The rhythm kept the shakes at bay and quieted the ringing in his ears. Cut-fan-bridge-tamp-repeat, the whicker of cards like the croon of a lullaby.

Broken glass glittered under neon lights, and overheads threw pools of light onto a sea of barroom debris. The jukebox had taken a couple of rounds early on, dying in a flash of sparks. Mahoney felt bad about killing the music, but worse about the vintage

Budweiser lantern. Busted chunks of plastic beer-advertising littered the middle of a coin-operated pool table, the miniature team of Clydesdales and the beer wagon they once pulled now reduced to a tangled mess. Mahoney found the dead sign more disturbing than the two cooling biker corpses, which said something about his personal issues that he preferred not to explore too deeply.

And speaking of not exploring . . . Why are the cops holding off?

Police officers stood by the doors, hands wrapped around pistol butts, glaring at him as he shuffled his playing cards.

After evacuating the club, checking the dead, and triaging the walking wounded, they had given him the hairy eyeball and backed away. The expected blue avalanche had failed to fall upon him. They appeared content to hold a perimeter, taking no further action.

This left Mahoney uneasy and off-balance.

Perhaps the shotgun and two pistols arrayed on the table in front of him had provided the boys in blue enough reason to avoid conflict. The guns weren't his, but the cops couldn't know that. All they could see was a crazy, bloody, beat-up bastard in a devastated biker bar—sitting in a playpen of broken furniture and crumpled bodies—who was shuffling cards at a table covered with weapons. Maybe the first responders were waiting for SWAT to come and drill him a new eye socket with a sniper rifle.

Mahoney snorted. *Don't kid yourself. You know what's going on here.*

For the last week he had been catching glimpses of a surveillance team—three people, minimum, changing cars and clothes, rotating ahead and behind . . . all the usual tricks. He had run a surveillance evasion route earlier that afternoon and believed he'd shaken the tail. But if they had tagged him with a drone, he never would have seen it.

Meddling federal asshats.

But what did it matter? Arrested, killed in a hail of bullets, or scorched to a cinder by a Hellfire missile, he remained, once and for always, now and forever, truly, deeply and supremely fucked.

Cut-fan-bridge-tamp-repeat.

Heavy footsteps foreshadowed a slow, ponderous approach. Mahoney's gut tightened. *Damn. I knew it.*

"Mr. Mahoney," came the dreaded gravel-crushing voice.

"Lofland." Mahoney tapped his deck into a neat rectangle. "What is it? You don't make Spy of the Month at the CIA and they send you to Shithole, USA?"

At six two and big around as a gun safe, Lofland, First-Name-Unknown, made the chair groan in protest when he sat. A government-issued bureaucrat, Lofland's dark features projected a soul-deadened weariness, as if he'd seen it all, done it all, and buried all the bodies afterward. He wore a travel-friendly suit, a white shirt, and a paisley tie that Mahoney assumed had come from a bargain bin at JCPenney about the time Ronald Reagan took the oath of office.

"I don't work for the CIA," said the man from the CIA.

"No. Of course not." Mahoney gestured with the deck. "Pinochle?"

"You made quite the mess here, Devlin. You want to tell me what happened?"

"Too much coffee. It makes me irritable."

"They say two men are dead. Six more injured. Cops aren't happy we're stepping in front of their raw meat. They want you served up on a stick, fit for roasting."

Mahoney shrugged. His hands felt steadier now, so he started doing one-handed cuts.

"It was the family, wasn't it?" said Lofland. "From the trailer park where you're staying."

"Wow. You're smart. You must be from the government."

"The dad was set to testify next week about one of these . . ." Lofland gestured vaguely to the wreck behind him. "One of these motorcycle enthusiasts. I'm guessing they took offense, but the guy wouldn't back down. Things . . . escalated."

"Escalated," Mahoney said with a snort. "Yeah. There was escalation all over the floor, the walls, the beds. Escalation dripped out the door onto the porch steps."

"You can't keep doing this."

"What? One-handed cuts? Sure, I can." The deck chose that moment to slip from his sore, shaky hand and cards spilled onto the table. "Well. Fuck."

"I have a job for you."

"I don't work for you, remember? I quit government service."

"You have a choice, Devlin—"

"A choice? That's a first . . ."

"—I can withdraw and leave you in the hands of the Graham County Sheriff's deputies, whereupon you will be handcuffed, arrested, printed, processed, and sentenced. The penalty for murder in Arizona can include death by lethal injection."

Mahoney repressed a shiver. Not at the thought of lethal injection—that didn't sound like a bad solution to his problems—but at the thought of being locked up again. Cold sweat broke out on his forehead.

"Or . . ." Lofland plowed forward with the irresistible force of a hydraulic press. "I have a job for you. Located in a beautiful slice of heaven in the piney woods of East Texas. No travel. No danger. A nice, quiet place that needs a . . . *caretaker* to watch over some . . . unique residents."

Mahoney noticed the hesitation and his instinct screamed: *It's a trap!* "I'd rather take my chances with an Arizona jury than take a job with the CIA."

Lofland quirked his lips in a brief smile. If he'd been playing poker, Mahoney would have folded and walked away. Instead, like a dummy, he sat there and waited for the river card. With the predatory gleam of a bear spotting a beached salmon, the hulking spy leaned in and said, "Zivon is there. We got him out."

Well.

Mahoney stacked his deck and tucked it in a shirt pocket.

Fuck.

PART 1

1

SIX MONTHS LATER

The glass door swung open, flashing sunlight in Mahoney's face. Backlit by afternoon sun, a halo appeared to shine through the woman's silky blond hair. Tall, with a swimmer's broad shoulders and narrow waist, she glided the short distance across the motel's strip of cracked linoleum separating the front desk from the entrance.

The woman's face was hidden in shadow until she reached the desk. She had clearly once been a classic Nordic beauty—perhaps a Miss Norway contestant with a straight, pert nose and eyes of luminous crystal. Strong cheekbones. Arched, dark eyebrows that contrasted with her pale hair.

As the backlight faded, it took all of Mahoney's self-discipline not to flinch. A red, rippled scar torqued her features from the corner of her left eye to her chin, splitting her lips into a skewed pinch that seemed to give her a permanent sneer. A Rembrandt burned with a torch could be no less shocking. A broken Ming vase repaired by a child with superglue and Scotch tape.

Motion to the side drew Mahoney's attention. It was only

then he noticed the woman's companion, a coltish, pale-skinned, dark-haired girl in that age between Barbie dolls and professional eye-rolling.

"Hello. Welcome to the Cottonmouth Motor Court."

"We would like a room," the scarred woman said. She carried a large purse of soft leather. It looked expensive. She pulled a roller bag behind her. It looked expensive, too. A backpack hung from the girl's shoulder by one strap. Quality of the backpack, unknown. "Twin beds. For me and my daughter."

The last sentence carried a tiny bit too much fake casualness. Mahoney resisted a snort of disbelief. *If this child is her natural daughter, the woman gave birth in junior high.* He swallowed his curiosity behind a professional mask.

Remember the rules, Mahoney. Don't get involved.

"Sure. I think we might have a vacancy." Which was an understatement, as only three rooms of the twenty-eight were occupied, including the one Mahoney lived in as owner-manager. "What brings you to town?"

Two kinds of people stayed at the Cottonmouth Motor Court: roughnecks and fugitives from Immigration. The road through town came from nowhere particular and went places no one wanted to go. Fair-haired Freya and her sidekick, Ilsa, were as out of place as a pair of diamond studs in a pig's ears.

"Not here by choice," the woman said. "Our car broke down. The man at the shop said this was the only place in town . . . ?" Her tone indicated she was open to better suggestions, and Mahoney didn't blame her.

"Fairly accurate," he admitted, dropping a registration card on the desk and spinning it to face her. "Fill this out, please. How long did Zee say it would take to fix your car?"

"Is that the mechanic? He didn't say. Just that it was bad."

Mahoney read the expression on her face as one of distrust.

"Zivon won't cheat you. He's not wired that way. He moves as fast as tectonic plates, but it'll be better than new when he's finished."

The woman dropped a hundred-dollar bill on top of the registration card. "We're in a huge hurry. It's urgent that we . . . get going as soon as possible." She looked back at Mahoney. "Is there a place I can buy a used car? Cheap?"

Mahoney amended his assessment. This woman wasn't merely distrustful. She was scared. Hunted. In trouble. The buzzing jangles that lived at the edges of Mahoney's perceptions tingled to life. He picked up his deck of cards from the desk and riffled through some shuffles.

"I can check around for you," he heard himself saying.

"Thank you."

The younger girl watched his hands manipulate the deck, eyes bright. A thin film of sweat broke out on his forehead. Benjamin Franklin's face studied him from the countertop. It was a new bill, crisp and clean. Vibrant green.

"What name?" He swept Ben off the desk.

"Pardon me?"

"For the registration?"

"Britte," the woman said. "Britte Thorpe."

"Okay, Britte. Devlin Mahoney, at your service." He retrieved a key with a plastic tag from under the desk. "Room twelve. Any luggage?"

"We left some things in the car."

"No problem," Mahoney heard his voice saying. "I'll go get it for you." *What the hell is wrong with you? Shut up, you moron.* The devil on his shoulder responded with, *I'm just getting her luggage. Good customer service.* The skin along his spine started to itch, followed by prickling itches up and down both legs. His fingers twitched for his cards. He repositioned the desk phone. Again.

"That would be very kind." She started to turn away, then paused and fixed him with her crystal-clear eyes. "And please, Mr. Mahoney. If anyone shows up, asking for us . . ."

"Asking for who?" Mahoney said with a bland expression.

For the first time, a ghost of a smile touched the woman's lips. The pull of her scar diminished a fraction when she smiled. "Thank you."

"Sure. No problem."

Britte Thorpe touched the girl's shoulder and they left. Mahoney watched the way the blond woman's hips moved in her jeans and electric current fired along corroded circuits. *Stay away and everything will be fine. Don't move.*

"Here," Mahoney said. "Let me get the door for you."

He rushed around the counter and made it to the door at the same time as Britte Thorpe. They engaged in an awkward shuffle-dance. Mahoney finally managed to get out of the way and point to room twelve.

"Right there, middle of the complex." He stepped out, as if to guide them further.

"Thank you," Britte said. "We can make it from here."

Mahoney retreated to the lobby and watched the pair through the glass door. He brought out his cards and riffled the deck, but oddly, as if by magic, the jangles had faded and the itching stopped.

"Just another guest," Mahoney said to himself. "Stay out of it and everything will be okay."

Britte Thorpe ground her teeth and stabbed the key into room twelve as if murdering it. What had possessed her to give up her name to a desk clerk of a scuzzy motel in a humid, mosquito-ridden town named for a *snake*, of all things? The name Stankovic knew her by.

"Have you seen a blond woman, goes by the name Britte Thorpe? Face like forty miles of bad road?"

"Oh, yes, room twelve. Right this way."

The clerk, with his quirky smile and twitchy hands, would no doubt give her up for a six-pack and a Slim Jim. She sensed no deep reservoir of strength lurking behind those off-kilter eyes, or a level of competence sufficient to resist even the smallest nudge from the kind of men that would be sent after her. All Stankovic's chief of security, Onye Dawali, would have to do is narrow his eyes and flare his nostrils and the clerk would flutter to the floor like the deck of cards he fanned about like a stage magician.

The mechanic was a different story. Zivon, the clerk called him. That mechanic had looked over her car and given her the initial assessment of "Is bad. Best to stay motel." He was built like someone who could throw the tow cable over his shoulder and drag her car into town without the truck. Slavic cheeks, crew-cut hair, and a comic-book superhero build. Britte smiled at the idea of the mechanic meeting Thomas and Kendrick. Not the two meanest bastards in Stankovic's employment, but the best trackers. If they found her car in Zivon's shop, the sheer size of the mechanic might give them pause.

Tap the brakes, sister. They're killers and Zivon is a mechanic in a backwater town. The guy will be a big, dead Russian in a heartbeat.

Britte opened the motel room door.

The room was depressing.

"Yuck," was Siobhan's assessment.

Britte agreed. Located in the middle of the U-shaped structure, the room was one of two dozen facing a central courtyard and a parking lot with a fenced-off pool. Two rows of identical red-painted, metal doors ringed the courtyard. On both levels, boxy air conditioners protruded from under curtained windows. Some of the doors bore war wounds from previous tenants—scratches and dents from either a drunken midnight barrage or police raids, she assumed. Inside, the room smelled of industrial cleaner and musty carpet.

"Hopefully we won't have to stay here long," Britte closed the door, and the room was plunged into near darkness. She switched on the light between the twin beds. "And if we're really lucky, there won't be any bugs."

Siobhan remained by the door, arms wrapped around her upper body. "What about . . . ? Do you think they can find us?"

"No, sweetie." Britte rushed to hug the girl. "I think we lost them around New Orleans. I haven't seen a sign of them in hours."

"How do you think they found us there?"

It was a good question, and one they had discussed to death over the last two hundred miles. After diving off Interstate 10, Britte had shaken the dark GMC Yukon carrying Thomas and Kendrick somewhere around Metairie. She had continued steadily westward, staying off the interstate through the bayous between New Orleans and Lafayette. From Lafayette onward, she had taken a series of random turns, driving deep into the pine forests of East Texas with one eye glued to the rearview mirror before beginning to relax and believe that, just maybe, they were clear.

But how the trackers found them in New Orleans remained a mystery. She had tossed her cell when she first grabbed Siobhan and made a run for it. Stankovic had never given the girl any kind of electronics, so they weren't being tracked by their phone's GPS. The next thing to do would be to go over every inch of their clothing and suitcases for an electronic tracking device, something she had meant to do several times, but had kept putting off.

Then the car overheated and the smell of scalding coolant and burning engine oil had invaded their air-conditioned cocoon. She brought the laboring car to a stop on the shoulder of a road she couldn't name, in the middle of a deep, murky, vine-covered forest of tall pines and twisty oaks. The air tasted faintly of skunk, and sweat broke out within seconds of exiting the car. With no phone, calling for help was not an option. Instead, they had hiked a good four miles to the decrepit town with the unlikely name of Cottonmouth City, and there found a gas station with an attached mechanic's bay called Zee Auto Works.

Siobhan switched on the motel TV and flipped through a dozen channels before settling on a laugh-track-powered sitcom. She sat on the edge of the bed. "Why would they name a town after a snake?"

"This is Texas, honey," Britte told her. "People here are strange."

"You think I could have a Coke?"

"Sure. I saw a machine by the lobby. Where the ice maker is. You need money?"

"No, I'm good."

"Okay, then. Grab it. Come right back."

"Are you scared?" Siobhan held her gaze, her expression wise beyond her years. Green eyes peered from under dark brows and midnight black hair. Not so much as a freckle marred her porcelain complexion. The child would be a stunner someday, no doubt of that. Assuming, of course, that she got away from Stankovic and never went back.

"Not a bit. We lost them, make no mistake." Britte fancied herself a master liar. After all, she'd had plenty of practice.

"Bring me a diet something, would you? Doesn't matter what. Right now, I need to pee so bad, I'm even willing to do it here."

"Turn the light on to scatter the cockroaches first." A saucy glint peeked from Siobhan's green eyes. Her grin reminded Britte so much of Ella's that it hurt. "And watch out for cottonmouths. I heard they come up through the toilet."

"That's not remotely funny, you know."

2

Mahoney approached the open bay of Zivon's garage. From under the hood of a modern sedan, mechanical things clattered and steel tools chimed. Mahoney didn't recognize the make and model of the graphite-gray car beyond something produced in this decade. His ability to distinguish vehicles fell off sharply for anything other than American heavy muscle and a few vintage sports cars with distinctive styling.

"What's the prognosis, doc?"

Zivon Zhivanevskaya peered around the open hood and regarded Mahoney with the gravity of a judge announcing a verdict.

"Head gasket." He pronounced it *het-guess-kit.* "Is blown."

"Sounds serious."

Zee retreated under the hood without responding, which Mahoney interpreted as an invitation to attend the patient more closely. Mahoney checked the bottoms of his flip-flops for any loose debris before venturing onto the silicon-coated, glossy surface of the garage floor. Vinyl mats covered both of the car's fenders, and a spotless rolling cart with gleaming tools had been pulled close to the bumper. Mahoney picked up a 14mm box end wrench from the cart and spun it around the tip of his middle finger.

"Put down tool," Zee said.

Mahoney kept twirling the wrench and leaned both elbows on the mat-covered fender. "How long?"

Zee straightened and plucked the wrench from Mahoney's finger. The tall Russian peeled off his rubber gloves and toed the foot pedal of a lidded trash bin to throw them out. "Depends on part. Eight hours delivery." He glanced at the digital clock on the wall. It read 4:20 p.m. "Thursday, fifteen hundred hours, minimum. Maybe Friday."

"Sometime day after never, then," Mahoney picked up a pair of needle-nose pliers. "What are these for? Pulling out fingernails? No? Okay so, listen up: The ladies are in a hurry. What if you cut some corners on the repair?"

Zee looked at Mahoney as if he'd suggested they have a kitten-strangling party. He retrieved his pliers and set them back where they belonged.

"Did you see that scar?" Mahoney sat himself on a padded stool with an oil-company logo.

"Of course."

"What do you think? Shrapnel? Car crash?"

"Glass bottle, maybe."

"Accident or assault?"

Zee deliberated over this question, wiping his already clean hands with a pristine pink shop towel. "Deliberate action, I would say. Is cut from here . . . to here, yes?" He ran a big finger from the corner of his eye to his lips. "Only one cut. No cosmotic surgery."

"Cosmetic," Mahoney corrected automatically, his eyes fixed on the quiet street. No traffic had passed, and none was expected. Typical Tuesday in Cottonmouth. "Now that you mention it, odd that someone with her looks wouldn't try to get that fixed."

Zee twisted his lips in a way that substituted for a shrug. "Money."

"Yeah, plastic surgery is expensive."

"Or she make point."

"What point? Beauty is superficial? 'I reject objectification.'"

"What is . . . objecti . . . ?"

"Being adored for your looks, like a piece of art, rather than a person."

"*Da*. Could be. But I don't think is so." Zivon picked up a landline phone and dialed a number from memory, speaking his thoughts as he completed the rote action. "I think is more . . . maybe defiance?" He circled his free hand in front of his face. "I see a look in her eyes. Of strength. Of 'fuck you, and your horse you ride to town, too.' Yes," he said into the phone, "this is Zivon. Please to send head gasket—make that full upper gasket kit . . . 2018 Lexus IS300. Two-point-zero. Yes. Yes. Yes. No, that is all. Expedited. Yes. Thank you." He hung up and looked at Mahoney. "Tomorrow by ten hundred hours. I ask for to rush. Nothing else happen, car ready tomorrow night. Tell them nineteen hundred, no earlier." The last was delivered with an admonishing finger.

Mahoney hopped off the stool and moved to the trunk. "That's great, Zee. Now, how do you open this thing? I need to deliver the lady's luggage."

Zivon cocked an eyebrow, the equivalent in a normal human of serious consternation.

"What?" Mahoney drummed a quick percussive solo on the trunk lid. "Don't look at me like that."

"Mahoney," Zee said as if the weight of Jupiter rested on

his shoulders. "Tell me you are not to be getting involved with this woman's trouble."

"No. What? Of course not. Look who you're talking to here."

"You know what happened when—"

"Hey, stop it, okay? This is nothing like last time, okay? Just a little extra service, man. She paid in cash, Comrade Cynic. I'm hoping for a big tip."

The sound of an approaching vehicle drew their attention to the street. A blue SUV cruised past, pausing as it came abreast of the shop. Two men in the front swiveled in their direction, taking a good, long look inside the garage. Zee and Mahoney watched the men watching them. Neither pair moved. After a moment, the vehicle cruised on. Mahoney's hand eased away from his waistband. From the corner of his eye, he noticed Zee doing the same thing.

"A Yukon," Zee said. "Nice car."

The Yukon traveled another three hundred yards before the brake lights flared again. A bad feeling crawled up Mahoney's spine, and his nerve endings started tingling with that familiar buzzing that preceded a full-blown jingling fit. He touched the cards in his pocket but didn't take them out. The sensation intensified when the Yukon's turn signal flashed and the car turned into the parking lot of the Cottonmouth Motor Court.

Mahoney sighed. "How did I know that was going to happen? Call Hannah, get her teed up for damage control. Then why don't you hop up onto the roof and cover me with one of your toys."

"Remember the rules, Devlin. Do not get involved."

Mahoney put on a hurt expression. "Zee. This is me, remember?"

"I saw Mr. Mahoney drive off in an old-timey Jeep," Siobhan said. She lay propped against her headboard, flicking through channels with the volume on low. "You think he went to get our bags? I need to get out of these nasty clothes."

Britte cracked an eye open and peered from under the crook of her elbow. She was laying on top of a patterned spread that had seen better days, like the days around when Sputnik had been launched. To her surprise, and despite the musty smell, overall she'd been satisfied with the cleanliness of the accommodations, and to her delight, the bathroom had been roach-free and generally well-maintained. *An extra half-star on the Yelp review.*

"I hope so," she said. "I need a shower and a change of clothes, too. Maybe there's a laundromat in town."

For a time, there was no sound in the room other than the faint laughs and chuckles from the TV. The air conditioner kicked on with a rattling wheeze. Britte drifted for a bit, the miles and miles of tension having taken their toll. Siobhan's voice snapped her back from the brink of sleep.

"He seemed nice."

"What? Who?"

"Mr. Mahoney," Siobhan said without looking up. "Did you see how he did those card tricks?"

"He seemed like a head case."

"But a good-looking head case, huh?"

"If you like 'em scruffy and slightly weird. I'll tell you something I didn't expect. When I opened my purse to find my lip balm, there was a hundred-dollar bill laying on top. The one I used to pay for our room. He must have slipped it back in when we were leaving. That little dance at the door. How strange is that?"

"Now that *is* strange," Siobhan said, her tone on the sly side. "I think he likes you."

Britte breathed a weak laugh that was more derisive

self-mockery than humor. Male attention was not exactly foreign to her, having been blessed with the kind of physical attributes men seemed biologically programmed to desire. Britte was not above—had not been above—using those attributes to her benefit, achieving both status and success with little effort and less sacrifice—success being defined as the material and superficial attainment of a pampered life. Since grade school, she had drifted on a cloud of approbation, sliding over, or around, the type of hurdles faced by the less fortunate. By the grace of her features, Britte had forged a cocoon of wealthy privilege. She had used her beauty like a knife, slicing out her pieces of life's cake and eating it whole, without regard for the future or the fate of others. Right up until . . .

Her fingers touched the tough ridge of scar tissue bisecting her cheek.

It served her right, this ugliness. Britte had no illusions about what kind of person she was, or what men wanted from her. In hindsight, all she'd ever purchased with her looks was space in someone else's world, beholden to a man for her life and luxuries.

And now she was marked. Broken. Branded. A disobedient pet spanked with a rolled-up newspaper and sent to the kennel without any supper.

If the desk clerk, Devlin Mahoney, desired her, it was because he thought he could get her at a discount. The once-valuable ornament known as Britte Thorpe was now cracked, her value greatly diminished. Ripe for bargain hunters. Maybe he thought a hundred dollars was his ticket to ride.

She found herself staring at the phone on the bedside table. *I should call. It's been so long. Ella must be worried sick.*

A knock at the door jerked her out of her thoughts, hard enough to pull a muscle. She exchanged wide-eyed looks with Siobhan, who sat frozen on her bed, cross-legged with the TV remote in her lap. Britte's motor control had deserted her. Muscles locked in a rigid spasm, she lay on the bed with her heart thudding an up-tempo beat. Then she remembered . . .

"The luggage!"

Britte's muscles unlocked and she slid off the bed. Siobhan managed a weak smile and ducked her head, so Britte ruffled her hair on the way past. *It won't be this way forever*, she promised silently. *One day you'll be able to hear a knock at the door and not wonder if this is it. If this is the day* he *catches up with you.*

She crossed to the door in three quick strides, threw back the lock bar, and pulled it open.

"Thank you, Mr. Mahon—"

Two men stood in the door. Her brain refused to process the reality reported by her eyes.

"Hello, Britte," Kendrick said.

"Ready to go home?" Thomas asked.

The phone at the counter rang at the exact instant Hannah Moshe was sliding into the booth opposite her husband, Asim, with her afternoon coffee. The phone ringing was rare enough, even at the peak rush during breakfast and lunch, when the diner might have as many as six paying customers. Now, at four thirty in the afternoon, well before the dinner rush, when she and Asim took their break to catch up, talk, and enjoy a cup of strong, black coffee . . . well, it had to be a telemarketer. No one they knew would be dumb enough to call at this time of day.

"Leave it," said Asim, looking up from the physics textbook laid out in front of him. "It's probably a telemarketer."

Hannah grumbled and slid out of the booth. "You know I can't."

"You and phones. Oy vey." Asim's use of Hannah's pet Yiddish expression brought a smile to her face. After eighteen years of marriage, the line between Muslim and Jew had long since given way to the bond between husband and wife.

"OK Cafe," Hannah said into the phone.

"Hannah," Zivon intoned with his typical end-of-the-world-as-we-know-it tone. "You should go to motel."

Her scalp prickled. "Why? What's he done now?"

"There is a woman . . . perhaps in trouble."

"Aw, for the love of God."

"She has a young child with her. A girl. Two men have arrived at motel in GMC Yukon. Blue. Florida plates. The woman's car has these plates. The men seemed very interested in car when droving past. Driving past, excuse me. I am to provide overwatch."

"Oh, this just keeps getting better and better."

"Da."

Hannah closed her eyes and counted to three. "Okay, Zee. I'll be right there."

Zivon acknowledged and the line clicked dead.

Hannah looked across the diner at her husband, who peered over his spectacles with raised eyebrows. His bow tie and button-down shirt looked incongruous under his stained chef's apron, but the man refused to dress in anything less formal. For a fry cook, he made a good scientist.

"Mahoney," she said.

Asim rolled his eyes. "Oh, for the love of Allah."

"I'll be back in a jiff."

I hope, she added silently.

3

Britte experienced the sensation of falling while standing still. The sight of Kendrick and Thomas standing side by side in the motel doorway, ebony and ivory statues signaling the end of her escape, sent her insides into freefall. From a distant galaxy, Siobhan squeaked in terror. Heat flushed her body and her mouth tasted like copper.

Thomas, white with brown hair buzzed into a flattop, stood with arms crossed to show off his steroidal upper arms. His cream-colored silk T-shirt bulged with muscle. Kendrick had less muscle but radiated a feral deadliness. He flashed his perfect teeth in a merciless grin.

"How . . . how . . ." Britte's words refused to come, her mind blank.

"That's funny," Thomas said. "She sounds like a lawn mower that won't start."

"How did we find you?" Kendrick asked. His wild, untamed mass of hair waffled in the breeze. He wore a tan sport coat and True Religion jeans. Gold chains hung down the V of his maroon shirt, unbuttoned to reveal a bare chest. "You were never meant to get away, is how. Surely not with the man's property. Always gonna find you, baby girl, no matter how far or fast you run."

Britte's dry throat clenched tight. She was oddly aware that this little tableau—her, Thomas, and Kendrick standing in the doorway of a shitty motel, with cool indoor air pooling out around her legs and the whine of a car's engine in the background—wouldn't last more than a second or two longer. She thought about slamming the door and throwing the bolt, but she must have given away the thought with her expression. Or maybe Kendrick was just too canny, as he pushed a foot into the threshold, barring any possible retreat.

"Sweetheart," Kendrick said in a honey-dipped voice, "What were you thinking? You know you can't take the man's property"—his eyes flicked to Siobhan—"or his talent, without there being . . . repercussions."

"Yeah," Thomas added, flexing his pecks. "Reaper-cussions."

"Shut up, Thomas," Kendrick said. "Come back easy, Britte dear. Make this hard and . . . mm-mmm. That won't be helpful at all."

The engine sound grew from a whine to a roar, and an honest-to-God vintage army Jeep squealed to a stop at the curb. The desk man, Mahoney, jumped out of the open vehicle, jogged around to the back and lifted out two suitcases. He extended the handles and rolled them onto the covered walkway.

"Room service," he announced.

Kendrick said, "Put those in our car, my man. The ladies are coming with us."

Mahoney stopped in his tracks, a perplexed look on his face. He parked the suitcases next to a support pole for the second-floor walkway. "But they just checked in," Mahoney said. He focused on Britte. "Is that true, ma'am? You'd like to leave with these gentlemen?"

Before Britte could say, "I'd rather light my underwear on fire," the desk clerk switched his attention to Kendrick. His eyes glittered and he held his head cocked a little to one side. "Sir, here at the Cottonmouth Motor Court, we take our guests' privacy very seriously. If Ms. Thorpe objects to your presence, then I have to ask you to leave."

"No, it's okay," Britte said. Misguided chivalry was about to get the desk clerk killed—Thomas or Kendrick would stomp him into paste without pulling a muscle. At least that was one act of violence that wouldn't be on her conscience. "I'll go with them."

Siobhan appeared at her elbow. The young girl's hand found hers and Britte gripped it tight. Her resolve hardened and she appealed directly to Kendrick. "Just leave Siobhan here. Say I was alone when you found me. You know what's in store for her, right? How could you wish that on anybody?"

"Not my place to say what happens. If it was up to me, we'd all go on about our business." Kendrick wagged his head, a man tasked with the impossible and given little time to do it. "Sorry, darling Britte, but everybody has to come home. Now, let's stop fooling around. It's hot, and we got a long drive coming up."

"Excuse me," Mahoney piped up. "I hate to intrude, but see, it's like this: They gave me a manual when I bought this place. *The Innkeeper's Guide to Running a Dump*. On page sixteen, Rule Eight clearly states, 'At no point shall the innkeeper allow a guest to be carried off by two thugs in an SUV against their will. Violence is authorized in these situations.' Now, please, gentlemen, don't make me resort to violence. Hannah says it's bad for me. Unbalances my chi, or something."

Had Britte's insides not been drained of life and replaced by liquid fear, she would have laughed. Mahoney stood no taller than five ten and weighed about a buck fifty. Lean and in shape, maybe, but not much more dangerous than a lamb chop in a lion's den. Thomas outweighed him by the mass of a small asteroid and, even if an aneurysm blew up in Thomas's brain right this instant and killed him dead, there was still Kendrick, who could kill a man faster than a drone strike.

Thomas cracked his knuckles. "Listen, dickface . . ."

"Dickface?" Mahoney touched his nose, as if alarmed. "Really? It's not that big, is it?"

"Enough of this bullshit." Thomas swung a fist the size of Kansas, clearly ready to swat this bug and move on with the main event.

Except Mahoney . . . swayed . . . or something, and the big man's fist met nothing but air. Then the desk clerk moved faster than Britte's eyes could follow. His body flowed, twisted, slipped, and jerked.

Thomas's head met the support pole so hard, the metal vibrated. The big man wobbled for an instant before plopping on his butt. Immediately, Mahoney was down on one knee beside him, a comforting hand patting Thomas on the back.

"Oh, dude," Mahoney said, "I'm so sorry, man. That's going to leave a mark. You should watch your footing around here. Maybe I should get rubber mats. Please don't sue me. I'll get you some ice in a towel in a minute, okay?"

"This is bullshit," Kendrick said with disgust. He reached under his coat toward the small of his back. "We're done here, motherfu—"

The Yukon's passenger side wing mirror exploded in a shower of metal and glass and bits of plastic. The sound of a rifle firing cracked the air an instant later. Britte pulled Siobhan down and shoved her out of the doorway. Kendrick made as if to run for the protection of the car's far side but another bullet exploded into the concrete inches from his feet, freezing him in place.

"I would stay put, if I were you," Mahoney said. "That's a

Spetsnaz-trained sniper who's an artist with a Dragunov." He stood and crossed to the door where Britte crouched. Gently, Mahoney eased her back from the door. "I'm sorry for this disruption of your lodging, Ms. Thorpe. Ordinarily management strives for a much more peaceful travel experience. I'll be right back. Please note that when you do your Yelp review. Wait inside."

And with that, he closed the door, blocking out a scene that Britte was still having trouble processing.

She and Siobhan shared a look. Britte was sure the girl's expression mirrored her own: dazed incomprehension.

"I can't believe it," Britte said in wonder. "Thomas, taken out by a *desk clerk.*"

Mahoney pulled the door shut on the two astonished women and turned to face the last man standing, who had remained stock still, one foot on the sidewalk, one on the parking lot tarmac. His partner was beginning to stir. Any second now he would—

"Blech!"

—vomit between his feet.

"Sorry again, Muscles," Mahoney said with sincerity. "I hate violence. I really do."

"Look, man," said the frozen guy. "I don't know what kind of game you have going on here. Got a sniper friend and some jujitsu moves, but this is not the time to be a good citizen, you hear me? What I'm saying is, the man I'm working for? You do not want to piss him off."

Mahoney waited a beat and said, "What do I call you? I'm thinking Goatee because of that marmot eating your chin. Or is that a chinchilla? I get those mixed up. So why are you here and what do you want with Ms. Thorpe and her child? Although, to be completely honest, I don't think they're related at all."

"Look, man—" The guy took a step in Mahoney's direction.

The Yukon rocked from a bullet through the rear passenger door. Goatee froze in place. A fine sheen of sweat coated his forehead. His eyes darted, trying to gauge distances and angles while not moving a muscle.

"I know what you're thinking," Mahoney said. "You're thinking you can dive to the ground, maybe roll behind the car, get the engine block between you and the sniper. But think about it. What's the endgame here? My man with the long gun? Right now he's in the zone. His heart is beating, like, once every two seconds, and his breathing is steady. He lives for this shit. He can stay up there all day, zeroed in. How long can you stay hunkered down while my guy punches holes in your car?" Muscles groaned but showed no further signs of wanting to reengage. Mahoney spared him a quick glance. "And I think your friend here has a concussion. Probably needs a hospital. Sorry, man. Really. I get carried away sometimes."

"Okay, okay," Goatee said. "What is it you want?"

"I'd like to talk about how I save your life."

"Say what?"

"All I have to do is touch my ear and—*boom!*—my sniper splatters your brains all over my parking lot. Have you ever tried to clean brains off concrete? It's really hard, since the blood soaks in and—okay, skip that. Anyway. In a few minutes, a nice little lady will show up and scream at me to shoot Muscles in the head and then . . . umm . . . you know. Zap you, too. We'll then bury you in an unmarked grave. And that's pretty much it . . . End of story . . . Finito."

Goatee's jaw hung open. "This is some crazy shit."

"Exactly," Mahoney agreed with an emphatic nod. "We're all

loonier than tunes. Crazy as glue. So here's the deal, Goatee Man: From this day forth, for the next four score and seven years, Ms. Thorpe and her . . . ward, protégé, whatever . . . are off limits. Out of bounds. Can't come out and play. You get in your GMC Yuke-thingy there and take Muscles to a doctor, please, possible concussion there, truly sorry—and go tell your boss you can't find her. And I would do that before the nice lady in the silver Toyota . . . Nissan . . . before the nice lady in the silver car shows up. She likes out-of-towners. They're good for the soil."

For a moment, Mahoney thought Goatee might make a play, the way the man's eyes shifted from Mahoney to Muscles to Zee's distant rooftop three hundred and ten meters away. Mahoney said, "Uh-uh," and made as if to touch his ear.

"Okay, okay," Goatee said. "We're gone. Come on, Thomas. Get your stupid, over-muscled ass in the car."

Mahoney held his ready stance until the GMC whale pulled out of the lot, turned right, and accelerated away. His relief didn't last long. Passing the gangsters' SUV as it drove away to the west, Hannah's silver whatsit wheeled into the motel lot. Mahoney could make out the thick mass of black hair mounded in a bun atop the Israeli woman's head.

The door opened behind him, and Britte Thorpe said, "They're gone?"

"Yes, ma'am," Mahoney said with a sigh. "But trouble ain't over. You may want to go inside for a bit longer. Hurricane Hannah has arrived, and you don't want to get caught in the storm."

"This day keeps getting stranger and stranger."

4

Britte didn't know whether to go back inside or stay put and learn what was making the motel guy so nervous. Mahoney, a ridiculous rescuer in his short-sleeved shirt and cargo shorts, flip-flops on his feet, looked like a roadie at a Jimmy Buffet concert. He produced a deck of cards from his pocket and soon had them moving in complicated cuts and shuffles.

A woman parked her car in the same spot Kendrick had just vacated. She stepped out of the vehicle and Britte goggled at seeing a middle-aged woman with threads of silver woven through her black hair, olive skin, and a waitress's apron tied around her waist. An order pad and straws in paper sleeves stuck out of the apron's pocket.

She held a pistol and wore an expression like she wanted to shoot somebody and didn't mind who took the first bullet.

The waitress saw Britte, rolled her eyes, and said, "Oy vey. No wonder," as if talking to herself.

Britte sensed Siobhan coming closer and motioned her back without turning. "Get in the bathtub, Siobhan. Lay down in it," she said, thinking the tub walls might absorb any stray rounds if bullets started flying.

"You might want to put down a towel first," Mahoney called out, then flashed Britte a look of apology. "I try to keep the tubs clean, but . . . well, better safe than sorry."

The gun-toting waitress pressed a cell phone against her cheek. "Yes, I've got it under control. You should probably get down here. Okay, thanks, Zee."

"Tell him to follow the guys," Mahoney said. "Make sure they leave town."

The woman nodded and repeated the instructions into her phone. She thumbed the screen and pocketed the phone.

"Right, then," the waitress said. "What's going on, Mahoney? In simple words, please. It's hot and my brain is already on fire out here. Who was it just drove off, and who is this shikse?"

Britte started to speak, but the woman stopped her with an upraised finger. "Him first. I'll get to you in a second."

Heat rushed into Britte's cheeks. She felt like she'd just been called down by the principal and found her mother waiting in the school office. Anger flickered then died, smothered by her fear.

"Hey, Hannah," Mahoney was saying in a bright, cheery tone. "I got it under control. Nothing to see here. Some guys were bothering my guests, so I handled it. No big deal."

"No big deal?" The woman slipped the pistol into a spare apron pocket and stalked up to the motel owner. Britte recognized the look of disappointment on the woman's face, having seen the same look many times from her mother. "Devlin, sweetie . . . Zee was shooting, wasn't he? He must have felt the deal was big enough, he needed to fire a warning shot. Huh? Or was he just target practicing on your motel?"

"Aw, you know Zee. He gets crabby if he doesn't get to shoot something. Seriously, I had it under control."

Hannah sagged, as if carrying the weight of the world. "You know the rules, Devlin."

"There is a *child* involved, Hannah," Mahoney said in the most serious tone Britte had heard from him all day. "What was I supposed to do? Let them take her?"

Hannah and the motel owner commenced a staring contest, which Mahoney apparently won. Hannah let out a long breath and said, "We should talk later, decide what to tell . . . you know who."

"Agreed." Mahoney flashed Britte a smile before turning back to Hannah. "For now, maybe you should get to know this young lady."

The woman smiled at Britte, all charm and warmth. "Let's go inside, *yekirati*, where it's cool."

Britte allowed herself to be led inside. She felt like she had walked out onto a lake of thin ice, which had begun to crack under her feet. Escaping Stankovic had been hard enough, and now she had landed herself and Siobhan in a town of snipers and gun-packing waitresses, not to mention a skinny motel desk clerk who could turn a hulk like Thomas inside out. Alice, through the looking glass, would be less confused.

The woman sat in the room's only chair and motioned for Britte to take a seat on the bed. "You can come out now, sweetie," Hannah called to the closed bathroom door. "No one's going to hurt you."

Siobhan must have been standing by the door because it opened right away, and the teenager poked her head out. When Britte gave her an all-clear nod, Siobhan came and sat next to her on the bed. Britte put an arm around the girl and pulled her close, feeling the slight tremors that coursed through her thin body. Acting brave for Siobhan's sake had helped Britte get through the past few days, and it helped now. She felt her own misgivings fade to a background-level hum.

"Okay then," the waitress said. "Let's start with basics. I'm Hannah Moshe, and I own the OK Cafe down the road. You met my friends, Devlin Mahoney and Zivon, who runs the auto shop. No one can pronounce Zee's last name, so I don't even try. What are your names?"

Somehow from the parking lot to the motel room, Hannah Moshe had morphed from an avenging angel with fiery eyes to a sweet grandmother radiating warmth as strong as the scent of baking cookies. Britte felt herself relax even further, the ice encasing her heart defrosting a few degrees.

"Britte Thorpe," she said. "And this is . . . my daughter, Siobhan."

"Oh, what a lovely name," Hannah cooed. "Are you hungry? Have you eaten? No? Oh, dear me. In a bit we'll go get some food, okay? Our cafe is called OK, not because the food is mediocre, but because ever since we moved to Texas, my husband fancies himself a cowboy. He's obsessed with the Old West. When we bought the diner, he insisted we put in all this cowboy decor and hung horseshoes and garbage on the walls—you should see it. He went crazy, I'm telling you. It looks like the Ponderosa exploded in there."

Hannah went on like that for a time, making small talk, engaging her and Siobhan in light conversation. Britte marveled at the woman's ability to put them at ease, and soon they were chatting like ladies at a tea party. After about ten minutes, she realized that the "waitress" was drawing out bits of information, including where they'd been, what roads they'd traveled, how their journey had gone . . . and then the questions became a tad more pointed.

"Okay, so," Hannah said at last. "Who were those guys and why are they chasing you?"

Britte noticed that the waitress had somehow scooted her

chair closer and was now almost knee-to-knee with her. She gazed into the woman's dark eyes and felt the need to talk swelling inside her. That pressure was blocked by . . . something. Shame, she supposed. Shame at what she had done. Shame at how she had come to this point. And fear, of course, which had been a part of her for so long, it felt like a thing living inside her, guiding her actions, coloring every decision. She wondered that she had any shame left, that it should appear now, in this tawdry motel so far from the gilded cages in which she had lived.

The fear, though—she had no need to wonder at that.

"That's not your business," she said at last. Siobhan flinched beside her, and Britte felt the girl turn to look at her. Britte refused to meet her eyes. "I . . . All I want is my car fixed so we can leave."

Hannah pursed her lips, and for a moment, Britte believed she would push it. If she did, Britte wouldn't be able to hold back—the need to spill her guts to someone, to ask for help, if not forgiveness, welled in her throat. Instead, the older woman said, "You know they're tracking you somehow, right?"

"Yes," Britte said. "The thought had occurred to me."

"We'll need to check all your clothes, your handbag, suitcases. I'll have someone check everything over. After that, we should move you to a safe place while Zee fixes your car. Are we agreed? Yes? Good. Stay here and let me go talk to the *tipesh*, Mahoney."

—

Kendrick Johnson powered the Yukon out of Cottonmouth City (and if that was a city, then he would shit in a cup and call it gold) and accelerated as the posted limit increased in increments. This being the South, Kendrick assumed the law would be twice as likely to rag on a Black man driving an expensive car, so he kept his speed a steady two miles under the legal limit. Soon, the signs of civilization, such as they were, disappeared and the road was swallowed in a tunnel of trees and vines and creepy shit. Kendrick hated the woods, hated country people, hated the country music playing on half the stations in Redneck, America, and really, really hated getting chased out of town right when the bitch and the kid were in his hands.

Fuck, that stung.

His partner, Thomas Pratt-Walker, had his seat reclined and was whining like a bitch about his head hurting.

"Serves you right, motherfucker," Kendrick told him. "You assumed Mr. Motel was easy, and he coldcocked you."

"Next time I see him," mumbled Thomas, "I'm gonna put him in the dirt."

Kendrick snorted. He had worked with Thomas for two years now, and his opinion of the man's intelligence, low to begin with, had never been given reason to improve. The bigger man had an animal cunning, and abnormally good instincts about which way a runner would bolt, or when things would go hot. Thomas's intuitive grasp of imminent danger had meant the difference between life and death more than once. Too bad his radar had been on the fritz today.

"Nobody's following," he commented.

"We need to get eyes on the motel," Thomas said. "Quick."

"Agreed."

Kendrick whipped the big SUV into a U-turn. The broken wing mirror bounced and rattled as he cut into the rough shoulder and powered the Yukon back toward town. There weren't a lot of options in the two-stoplight city, but on the way out, Kendrick had noted a side street that looked promising.

Out of sight from the motel, the secondary road led off into a neighborhood of ratty homes with yards covered in cars and kids' toys. He turned onto the street, marked with a simple sign that read CR-22, and bounced along the potholes until he found what he was looking for. Kendrick eased the Yukon into a small plot of land occupied by a wood-frame house. Once white, the abandoned home had been stripped by wind and rain and likely vandals, leaving it windowless and open to the elements. A tree growing through the foundation had sprouted limbs out through a window, and weeds were busy swallowing the rest. Kendrick rolled the Yukon around the side of the house, forcing his way through brush up to the car's bumper and praying he wouldn't run over anything sharp enough to rip up a tire.

Behind the place, the remains of a shed had collapsed into a pile of bare boards and rusted tin. Kendrick caught a flash of brown as an animal of some kind zipped into the maze of gray debris.

He braked to a halt and threw the shifter into Park.

"Okay, Thomas, the motel is about a mile thataway," Kendrick said, pointing east. "Get yourself on over there and find a way to get eyes on."

"Why me? Why don't you go?"

"If these rednecks see me ambling across their yard, they're liable to shoot my Black ass. I won't even get close before someone sics the law on me. You're just another white boy, got a boo-boo on his head and lost his way. And I got to call the boss. You rather do that instead?"

"Stankovic or Dawali?"

"Dawali, dipshit. Do I look stupid enough to call Stank direct?"

The big man groaned but opened his door and got out without further comment.

Kendrick tapped a contact using the car's Bluetooth connection.

"Dawali," said the voice on the car's speakers.

In short phrases, devoid of emotion, Kendrick briefed the head of Stankovic's security force of the situation in Cottonmouth City. He ended with, "Thomas is getting his ass on back there. I expect to have eyes on the motel in a few minutes."

A long moment of silence followed, then Dawali spoke in his clipped, precise English. "We must assume the tracking device is compromised."

"I don't know how—"

"Because you have arrived at their exact location twice now. Do not underestimate Thorpe. Despite her recent position in the household, she is quite intelligent, and obviously resourceful. She will have to conclude there is a tracking device on her person and take steps to find it or leave everything behind. If not, all the better for us. However, we cannot take that chance." Dawali paused and Kendrick remained silent. "This situation with the sniper and the other man . . . it is very unusual, and this makes me uncomfortable. We have access to some contractors in Houston, though it will take up to four hours to arrange backup. It is imperative you not lose contact with Thorpe and the girl. If you lose surveillance, it will be bad. You must obtain a different vehicle. Will this be a problem?"

"Finding a car? No," said Kendrick, thinking of the broke-ass places he had passed, yards filled with vehicles of every description. "They know our faces now, so a close tail could be tricky. But we'll handle it, one way or another."

"I will be in contact once I have an ETA on your backup."

The line went dead before Kendrick could acknowledge, though that wasn't a surprise. Dawali wasted little time on niceties like hello and goodbye. He was the most focused hard-ass Kendrick had ever known, and truthfully was the one man in the world who scared him more than cancer. No, correction.

Second man. Dawali's go-to executioner, Bridges, made Kendrick's stomach go cold every time he saw the zombie-eyed giant.

As the saying went, failure was not an option.

They had to retrieve the man's property or keep running until they fell off the edge of the earth.

5

Mahoney was practicing stacking a royal flush with his marked deck when Hannah and Zee entered the lobby, one right after the other. He dealt three hands of draw poker, face up: two pair, sixes and sevens; a full boat, eights over threes; and his hand—the ace, king, queen, jack of spades . . . and the nine of diamonds. *Well, shit.*

"Maybe you should stick to gin rummy," Hannah said. "Or maybe Go Fish. A kid's game, ya'know?"

"Is there an implied rebuke there, Hannah?"

"Not so implied. More like 'What the fuck were you thinking?'"

"I tried to follow, but too late. They are gone." Zee hulked over Hannah's shoulder like her own personal Terminator. "Why no kill them? Solve problem."

"I ran out of bullets murdering the last batch of tourists who came through," Mahoney said. He gathered the cards and tapped them back into shape.

"Devlin, my little *mensch*," Hannah said with concern crinkling the corners of her eyes. "That woman spells nothing but trouble for us. We don't know who she is, where she came from, or the type of people who are after her."

"The plates are Florida," Zee said. "Also, on Yukon."

Mahoney switched to his deck of plastic-coated throwing cards.

"You know the rules about drawing attention to us," Hannah said.

Mahoney snapped a throw and the card bounced off the dart board seven feet away. "Shit. Hey, Hannah, put a pin in that, okay? What was I supposed to do, with a kid involved? Huh? Tell me." Hannah and Asim had never been able to have children and kids were her soft spot. Mahoney knew he was playing dirty by invoking the child, but he'd taken all the crap he felt like taking about The Rules. The bells started ringing, deep in the corner of his mind, a sure precursor to a full-on buzzing, nerve-jangling cacophony. Mahoney clamped down and willed them to silence.

"Okay. All right," Hannah acknowledged. "You have a solid point, Devlin. I'll give you that."

Hannah laid a hand on Zee's shoulder. "Go fix the lady's car, please. And go over it with a fine-tooth comb for any tracking devices. Sooner is better. Thanks, love." She turned to Mahoney. "We need to move them. This place will be ground zero if the Bobby Twins come back."

"Bobbsey Twins." Mahoney zipped another throwing card. This one stuck for a second, then fell. "And you are correct. I'll reach out to Hans. He has that place he calls a hunting cabin back in the woods—you remember, we all went there, last Committee meeting? In the meantime, you call Chan. Get him over here so he can run his thingie over the woman's stuff. Wait, that didn't come out right."

He cocked and fired another card. Another bouncer.

"This has the potential to be a big mess, Devlin," Hannah told him. "You should call Lofland."

"Um . . . no thanks, Mom," Mahoney responded. A third throwing card spun, missing the board completely, though it did stick in the drywall. *Small victories.*

Hannah glared poison darts at him. She took Zee by the elbow and said, "Come on. Let's get to work before I shoot this one in the face."

Mahoney tried one more time for good measure. The throwing card stuck in the double-one slot.

Great. Snake eyes.

Kendrick prowled on foot until he found a house set off by itself. A two-toned, mid-seventies Ford LTD was parked in the driveway, and a mid-seventies man was parked on the unscreened porch. Both looked old but well-maintained.

"Hey, man," Kendrick called, all teeth and good fellowship, as he approached the porch.

"Hey, man, yourself," said the man, who squinted his wrinkled eyes filled with a lifetime of suspicion, no doubt related to a lifetime's worth of smiling strangers. He had a rough face with a bent nose, like he had been in more than one scrap in his life, and cheekbones ridged with scar tissue. He held a plastic glass of what looked like lemonade in one gnarled root of a hand. "You sellin' something? 'Cause if you are, I ain't buying."

"Hopin' to buy something, actually." Kendrick twitched his head in the direction of the car. He slipped into a corn pone speech pattern, hoping to put the old man at ease. "What would you and the wife think about selling off that old Ford? I'm in a serious hurry for a vehicle, and I'd make you a good offer."

"Ain't no wife to consider." The man sipped his drink and ice rattled. With a no-bullshit tone he added, "And ain't no way I'm selling off my car."

"No wife?" Kendrick put on his astonished face. "You live all by your lonesome?"

"I do."

"Well, that's too bad. And too bad about the car. Truth is . . ." Kendrick dipped his head. When he looked back up, his hand appeared from under his jacket. Holding his nine.

He shot the old man through the bridge of his bent nose.

"Truth is, I didn't have no money anyway."

Kendrick waited a beat, but it appeared no one heard the shot. Or cared about it, more likely. This was a rural community—probably every peckerwood in three hundred square miles fired off pistols once a day, just to clear dust out of the barrel. Kendrick tucked his piece away, careful of the warm slide up against his back. He stood there a moment longer, eyeballing the old man sprawled on the porch, arms and legs laying every which way.

Damn, I should have asked him where he kept his key.

He had his hands in the dead man's pocket when his cell phone chirped with an incoming call. He cursed and dug it out.

"Speak," Kendrick said.

"I got a good spot," Thomas said. "There's a building for the Chamber of Commerce, used to be a Dairy Queen with, you know, the big window in front? Nobody's been in here Chambering or Commercing in a month of Sundays. I have a great view of the front of the motel. A little while ago, this woman came out of Britte's room—short, chubby, dark hair. Never seen her before. She goes into the office and a second later, a man the size of a redwood tree shows up and follows her into the office. He's carrying a rifle, so I'm guessing that's our sniper. Nothing else is happening right now."

"Cool," Kendrick said. "Hang loose until . . . Hold on. The other line's beeping. Oh, it's Dawali. Hold on and I'll conference you in." Kendrick tapped the appropriate keys. "Hey, boss. You're on with me and Thomas."

"Status," Dawali demanded.

"Thomas says no movement." Kendrick said. "We have a clean car for surveillance."

"Three men are en route to your location. ETA is approximately three hours."

"You really think that's necessary? I mean, we go in there hard, blow away the clerk, grab the girl—"

"No. Nonlethal force only."

"Say what?"

"Are you shitting me?" Thomas added.

"No firearms," Dawali said. "If the woman or girl are injured in any way, you will be held responsible. My advice would be to jump on the first ship headed to a far corner of the world and bury yourselves in a tomb. You have been told this before."

"Yeah, but that was before a sniper—"

"Stop talking." After a moment of silence, Dawali continued, "The extra personnel are to be used to overwhelm the opposition. I expect you to neutralize the sniper and effect the recovery of the property and the women. You will do this without firearms. Am I understood?"

Kendrick pulled a face as if he'd bitten something very nasty. He stepped off the porch, away from the slowly spreading pool of blood threatening his shoes.

"Understood?" Dawali repeated.

"Yeah, yeah," Kendrick said. "I get it."

"Sure," Thomas grunted, though he sounded anything but sure.

Dawali clicked off with typical abruptness. After a moment of silence, Thomas said, "He gone?"

"Yeah."

"No guns?" Thomas muttered. "That's bullshit."

"Agreed."

"I mean, I owe that fucking desk clerk, big time."

"I know, but you heard the man. You'll just have to take it out on Britte."

Thomas breathed hard into the phone. "Oh, hell yeah."

Mahoney knocked on the door to room twelve. When Britte opened it, Mahoney's heart double pumped at the sight of her, as powerful as seeing his prom date for the first time.

"This is Mr. Chan," Mahoney said, indicating the man standing next to him. The latter carried a small, black case and possessed the demeanor of a high school chemistry teacher. He wore a Hawaiian shirt with a loud print over a white T-shirt and polyester slacks. Sensible black shoes gleamed from his feet. "He's an expert in electronics."

Chan grinned. "Expert gives me too much credit."

"Very nice to meet you," Britte said. She stood aside and Mahoney led Chan inside. He crossed to the corner of the room, while Chan went to the bed and unzipped his case.

"Mr. Chan will inspect your stuff and find any bugs."

"Many tracking devices," Chan said, as he poked around in his bag, "are GPS-based, and send signals intermittently, such as two times per day. This helps them to conserve batteries. Unfortunately, they can only be electronically discovered while actively transmitting." He removed a device that resembled a walkie-talkie, with a longer than normal antenna. "For most detection equipment. The good news is that trackers are not as small as pictured in most movies and TV shows. Those as small as a button, for example, have a limited battery life and short range. You have no cell phones or other devices connected to the internet or cellular network, correct?"

"No, nothing." She looked at Siobhan, who shook her head.

"I even gave up my Nintendo," the girl said. She didn't sound happy about it. Siobhan spoke with a country twang common to rural people from Arkansas to West Virginia, completely different from Britte Thorpe's bland Midwestern English. The discrepancy added weight to Mahoney's working theory that they weren't related at all.

"This is a tool of my own design." Chan switched on the device and fiddled with the knobs. "Patent pending," he added with another small, tight smile. Chan swiped the device over his own bag and received a happy beep. "Good, we are calibrated. Please, Miss, allow me to examine your possessions?"

"Of course."

Chan started with the suitcases, laying unopened on one of the twin beds. He spent several minutes going over the outside of the two bigger cases, then asked permission again before unzipping them and running his device over the contents. Mahoney inspected his nails rather than peek at whatever might be inside.

The device remained silent.

When Chan reached for the third case, the one Mahoney remembered her dragging into the lobby, Britte jumped up and said, "Please don't open that."

Chan hesitated, then nodded. "No problem. Here, I will show you how to use this and you may examine the contents in private."

After some instruction, Britte took the case and the bug finder into the bathroom and closed the door. Two minutes later, she emerged and handed Chan his gizmo.

"Your handbag?" Chan asked.

Britte pointed with her chin at her purse, where it sat on the table between the beds. Chan swept his detector over the shoulder bag and the device immediately beeped. It did so again and again as he zeroed in on the base of the purse. "I believe we have discovered the source of the signal."

Mahoney slanted a look at Britte, who had gone even paler than her normal complexion, which seemed impossible.

"I've had that bag for two years," she whispered. "Milos gave it to me."

Milos? Mahoney quirked an eyebrow. *Milos who?*

"You should leave it here," is what he said aloud. "Don't let them know we found it."

Britte blinked several times. "Okay."

With sincere apologies, Chan emptied the purse and ran his scanner over the contents, getting no beeps. He scanned the bag and the device chirped. "I believe the purse itself is the culprit," he said. "May I check your persons?"

First Britte, then Siobhan, stood as if being wanded by airport security. The detector remained silent. Putting the device away, Chan pronounced them all clear.

"Okay, thanks, Chan," Mahoney said. To Britte, he added, "We need to move you somewhere your pals won't find you. You up for a little road trip?"

The blond woman visibly pulled herself together. "Can't wait."

"Okay, leave the purse. I'll throw your stuff in the Jeep and we can blow out of here."

Siobhan jumped up. "I want to ride in the back!"

"And so you shall," Mahoney agreed. "Extra bouncing has been approved."

"Where are we going?" Britte asked.

"My pal has a hunting cabin in the woods. It's private, clean, and well-stocked with everything a pair of desperadoes need for a little R and R while their car is being fixed. Trust me, once we lose the tracker, those guys will never find you."

Britte looked a bit dubious at his assurance, and Mahoney couldn't really blame her. His appearance wouldn't inspire confidence that he could manage delivering a pizza, let alone an escape from a pair of tough-looking bastards like Goatee and Muscles. But that was okay with Mahoney. Trust was earned by deeds and results, not appearances and words.

"Oh, I almost forgot," Mahoney said to Siobhan. "I think there's even an Xbox hooked up to a big screen."

The look of wonder on the girl's face was priceless.

—

"You call this a cabin in the woods?" Britte couldn't have been more stunned had she found an emerald in her morning cereal. The massive house set among the tall pines resembled an Aspen ski lodge, featuring picture windows and a grand entrance of rough-hewn stone and redwood timbers overlooking a driveway large enough to accommodate a marching band. The grounds were covered in a carpet of pine needles. Birds dodged and danced through the trees.

"Look!" Siobhan seized Britte's shoulder from behind and breathlessly pointed to her right. A pair of deer watched them from the forest.

Mahoney shut off the Jeep. A soft breeze caressed Britte's cheek as the last light of day seeped from the sky. Silence crept in, soothing her nerves.

"Wait until you see the inside," Mahoney promised. "Hans doesn't really have a solid grasp of the whole 'cabin in the woods' concept."

Mahoney's assessment proved correct.

The cabin interior would satisfy the taste of any Condé Nast editor or new money dilettante. Mahoney opened the door and bowed her in before him with a maître d' flourish. Britte stepped into a living room as large as a basketball court, with sofas and armchairs in plush, white leather. Side tables and an adjoining dining room glittered under track lighting. Sculptures occupied every surface, and brilliantly colored art hung from the walls, spotlighted with individual fixtures.

Mahoney stood at her shoulder as she stood gaping from the entrance. "Pretty cool, huh?"

"It looks like a modernist's wet dream."

"Wait until you see the kitchen."

Britte followed Mahoney, only half-listening to his tour of the cabin, her brain fogged with a through-the-looking-glass sense of unreality. That this oasis of luxury should appear less than an hour after being cornered in a dumpy motel by Thomas and Kendrick, as though delivered by an act of a kind and benevolent god, struck Britte as suspicious. Kind gods did not exist, and acts of benevolence came with a hefty price tag. Always. There was no such thing as a free lunch—a phrase she had not understood until recently, when that particular lesson had been stamped into her face. For a moment she wondered if this whole setup was one of Milos's pranks, with everyone from Mahoney to the mysterious sniper playing a part in an elaborate production. Britte snorted at her own paranoia. No, Milos would have no need to go to these lengths to send a message.

But the doubt at her good fortune remained very much alive in her heart.

When Mahoney pointed to a hallway leading off the main room and said, "You can have the master bedroom," that kernel of suspicion flared white-hot. How long before the scruffy motel man made his move?

Oh, by the way, there's only one bed. Guess we'll have to share.

Britte suppressed a smirk. Was that the price tag for her salvation? It wouldn't be the first time she had received an offer of help that came at a cost.

She caught a glimpse of Siobhan through the living room windows as the girl stalked toward the ambling deer. The animals seemed in no hurry to leave, though they kept their distance from the teenager, moving a few steps away every time Siobhan got too close. Britte dismissed Mahoney from her mind and crossed to the open door.

"It's getting dark, sweetie," she called out. "Time to come inside."

Siobhan obeyed with an uncharacteristic sulky frown, leaving the deer and returning to the house with the trudging step of the damned. World-wise beyond her years, the girl understood her fate should she fall back into the hands of Milos Stankovic. She rarely pushed back against anything Britte asked of her or showed signs of becoming rebellious or unruly. The hours of constant danger had obviously worn down her reserve of good cheer. Britte couldn't blame her a bit—she herself felt ready to crumple with exhaustion.

Mahoney's voice drifted from the kitchen, slicing through her brain fog. "Hey, anybody hungry? I brought stuff to make spaghetti and meatballs."

Siobhan's eyes popped wide. "Yes!"

The girl laughed out loud when Britte's stomach growled like an angry lion.

6

Four hours.

It had been four hours and Mahoney had yet to feel a trace of the jangles. A four-hour break was relief akin to a sudden and complete cessation of itching for someone afflicted with a poison ivy. That buzzing, twitching, nervous tingle, which often started as the sound of bells ringing at the edge of his hearing and would soon be followed by the sensation of mice skittering across his skin. It could broil up to a full-body dyskinesia, akin to an acute attack of Parkinson's if he couldn't escape the triggering event or soothe himself with his cards.

The jangles were often triggered by any personal interaction with other humans, where Mahoney had to behave in a relatively normal manner for any length of time. The time required for a standard motel check-in was about the limit of his ability before the first tinkling sound announced the start of the race.

Hi-how-are-you-how-many-keys-would-you-like?

Mahoney called it the Hilton Line, and he listened for those bells with the diligence of a sentry on duty at a nuclear missile base.

Avoidance was his preferred treatment. No prolonged conversations. No small talk. Online shopping wherever possible. Email. Email was great. In situations where he couldn't extricate himself from a conversation—like when a guest showed up in the lobby and wouldn't leave without discussing the minutia of travel aches and pains, weather, and whatever the hell the current president was up to—then Mahoney resorted to his ever-present deck of Bicycle playing cards. Shuffling, bridging, stacking, floating, and cutting those rectangular bits of pasteboard kept him from losing his shit on a daily basis.

Maintaining a Shit-Not-Lost status was much desired by the Committee, claims adjusters, and coroners.

Somehow, the presence of Britte Thorpe and Siobhan Last Name Unknown had kept his nerves from going on a visit to Jangleland (located between Newark and Hell on most maps). The experience was . . . unique.

After loading up a plastic bag with the contents of Britte's purse, they had traveled to the hunting cabin together, fixed a meal together, eaten together, and cleaned up the kitchen together, and not once had the tiniest tingle rippled across Mahoney's skin. He had remained calm for four hours and counting, the clock ticking away quiet seconds and Mahoney's nerve endings resting comfortably, lulled into a Britte-induced slumber.

Amazing.

The girl was in the game room, ensconced in front of a seventy-inch TV tuned to an animated movie filled with happy music, though the last time Mahoney had checked, Siobhan's eyes were closed, and gentle snores fluttered her lips. Mahoney pulled a blanket from the spare bedroom and spread it over the sleeping girl. He experienced a rush of paternal warmth.

Mahoney sat in a chair near the big front window, pretending to flip through a celebrity gossip magazine.

Hans Schlichter—former German SKS badass, who had single-handedly drilled the foreheads of six members of an Al Qaeda bomb-building cell in Frankfurt with 9mm, 130-grain bullets, and owner of this "hunting cabin"—had a serious obsession with American television and movie actors. He could flip channels and, within eight seconds, identify the name of the movie, its director, and the lead actors. Mahoney, after eight minutes of page flipping, didn't recognize a single face.

To his right, the window reflected the room: an open space with a sofa and two chairs covered in soft, creamy leather. Chrome-and-glass coffee table. Gas fireplace with colored flames that gave off no heat but looked pretty. He was very aware of the black night stretching away on the other side of the glass, and he desperately wanted to close the drapes . . . except there were no drapes. That the glass was bullet resistant did little to ease his paranoia. He felt like a fish in a well-lit aquarium.

And yet, despite the feeling of being watched from the darkness outside . . . no jangles.

The Sig P365 digging into his hip helped as well. Nothing calmed the nerves like ten rounds of 9mm Silvertip hollow point.

Britte Thorpe huddled directly opposite him in a cream-colored armchair, sipping from a cup of steaming decaf. To this point, nothing had thawed the woman's icy shell—not Mahoney's special recipe spaghetti and meatballs, his atrophied skill at witty banter, or the hot coffee with a dollop of Irish whiskey. She watched him with the wariness of a once-beaten cat, willing to tolerate his presence as long as he kept his distance, but ready to scratch his eyes out at the first sudden move.

She spoke after a long silence. "Who are you people, exactly?"

Mahoney twitched, rattling the magazine in his hands. He had half-expected, half-dreaded the question all evening, knowing that Britte Thorpe's curiosity would get the better of her sooner or later, and knowing that to satisfy her, Mahoney would have to violate one of Lofland's prime directives: *Thou shalt not reveal the nature of Cottonmouth to an outsider.* No answer presented itself that didn't involve breaking that commandment over his knee and scattering its remains.

He put on an innocent face. "People?"

Britte narrowed her eyes in a *Don't fuck with me* look.

"Oh, you mean Hannah and Chan?"

"And the auto mechanic who doubles as a sniper and the hotel desk man who can turn a guy twice his size inside out. Thomas can . . . well, never mind. But he's strong as an ox."

"Look . . . Britte . . ." Mahoney leaned forward over his knees. He rolled the magazine into a tube and used it to tap out a quick rhythm on his palm. "Some stories aren't mine to share. And my life here is dependent upon me following certain . . . rules. But I'll cut you a deal. Let's go one for one. I'll give you one straight answer to a question—within the limit I feel comfortable—and in return, you do the same for me."

Britte shifted in her seat. Set her cup down on the side table and cleared her throat. She looked away, hiding the scarred side of her face, something Mahoney had noticed her doing all evening. "You first."

"Okay . . . umm." Mahoney gathered his thoughts. Picked his words with care. "You've heard of Sanctuary Cities, right? Places where the city decides they'll protect illegal immigrants from Immigration? Well, Cottonmouth . . . is a Sanctuary City for people of . . . a certain, um, specialized background. And that's all I can say. I promise. And that's saying more than I'm supposed to."

"You'd tell me, but you'd have to kill me?"

"Worse. Banish you to a small town in East Texas."

Mahoney's attention was drawn to the picture window. He could see nothing past his reflection.

"I really wish Hans had installed drapes," Mahoney said, half to himself.

"Excuse me?"

"Nothing, sorry." Mahoney dragged his focus away from the darkness outside. "Okay, your turn. Who are you running from?"

Britte pulled in a quick breath through her nostrils, flinching as if struck. Her head dropped, blond hair curtaining her face. She studied her nails without answering. Mahoney let the silence drag out, happy enough to give the woman her space. He kept quiet about the briefing Hannah had sent him via text. Zee had pulled the car's registration information, and Hannah ran a background check on the vehicle's owner. It was an old interrogator's trick: ask a question to which the answer was already known in order to validate the subject's honesty. He felt slightly sleazy using it here, but not enough to come clean about how much he knew.

"Milos Stankovic," Britte said at last.

"Never heard of him. Is he your ex?"

A ghost of a chuckle came from behind the curtain of hair. "No. Yes. It's complicated. He's the world's biggest bastard. And I did his bidding for years." She looked up and fixed him with her crystal eyes. Direct and unflinching. "So what does that make me?"

Kendrick met the contractors three miles away from the cabin in the woods where Britte Thorpe and the girl were hiding with the motel guy. He left Thomas on watch, hunkered down in the briars and mosquitoes, while he drove the old Ford LTD down to meet the boys from Houston. Kendrick arrived at the correct mile marker and only had to wait seven minutes before the contractors' car—a black Chrysler 300—rolled off the two-lane onto the shoulder. Kendrick threw up a hand as the other car's high beams damn near fried his eyes out.

"Cut the shit!" he yelled into the windshield. Whether they heard him or not, the lights went out, leaving purple spots dancing in Kendrick's vision. He blinked hard and climbed out of the musty, old-man-smelling car.

According to Dawali, the "contractors" were three mid-to-senior lieutenants from the 52 Hoovers. Real OGs who knew how to use the front sight on the pistols they carried. These were outlaws who had survived feuds with Bayou City gangs like the Treetop Bloods, Tango Blast, Latin Kings, and the Texas Syndicate. They had been baptized by fire and anointed in blood. Prison? Been there, got the orange jumpsuit.

Kendrick met the contractors in the neutral ground between the two parked cars. They came in three sizes, Small, Medium, and Large. Medium styled his hair in tight rows, Large was shaved bald, and Small slicked his hair down tight. Other than those small differences, they could be clones. Medium moved ahead of the pack and offered a chill look.

"Nice ride," he said, his tone riding a razor's edge challenge, balanced between dissing and funning.

"Yeah, it's low rent." Kendrick met the look with some sharpness of his own. "But I killed the last guy who drove it."

The trio exchanged sly grins and Medium offered his palm for a dap. "L'Quan," he said. "And this here is Tie-Die and Maurice. Don't call him Mo."

"You all understand the operation."

L'Quan waggled his hand. "The general outline."

"We're fixin' to bust in this house. Inside is a white dude who has some moves. There's also a snowflake and a little girl. We want the girl alive and in one piece. She gets a scratch, you might as well put your gun in your mouth and pull the trigger. And speaking of guns . . . there won't be any on this operation. The only one we got to worry about is the white dude, and he hasn't flashed any weapons so far beyond some fancy kung fu shit. The woman may bite and scratch a bit, but that's all. The girl is not to be touched. Period."

The three bangers exchanged looks.

"Yeah," Kendrick said, "I know ditching your guns is like pulling off your peckers and leaving 'em at home, but this is a precision operation, not a Saturday night out on the town. Won't be no spraying a TEC-9 out the back window of your car."

There was some more shuffling and hemming and hawing, but in the end, L'Quan and his boys agreed to the terms, as Kendrick knew they would. Dawali commanded a lot of respect in crime circles from coast to coast. Throwing in the towel and leaving Kendrick hanging meant their boss would lose face with Dawali, as well as losing any chance of future revenue opportunities. The last thing these chumps wanted to do was insult their boss by walking away.

Once it was clear the 52 Hoovers were in, Kendrick said, "Okay, y'all follow me." He turned to get back into the LTD, then paused with a finger in the air. "Hey, wait, I forgot to ask: Any of you boys know how to use a flash-bang?"

7

Mahoney leaned forward, unsure he'd heard what Britte said. "Biggest bastard in the world? How is that possible? Did he win a contest or something? Or is that just what is says on his LinkedIn profile?"

"It's not funny. Besides, you're out of questions for your round." Exhaustion smudged her eyes and Britte slumped in her seat. "Who are you? And try for honesty, okay? I'm told it's the best policy."

"Yeah, well . . ." Mahoney grumbled. "I just think I'm getting shortchanged on the answer to my question, that's all."

"Oh, and your 'Sanctuary City' was a full and complete response?" Britte arched an exquisitely expressive eyebrow. With one look, she cataloged Mahoney's beach bum attire and poor attention to personal grooming and managed to convey: *You're a desk clerk in a motel in East Jesus, Texas, population sixteen on a good day and you look like cat barf.*

"Um. Okay," Mahoney acknowledged. "Fine. Your turn. What was the question again?"

Britte smirked. The gesture must have tugged at her scar,

reminding her that he could see it. She twitched and turned away, presenting the undamaged side of her face to him. Mahoney couldn't think of a way to tell her the scar didn't bother him, so he kept his mouth shut. They were like two strangers sharing a car filled with dynamite. If he didn't steer carefully, they would go off a cliff and land in a ball of flame.

"Who are . . . How did . . ." Britte stuttered her way toward the question Mahoney dreaded answering. "Look. I'm not stupid. A guy your size doesn't manhandle Thomas unless he's had training. A sniper doesn't just happen to be all set up and ready to shoot. Another guy has a case full of bug-detecting spy gear! Not to mention Hannah Helpful, who is . . . who is . . . hell, I don't know what she is."

Mahoney waited, a pleasant, bland smile plastered on his face.

"Who. The fuck. Are you?"

"If I said the Justice League, would you hit me? Okay, okay, look"—he put his palms up to stave off her withering glare—"there are just things I can't talk about without having you undergo a blood ritual at a crossroads under the light of a full moon. Can I . . . can we leave it at: I'm one of the good guys?"

"There are no good guys. That's a fairy tale for children. Everybody wants something. So let me retract my question and ask a different one."

"Okay, shoot."

"What's this protection going to cost me?" Britte waved a hand around the *Modern Interiors* room. "This stuff isn't cheap. Snipers and martial arts experts aren't free." She stood and spread her arms, offering herself for inspection. "Is this what you want? If so, quit beating around the bush and make your pitch."

"Huh? What—"

"Frankly," Britte raised her voice. "Can I write a check and skip the messy exchange of bodily fluids? I'm really, really tired and not a good enough actress to pretend I'm enjoying it."

"Wait a sec—" Mahoney lifted his hands to surrender, but Britte had grabbed the wheel of their little trust-mobile and yanked it toward the cliff.

The cell phone in his pocket buzzed. Mahoney held up a finger to say, "Hold that thought" and glanced at the caller ID. *Ah. Saved by the buzz.*

"Talk to me, Hans."

"Right-oh," said the German, who had learned his English in Britain. "There's a bloke watching from the woods. His mate drove off a few minutes ago and has not returned."

"I told you I had a tail."

"Now would be—"

"A tail!" Britte cried. "How did—"

Mahoney forestalled her with an upraised palm and tucked the phone tighter against his ear. "Say again."

"I said, 'Now would be a good time to take out one of these wankers.'"

"We need one alive, Hans. Don't kill them both, okay? They can't answer questions with their throats cut."

A long pause. "Of course. I would never think to do otherwise."

"Okay. Yeah. Sure. Do you need a hand?"

A dead line answered his question.

Hans Schlichter, former *Oberleutnant im Kommando Spezialkräfte*, tapped his earpiece and killed the connection without bothering to answer Mahoney's ridiculous question. *Need help?* With one "tango," as the Americans liked to call them? A hulking beast, to be sure, but the watcher in the woods operated with all the stealth of . . . of a clothes dryer full of tennis shoes.

Hans improved his English by inventing similes. He liked trying them out on Mahoney, who appreciated words the way a . . . a vampire drank blood.

He edged forward through the thick undergrowth. Tricky with one prosthetic leg. Night vision goggles rendered the forest in shades of green and black. Purchased online, the goggles's commercial-grade optics were not nearly the quality to which he had grown accustomed in the elite special commando unit of the *Bundeswehr*—the German Army. Using these was like observing the world through toilet paper tubes at twilight. *Good one . . .*

The optics were sufficient, however, to reveal the tango sitting on a stump on the verge of the driveway, fifty meters from the cabin. The way the drive curved, he was out of sight from the cabin's front door, though situated such that he could maintain a reasonable surveillance of the cabin through the trees. In all, not a terrible position, but not optimal. There were many better locations from which to set up an observation point, but they would require lying prone among the weeds, something which this person clearly showed no inclination to do. The bulky, over-muscled man slapped and scratched and cursed so much, he may as well have worn tambourine earrings and danced an Irish jig. Hans had stalked closer to his prey ever since the second tango had gone away. So far, the target had ventured no more than two feet into the surrounding forest, and that was only *zum Pissen.*

Where had the second man gone? The pair had left their vehicle at the juncture where the driveway met the main road. Hans heard the engine start, though it would be wishful thinking to believe the man had gone for good. More wishful thinking to assume he had gone far at all. The possibility remained that the second man had circled back to check for observers such as

Hans. If the other man was better in the woods than this cretin, Hans might be walking into a trap.

He considered his approach. The artificial leg slowed him, but not by much. He had looped around such that he now occupied a position across the crushed-rock road from the tango. The man was silhouetted by the glow of cabin lights, which played hell with the NVGs. If a random beam of light struck his eyes at the wrong moment, it could fuck up his entire night. Plus, crossing the road in stealth would be difficult. The gravel underfoot would crunch and give away his approach long before he was ready. With no way to feel the terrain under his prosthesis, he couldn't guarantee silence. It would be better, then, to slither back a few meters and go right, paralleling the driveway until it was safe to cross, then close the distance on the other side. The rest would be simple. Mahoney had said he wanted one left alive, and he preferred it to be the *Schwarzer*, who seemed to be the brains of the operation. This one was expendable.

Hans touched the hilt of his Gerber Mark II. Sixteen-point-five centimeters of German steel, driven into the brain from below the right ear would rid the world of one extra-large piece of *Scheiße*.

Fifteen minutes later, Hans drifted through the trees, silent as fog on a still morning. By his calculation, he could cross without giving away his presence. A scuff of gravel and a low-voiced comment froze Hans with his prosthetic leg lifted to step over a thick tangle of vines.

The question of where the second man had gone became evident a moment later. Hans eased back into the brush as four men walked up the driveway. Arrayed in a loose scrum, the group appeared as green ghosts through his goggles. Making out individual features through the cheap NVGs was impossible, though Hans was sure that at least one of the arrivals was the *Schwarzer*—the one Mahoney wanted alive. The man had a distinctive gait, almost a strut, as if he owned the world and everything in it. The three newcomers scuffed along behind the leader, their heads on a swivel.

Reinforcements. *Scheiße. This is bad.*

Hans tensed when one looked directly at him, only letting his breath out when he realized the man wasn't wearing night optics and would see nothing but blackness this deep into the forest. The group passed his position and carried on without stopping, no doubt on their way to linking up with their spotter.

An engagement would be difficult. In addition to his knife, Hans carried a suppressed Walther P22. A great pistol for assassination, though not so good for an extended firefight against multiple opponents. The suppressor and subsonic loads squelched the report down to that of an air pistol, or about as loud as snapping your fingers. The .22 would require close-range head shots to be sure of a kill, meaning Hans would have to rush up the gravel road, making as much noise as a lorry full of pots and pans, then place four shots with exquisite precision before any of the four reacted.

At one time, before the injury, he had been among the best in the world—Hans knew this to be true, without false pride, having tested himself against elite operators from around the globe—but attempting four kills at spitting distance at night through crappy NVGs against armed opponents? Besides, he had not been operational since the 7.62 rounds had blown up his leg. He had lost a step, so to speak. No. Mama Schlichter did not raise a *Dummkopf.*

Hans mouthed a long stream of German obscenities. *So* blöd. *So stupid. One of us should have anticipated the enemy team would bring in reinforcements.*

And yet, no one had. Out of practice . . . out of the field too long . . . whatever it was, it was nothing but plain stupidity. And backup was at least thirty minutes away. Zee, Hannah, Chan, and all the rest, tucked in their safe houses all through the shitty little town of Cottonmouth, assuming Hans and Mahoney could handle a pair of garden-variety street thugs by themselves.

Mahoney. *Scheiße.*

Hans huddled over his phone to mask the light. *Cell phones for field comms. Verdammt. This is no way to run an operation.* He tapped Mahoney's number. The ring sounded in his Bluetooth earpiece. Another ring.

And another.

And another.

Pick up the phone, Mahoney!

Scheiße!

Mahoney faced Britte Thorpe—who stood before him, hands on her hips and her neck flushed red from anger—with his mouth open but no words coming out. He had plenty to say but his thoughts had jammed together like the Manhattan Tunnel on the last Friday before Christmas.

The phone in his pocket buzzed with an incoming call. He ignored it.

Why hadn't he seen it coming? That Britte Thorpe would jump to the conclusion he expected a little *quid pro sex* for his protection. She was a devastating, thirty-megaton sexual warhead. She could walk into a ballpark and every male in the stadium would faint from sudden onset erection. How could she not have a jaded view of a man's motivations?

But the truth was that he was turned on in a completely different way. Like a car left to gather dust in a barn and cranked up for the first time in years, his engine was sputtering, chugging, and running rough. But at least he was running. And he assumed being switched on, mission focused, had been the catalyst that quelled his cantankerous, raw, buzzing nerves like nothing had in months.

His phone buzzed again. Mahoney shut it off without pulling it from his pocket. *Damn it, Hans. Not now.*

"Come on, Mahoney," Britte demanded. "I'm tired and I want to get this over with."

"Redemption, Britte," he said. "Ever feel the need for redemption? Like you've done so many bad things, that no matter how many good things you do, you'll never wipe the stain from your soul?" Mahoney read the slight change in her posture that told him he had registered a hit. "You're not the only one who needs to make up for past sins, Britte. I've done things . . . terrible things . . ." Easier to sell the story when there was a thread of truth. "Everybody has a past. Some of us have to balance scales so heavy with guilt, every good deed is a grain of sand in comparison."

"So that's what I am?" Britte scoffed. "A good deed?"

"I'm guessing that altruism is probably something you've rarely experienced." Time to weave in another thread of truth. "And I'd be lying if I said I'm immune to your charms."

"Charms!" She added a mocking laugh. "Oh my God. Charms."

"Look, Britte. Keep your clothes on, okay? Keep your money. When this is over—"

A tremendous bang shook the house. The front door blew open with a billow of white smoke. Mahoney whirled, reaching for the pistol at his hip. An object sailed into the room, bounced, and clattered to a stop. Mahoney recognized it in the microsecond before it exploded.

Oh, shit.

8

Mahoney had once observed a Marine Corps training session on breeching a room using a flash-bang grenade. As with everything in the Marines training regimen, the procedure for tossing a flash-bang had been broken down into simple steps and those steps practiced in a strict, orderly, military fashion until they were burned into muscle memory. Spoon held against the web of your hand, pull ring facing out. Look. Pull. Throw. A gentle but firm underhanded toss into the room, not too far, not too close. Do not bounce it off the door frame. Do not rebound it off the furniture and back into your lap. The delay from spoon release to explosion was between 0.75 and 1.5 seconds. Wait for the bang.

Pain is experienced at any sound above 130 decibels. A flash-bang delivers a pulse of sound upward of 175 decibels.

The grenade—a cylinder about the size of a can of Red Bull—rolled across Hans's pure-white marble floor. It detonated less than ten feet from where Mahoney stood.

Even with his eyes squeezed shut, the flash lit up his eyelids with supernova intensity. The bang stabbed his brain with icepicks of sheer pain. It felt as if his ears had been stuffed with firecrackers. Mahoney staggered. He kept his feet under him with an act of will and pulled his weapon using a little muscle memory of his own. Purple dots dazzled his vision. He blinked, felt loopy, like a prizefighter on the ropes, waiting for the knockout punch.

Three guys.

In the room. Coming through the hazy smoke.

Targets.

Point and shoot. Point and shoot.

Twin needles of fire burned in his chest. His body convulsed. The world turned red, then—*blink*— The ceiling. He was on—

The floor.

Not good. So not good.

Fire flared through his chest again, seizing him up, as if he'd stuck his tongue in a light socket, except the voltage came through twin fishhooks stuck in his chest. Mahoney recognized the sensation. He was being Tased. It hurt like fuck, same as it did back then, when the Chechen interrogators took turns shocking him until he passed out. *Funny how you never get used to peeing your pants.*

He blinked.

One guy, standing over him. Lighting him up with a Taser. Black guy. Never seen him before. Muscles (the one Britte called Thomas) appeared next to him, two faces side by side, looking down from Mount Kickass. Big Thomas, from the motel. Nasty grin on his face. Mouth moving with soundless words.

I'm gonna stomp you to death!

A size ten shoe cracked down on Mahoney's right forearm. Pain signals tried to get through his snarled up nervous system. Mahoney barely registered it. That's gonna hurt later.

Thomas yelling: *Zap him again!*

Fire ruptured inside him. Mahoney jerked and twisted and

jiggled like electrified spaghetti. Thomas kicked him in the ribs. Mahoney felt a bone crack.

His muscles had turned to jelly. All his nerve pathways had shorted out. Coordinated action was out of the question. How many jolts? At least three. Random thoughts blipped through his head. *Maybe this will cure the jangles, once and for all. Blow all the circuits in my brain.*

One last kick and Kendrick pulled Thomas away. They exited his field of view.

Get up, get up, get up, getupgetupgetup! Another jolt galvanized his muscles.

Shouts. Faintly heard over the ringing in his ears. Angry. Excited. Taser-guy's head jerked. He toppled like a tree, eyes bulging. Mahoney felt the thump when Taser-guy hit the floor. Didn't hear it.

Hans appeared, his pistol spitting. Another guy dropped.

Mahoney managed to roll his head to the right.

Saw Britte over Thomas's shoulder. Saw Kendrick pulling Siobhan out of the game room, disappearing down the back hall. *No. No fucking way. Move, Mahoney!*

He was a meat puppet, all his strings cut. Screaming inside his head. Coming apart.

Where are you, Hans?

A third tango was down, but so was Hans. The German rolled on the floor. Clutching his leg. Out of the fight. Just like Mahoney.

Britte, gone. Siobhan, gone.

Fuck.

"*Get your lazy ass out of bed! You'll be late for school!*" Ma's voice, yelling from the kitchen. Mahoney rolled over and tried to go back to sleep. The bed was hard. Cold. Nausea turned his stomach and a cold sweat flushed through him from head to foot. His crotch was wet. *Ah, Christ. Did I wet the bed? Oh, man. Ma's gonna rip me a new one.*

"Get up, Mahoney! Get up!"

"Five more minutes, Ma," Mahoney mumbled. "Gimme five more minutes."

"Get the fuck up, Mahoney!"

Ma's voice sounded harsher, more masculine than it should. Has Dad come home? No. Impossible. Dad was dead. Killed in Desert Storm. Silver Star. Triangular flag on the mantel.

Mahoney cracked a sticky eyelid. White marble cooled his cheek. He was on the floor, twisted into a pretzel, pain seizing him from hair to toenails. It was like waking up with a charley horse in every muscle. Close enough to touch, a dead man's eyes stared back at him. They were already filming over, as if white curtains were being drawn over his final act. A man's voice yelled at him to get up, get moving.

That last part clicked a switch. Britte. Kendrick and Thomas—along with some extra goons, invading the cabin. Flash-bang. Tasering.

Oh.

Hans, not Mahoney's mother, was yelling at him.

"Move, gott-dahmit!" Then his tone changed. "Hannah! It's Hans. Things have gone teats up. I am injured, GSW, right thigh . . . *Ja*, in my bad fucking leg! Mahoney is down, injuries unknown. Three unsubs, KIA. Two unsubs have escaped with the principals. Whereabouts unknown . . . Yes . . . Yes! . . . No, I don't know. *Mahoney!* Get up!"

Mahoney summoned his focus and built a sentence, word by word. "Tell her. To put Zee. On Highway 379. Overwatch."

"*Ja.* Wait, Mahoney is mumbling something. He may be coming around. Mahoney! What is it?"

"Overwatch!" Mahoney said, louder. Life was returning to his muscles. The ringing was fading from his ears. "Zee! Highway Three Seven Niner!"

Hans repeated Mahoney's direction.

There came a pause during which Mahoney unkinked his arms. He pushed himself into a sitting position. His right arm screamed and buckled under him. The room tilted and swirled. He caught himself a second before face-planting into white Carrara marble. *The blood makes a nice contrast . . .*

Hans was propped against the wet bar, a field-expedient tourniquet around his right thigh and a phone pinched against his shoulder. His expression was not encouraging.

"Mahoney," he said at last. "Hannah is saying *nein*. This is not our fight. You are risking everyone. We are not to get any more involved. These are the rules, Mahoney," he said, clearly repeating Hannah's words. Hans pinched his lips in a near-apology. "You knew the rules. We cannot get involved with this mess any longer. Uh-huh. *Ja. Ja. Ich verstehe.*"

"Fuck. That." Mahoney's face hardened. He forced his legs straight. He tried flexing his right hand, which brought tears to his eyes. *Good thing I'm a lefty.* "How long?"

Hans glanced at his watch. "Six minutes."

A six-minute head start. "Vehicle?"

"Unknown," Hans said. "Probably parked at the end of the driveway."

A five-minute walk to the end of the driveway. The drive terminated at a county road which meandered in a loop, connected at both ends to Farm-to-Market Road 379. At top speed, it would take either ten or twenty minutes to reach 379, depending on direction. At 379, if they turned right, they would pass back through Cottonmouth in less than ten minutes. Another fifteen and they would reach US 190, an east–west two-lane blacktop through the pines between two national forests. It would take a lot of country backroad driving to reach a major interstate. It was the least likely option, though having an observer watching the highway through town would cover that bet.

Turning left would bring them to the four-lane US 96 in about five minutes, and from there they could reach Beaumont and Houston to the southwest, or points north, eventually Dallas or maybe Shreveport. If they reached US 96 before Mahoney caught up, the choice of roads went from two to infinity very quickly.

"Hang up. Call Zee." Mahoney said. His vision tunneled and his stomach turned over. He bent over, left hand on his knee, right arm hanging limp, and practiced breathing with a knife stabbing his chest. At least one rib was broken, for sure. His forearm ached and throbbed in time with his pulse, and a huge red swollen knot was developing midway between his wrist and elbow. He suspected a broken bone there as well. For a moment, he couldn't recall how it came to be injured, then—*Oh, yeah. Tommy stomped it. I owe him one.* He focused on Hans. "Tell him . . . Tell Zee . . . to pretty please watch . . . the road . . ."

"Do not throw up on my floor," Hans warned.

Mahoney shot him a dirty look. "Blood and brains, you don't mind, but a little puke upsets you?"

"Getting shot upsets me. This is all your fault."

"Don't get your lederhosen in a twist." Mahoney found his Sig a few feet away. He clamped down on the nausea rising from his gullet and retrieved the pistol. He mopped cold sweat off his face with a sleeve before fumbling through a magazine change, swapping for a full one. Four rounds fired—when did that happen?

He hitched his chin at Hans. "I didn't shoot you, did I?"

"*Nein*. It was him." The German indicated the smallest of the three dead men. "You were already down when I came in."

"I'm going after them," Mahoney said, stumbling toward the garage door on jelly legs. "This is on me and no one else. Please, Hans. Call Zee. Ask him to watch—just watch, okay?—the road through town. If they go that way, call me."

Hans glared at him for a moment longer, then his expression softened to one of pity. "You're an idiot, Mahoney. All right, go. I will call, though I promise nothing."

"Thanks, Hans," Mahoney said without looking back.

"Mahoney! Do not touch my car!"

"Sorry, Hans," Mahoney called back. "Ears ringing. Can't hear you."

"Mahoney! . . . Mahoney! Gott-dahm you, Mahoney!"

Two choices of transportation awaited Mahoney under the fluorescent lights of Hans's garage: Mahoney's 1947 Willys Jeep or a Porsche 911 GT2 RS Weissach. The dirt-crusted, oil-dripping Jeep sagged on its springs, as though embarrassed to be in the same garage as Hans's seven-hundred-horsepower bullet on wheels. Both vehicles had four wheels and could convey people from point A to point B by means of an internal combustion engine. There the similarities ended.

Hans cherished his Porsche the way Midas coveted gold. Mahoney, who knew nothing about cars, had listened over and over as the German had recited stats, dimensions, and performance envelopes for the gleaming white road-rocket with its iridescent black accents and airfoil spoiler. He had forgotten all of them except the horsepower rating and the number of cup holders.

With his bum right arm, operating the Jeep's cantankerous

shifter would be pure hell. The Porsche had an automatic transmission. The Jeep's top speed of fifty miles an hour versus zero-to-sixty in a hummingbird's heartbeat? No contest.

Hans kept the keys on a hook by the door, next to the automatic garage door button. Mahoney sank into the buttery-soft seat, fired up the Porsche, and reached over awkwardly with his left hand to drop the shifter into gear. The throaty rumble of the rear-mounted engine vibrated up Mahoney's tailbone as he fumbled the seatbelt into place.

When he goosed the accelerator, the Porsche's ass twisted sideways before firing out of the garage like a cruise missile. Mahoney fishtailed down the driveway, fighting to find the accelerator's sweet spot that would keep the car moving forward without the rear end trying to spin out of control. He hit the end of the driveway and executed a drifting left onto the county road before aiming the Porsche down the middle stripe and stomping the accelerator.

Mistake.

Mahoney's head snapped back as the Porsche shot away. The car devoured the road and begged for more. Mahoney one-handed the steering wheel, white-knuckled grip feeling every pebble and pit in the asphalt. He never claimed to be a "driver"—having in fact nearly failed the evasive driving course during training—and the nuances of handling a seven-hundred horsepower beast took more concentration than he felt like giving. Mahoney reluctantly backed off the gas and slowed the sports car below the speed of sound to allow his mind and his stomach the chance to catch up.

He had taken the left instinctively, that being the shorter route to 379. Which way from there? Back to Cottonmouth, or left again and race flat out to the main highway? *If I was them, which way would I go? And what are they driving? How will I know when I've caught them?*

On the drive from the motel to the cabin, Mahoney had clocked an older model Ford sedan on his tail almost from the moment he pulled onto the main road. Would they be in that car, or their Yukon, or something else entirely? It was possible Kendrick's crew had transferred to a vehicle provided by the backup hitters, leaving the Ford in a ditch somewhere. If so, he was screwed.

While fighting to keep the willful Porsche out of the ditches, Mahoney also battled a stomach-turning cocktail of guilt, despair, and failure. Britte and Siobhan may not have trusted him—Britte had said as much—but he held the delicate crystal vase of their well-being in his hands . . . and he'd dropped it. The look of terror on the girl's face as Kendrick dragged her out of the game room looped in a repeating instant replay in Mahoney's mind. The buzzing of the phone in his pocket had no doubt been Hans, calling to warn him of the attack. So intent on making a connection with Britte Thorpe, he had ignored the call, not heard the warning, and therefore was unprepared for the attack.

Stupid. Stupid. Stupid. So much for being a well-trained covert operative. Hi, my name is James. James Bungle. No disaster is so bad I can't make it worse.

The tinkling chimes of his rattletrap nerves started playing at max volume—a sure precursor to a full-on shivering fit. *Not now!* he begged himself. *Please. Not now.*

The phone in his shirt pocket buzzed. Mahoney forced his right hand onto the wheel and eased back on the gas, rolling to a stop at the intersection of the unnamed county road and Highway 379. He plucked out his phone and read the caller ID. Hannah. Mahoney declined the call. The last person he wanted to talk to—other than Lofland—was Hannah Moshe. There was no formal hierarchy among the "special" residents of Cottonmouth, though in theory Mahoney was more or less in charge, with Hannah running a close second. She practiced stuffing her opinions up Mahoney's nose with the sharp, unrelenting pounding of someone who has all the answers. That she often used logic and facts to back up her argument didn't make him like her any better.

Mahoney tucked the phone away and took a deep breath. Decision time. The Porsche idled in impatient fury, anxious to move. Did they go right toward Cottonmouth, or left to US 96? Traveling through Cottonmouth made the least sense, logistically speaking. One, Kendrick would be wary of entering the sniper's sights again. Two, it would take much longer to reach an interstate highway. Three . . . well, there was no three.

Pretty thin, Mahoney. Pretty thin.

He closed his eyes and tried to clear his mind. Deep breaths. The jangles receded to the sound of distant church bells. He peeked at the time. Best guess, Britte's captors were less than ten minutes ahead. In the Porsche, he should be able to overtake them before they reached 96. If he guessed wrong, there *might* just be time to reverse direction and catch up before they passed through Cottonmouth and reached US 190.

Screw it. Left it is.

Mahoney hit the gas and unleashed the beast. The Porsche roared away into the night.

9

"We heading back to that podunk town?" Thomas asked from the backseat. He had both feet propped on Britte Thorpe, who was crammed into the footwell of the LTD. He had one big arm looped around the kid, whose stunned eyes stared into space. Kendrick, seeing her thousand-yard stare reflected from the rearview, found it a little creepy. He hoped her funk would wear off before they got her back to Florida. Stankovic might take it badly if he thought they'd abused the kid.

"Yeah, we are," Kendrick said. "All our shit is in the Yukon, and I damn sure don't want to drive for long in a stolen car. Did you pat her down? Did she have it?"

"Yeah, I got it." Thomas held up a palm-sized velvet sack. "Man, who was that guy in black? Dude dropped those bangers like shooting ducks on a pond."

"How the fuck would I know. Maybe the sniper?"

"That makes sense. Fucking guy could shoot. Came out of nowhere and started capping dudes with a silenced piece. Like, some real James Bond shit. First guy went down, and I was like, fuck this. Grabbed the woman and ran out the back."

"Uh-huh," Kendrick said.

"Those guys did good, though. Like, storming the front door and taking all the heat while we snuck in through the back."

Kendrick grimaced without speaking. Big Tom liked to chatter after a gig—it helped him come down. Didn't mean Kendrick had to respond.

"Even the fuckin' clerk got off a coupla rounds after being hit with the flash-bang. The Taser put him down though. Did you see it? The way he flopped around on the floor? L'Quan kept hitting him with the juice. *Zzzt! Zzzt!* Fucker was tough, gotta give him that. Kept trying to get up, even after I stomped on him a little."

"You see who fired that last shot?"

"Nah, man," Thomas said. "But I think one of Dawali's guys? He must have, like, had a piece on him, even after you told them no guns. I was already running by the time that happened, so I didn't, like, see it. Just a guess."

Kendrick nodded. That sounded about right.

"Fuck, you remember where we hid the Yukon? All this redneck shit looks the same." Kendrick slowed as they passed the Cottonmouth City limits. Population 286, according to the sign. Kendrick wondered how many of the 286 were like the desk clerk and the sniper. Just those two? Maybe they were two old boys, back from Iraq, learned their shit in the Marines and came home to this little piss-pot town. They saw a chance to play heroes again and jumped on it, like they were missing the action and needing that little boost to feel alive again.

"Keep going," Thomas said. "Sign said CR-22."

They passed a Chinese restaurant with a flashing Open sign in the front window. The rest of the town may as well have been deserted. Darkness shrouded closed or abandoned storefronts along the main drag. Five buildings, dating from the Great Depression and patched with materials of later eras, comprised the single block of "downtown" Cottonmouth. All of them appeared to have gone out of business about the time Sonny and Cher broke up.

Beyond the center of town, buildings thinned out to odd little collections of businesses. Kendrick saw a thrift store, a laundromat, a gas-station-slash-convenience-store, an attorney's office, and a few structures with no current occupant or visible purpose. The motel was a mile or so farther down the road.

"Slow down," Thomas said. "It's just up here. See that real estate office? Right before that."

"Real estate. Shit," Kendrick said with a sneer. "Who the fuck would buy property around here?"

The Yukon was right where they'd left it, the right mirror still dangling from a wire, and a bullet hole in the rear passenger door. They had to conceal that somehow. Only thing worse than driving a stolen car was driving one with a bullet hole in it. Be like a big neon sign to cops all across three states—Here Be Criminals!

"Call Dawali," Thomas suggested. "Maybe he can send the Gulfstream to meet us at a local airport somewhere close, so we don't draw cops like flies on shit."

That was actually a good idea. Two days and three nights on the road, sleeping in shifts in the back of the SUV, followed by post-fight fatigue, had left Kendrick feeling sluggish. His thoughts were processing one at time, in slow motion, as if he'd smoked weed or something. They kept a few tabs of meth in the glove box of the Yukon for situations like this. Kendrick hated taking meth—it made him itchy and nervous, and afterward he crashed like a derailed freight train. But itchy was better than dead or jailed because he hadn't thought of something he ought to.

"Get the women secured," Kendrick said. "I'll call Dawali."

—

Mahoney's phone buzzed multiple times before he recognized it over the vibrating rumble of the Porsche. He risked a peek at the display and saw it was Zee calling. Holding the wheel with his swollen right hand, Mahoney fumbled the phone up to his ear.

"What's up, Zee? You see anything?"

"Mahoney. I am not calling. You have not heard from me. I am not in the parking lot of Chan's restaurant, and I am not using my night scope to watch traffic for you."

"Okay, fine. What are you *not* telling me?"

"A green sedan drove past my position at twenty-one-forty-two hours, heading northeast. Other occupants in the rear."

They went the other way. Dammit!

"Roger that, Zee. I owe you."

He had traveled fourteen miles at speeds between eighty and one thirty. Elapsed time since turning onto 379 . . . eight minutes. Now he had to cover that same fourteen miles back in the other direction and add another ten or so on top of that to reach Chan's place . . . call it twenty-five miles . . . in under ten minutes. Then add on however much distance Britte's captors had tacked on since then.

Mahoney spat curses as he dropped the phone in his lap and spun the Porsche in a tight arc. The car shuddered through a one-eighty and Mahoney slammed the accelerator to the floor. Rear tires squalling, blue smoke spewing, the rear end squatted like a big cat and the sports car blasted off in the opposite direction.

Mahoney recalled Hans mentioning the car's top speed as somewhere around two hundred miles per hour. Professional driver on a closed course kind of speed. The farm-to-market two-lane was far from a closed course—even this far out in the boondocks, there was enough traffic to be annoying, with limited sight lines and significant curves. Smashing the 911 into the back of some farmer's pickup wouldn't help anyone.

Still, Mahoney found his foot settling heavier and heavier onto the pedal, the car drifting farther and farther into the curves, and the needle of the speedometer quivering into unknown territory on the far right of the dial. The road tunneled into a blur, and his left hand tingled with the strain of his death grip on the wheel. He was far outrunning his headlights. If a wayward deer appeared before him, there would be a messy explosion of buckskin, fine German craftsmanship, and Irish American intestines.

Mahoney gritted his teeth and prayed.

With Thomas's feet pressing into her back and her middle squeezed by the old car's transmission hump, Britte was having trouble breathing. A desiccated Corn Nut was embedded in the carpet an inch from her nose, along with a crumpled Peanut M&M's bag and a gas station receipt. A scent akin to old gym socks invaded her sinuses. As the Ford swayed and jounced, acid reflux burned in her chest, and she swallowed convulsively to keep the vomit down.

Her physical discomfort paled in comparison to the chains of dread that weighted her spirit. Hope, or something faintly resembling it, had begun to crawl from the deep grave in which she had buried it. For a few moments, Britte had entertained the idea that they might just have made it. With Mahoney and his strange crew, she had begun to believe she might have some allies. That she might stand a chance against the house odds.

She had gambled against Milos. And lost.

Now she would pay the price, though that equated to very small stakes compared to Siobhan's fate. Britte had long since given up the possibility that her own existence had any value, except as a coin she might spend to spin the wheel in protection of another. And like any gambler, when the house took her last chip, it felt a lot like . . . relief. *Of course you lost*, said that tiny voice in her head. *What were you thinking? No one beats the house.*

At least now she had no more decisions. No more tension. She felt nothing, as if hollow on the insides, all her emotions scooped out. Exhausted. *Ella, I am so sorry. I will miss you the most.*

The car rolled to a stop. Kendrick and Thomas had been talking, saying something about Dawali. Britte missed it.

"Come on, ladies," Thomas announced. "Time to change cars."

The old Ford jolted and squealed as Kendrick got out, then opened the back door. Warm, muggy air rolled into the interior. Thomas acted the clumsy oaf climbing out, making every effort to stomp on her extra hard, with obvious malice. He giggled when she gasped. Siobhan avoided stepping on her, muttering "Sorry" when her toe cuffed the back of Britte's head. A moment later, Thomas was dragging Britte out of the car and spilling her into the weeds of a dark yard behind an abandoned house.

Thomas yanked her upright.

It's over. Why fight it?

No one was coming to save her. Her last view of Mahoney was of the scruffy little would-be hero convulsively twisting on the floor of the cabin with glassy eyes and a wet crotch. If he wasn't dead, he was close enough as to make no difference. His rescuing days were over, and whatever "skills" he possessed were inadequate compared to the ruthless determination of Milos's gangsters.

Fuck you, Mahoney, for making me feel like I had a chance.

The back door of the Yukon yawned open.

"Get her inside," Kendrick said.

"Aren't we supposed to finish—"

Kendrick jerked his head at Siobhan, silencing Thomas with

an unreadable expression. "Not where she can see, okay? Girl's already freaked enough. We don't need that shit right now."

Siobhan eyes flickered to Britte's. The girl had appeared catatonic up until that second, though in that tiny moment of connection, Britte realized her dull-witted look had been an act. One second, she was standing as dumbstruck as a cow, the next—

Siobhan was sprinting full-out, legs pumping, pulling away fast.

"Hey!" Kendrick yelled. He started after Siobhan. Britte's foot hooked his ankle and he sprawled on his face with a heavy thump. Kendrick burned her with a glare as he scrambled up and kicked into motion. The skinny man was fast, but Siobhan was flying. She disappeared around the corner of the house, running for the road.

Go, girl! Go—!

In the instant before Thomas's big fist crashed into her temple, Britte realized she was grinning.

—

Shelly Ann Mott, renamed Siobhan for her "new life," ran into the pitch blackness in front of the abandoned house and powered toward the narrow country lane at the end of the drive, putting some serious distance between her and Kendrick, who was probably the faster of the two dickheads. Thomas, for sure, would never catch her. Bench press a John Deere, maybe, but a run a hundred yards flat out? No. And Shelly Ann could haul ass on two feet. She had run track at Livingston Junior High, beating out all but a couple of girls for the fastest times in the 800 and 1500-meter events.

That was in the Before Time.

Before she ran away from home. Before she met Dean at the Memphis bus terminal and accepted his offer of "help." Before they had renamed her Siobhan—pronounced Sheh-vawn but spelled like Sea-o-bon—and she had gone along with it, thinking it made a pretty cool name. Elegant and foreign sounding.

Before she ran away from home, Shelly Ann had never been a dozen miles from the trailer park where she lived with her vodka-soaked mom and a procession of meth-addicted prospective stepfathers. Smart enough to know that Dean's help came with strings attached, she had believed herself equipped to beat the odds and avoid dope and turning tricks . . .

Watch where you're going, stupid.

Running in the dark like this, her biggest worry was tripping over some hidden obstacle in the tall grass or stepping on a rusty nail. She couldn't make top speed until she hit the road. Kendrick barked a curse. His footsteps pounded the turf. Close. Too close. Shelly Ann hit the road and put on a burst of speed. The drive from the main road to the abandoned house had been under a mile. A couple of houses had appeared occupied—porch lights shining, cars in the yard—but she couldn't risk the time it would take to run up, pound on the door, and hope someone answered before Kendrick caught up. Besides, knowing Kendrick, he would just shoot whoever answered and call it a job well done.

No. Making it to the main road was her only option. Turn left and race back to the Chinese restaurant—the only place in town that seemed occupied at this hour. No way Kendrick would cap a room full of people. Hopefully.

Shelly Ann punched it into high gear. Knees up, arms pumping. Heel to toe on the pavement and kick it out. Just like Coach taught her. She was breathing right, hitting her runner's stride. *Screw you, Kendrick!*

She felt bad about leaving Britte. The scarred woman had been her only real friend in Stankovic's compound, as well as the reason for being taken from Dean and sent south to live in the Florida mansion, a hostage to Britte's continued good behavior. She had been the one to explain Shelly Ann's true future, the fate Stankovic had intended for her if Britte failed to do the master's bidding—a life on the streets, strung out and hustling in truck stops for fifty bucks a trick. Britte had been the one who had risked everything to get her away. In that last glance before Shelly Ann had made a run for it, she had met Britte's eyes and asked a silent question. Britte had answered back with the tiniest of nods. *Yes! Go!*

Still, it didn't feel right.

She chanced a glance back.

And her stomach fell.

The lights of the black SUV swung out of the drive and onto the road, pinning her in their twin beams. The Yukon roared up behind her.

10

"Sit there and behave," Kendrick said after he had zip-tied the girl's hands to the passenger side armrest. "You twist around too much, you're gonna bruise yourself, and that won't do anybody any good. How is she?" he asked Thomas, who had tossed Britte into the backseat like a sack of dogfood, then climbed in beside her.

"Out cold," Thomas responded.

Kendrick climbed into the driver's seat, buckled up and threw the SUV into gear. The dashboard clock read eight minutes until 10 p.m. What with retrieving the Yukon, chasing down the girl, then getting everybody situated, almost thirty minutes had elapsed since they stormed the cabin. Way too long. If the sniper and the clerk had reached out to the cops, there could be roadblocks going up on any of the major roads out of Redneckville. They could be driving into a trap, no matter which way they went.

Kendrick pumped the brakes as he approached the intersection with 379.

"Which way we going?" Thomas asked from the back. "I don't want to get anywhere near that sniper dude."

"Question is, was the shooter at the cabin the sniper?"

"Had to be. I mean, who else, right?"

"If it was him, and not some other yo-yo, then the way north is clear."

"And south means going back past where we snatched these two."

"Where all the police activity will be."

"Shit," said Thomas. "You think they called the cops?"

"If so, we could be fucked, no matter which way we go."

After a long exhale, Thomas said, "Fuck it. Head north."

"Agreed."

Kendrick spun the wheel and steered the GMC into a right turn. He hit the gas, and the big V-8 powered the car onto the highway. Ten minutes, maybe less, and they would reach a cross-road that would carry them east or west, and finally, maybe, get them the hell out of this backwoods nightmare.

Kendrick tapped the in-cabin display and scrolled down to Dawali's contact number and touched it.

"Tell me you have good news," the security chief said without preamble.

"Mostly good," Kendrick admitted. "We have the woman and the girl with us. And the package. The girl's fine. Say hello, sugar . . . No? She's shy, boss. But not a scratch on her. Thomas had to lay out Britte, since she was causing a ruckus. But that ain't the bad part . . ."

"Spill it."

"We may have some heat on us. Those three gunslingers you sent are down, probably dead. The motel guy is down, but probably not dead. He had backup, a hitter with some moves. May be the same guy that took a shot at us earlier. Either way, if they bring in the cops, we may be screwed."

"Mr. Stankovic can produce paperwork affirming he has

custody of the minor, though it won't withstand deep inspection. Our bluff will be that you were tasked to find and retrieve her from her abductor. This approach . . . would be messy, to say the least. Plus, all the exposure . . . No, involvement in the legal system is not optimal. I'll call you back after I confer with Mr. Stankovic."

Uh-oh. I know what that means. The cost of the operation had to be mounting, what with paying off the bangers, and all the other bits and pieces. If the lawyers had to get involved, the cost would skyrocket. There came a time, the juice wasn't worth the squeeze. *They're gonna cut their losses. Cheaper to find themselves a new diamond mule and turn the girl out or drop her in the same hole as the woman.* Kendrick glanced at the teenager, who had gone back to her spaced-out look. *Damn, I hate killing kids.*

Mahoney reached the Cottonmouth City limits at 9:55 p.m. Nothing was open besides Chan's restaurant and the EZ-Shop convenience store. The road changed names to Pecan Street between the city limits, and two stoplights controlled traffic as it cut through downtown Cottonmouth—one at Simmons Street and one at Miller Road. Rarely had Mahoney seen more than one car stopped at either of the lights, though of course now, when he was racing the clock in a land-bound missile, the Cottonmouth equivalent of a traffic jam clogged both lanes, coming and going, at the Pecan and Simmons intersection.

The speedometer read somewhere between ninety and one hundred miles per hour as Mahoney rocketed toward the intersection. The light was red, and two cars were stopped ahead of him. In the oncoming lane, another car waited. Buildings blocked the view of any cross traffic via Simmons. If vehicles were approaching from the sides, Mahoney wouldn't see them until they T-boned his ride.

Brake lights grew from twin dots to giant eyes in seconds. His foot eased off the gas, chafing at having to stop for a red light.

The obvious solution presented itself. Don't slow down. Blow the light. Go around the cars in this lane, whip to the side to avoid the head-on with the oncoming traffic. Juke left, juke right, nothing to it. Pray there's no cross traffic. The safe and sane Mahoney riding on his shoulder screamed a warning.

"Screw it," Mahoney said.

He twitched the steering wheel left. Headlights flooded his windshield. He blew past the waiting cars and into the intersection, powering toward a head-on collision like a speeding bullet, attempting to fit the Porsche through the eye of a needle in a microsecond. Horns blared. Mahoney registered a snapshot image of a white face goggling from the other vehicle. Tires squalled. He fought to keep the car out of a spin. His broken rib screamed at him. The Porsche fishtailed, wobbled . . . and straightened out.

And he was through.

There. That was easy.

The light at Miller was red too, but no traffic waited there. Mahoney blew through in the blink of an eye. He juddered over railroad tracks and then opened up the throttle again as the road flattened out. The Cottonmouth Motor Court blurred past on his left, then Zivon's garage on his right. The city limits sign blipped by. *Thanks for visiting Cottonmouth! Come back soon!*

Sweat soaked his armpits and dripped from his hair.

"Nothing to this driving thing," he said to himself. "I don't know why Hans makes such a big deal about it."

—

Britte Thorpe played back the conversation between Kendrick and Dawali, trying to spin it in her own mind to reach a conclusion other than the obvious. She knew how Milos's mind worked. At a certain point, he would cut his losses and move on. Expedient, pragmatic, and ruthless. Those were three words coded into his operating system. The chance either she or Siobhan would make it through the night was fading with every tick of the clock.

Slumped in the backseat, on the passenger side, with Thomas camped next to her, she kept her eyes closed and feigned unconsciousness. Her cheek rested against the cool leather of the Yukon's door. The position strained her neck and shot pain down her spine whenever the car hit a bump, which seemed to happen every three seconds. However, any movement on her part would give away her one slim advantage of surprise. If Thomas thought she was unconscious, he wouldn't be prepared when she attacked. Her legs were already positioned correctly.

Over the years, Britte had tried a number of fitness routines—yoga, Pilates . . . and three months of kickboxing classes. She knew how to deliver a heel strike. If she timed it perfectly, and everything went her way for once, she would get in one solid kick, maybe two, before Thomas could react. If she connected with his chin or his nose on the first blow, blinding him with pain, she had a chance. A few more heel strikes to the face would put Thomas out of the fight for long enough to . . .

To what? What do I do then?

The door locking button was inches from her nose. The locks had thunked into place moments after they started driving, either due to Kendrick hitting the switch or an automatic feature activated when the car moved. The question was—had Kendrick engaged the child safety lockout mechanism, which would prevent someone in the backseat from unlocking the door? And if not, what was she going to do? Jump out of a moving car? With her luck, she would either be run over by another car, or smash her head open like a discarded pumpkin.

And she would be abandoning Siobhan, which is exactly what she had tried to avoid.

If she squinted her right eye, she could just make out some strands of the girl's dark hair in the narrow crack between the seat and the door. "*Do as you're told,*" Milos had said, "*or I'll have her turning tricks before nightfall.*" And he had played her just right. No way could Britte condemn the girl to that kind of life.

Kendrick's voice came from the front, "This whole state can go straight to hell. I never want to see this ass-backward place again, as long as I live."

"Amen to that," rumbled Thomas. "Although, looks like mission accomplished, huh? We got what we came for."

"Hotel guy and a *sniper.*" Kendrick's tone carried a thick layer of disgust. "Man, that's some crazy shit. Hold on . . ." The sound of a ringtone burbled through the car. Kendrick picked it up rather than put it on speaker. "Yeah? . . . Uh-huh . . . Yep . . . You sure? . . . Okay, then. Later."

Britte failed to make out the direction of the conversation from Kendrick's tone. However, when the car slowed and the sound of the road's shoulder rumbled as Kendrick pulled over, Britte's throat squeezed tight. The word had been delivered. Cut the loose ends. Move on. If she didn't act, the next few moments would be Siobhan's last on earth. And hers.

Damned if I let that happen.

Mahoney hated the Porsche, and the Porsche hated Mahoney. Controlling the car at one-hundred-plus miles per hour on a twisty, corncob road worked every muscle in his body. Sweat saturated his shirt and dripped from his eyebrows. No matter where he rested his right arm, it ached with a constant, eye-watering pain. No position could help with his cracked ribs, either, as the GT2's sports-tuned suspension found every bump in the poorly maintained asphalt and magnified the sensation. The shoulder strap pummeled him like a prizefighter going for the body. His left arm ached from the constant strain of keeping the car out of the ditches. The willful beast seemed to be fighting Mahoney, as though resentful that he was not a more experienced driver.

Some guys would give their left arm for a chance to drive a 911 GT2 RS. Mahoney was ready to trade both arms just to get out.

Traveling northeast from Cottonwood, Highway 379 became County Road 480, which meant it was built by the Romans, patched with Silly Putty, and followed property lines laid down by Sam Houston when Texas was a part of Mexico. The carcasses of opossum, skunk, raccoon, and armadillos provided mushy speed bumps that Mahoney mostly dodged.

Three minutes after leaving Cottonmouth behind, he gritted his teeth and forced the Porsche through a tight curve—the warning sign advised the curve to be handled at 35 mph. Mahoney took it at twice that speed, then hammered down on the gas.

Traffic, thankfully, was nonexistent. He had passed one vehicle but Mahoney blew by it so fast, the pickup truck appeared to be going backward in time.

No matter how fast he pushed the shiny white sports car, the sick, squirmy feeling in his gut wouldn't go away. Repeating like the chorus of a bad rock song, the same lines cycled over and over in his head . . .

I'm too late; I'm too late.

Oh Lord, don't let me be too late.

Britte kept her eyes closed.

"Friendship Baptist Church," Thomas said, apparently reading from a sign. "Why're we stopping here?"

"Because," Kendrick said.

Her mind raced through various scenarios, none of which ended with her and Siobhan escaping alive. If she kicked Thomas and ran the instant the door locks clicked open, she *might* get away, but Siobhan was as good as dead. If she waited until everyone was out of the car before making a break for it, somehow dragging Siobhan with her, then Kendrick would shoot them both in the back before they made ten yards. Which left her with one option . . .

"Okay, ladies, time to get out," Kendrick said as the car came to a halt. "Boss man said you're free to go."

"Say what?" Thomas demanded. "We're just letting them go? After all this shit?"

"Wake her up," Kendrick told him. His voice had taken on a false undertone of cheeriness. Leather creaked and plastic snapped. "She's probably playing possum anyway. And you, sugar. Unbuckle your belt. Come on, Thomas, let's give the ladies a hand out of here."

The locks clicked again, and the driver's door opened. Britte felt the car shift as Kendrick climbed out.

"Wake up," Thomas growled. He shoved her shoulder. "Wake the hell up, Blondie."

Britte pretended to come to, groggy and disoriented. "Where are we?"

"Get out of the car," Thomas said, shoving her against the door. "You're going for a walk, looks like."

The door opened and Kendrick was there, dragging her out. She stumbled a bit, only half-pretending. She shivered, though the outside air was muggy and still. Siobhan appeared next to her, and Britte threw an arm over the girl's shoulder. The child's tremor matched her own.

"What's going on?" Britte didn't have to work at adding a fearful tremble to her voice. Electric terror buzzed through her all the way down to her fingertips. She used the moment of pretend confusion to take in the surroundings.

The Yukon's interior lights spilled from the SUV's open doors, illuminating a circular space in a small parking lot behind a single-story frame building—apparently the Friendship Baptist Church. The surrounding night was as pitch black as she had ever seen it. Humidity clogged the air and clouds hid the stars. No moon, either. Thick stands of trees bore silent witness to the scene, shadowed spectators, stoic and uncaring. Night bugs quizzed the darkness.

"Go on," Kendrick said. "Get to walking. It's been fun, but we gotta get on the road."

He had the decency not to display a weapon. Were they really letting them go?

No. Kendrick wouldn't need to get out of the car just to send them on their way. Two steps away, maybe three, and the gun would appear. A bullet to the back of each of their heads would rid Stankovic of two potential witnesses.

Britte gripped Siobhan and pulled her tight, trying to communicate her plan without words. They shared a look. Siobhan's face glowed ghostly white and she swallowed convulsively. Britte turned on her high-wattage smile.

"It's okay, honey," she said. "I've got you."

Siobhan rewarded her with a flicker of hope in her eyes.

With that, Britte spun the girl away, putting herself between Siobhan and the men and pushing Siobhan in the back. "Run!"

Siobhan took off like a deer. Britte ran behind her, dodging and weaving to block Kendrick's aim. If she could only buy a few seconds, Siobhan could make the darkness of the forest and get away. The girl was fast. Already she was a car length away and adding to her lead with every step. "Go!" Britte cried, not sure if she was speaking out loud or only in her mind.

A hammerblow hit her in the back and Britte pitched forward. Hot gravel slammed her palms and burned her cheek. It felt like an axe had been buried in her back. She couldn't breathe. More shots banged out.

Britte felt the world go away, fading out like the end of a sad movie, the title to which she couldn't recall.

Mahoney saw the flash and thought it was lightning. The weak flare of light pulsed from behind a dark building, once, twice, and then he was past it, the Porsche gobbling up road faster than his brain could interpret the meaning of the tiny flicker.

Gunshot.

His foot stabbed the brake before he consciously recognized the faint report. The 911 stood on its nose. Pain exploded across his chest as the seatbelt carved a line from collarbone to waist. The rear end broke loose amid a scream of burning rubber. The Porsche spun. Headlight beams sliced the darkness, and smoke billowed up around the car in blue clouds.

The car rocked a moment, then rested.

Mahoney blinked watery eyes and drew a breath despite the knife stabbing his ribs. Orientation with the real world required a moment's concentration. The car was angled across the road, nose pointing at the forest. The building from where the gunshots came was behind him and to his left. A hulking shape, vaguely outlined against a black background. A hundred, hundred-fifty yards away.

He gentled the accelerator to get the car moving again. It

wobbled and bumped onto the ragged shoulder. Something scraped the underside and Mahoney winced. *Sorry, Hans.* Then he was moving again, gaining momentum.

It was a church. A small cross stood at the building's apex. Set off the road in a clearing, with a paved lot on the side, and some sort of sign out front, the church grew larger in his headlights. More light glowed from the rear of the building. Someone else was parked there. Someone shooting a gun, based on his earlier impression.

He wheeled the Porsche into the lot and cut the car around the side in a semicontrolled drift.

And there was Thomas. And Kendrick. Both standing a few paces away from a parked SUV. Weapons dangling. Eyes goggling at the apparition of a sports car in their private little shooting gallery.

Mahoney stomped the gas and the car surged forward. He aimed for the pair of men, intending to cut them both down like wheat. Kendrick reacted faster than Thomas.

Kendrick dove for the SUV, rolling away at the last instant. Thomas was as slow as he was big. The Porsche scythed his legs at shin height, and the slab of beef slammed into the hood, then the windshield. Safety glass crunched in a spiderweb. Blood splattered the windshield like so much tossed paint. Thomas's loose body tumbled away, and Mahoney slued the car to a stop.

With his right arm fucked, he ignored the shifter, letting the car roll forward in low gear. He fought his way free of the seatbelt, yanked the door pull, and tumbled free. Rough gravel scraped his palms, his elbows. Freakish pain blinded him when his broken arm hit the ground.

He was up before he realized it. Weapon somehow drawn.

A shape struggled upright, outlined against the interior lights of the SUV. Kendrick squared up at eight yards. A perfect silhouette target. Concussion and heat slapped Mahoney's cheek as a bullet blistered by. Mahoney aimed one handed. Shots banged out on long tongues of fire. Kendrick flew backward, thudded into the SUV's rear door.

A high-pitched whine in Mahoney's ears blocked out all other sounds. Kendrick gasped out black bubbles and stirred as Mahoney approached on silent footsteps. The man looked up and said something, his lips forming words that Mahoney couldn't hear. He heard nothing, not even when the pistol bucked in his hand and he put the final shot between Kendrick's eyes.

Mahoney shuddered and let his hand drop.

A quick check of Thomas confirmed Mahoney's initial impression that the big man had died on impact. His crew-cut head was split open like an over-ripe tomato, features distorted as if a mask had fallen loose.

The taillights of the Porsche drifted away, following its high beams. The sports car rumbled along at a walking pace, driver's door sagging open, headed toward the East Texas woods like it wanted to see what was hidden there, but was in no hurry to do so. Mahoney sympathized with the car—there were things he needed to see but didn't want to. Nothing else stirred in the dark lot—not a breath of wind, nor a single human motion.

"Britte! Siobhan!" Mahoney's eyes adjusted to the darkness and details congealed.

Two shapes lay close together, a dozen feet away. Unmoving.

Mahoney jogged on wooden legs.

One was Siobhan. Tumbled into a rag doll heap, the girl appeared to be sleeping. Mahoney couldn't see a trace of a wound. He touched the girl on the shoulder and rolled her onto her back. Blood matted her hair and Mahoney's heart seized. A soft wheeze came from the girl's lips. Somehow, she was still breathing.

Britte lay close by, facedown, a splotch of darkness staining the back of her blouse. When Mahoney touched her on the neck, warmth met his fingers, along with the sensation of a stuttering breath. He blinked in surprise, and strange emotions crashed through his soul. Relief, dread, heartbreak, joyfulness—all hit him at once. He wanted to laugh and cry with the same breath.

He ran for the Porsche.

11

Mahoney perched on the edge of a green sofa and studied the rust-red bits of dried blood that flaked from his hands and floated to the hardwood floor like so much gory dandruff. His right arm throbbed in time to the beat of his heart. A post-traumatic body ache soaked his over-strained muscles.

He sat in a waiting room that was once a living room, in a clinic disguised as a house, built in a refugee camp masquerading as a small town, in which broken people pretended to be normal citizens. From the outside, the clinic appeared as nothing more than a modest, three-bedroom frame house nestled among pines on the fringes of Cottonmouth. Inside, modern medical gear revealed its true purpose.

A male voice drifted down the hall from the open door of an examination room, originally a guest bedroom. Hans, doped to the gills, warbled snatches of German drinking songs, mixed with off-color commentary about the sexual preferences of former commanding officers. He had been getting his leg patched up by the on-call trauma team when Mahoney had barged in, carrying a ghost-pale Britte, her bright red blood seeping through his fingers.

The medical team had stabilized Siobhan as best they could, then evac'd her via helicopter to a trauma center. In the master bedroom that was now a fully loaded operating theater, Doctor Morgenstern and his competent-but-always-frowning nurse had been operating on Britte Thorpe for the past two hours.

An electric buzz-click announced the front door unlocking—the keypad was hidden behind a porch decoration—and Hannah Moshe entered the room, followed by her husband, Asim. Like all good spies, Hannah could pass unnoticed in a parade of one. The former operative for Israel's Institute for Intelligence and Special Operations dressed like a small-town businesswoman and wore her curly, black hair done up in a bun atop her head. She was the woman who brought cookies to the PTA meeting, and baked challah for Shabbat. Her Muslim husband was as dapper as his wife was frumpy. Never without his bow tie and suitcoat, Asim Suleimani was a slight man with a shy smile and intelligent eyes hidden by thick, round glasses. As far as Mahoney could tell, the couple had been deeply in love for the last thirty years, dating back to when Hannah recruited the Iranian nuclear physicist as an asset for the Mossad.

"Zivon is finished sanitizing the site," Hannah glared at Mahoney, transferring her angry look to her husband when Asim brushed past her and laid a hand on Mahoney's shoulder.

"How are they?" the small man asked.

Mahoney shrugged. "No word yet. I guess that's a good sign."

"Yes. That is a good sign."

"Do not coddle him," Hannah snarled. "It is his fault we have this mess."

A spark of annoyance fell on damp tinder at Mahoney's core and failed to ignite. He was too tired for a fight. He shook his head and scraped a thumbnail through the dried blood on his hands. Red snow fluttered to the floor. It reminded him of the biker bar.

Why are my hands always covered in blood?

"Hannah," chided Asim. "Mahoney did the only thing a man could do. Was he just to stand by and let the outlaws take the woman and the girl? Would John Wayne do this? Gary Cooper?"

The Israeli woman stamped her foot. Hannah was the only woman Mahoney knew who ever did that. It made him smile, despite the block of ice inside his chest.

"This is not one of your Westerns, my husband. This is our life, too!"

"Well, hell, Hannah," Mahoney said, standing up. "I'll just go shoot her now, okay?"

"Don't be a jackass," Hannah huffed. "I was only saying, good reasons notwithstanding, we have a situation on our hands. Dead bodies everywhere. Hans is wounded. The child is injured and may not live. The woman's status is unknown—"

Hannah broke off when Doc Morgenstern appeared. Scrubs patched by sweat and stained by blood, the doctor stood in the entrance to the back hall, wiping his hands on a green towel. At his shoulder appeared the lemon-faced Nurse Wilma—Mahoney had never heard a last name. Morgenstern and his dour nurse provided medical services ranging from routine checkups to emergency intensive care. The doctor was the archetype of every white-haired, wise, no-nonsense physician ever produced by central casting. Mahoney often wondered what Lofland had leveraged to get a first-class doctor like Morgenstern to live in this little backwater town. As the personal physician for the smallest private practice in the world, the guy had to be making more per patient than the entire staff of MD Anderson averaged in a year.

"Barring complications," Morgenstern said to the room at large, "The patient should make a full recovery, though range of motion in her left shoulder will be limited. The amount of limitation will be defined by the quality and duration of physical therapy. The bullet struck the scapula and was deflected upward, through the trapezius muscle. Most of the surgery involved removing bone shards from the wound."

"Any word on the girl?" Mahoney asked.

"I haven't had time to check. I'll do that next."

Mahoney nodded to the back room. "Is she awake?"

"Of course not. The patient is in post-op recovery and will regain consciousness at her own pace."

"Great," Hannah said. "Glad that's settled. Mahoney, you need to come with us."

"Why?"

"Lofland's here. He wants to see you."

"Oh. Wow." Mahoney glanced from a firm-jawed Hannah to a sheepish Asim. "That was fast."

"Not really," Hannah said. "I called him yesterday first thing." Mahoney's face went dark. "What?" she nearly shouted. "I had to! And you can see I was right. This situation is completely out of control."

Mahoney levered upright, cradling his right arm.

"What's wrong with your arm?" Morgenstern asked.

"Broken, I think."

"Were you going to mention it?"

"Depends." Mahoney looked at Hannah. "Is my insurance coverage still good?"

"Go on, Mahoney," she said, not without pity. "Get your arm seen to. Lofland can wait."

Dawn was near by the time Hannah drove them to the back lot of the grandiosely named Mercantile Building in downtown Cottonmouth. During the roaring age of post–World War I

America, the two-story, red-brick structure at the corner of Miller and Pecan Street had been a prestigious office, a vital and vibrant business place for attorneys, accountants, and architects. The seismic shifting economic plates that had rendered so much of Small Town, USA, into sallow, decaying corpses had left the Mercantile a hollow shell—at least, by all outward appearances.

A tired streetlight struggled against the darkness of the parking lot. Hordes of black crickets partied the night away under its weak, gray illumination. Weeds broke through the asphalt and broken glass glittered. A new Yale lock on the rusted-red back door turned without resistance when Hannah applied her key. The door groaned open, and Mahoney followed Asim and his wife into a gloomy hallway, littered with dust and spiderwebs. Hannah clicked an ancient switch and a weak overhead bulb flickered to life. The door boomed shut behind them and Mahoney twisted the thumb turn to lock it.

At the end of the hall, a steel door awaited them, and here, all pretense of abandonment vanished. Secured by an electro-magnetic, biometric lock, and thick enough to shrug off an RPG, this interior door separated facade from reality. Government contractors, flown in from parts unknown and working under the cover of night, had transformed the Mercantile's interior into a modern office suite befitting a midlevel government agency, suitable for GS-13 and above. Beyond the door lay an open foyer with a reception area / waiting room filled with bland furniture. Four well-appointed offices flanked the foyer, two per side, each enclosed behind solid-core wood doors. A conference room with seating for twelve took up the far side. There were no windows, and the entirety of the enclosed space was shielded from electronic eavesdropping, like one giant SCIF—a sensitive compartmented information facility.

The door to Lofland's office stood open, so Mahoney went

in without an invitation. He also closed the door behind him without waiting for instruction and took a seat before Lofland told him to.

Bosses like it when you show initiative, right? Look at me, being a self-starter.

Across the desk, Lofland two-finger tapped his laptop's keyboard without acknowledging Mahoney's presence. As far as Mahoney could tell, Lofland didn't have a title or a life beyond his duty as liaison to the Island of Misfit Spies. In his mid-to-late-fifties, Lofland wore his hair cropped short, carried a beer keg belly on stout legs, and smoked cigars the size of cruise missiles.

Lofland settled the laptop's screen down with a soft click and regarded Mahoney with tired eyes. A gold ring glinted from his pinkie finger when Lofland tented his hands.

"You are quite the spectacular fuckup, aren't you?"

"Well, 'spectacular' is a bit harsh, don't you think? Remarkable. Breathtaking, maybe. But spectacular—"

"Shut up, Mahoney." Lofland rubbed his face and his chair squealed when he leaned back. "We have six dead and three wounded. Dead civilians."

"Wait." Mahoney counted on his fingers. The fog of painkillers made thinking as difficult as putting together a puzzle while blindfolded. "Three at the cabin . . . the dynamic dumbasses . . . that's five."

"Zivon backtraced the SUV's GPS and found the green car the subjects used. Followed that back to body number six. A resident of this shithole named Thurgood Marshall Smith, shot in the head on his porch. Another crime we can lay at the feet of your dynamic duo of would-be kidnappers."

"Damn. I knew Thurgood. He was good people."

"As is the child, I'm sure."

"Fuck you, Lofland." Bitterness welled up inside Mahoney

like the taste of burned coffee. "You know I didn't want that to happen. I was trying to protect them—"

"And look how that turned out."

Mahoney hunched, as if taking a punch to the gut. Guilt twisted the breath out of him in a long exhale. His head throbbed. "Great mic drop, Lofland. But why would they do that? Why kill them?"

"Eliminating witnesses," Lofland said "Cutting their losses. Or as punishment. We found this in one of the dead guys' pockets." He tossed out a velvet sack, from which tumbled a trio of glittering stones. The size of the sack indicated more stones lay inside. "Presumably the woman stole this from her boss. Most criminals don't take kindly to people stealing from them." He flicked a hand as if brushing off a gnat. "But, really. Who the fuck cares?"

"Wait. Seriously . . . ?"

"You should have stayed out of it. But, no. You had to play white knight, didn't you? And now you have brought attention to yourself, and this community, Mahoney. What's the number one rule of your new life? What did we agree to, back in the day? Two words. Say them after me: Stay. Hidden."

"Look, Lofland—"

"And this is your second strike, isn't it? The last time it was some trucker beating on a prostitute, as I recall, there in your motel. You recollect how that turned out? Had to bury the body . . . repaint the room, replace the carpet . . . pay off the hooker to keep her mouth shut . . . Any of this coming back to you?"

"Lofland." Mahoney studied the cards in his hands, holding them awkwardly with his right arm trussed in a sling, not remembering how they got there. "Listen to me carefully. You may own the pink slip on my life. I totally get that. Rescued me after I escaped that Balkan vacation retreat. Paid for my rehab. Set me up here as my own boss and gave me a town full of new

BFFs. All that is a debt I believe I paid in advance, but forget it, it doesn't matter. You own my ass, is what I'm saying."

"Yes, we do," Lofland agreed. "Glad you remember—"

"But," Mahoney interrupted, holding up a finger to forestall the thunderous mountain of ass chewing Lofland was building up to. "But . . . you don't own a single piece of my soul. And I will not. Absolutely. Ever. Walk away when someone needs me."

With that he got up and walked out.

Mic-fucking-drop that, asshole.

Mahoney marched through the reception area, ignoring looks from Hannah and Asim, and shouldered through the interior door without stopping.

Feeling as self-righteous as a Knight Templar on a holy crusade by the time he hit the outer door, Mahoney burst into the parking lot behind the Mercantile Building . . . and skidded to a stop. He double blinked, shifting mental gears. The lot was empty except for a gray sedan, some litter, and about a billion crickets. He rotated in place, turning in a small circle for a couple of heartbeats before it hit him.

He had ridden here with Hannah and Asim.

His Jeep was at Hans's place.

Mahoney considered trashing what was left of his dignity by going back inside and begging for a ride. The imagined looks of the people inside . . . Lofland's derision . . . Hannah's disdain . . . Asim's pity . . .

Mahoney started walking. Dead crickets crunched underfoot.

12

Mahoney walked back to his room at the motel and flopped on top of his bed without taking off his shoes. He slept for four hours, got up, showered with his arm in a trash bag, shaved with one hand, and had his assistant manager drive him out to Hans's cabin to retrieve his Jeep. He ditched his sling and shifted gingerly. He was back at the clinic before 6:00 a.m., only to learn that Britte was still mostly out of it and too groggy for coherent speech. Too out of it, he judged, for news of Siobhan's near death to penetrate the fog of drugs in her system. Mahoney patted her hand, avoided eye contact, and slunk away.

He ate breakfast at the OK Cafe—Falafel Waffles, an Asim specialty—which was prepared and served by the diner's backup staff, as neither the Iranian scientist-turned-cook nor his Mossad agent wife were present. Another confrontation avoided.

A text from Zivon killed his run of luck.

MB @ 0800. Comm mtg.

Mahoney translated the message as "Be at the Mercantile Building at eight a.m. for a Committee meeting."

"Ten minutes," he muttered into his cooling coffee. "Great. Thanks for the notice."

A few days after his introduction to Cottonmouth, Mahoney had slipped into the role of chairman for a then-nameless group of nonelected officials who oversaw the "special" residents of their little backwater hideaway. The agenda at these irregular council meetings was loosely arranged around four major topics: Security, Infrastructure, Logistics, and Intelligence. This body had little or nothing to do with the running of the city, but everything to do with protecting the community of broken operatives, retired spies, and foreign defectors who had been settled in Cottonmouth by a benevolent but paranoid federal bureaucracy. Although constantly watched, electronically monitored, and in all other ways kept on a tight leash by government minders like Lofland, the collective of former spooks felt obliged to remain diligent to protect their own interests—or to assuage their paranoia. Spies being spies, they obsessively gathered information, assessed threats, and managed dozens of conflicting agendas to avoid the type of ego-driven explosions that would tear apart their safe haven.

Within minutes of his first meeting, Mahoney had dubbed the group the Double-Secret Committee of Retired Super Spies.

The full name never really caught on, but "Committee" became the unofficial shorthand designation.

Mahoney paid his check and hopped into his Jeep for the quick drive to the Mercantile Building. Six cars were parked in the lot behind the Mercantile, which meant at least that many Committee members were already present, not counting Lofland. Mahoney left his Jeep on the street and walked around back. The cricket jamboree had wound down, leaving behind a few sluggish hoppers and a lot of crunchy corpses.

Mahoney found the conference room jam-packed. Word of

last night's action had obviously burned through their tight-knit little community like a bonfire in an oil refinery.

Nothing draws the spies out of the woodwork like a good gunfight, followed by a car chase and a killing. Probably hoping to get a contact high from the smell of blood and gunpowder.

The room fell silent as he entered. Mahoney smirked when he noticed the only two vacant seats left were the ones just inside the room, with their backs to the door. The Wild Bill Hickok seats, they were called.

"Mornin' folks." Mahoney grinned with the sincerity of a TV preacher. Nine pairs of eyes tracked him as he claimed one of the two remaining places. "Is this the day I get voted off Spook Island?"

Hans groaned and shifted in his seat. "Mahoney, if I could get out of this chair, I would kill you."

"My grandmother used to say the same thing." Mahoney, with air from the open door stroking his neck, resisted the urge to look over his shoulder.

Lofland sat at the far end of the table and toyed with an unlit, turd-colored Cuban missile. His expression suggested a bullet to Mahoney's head might be on the agenda.

Zivon loomed to Lofland's right, tall, blond, and grim. Then came Roxy Clark, a Brit with tie-dyed hair and each fingernail painted a different color. She wore the scent of C-4 like a perfume. Hans was next to her, disheveled and bed-headed. The German leaned his chair back against the wall, his bandage-wrapped stump poking from the leg of his shorts. His crutches leaned against the chair next to him. Directly to Mahoney's left, a Syrian named Abdul Abassi toyed with a pen, spinning it in circles on the table like a top. Abassi had been the longest-running and best-placed CIA mole inside the Libyan government and escaped that country seconds ahead of a mob who were in the process of overthrowing the government. Now he spent his days playing first-person shooter videogames with online strangers.

Hannah and Asim sat on Mahoney's right, with the unassuming Chan in his ever-present Hawaiian shirt next to them. Rounding out the table was a former SEAL named Billy McCurry, a man who carried a price on his head so big, anyone who claimed it could buy an island in the Caribbean. Twice a week, McCurry came by Mahoney's motel to swim laps in the pool. A twenty-year veteran of the war on terror, McCurry's dark skin was a quilt of scars, and his knees resembled brown dress socks filled with gravel.

Lofland wasted no time on preliminaries. "The situation summary is this: Mr. Mahoney intervened in a civilian law enforcement matter. As a result of that intervention, six civilians are dead, two are wounded, and Mr. Schlichter has sustained an injury—"

"And so has my car," Hans blurted. He glared at Mahoney with bleary red eyes. "It was injured as well."

"That's all right, dearie," Roxy patted Hans's stump. With a cheeky grin she added, "We've all seen Mahoney drive. I'm sure he didn't mean it."

"Yes," Mahoney said. "Yes, I did. I meant the hell out of it. As a murder weapon, your Porsche pulls a little to the right, Hans."

"One of the civilians is a juvenile female," Lofland continued in a monotone voice, as though reading from a teleprompter. "She has been airlifted to Houston for treatment. The wounded woman is expected to recover. Ms. Moshe, intelligence update, please?"

"We ran the prints of the dead men, and all members of the opposing force have been identified." Hannah cleared her throat and peered through her reading glasses at a sheet in front of her. "Maurice Damian Martins, L'Quan Elroi McCarthy, Tyrahn Deshawn Blankenship, Kendrick Johnson, and Thomas Michael

Pratt-Walker. The first three were all known members of the 52 Hoovers, a chapter of the Crips, and all with rap sheets long enough to bind a mummy." Hannah glanced up and twitched a frown when no one laughed at her joke. "The other two were bigger fish. The FBI has files open on both individuals. Johnson and Pratt-Walker have been linked as employees—enforcers—for Milos Stankovic."

"Stankovic?" Mahoney smirked. "I can't get over a bad guy with the name *Stank*-ovic?"

Hannah skewered him with an evil-eyed glare.

"Shut up, Mahoney," Lofland said. "Ms. Moshe, please proceed."

"The file on Stankovic," Hannah said to everyone else, studiously avoiding Mahoney, "reads like a trip through the sewer of human depravity. He got his start in Africa, in the DRC . . ."

"DRC?" Roxy asked.

"Democratic Republic of Congo. Born in the Sudan to ex-pat Bosnian parents, he somehow slithered into the diamond smuggling business, specializing in moving conflict diamonds from African mines, through Surat, India, and into the West. There is some suggestion that his partners in this operation include terrorist organizations in central Africa, such as Boko Haram."

Lofland picked up the briefing. "No proof, but plenty of coincidental evidence. Once established in the trade, Stankovic moved to the US, primarily, though he owns houses all over the world and prefers to spend most of his time on his yacht. Entertaining. Assume I just used air quotes."

Lofland cracked a tiny smile.

"Hysterical, Lofland," Mahoney said. "You should try stand-up."

Hannah Moshe resumed the presentation. "For reasons

that remain unclear, he branched out into a more prurient trade. First it was so-called gentleman's clubs—both extremely high-end as well as the trashiest all-nude stink holes from coast to coast—then he added an entire organization dedicated to the production and distribution of pornography. Most recently, he has made inroads into organized prostitution rings throughout the South. If a woman—or a man, for that matter—can be exploited, degraded, sold, or rented, then Stankovic's organization has a significant market share of the business." Here Hannah paused for breath and looked around the table, even meeting Mahoney's eye before continuing. "He has teams of 'talent scouts' searching all the usual places for recruiting both for street walkers and adult film talent." Hannah made a sour face. "Including girls as young as fourteen."

"Siobhan." Mahoney found his card deck in his hand. He fluttered through a cascade. Tough to do with an aching hand.

"Yes," Hannah said. "Odds are that is where the girl comes into the picture. Though why she is traveling with Thorpe is not clearly understood."

Billy McCurry, the ex-SEAL, slapped his hand flat on the table. "Shit, Mahoney. Your only problem is you didn't kill enough of them."

"Too bloody right," Roxy affirmed. "The man needs a string of det cord applied to his cock."

"Stow it," Lofland said. "This is not about yet another rotten fleck of dog vomit staining our nation. This is about a potential security breach that we need to contain."

"If this is such a bad man, the FBI knows so much about him . . ." Abassi said, "Why is he not . . . ah . . ." Abassi crossed his wrists. "Locked up, yes?"

"Good question." Hannah shuffled the few thin pages in front of her. "Except for the prostitution and, if true, the use of underage girls, nothing related to Stankovic's sexually oriented businesses is against the law. The FBI is interested in his diamond smuggling operation and couldn't care less about bringing down a . . . a what? A pimp?" Hannah shook her head. "Even so, the file on Stankovic was placed in 'Pending, Not Active' status. The last recorded document added to the file was in October, two years ago."

"What the everlasting fuck does that mean?" McCurry asked.

"It means," Lofland said, "that priorities at the Bureau shifted. Resource constraints being what they are, it is quite possible that hotter, larger cases are being worked first, with this one languishing until somebody has time to get around to it. This case was being worked out of the Tallahassee office, so for all we know, something of greater urgency sucked away all the manpower."

"Or somebody spiked it," Mahoney said.

Abassi frowned. "Explain 'spiked.'"

"Somebody higher up the food chain, maybe the SAC or somebody at Justice, said leave Stankovic alone."

"Why would you think that, Mahoney?" McCurry asked. "You know something we don't?"

"Because Mahoney is paranoid," Hannah said. "Everybody has the fix in, as far as he's concerned. There's absolutely no trace of a supervisor suspending this investigation. Everything just . . . stopped. Like Lofland said, it was probably a resource issue."

"It's not like somebody would sign their name to it, now would they, Hannah?" Mahoney fumbled a one-handed cut and his cards spilled into his lap. "Shit."

"Again," Lofland said, "we're chasing down a rabbit hole. Mr. Zhivanevskaya, you cleaned up the field of engagement. Please give us your assessment of the OPFOR."

Zee fixed his eyes on a point beyond the room and recited like a man reading bullet points off a PowerPoint. "At cabin, three KIA. All armed with the nonlethal weapons. One armed with handgun. Nine-millimeter. One round discharged. One expended flash-bang grenade found. One Taser fired, unknown the number of discharges—"

"Seventy billion," Mahoney said.

"All KIA, dispatched by small caliber weapon, wielded with the greatest of skill." Zee broke off to bestow upon Hans a respectful nod. The German sat straighter in his seat. "The OPFOR executed poor tactical assault. Stood all together. They did not plan for the rear guard."

"Cannon fodder," McCurry said.

"Just so," Zee allowed. "At the secondary site, two OPFOR KIA, two civilian WIA. The woman and the girl were shot from behind, apparently while fleeing." Mahoney cringed at the clinical nature of Zivon's report. "Two 9mm handguns recovered, both with multiple discharged rounds. One subject, the white male, died of the blunt force trauma—"

"Blunt Porsche trauma is what I heard," Roxy interjected.

"—and the Black man suffered many gunshot wounds. Killed by quantity of bullets, not placement."

"It's the result that counts," Mahoney grumbled.

"SSE conducted. Material delivered to Chan for the analyzing. Assessment: OPFOR is armed okay, trained not so good, and motivated by the profit. This is not to say they are not a danger. Gangsters can be danger, yes? Assessment ends."

"Get to the part about my car," Hans moaned. "Where is it? What did Mahoney do to it?"

"In my garage." Zee shrugged. "Is possible we save it. Maybe yes, maybe no."

"Oh, come on," Mahoney muttered. "I didn't hit the guy that hard."

"Mahoney." Hans pointed his finger like a gun. "I'm going to strangle you."

"Have to catch me first, Hopalong."

"I swear to God, I should knock your heads together . . ." Lofland trailed off, muttering something about a room full of third graders. Mahoney resisted the urge to say, *He started it.*

"We need a threat assessment," Hannah said.

Lofland nodded. "Agreed. How likely is it this community is compromised? Mr. Chan, anything on the material provided by Mr. Zhivanevskaya?"

If the Chinese spy had a name other than Chan, Mahoney had never heard it. Bland, round-faced, and modest, Chan was to electronic espionage like Nicola Tesla was to electricity. Mahoney was in awe of the man's skills. Chan could eavesdrop on a phone booth in Kazakhstan with two tin cans and a piece of string, or Trojan Horse his way into Fort Meade's most encrypted servers using a Commodore 64 and a 9600 Baud modem.

Chan acknowledged the room with a slight tilt of his head. "Cracking the phones proved easy. Most used the thumbprint," he wiggled his thumb to illustrate, "and Mr. Zee had thoughtfully removed those and brought them to me."

Mahoney shuddered at the gruesome task of matching severed thumbs to phones. *This little piggy goes to iPhone, this little piggy goes to Samsung . . .*

"We downloaded hundreds of phone numbers and texts, of course," Chan continued. "Mr. Zee suggested we concentrate on the two main actors, Johnson and Pratt-Walker, and that we have done. As to the phone numbers most frequently called, and their contact lists, we were not sure how . . . ah, diligent you wished our inquiry to be . . ."

Mahoney smiled. Translation: *How many federal laws did you want us to break by hacking private cellular data to run down the identities of the callers and contacts?*

Chan continued. "A cursory examination shows contact

was made between Johnson and a person identified in his contact list as OD."

"Cross-referencing with the FBI file," Hannah said, "we believe this to be Onye Dawali, one of Stankovic's top lieutenants."

Chan inclined his head in Hannah's direction. "Just so. An analysis of the text messages and call logs reveals the . . . unusual nature . . . of the situation these two encountered when attempting to retrieve the female subjects. OD, or Dawali, if you will, took command of the situation and ordered reinforcements dispatched."

McCurry paddled the table in a two-handed drum roll. "And then when things went to shit, the bad guys decided to ditch the witnesses and move on. And would have gotten away clean except for Lancelot riding up in his shiny white Porsche."

"Lancelot?" A crease formed between Zee's eyebrows. "Who is Lancelot?"

"American word for car thief," Hans muttered.

"Two things," Lofland said in his portentous manner. "One, we may have come to the attention of a criminal by the name of Milos Stankovic, who will no doubt wonder what happened to his people . . . and to the witnesses he wished dead. Two, civilians have been exposed to several of you and are aware that you are more than you seem. Both of these circumstances need to be managed."

Mahoney jumped to his feet. "Wait a fucking minute! Tell me we're not in cover-up mode. Stankovic needs to be dealt with. He's not going to just fold up and disappear without trying to get his diamonds back, at the very least."

"Mahoney," Lofland said. "Despite popular fiction, the government does not go around terminating innocent citizens because they are inconvenient. It's much less fuss to buy them off. I will have a talk with Ms. Thorpe when she's able to—"

"About that," Hannah interrupted. "I . . . we . . . recovered the woman's prints from her luggage. Her real name is Bridgette Knudsen, from St. Paul, Minnesota."

Lofland waved off the distinction. "I will recommend to my superiors that we develop an intelligence package on Stankovic. Passive only. We will gather this information only to defend against any aggressive response from him. No direct action is sanctioned. Understood, Mahoney?"

Mahoney remained standing. He gathered his cards and rapped them into a brick. His jaw was tight, face hot. Fortunately, his hands barely shook at all. There was no sign of the ringing in his head.

"Mahoney?" Lofland barked. "Do. You. Understand?"

"This is not a crusade, Mahoney," Hannah said, not without sympathy. "You cannot save everyone. Not every wrong has to be righted."

"No," Mahoney snapped. "Of course not. God forbid we hurt a scumbag's feelings."

13

"I'm with Mahoney," Roxy said to the collected members of the Committee. "This bloke, Stankovic, doesn't deserve to be breathing my bloody oxygen. I say Zee shimmies up a tree and blasts his bloody lights out from a mile away." She twiddled her fingers and waggled her eyebrows like a cartoon villain. "Or he gets a gelignite special delivery from Mother Roxy."

"Oo-rah," said McCurry.

"This is not a Star Chamber," Lofland stamped his words with authority. "This is a community that exists by the pleasure of the United States government. I shouldn't have to remind anyone of the terms of their individual agreements, all of which expressly forbid unlawful activity, no matter the precipitating action. In simple words, Mahoney, you step a toe out of line, and I'll stomp on it with my size twelve government-issued Oxford shoe. Rein it in and let's get straight on the Rules of Engagement."

Mahoney's jaw dropped. "The Rules of . . ."

"He's a diamond smuggler and a creep, nothing more. Rule One: There is no engagement. Period. I will make some calls and try to learn why the investigation is stalled. In the meantime, we have a freezer full of bodies we need to make disappear."

Chan raised a finger for attention. "The phone records show Johnson and Pratt-Walker called the person known as 'OD' after they left the cabin with the women. They would have reported the deaths of their gang companions, yes?"

"I would assume so," Lofland said.

"Given the timeline, they were dispatched by Mr. Mahoney before another call was made," Chan added, then paused like a teacher waiting for his students to catch up.

Hannah was the first to respond. "They never got a chance to call in. Their boss doesn't know they're dead."

"Both of the men's cell phones," Chan said, "have received numerous calls and texts from OD. The texts are requesting a status report. We could easily respond via text and . . . ah, craft the narrative."

McCurry belted out a laugh. "Say, 'Took the money, took the women, headed for Mexico. 'Kay-thanks-bye.'"

Chan inclined his head to McCurry, a slight smile curving his lips.

"Maybe not quite so obvious." Mahoney pinched his lip, eyes boring a hole in the table while he thought. "Assume for a second that Stankovic's people can track their people's phones, using a Find Me app of some kind . . ."

"There is such an app installed," Chan said.

Mahoney looked up. "Then how about we send an 'all-ok' message every day or so, but carry the phones farther and farther away? Make it look like they're making a run for it?"

"The purpose?" Lofland asked.

"Buy us some time for you to make your calls," Chan said. "Send Stankovic on a . . . ah, a wild chase of the geese. While he may not believe they have deserted him, he can never know for sure."

Hannah, for once, seemed to agree with him. "It is misdirection. It is what we do, no?"

"I like it," Roxy said. She winked at Mahoney privately, conveying a message he failed to interpret. "All in favor say 'aye,' and let's get out of here. I'm late for my brew up."

Lofland nodded once and fixed his attention on Mahoney. "This is your mess, so you get to make the run with the phones. Get what you need from Chan and get out of here. If Stankovic checks, he needs to see his people on the move, not sitting in Cottonmouth."

"Sure," Mahoney said. "Can I take the Porsche?"

"Noooo!"

The scream ripped out of her guts. A rusty railroad spike stabbed through her shoulder and pain skyrocketed, exploded, and rained fire throughout her body. But it didn't matter. She welcomed pain. She deserved it, and more. The morphine cloud burned away as Britte clamped the damp pillow around her face and screamed again. Monitors blipped and chirped in anxious frenzy.

Mahoney stood by her bed, one arm in a sling, hollow-eyed, with a hangdog look about him. She lay on her stomach, the bandage adhesive stretching and pulling at the skin of her back. An IV needle was taped to her hand. He hadn't wanted to tell her what had happened, but she'd pushed and pushed . . . and now she wished she had left it alone.

"How could you?" Britte croaked. "How could you let it happen?"

"I . . ." For once, words seemed to fail the man. He looked out the window, refusing to meet her eyes.

"We trusted you. You said we'd be safe. And now Ella is in a coma because of you."

A cloud of confusion passed over his face and Britte realized that she had called Siobhan by her sister's name but was too sick and hurt to care.

"Get out of here!" Britte's eyes burned and watered. Odd, she had long since thought herself incapable of tears.

Mahoney nodded once. Then turned and walked away.

Hours later, the last golden light of day tinged the curtains. A single wall sconce lit the bedroom and the medical monitors flickered in greens and reds. Britte floated on a morphine cloud, forced to remain facedown since every time she tried to roll over; lightning shot through her shoulder blade and lights danced in her eyes. She had vague memories of the passing hours. Both the doctor and the nurse had been in, fussing over vitals or forcing her to blow into a plastic doohickey with a floating ball to test her lung capacity. Her sweaty hair itched, and a thick, pungent body odor accompanied the perspiration soaking her sheets.

The woman called Hannah may have visited her. Britte couldn't recall clearly or trust the things she could recall. Dope always did that to her, mixing reality with dreams in such a way that she couldn't separate the two. Except for the memory of Devlin Mahoney coming to tell her that Siobhan was in a coma. That stood out, clear and sharp as jagged glass. Things faded after that.

At one point, she was sure Milos had visited, impossible as that was. He appeared as he had the first time she'd met him—at a nightclub in Montreal. Broad-shouldered, tapered waist. Brooding eyes and midnight black hair. Matching beard stubble. Obviously rich, but not flaunting it.

He lit a cigarette in defiance of the club's no smoking policy. No one challenged him. "Do you like to sail?"

"Of course," she said.

"Then come, let us go for a ride on my boat."

Boat. The craft was three times as large as the house she'd grown up in.

The party on the yacht never ended, or so it seemed to Britte in those days. Milos and his friends. Men of power. Influence. Fame. And wealth. Britte mingled with rock stars and sports heroes. Movie stars and tycoons of industry. An infinite variety of dope awaited consumption, laid out in a buffet: coke, pot, hashish, X, and designer drugs with no street name. Thousand-dollar-a-bottle champagne. All of it free.

Free. Britte snorted and fresh dampness soaked her pillow. Nothing was free.

There were women, of course. Competition? Hardly. A dozen or more of the most exotic beauties, wearing shoestring bikinis and predatory smiles. Decorations. Adornments. Playthings. And Britte was the Queen Plaything, jealously guarding her place by Milos's side. She was eighteen, still growing into her beauty, tragically inept at sex. Her lovers up until then had been boys, gangling and awkward, and all on a hair-trigger. Not Milos. Milos had taught her so many things in the bedroom.

Siobhan was on the boat. No. Wait. That wasn't right. Siobhan came later. All the girls were young, of course. Not Siobhan's age, but many not old enough to buy a beer on their own. Britte wasn't looking at IDs back then, only threats to her position. Her job was to be near Milos, to please him, and to enjoy herself. He was her teacher, her guide, her mentor, and she the eager student. Ever obedient. Ever diligent and attentive. Under his tutelage she thrived. Matured. And lacked for nothing.

She saw it as a natural progression as he eased into a management role. Jealousy faded away with sinecure and Milos took other women to bed. Often it was Britte who invited them into his arms, and at times even joined in. Somehow, she morphed from Queen Plaything to Mistress of the Harem, organizing and managing the gaggle of women who surrounded Milos and his guests.

"How are you feeling?"

White-haired Monroe . . . No, Morgan . . . Morgenstern. The doctor. He peered at her over the rims of his half glasses. Britte pulled her focus into the now. Formed words with a thick tongue.

"Hazy," she said. "Everything's hazy."

Poking and prodding. A blood pressure cuff squeezed her arm.

She blinked. Somehow it was late at night. They had dimmed the sconce. The silence of deep darkness seeped through the curtains.

Milos sat in the chair, angled into the corner by the window. Cigarette smoke ribboned up from his hand. He flicked the butt with his thumb and ash sprinkled to the floor. Should he be smoking here? There was an oxygen tank close by. No, of course he could. They were at the villa. An ocean breeze lifted the smoke, carried it away. They were on the patio, and she stood hip-cocked and bold under the Florida sun.

"I need you to do something, my love," Milos said.

"Of course," she told him. Britte wore a Retrofete Auris dress in a sunny, tie-dye pattern, and Louboutin slingback pumps with spike heels. Her bodyguard, Thomas, waited patiently by the sliding glass door leading into the sunroom. She stood with her back to the railing, ignoring the opulent gardens. Farther away, beyond the security wall, the grounds tapered to a white-sand beach. Palm trees nodded. The sun warmed her bare shoulders.

Milos sipped from a champagne flute, using the hand holding his cigarette. The smoke curled over his forehead. "I have a very special request."

A slither of unease wound through her midsection. Special request?

"Tell me, darling," Milos continued. "How do you feel about smuggling diamonds?"

Britte snapped awake, the memory fresh as if it happened yesterday. Her pillow was soaked. Why was she crying? It's not like she didn't know how he made his money. Smuggling. Pornography. Prostitution. Exploitation. It was not the most heinous of crimes, and moving a few ounces of diamonds was not nearly as fraught with peril as an equivalent amount of heroin. Britte could have walked away at any time. Walked away from her Maserati and her wardrobe, and her never-ending supply of cocaine, and struck out on her own. She was intelligent, poised, capable. But . . . twenty-six years old, with no degree, and trained to be the toy of a sugar daddy . . . what was she going to do? Wait tables? Flip burgers?

Besides, she was in love with him. And she thought he loved her back.

So she'd done it. Run after run from India—the gem polishing capital of the world—to Europe, the Mideast, and the Americas. Small packets of unregistered diamonds hewn by near-slave labor from mines in Africa and sold to fund civil wars, terrorism, and other acts of criminality. A diamond was a rock, nothing more. To whom and for whom her lover sold them mattered not a bit to her.

Until Milos hit her one time too often and she tried leaving him.

Her face flamed at the memory of the broken bottle that he slashed her with. She had laid all night on the deck, blood soaking the cedar planks, and wept with pain and humiliation. In the morning, Milos had thrown a towel at her feet and told her to get cleaned up, she had work to do. Two days later, Siobhan appeared, giving Britte no choice but to live with the pain, the disfigurement, and to do whatever Milos said for as long as he found her useful.

Britte's shoulders convulsed with her sobbing and outrageous pain hammered her back. The monitors beeped unhappily. She cried harder and the knot of agony twisted tighter. She reveled in it. She deserved it. Britte levered herself upright and slammed her body back down. She twisted and rotated her arm until white-hot waves of pure electric lightning washed through her. It wasn't enough. She deserved worse. Much worse. Britte pushed at the sopping mattress, tangled in the sheets. She wanted to fall on the floor. She needed to feel her wound split open, be bathed in sure pure torment—

"Hey, what are you doing!" The nurse rushed in, followed by the white-haired doctor. She grabbed Britte, held her down. "Stop that!"

Britte shrieked so hard, her jaw ached. Her throat burned. Fire roared through her and every muscle cramped into tight knots of wet rope. The doctor and nurse were shouting. She couldn't hear them over her own screaming. A needle pricked her buttock and a coldness spread outward from the injection site.

She screamed at them to stop. Or maybe it was only in her mind that the words formed. *No! Don't you understand! Don't make the pain go away. I need the pain. I need the . . . pain . . . I . . . need . . .*

the pain

PART 2

14

Onye Dawali found his boss taking breakfast on the patio overlooking the compound's Olympic-sized pool. Milos Stankovic, having swum fifty laps as the sun came up, now sat before a plate of fresh fruit, a cup of Crema D'or yogurt from Hokkaido, and a carafe of Ethiopian dark roast. The morning sun glinted off his damp black hair, making it appear oiled. With his chiseled chin, hawkish eyes, and broad shoulders, Stankovic could have made the cover of a rugged, outdoorsy men's magazine, or starred in a series of action films.

Dawali stopped at a respectful distance, hands crossed in front of him as though at parade rest. His many years in the Sudanese Armed Forces had ingrained a habit of military bearing that still influenced his posture.

"Coffee?" Stankovic asked.

"No, thank you, sir."

Stankovic switched off the tablet propped up by his plate and fixed Dawali with his brooding, heavy-lidded stare. "Then tell me you bring at least a small bit of good news this morning." He gestured at the tablet. "The market is trending down, the jobs report is weak, and the deficit continues to grow. Have you solved the mystery of our missing men?"

"This is what disturbs me, sir. We tracked their cell phones to the Mexican border, then they were obviously switched off, or destroyed. We have had no contact in twenty-four hours."

"Nothing."

It was a statement, not a question, so Dawali remained silent.

"Have they run away, Onye?"

Dawali shifted and looked away. "I . . . do not know. My instincts say no. All communication was via text, and only short messages. The style was not congruent with Kendrick's normal messaging. Plus, he would not answer my voice calls."

The sea breeze ruffled the patio umbrella and carried with it the aftertaste of salt. A screeching gull wheeled and dived for the ocean. When he at last spoke, Stankovic's words came freighted with a heavy load of disapproval. "Someone is trying to mislead us."

"Yes, sir. I have people researching through various databases for any other anomalies related to Cottonmouth, Texas. After London and his team finish their current assignment, he will be leaving to infiltrate the town and attempt to learn more."

"Good, good. And has the situation with Catano resolved?"

"As we speak," said Dawali, checking his watch.

"I will reach out to some people I know, as well. Some of our A-list clients have greater access to information. They may prove useful. One way or another, Onye, I believe we should get to the bottom of this little mystery."

"And if our team has been compromised or killed?"

Stankovic squinted into the horizon a moment before replying. "I don't want to go to war without profit, but Britte and the girl are a security risk, and they have stolen a not insignificant amount of merchandise. If they are being harbored by the people of Cottonmouth . . ."

"Then we should take the appropriate steps to neutralize this risk and recover our property."

"Exactly," said Stankovic. "And Onye . . . I don't care if you have to burn the whole town down to ashes to do it."

Dawali checked the urge to salute. "Very good, sir."

Victor Catano woke up in the same bed he had slept in as a teenager. The room was now a "guest" bedroom, though the chances of his mother having guests approached a negative number. Junk and boxes of junk covered every surface and made the path between the bed and the door a hoarder's maze. Dust coated every surface and puffed to life every time he brushed up against something. It was killing his sinuses.

Light streamed through the crack in the curtains and slashed across his pillow. No doubt what had woken him. Victor threw off the covers and swung his feet to the floor. Scratched his shaggy chest. Took a moment to pause and reflect.

Look at me—thirty-two years old and hiding at Mom's house.

"Fuck you, Britte Thorpe," he said, not for the first time and probably not the last. The rotten bitch had played him like a bagpipe. *Save me*, she said. *Save us.* Making him think they had something, that they might build a life together if they could get away from Stankovic and his people. All they needed was enough money to get away and stay hidden. "*And you have access to the vault, right?*"

So what had he done? Fucked himself, that's what he'd done. Put together the plan that sprung Britte and the girl from the island, along with a handful of flawless and near-flawless stones, all in the one- to two-carat range. Used his position on Stankovic's security team to line up the boat, the car, and the diamonds.

Yeah, the woman had made some suggestions, sure. Contributed a couple of good ideas. But it was his plan.

"You know what will happen if they catch us," he had said.

"Then you better not let them catch us," she had told him. She'd looked at him with those soft eyes, so innocent and blue-gray, and after that he had sure lost all control.

They had snuck out in the dead of night, a mouse's fart away from getting caught more times than he cared to remember. A wild boat ride to the mainland to where Victor had stashed a car. As they zoomed away along dark highways, the heady thrill of escape sharpening all their senses, they had chattered nonstop. Britte and the girl sang along with the radio. Victor had never felt so alive. Protecting his woman and taking her away from danger.

The girl was admittedly a third wheel messing up Victor's dream of a new life. He planned to ditch her at the first opportunity. Who needed a kid hanging around when they were trying to build something together, the two of them? Of course, they would hide for a while, let the heat die down. Once Stankovic and Dawali lost interest, then they could sell off enough stones for the cash to fix Britte's face. It was the one piece of the picture in his head that was out of whack. Fix her scar, and the woman would be back to stunningly beautiful. The kind of woman he'd be proud to have on his arm. And she'd be grateful. Always grateful to the man who rescued her. And Victor could mold her like clay, shape her into the best wife a man could have.

Then came the morning he woke up alone.

Her room was empty. So was the girl's. Loopy from the dope she'd slipped him, Victor had stumbled around the motel in Tallahassee, trying to figure out where the woman had gone. And his car. And the diamonds. And his cell phone. And his pants. Two hours later, after reality had sunk its claws into his chest, he had done the only thing he knew to do.

He'd called his mom to come get him.

"Fucking bitch," Victor mumbled and scrubbed the sleep from his eyes. Now he knew why she'd insisted on her own room. In a falsetto voice full of self-mockery she said, "We should wait until we're safe and I've gotten my face fixed. I can't be with a man looking like this."

A thud from the other end of the house startled him out of his reverie. Either a door had been caught by the wind and banged shut, or something heavy had fallen. It sounded like it came from the living room, and there wasn't anything heavy there, unless he counted his mom. It was not nice to think of her that way, but the woman could stand to lose a few.

"You okay, Ma?"

No answer.

Victor had slept in his boxers. His pants were in a wad on top of a stack of U-Haul moving boxes. He was reaching for them when his door slammed open.

"Ma! Do you mind?"

It wasn't his mother. The towering figure of London Bridges ducked into the room. Tall and relentless as a tax audit, Bridges had dreadlocks down to his shoulders, and his biceps resembled an anaconda swallowing a pig.

"Your mother is dead," Bridges said in his lilting African accent.

"Wait, wait, wait—" The words bubbled from Victor. He held out his hands like a traffic cop, and warm wetness spilled down his leg. "Stop. Just stop, okay. You don't have to do this, man. I . . . I . . . didn't mean to—"

"I'm not here to kill you," Bridges said.

"Wait. What?"

"I am not here to kill you," Bridges repeated. The tall man glided through the maze of boxes, his expression as bland as ever.

A dozen emotions trilled through Victor's chest, rattling his heart with rapid-fire intensity. Utter, bowel-loosening terror gave way to relief, then hope, followed soon by despair as he realized there was no way he was getting out of this alive. It had to be a joke. Bridges was toying with him. He had witnessed Dawali's top enforcer slice open a man's stomach with care, then pull the man's intestines out in a big, slimy, looping mess. Bridges had kept the man alive long enough to witness the murder of his family. Only then had he been allowed to die.

"Don't kid me, man," Victor pleaded. "I know I fucked up. All I can say is I'm sorry. I want to . . ."

Victor's throat clenched up when Bridges slid his eight-inch Bowie from the sheathe at his back. The blade gleamed bright silver in the streaming sunlight.

"I said I'm not here to kill you," Bridges said. "Not that you would escape punishment. You thought to take the boss's woman, as if you were a man who thinks not with his head, but his prick." Bridges lifted the knife, seemingly admiring the flash of light off the blade. "Mr. Stankovic has ordered that I remove this offending organ, along with the two tiny peanuts you call balls."

Victor must have fainted then, because the next thing he knew, he was back on the bed, Bridges leaning over him. Cool air on his balls told him his shorts were gone. Two of Bridges men were in the room, holding his arms. Two more held his legs. It was very crowded in the small bedroom and many stacks of boxes had tumbled into heaps. The men had trampled all over his mom's belongings. Victor twisted, trying to hide his privates from Bridges's enormous hand. But it was no use.

Victor screamed.

And screamed, and screamed, and screamed.

15

It had taken London Bridges three nights to cover the motel with a dozen concealed cameras. He trusted no one else to do this task. His team had been dispersed throughout the county, renting rooms in motels as dingy as the target location. To avoid suspicion, the six-man team broke up into ones and twos, and left their equipment stowed in their vehicles. Bridges was the only one who entered Cottonmouth, and then only under the cover of darkness.

Each 1080p camera was solar powered with integrated batteries, and contained its own wireless SIM card, so wiring wasn't necessary. The difficult part of the job was to find surveillance points that offered good coverage, exposure to sunlight, and yet remained undetectable by the target. Sometimes placing the unit meant hiding it from sunlight as well, and this required running a wire to a separate solar power panel located some distance away from the camera. Though the cameras were small enough to fit inside a soda can, an observant target might spot them. Bridges never underestimated the sensitivity of surveillance targets to changes in their environment. Any object introduced to the landscape tended to snag the eye of even an untrained observer, thus placement required a cautious scouting of the terrain, some trial and error, and a tremendous amount of stealth. He made no physical movement without thought, care, and planning. Hours of observation went into every night's installation, requiring Bridges to lay belly-flat among every imaginable—and unimaginable—hiding spot to map his approach to the sites.

He had spotted enemy surveillance—observation posts—twice, in different locations. One on the main road, overwatching the highway, and one near the motel. Having to account for enemy OPs added a powerful degree of difficulty to the work.

After patient, methodical placement and testing of his entire network, including verification of the signal strength of each wireless cellular connection, Bridges had withdrawn to a town twenty-five miles away from Cottonmouth, where he had set up his home base in a chain motel that was light-years better than the sleazy motor court shown on his laptop. He didn't notice the furnishings. Didn't care. Bridges had little interest in anything other than his primary function. A bug-infested blind deep in the Sudanese wilderness, or a carbon-copy motel room in the American heartland, they were nothing but background noise. Places to do his work. Bridges was a point-and-shoot weapon, designed for two purposes: Find people. Kill them.

The sun beat down and turned the pool's surface into a sparkling field of blue ice. It was an oppressive, sweltering day, and the motel owner paused to wick the sweat off his forehead.

Bridges watched.

After installing the covert surveillance devices, Bridges had driven every mapped and unmapped road of the county, from lamppost to landfill, looking for traces of Kendrick and the others. He had visited eight cemeteries and walked the rows, looking for fresh graves and found nothing . . . until cemetery number nine. Discovered more by accident than intent, he had nearly driven past the tiny signpost marking the graveyard. In the overgrown, weedy grounds, among the untended and forgotten graves, he had found six plots of recently turned earth. One was marked with a name on a fresh-cut headstone. Thurgood Marshall Smith, eighty-two years old. Rest in peace. Five other graves lined up next to the marked one. Kendrick had reported the Crips as dead, so that accounted for three. But who occupied the others? The two women and either Kendrick or Thomas? Or were Kendrick and Thomas down in the dirt with an unknown person? Only way to know for sure was to start digging.

Bridges had returned with shovels and his men. They uncovered the three gang members, then Kendrick, and Thomas. From the sixth grave, the one marked with Smith's headstone, they unearthed an old man. Shot in the forehead. No woman.

As he crisscrossed the county, Bridges kept an eye open for the cabin where Dawali said the freelancers had been capped and identified two possible sites. He installed cameras at both. He also found eight Yukons like Kendrick's and half that number of Chrysler 300s—the freelancers' ride—and compared them to the license tags he had copied down. All checked out as belonging to local people.

Motel Guy was the one solid lead, so London sat in his room as if carved from granite and watched his laptop as the guy went about his business. Bridges had been watching for three days, blinking rarely, moving little. The video cameras recorded to a cloud server upon detecting motion, and they were equipped with excellent night vision capability, so Bridges catnapped, then reviewed the recorded motion events upon waking. He ate protein bars and drank bottled water.

He missed nothing.

For the past three hours, Motel Guy had been out and

around sprucing up the place. More activity than Bridges had seen in a while. Bridges's pulse remained steady, his face impassive. He remained still as a stone.

And watched.

Mahoney upended the pool skimmer into the bushes lining the motel's street-side parkway, and a dozen chlorinated June bugs drizzled out. Hundreds of the brown beetles committed suicide-by-drowning during the spring and summer, clogging the filter baskets with their crunchy corpses. Mahoney fished out the last dead bug clinging to the bottom of the net and dried his hand on his shorts.

He had long since ditched the sling and the plastic cast on his right arm. Morgenstern had called it a greenstick fracture, so it wasn't like the bone was broken-broken. But it wasn't quite unbroken either. And it ached with the effort of handling the pole.

It was nearly 4:00 p.m. and Mahoney had been in motion since seven that morning. So far, he had trimmed the hedges, blown the parking lot clear of debris, power-washed the windows, and skimmed the pool in preparation for a chlorine shock. He had driven Perla, the weekday maid, into a Spanish-soaked fury with his fussing and nitpicking. He knew he was being a jackass, but just couldn't seem to stop.

Morgenstern had called in the morning to say he was kicking Britte loose from the clinic and dropping her at the motel until Lofland came up with a final decision on what to do with her. Mahoney hung up the phone and jumped into action like a newlywed whose mother-in-law was coming for a first visit.

In the two weeks since Mahoney had pitched Thomas's and Kendrick's phones into the Rio Grande and returned to

Cottonmouth, he hadn't seen Britte once. A complicated knot of emotions held him captive, tied his feet together and prevented him from taking one step in her direction. She blamed him for getting Siobhan hurt, and rightfully so. Hell, he blamed himself.

And now she was on her way. Mahoney half-dreaded—no, more like 90 percent dreaded—the confrontation that was sure to follow. The jangles hovered at the edge of his consciousness, held at bay only by furious activity. *What do I say, what do I do, how do I act*—every time his mind found those tracks, he purposely and forcefully derailed the train of his thoughts.

Mahoney hung the pool net in its brackets and scrubbed his face with damp palms. Chlorine burned his eyes. He welcomed the pain—it brought focus, and focus drove purpose. Purpose kept him from diving into the pool and drowning himself with the June bugs.

His neck hairs prickled. He felt eyes on him. He always felt eyes on him, so this sensation was nothing new. The feeling was more intense than usual, which could be a factor of his abundant psychosis coupled with the low-level irritation of allowing a loose end named Milos Stankovic to scrape the raw nerves of his paranoia, or it could be the demons populating his subconscious had been stirred to angry life by guilt and self-loathing. PTSD mixed with abject failure blended up his favorite flavor of neurotic cocktail.

Neither Hannah nor Lofland had shared any details of their inquiry into Stankovic. All he heard from them was "be patient and remain calm," like he was a toddler asking when they would get to grandma's house.

Are we there yet? No. Shut up and eat your cookies.

Had Stankovic bought the ruse, that his henchmen had flown off to Mexico? On the yes side of the ledger, there had been no strangers with Florida plates appearing, asking about a muscle-head and a gangster. Traffic returned to normal at the Cottonmouth Motor Court, which was to say it had trickled down to nothing.

A whole bunch of green, crawly sensations he called the Mahoney Willies lay stacked up on the other side of that same ledger. Nothing concrete at all. A feeling that things weren't right. Was the *absence of evidence* evidence? His gut was telling him they hadn't seen the last act of Stankovic's play.

The sound of a car pulling in grabbed Mahoney's attention and caused a mild heart flutter, which Mahoney ascribed to overwork, or possibly heat stroke. A green, midsized car rolled to a stop in front of the motel. There was a blond head in the front passenger seat. Mahoney's gut clenched.

He brushed his hair back and forced a smile.

16

I have found the woman.

Bridges hit send on the text to Dawali, then initiated several more text messages in rapid succession, alerting his team and issuing orders. His fingers tapped letters without missing a beat. No change in breathing. No adrenaline. That would come later, once he engaged with the target. When blood flowed, that was when Bridges's heart raced.

Dawali responded within seconds. *Sit rep.*

@ motel. Team moving in.

Call it a day.

For the first time in days, the ghost of a smile touched Bridges's lips. *Call it a day.* Code from the past, the heady days when his Popular Defence Force unit worked with Captain Dawali of the 6th Infantry Division, Sudanese Armed Forces, in joint counterinsurgency operations. That particular effort targeted the eradication of Sudanese Liberation Army support infrastructure, part of which entailed the systematic destruction of villages in and around the Nyala region of South Darfur known to be non-Arab or sympathetic to the SLA, or both.

After a successful raid—when black plumes of smoke filled the sky and bodies littered the ground, and the men were sated by violence—Dawali would join Bridges in sharing a smoke. The young captain would clap Bridges on his shoulder and say in English, "Job well done. Time to call it a day."

Bridges interpreted Dawali's text as, "Kill everyone, burn everything." With only six men and nothing but small arms, Bridges's options for destruction were limited. But how hard could it be to kill one woman, the motel guy, and any others who interfered, then burn the motel to the ground with all the evidence inside? Kendrick had failed, but then Kendrick was a criminal and not trained for combat. Bridges was not a criminal.

Bridges was a soldier.

For Britte, coming back to the ratty motel was bittersweet. The "hospital" room provided little in the way of distraction—no television, no radio, no internet—so after the grayed-out static of painkillers left her head, she had nothing but time to think. Her thoughts had chased around inside her head like frightened birds trapped in a cage. Twisted and tangled in sweaty sheets, she tied herself in chains of guilt, dug a deep pit of self-pity and jumped in headfirst. She wanted to put it all on Mahoney. She and Siobhan were doing just fine until he stepped in and tried to be a hero. That blame game lasted until she circled back to Thomas and Kendrick showing up at the motel room door. Had Mahoney and his friends not intervened, the result would have been approximately the same. She would be dead, and Siobhan either dead or handed off to some pimp to be turned out. Was laying in a coma better or worse than life on the streets? And who was Britte Thorpe to make that decision for someone else? She was no one's role model.

At the time Britte had concocted her plan to escape from Stankovic's compound, taking Siobhan with her had seemed the most moral choice. The right thing to do. But now Siobhan was injured, potentially never to recover, her future irrevocably altered . . . and it was Britte's fault, no one else's.

Wilma wheeled her car into the motel parking lot. The bounces jarred Britte's shoulder, stabbing her in the back with knives of ice. Seeing the dismal place again raked up the freshly buried memory of the last time she had been here, with Siobhan. Both of them sneering at the cheap fixtures and potential biohazard waiting in the bathroom. She closed her eyes and let the memories play out, absorbing the hurt, then letting it flow out through her nostrils as she breathed.

The car stopped. Britte opened her eyes and Mahoney was there, standing awkwardly by the pool, like the last kid on the playground waiting to be picked for a team. Odd, but she had forgotten what he looked like. In her mind's eye, he had morphed from a person into a sterile mannequin, an object onto which she projected her emotions. A whipping post, for a time, until she stopped trying to blame everyone but herself.

His black hair begged for a cut and a comb, and judging by the dark stubble on his cheeks, a razor wouldn't hurt either. Lanky and lean, with ropey arms and cobalt-blue gunslinger stare, Mahoney reminded her of a cowboy dressed like a beach bum. The Marlboro Man lost backstage at a Jimmy Buffett concert.

Wilma put the gear shift in Park and set the brake. She got out without saying anything, which didn't surprise Britte. The nurse acted like she paid for words by the letter. Another reason Britte had spent so much time in her head lately—there was no one to talk to. Wilma opened the car door and helped Britte disengage from the seatbelt and climb out, taking care not to jostle her arm in its blue cotton sling.

Britte Thorpe had considered and rejected a dozen ways she wanted to greet Devlin Mahoney. Everything from a sharp slap across the face to a cool handshake was on the table.

She surprised herself by pulling him into a one-armed, sisterly hug. "Hey."

At first it was like hugging a wooden puppet with tangled strings, arms akimbo, and then he patted her gently on the back.

"I'm so sorry," he said into her hair.

"I know. Me, too."

She released him and he stepped back.

"Here," Wilma said, holding out a small bag to Mahoney.

"What's this?"

"Meds. Bandages."

"What for?"

Wilma's expression would have melted pack ice. "Try not to be an idiot, Mahoney."

"Always a ray of sunshine, Wilma."

The nurse rounded her car and got into the driver's seat without responding. Mahoney bent over and waved at her from the passenger window. "Pleasant as always, Wilma. Have a nice day. Say hi to Fred and Pebbles."

"Behave yourself," Britte said. "She's really nice once you get to know her."

"Stockholm syndrome. You need deprogramming. Come on."

Mahoney led her into the motel lobby, past the front desk, and through a cluttered closet of an office. At the rear of the office, a door opened into a small apartment. The living room was decorated in Midcentury American Goodwill, including a solid green sofa, a walnut coffee table, and a cracked leather easy chair. A thin credenza against the wall acted as an entertainment center. Arranged on top of it, from left to right, was a boom box CD player, a small flat screen TV, and a turntable.

Albums and CD cases fought for space on the lower shelf. The kitchen was set off by a countertop, and a four-seat table filled the left corner of the space.

"You get the bedroom." Mahoney gestured to a short hall in the middle of the back wall. "I brought your stuff back . . . back from the cabin. It's all there. The money, too. And Zee fixed your car. The keys are on top of your suitcase."

She nodded. The tight band of tension around her chest loosened a couple of notches.

"So," he said.

"Well," she said.

The strong fragrance of industrial cleaner permeated the room. Every surface, though old and worn, appeared to have been eradicated of the tiniest molecule of grit and grime. Britte wondered if Mahoney always kept it this way or was it just for her benefit. She suspected the latter.

"You want something to drink?" Mahoney asked.

"Just water."

"I only have tap water. I wouldn't recommend it."

Britte settled on a diet ginger ale from the machine out front. Mahoney brought it back to her, along with a Dr Pepper for himself. Britte settled on the sofa. She swallowed a pill along with a swig of ginger ale. The easy chair creaked when Mahoney eased onto the seat's edge, poised as if to take flight at any sudden movement. He combed his fingers through his hair, which turned the tangle into a muss. He looked at her. Looked away. Sipped his soda.

Britte broke the silence. "What are you supposed to do with me?"

"Huh?"

"I mean, I've seen behind your mask, Batman. I know all of your secret identities . . ."

"Oh, right. That. Yeah, uh, there's a guy named Lofland.

He's a bit of a prick, but not too bad as government drones go. He's coming by tomorrow and bringing a bunch of NDA paperwork for you to sign. Espionage Act kind of stuff. I would say get a lawyer to read it over, but that wouldn't make a difference. The outcome is simple: Sign the docs and you're free to go. Don't sign and it'll mean a prison in some far away land." His expression turned distant, unfocused. "Trust me," he added in a small voice, "you don't want to go there."

"So, on the bright side, no shallow grave."

"Could be worse," he said. "You could be sentenced to spend the rest of your life in Cottonmouth."

"Is that what you are? Sentenced?"

"Uhh . . . more like a work-rehab program for me."

"And the others?"

"A real mixed bag, I guess you'd say. You met Hannah, right? Well, she fell in love with her asset, an Iranian physicist named Asim. When the Mossad found out she was sleeping with her agent, they threw a hissy fit. Since a Jew living in Iran was problematic, she reached out to a CIA contact, and voilà, here they are. Been married twentysomething years, those two."

"And the mechanic? I forgot his name . . ."

"Zivon? Ex-Spetsnaz sniper. He became . . . disillusioned with his government while serving in Crimea and the Ukraine. He won't say, but rumor has it he was all lined up to take a shot at the Russian president when the FSB came for him. He escaped and was caught crossing the border into Kosovo. Long story but we wound up in the same place. And then both of us came to live a life of luxury in East Texas."

"Amazing," Britte said while fighting a yawn. Dr. Morgenstern had switched her off narcotic painkillers to something non-addictive over a week ago. Whatever the new stuff was, it knocked her out pretty quick.

"Hey," Mahoney said, jumping up. "Go take a nap. Get a shower, whatever. There's new soap and towels and whatnot in the bathroom. Your suitcase is in there, so you can change if you want."

Britte picked at the blue cotton scrubs she wore. "And give up an outfit like this?"

"Later on, we can get some dinner over at the OK Cafe. You up for fusion Tex-Arabic?"

"Fusion what?"

"It's like all the worst of Persian cooking mixed with tacos and burritos. Lamb and saffron enchiladas. Things like that."

"Oh, yummy," Britte said. "I can't wait."

"And afterward, I'll make you a nice Pepto-Bismol smoothie. Do you need any help with . . . with . . ." Mahoney's hands semaphored across his body. "With . . . you know?"

"Do you want me to bunt, coach? Or are you offering to help me undress?"

"Un— No! I mean . . . Can you . . . With your bandage . . . Hell. Never mind." He scrubbed his hair and said, "I moved my stuff to Room One. To the left as you come out. If you need me, dial eight, then zero-zero-one." He spun on a heel and headed for the door, throwing over his shoulder, "Eight o'clock for dinner, okay? We'll celebrate your last night in Cottonmouth."

Then he was gone and Britte was alone for the first time in what felt like forever. She sat there and let the silence soak in, and her eyes grew heavy. There were no windows in the room and no way to tell the passage of time. Britte slumped onto her good shoulder and let sleep take her.

London Bridges directed his team to collapse on Cottonmouth while he remained in place, watching the monitors in case Motel

Guy and the woman moved. After entering the office, Motel Guy emerged eighteen minutes later. He had then gone directly to a motel room next to the office and disappeared inside. That was at 4:20 p.m. Three hours and six minutes ago.

Bridges's men were stationed at predetermined points throughout the small town, overseeing all possible routes into and out of the area. A final text from Muhtadi confirmed he had eyes on the motel. With his surveillance net complete, Bridges shut down the laptop and packed his gear into two duffel bags. He carefully rolled his prayer mat and stowed it on top of his spare clothes. Within eight minutes he was out the door and in his vehicle.

At the speed limit, it was a thirty-minute drive to Cottonmouth. Bridges intended to obey that limit. Getting pulled over with a trunk full of weapons while dressed in black tactical gear would add complications he could not afford. Before starting off, Bridges opened his laptop and connected it to the Internet via an air card so he could keep an eye on the motel while driving.

Having to stay so far away from the objective irked Bridges. There was a real risk his target would move and be lost during the shuffle between the time he spotted the woman and the time his team could close in. Bridges had opted to accept the risk, as the fate of the previous team had proved that his opponents had tactical acumen. A close-in surveillance would almost guarantee their detection, blowing the entire operation.

So far, everything was going better than he could have hoped.

Light faded from the sky as Bridges drove. The darkness here in rural Texas reminded Bridges of his home in Sudan—the sky full of stars and the moon bright enough to hurt the eyes. Other than driving an American sedan over well-paved roads, he might have well been back in North Darfur, on his way to cleanse a village of rebels and infidels. The target in this case was more limited, of course, and specific rather than general. There would be no burning of the entire town. He and his men would have to make the hit, then scatter to the winds, unlike the old days when they would ride in trucks back to their base, full of laughter, high on gunpowder and khat, recounting the action blow-by-blow.

This was America. He was a contractor here, doing a job, not a patriot doing his duty.

So be it.

His cell buzzed with a call. Muhtadi.

"Yes?"

"They are moving."

"Keep watch. I am eighteen minutes out."

17

Whenever Mahoney ate at the OK Cafe, he felt like an extra on the set of an old-timey western. Wagon wheel chandeliers hung from the ceiling, and artwork by Remington and Russell adorned the walls. The diner featured twenty tables of knotted pine. Six booths ran along the front window, which was covered up to shoulder height by a frilly, red-checked curtain. At the counter, stools were lined up in the style of a saloon, though instead of whiskey bottles and a mirror behind the bar, there was a cut-through window into the kitchen. A sweeping pair of cattle horns decorated the wall above the cut out.

Mahoney had heard that Hannah had drawn the line at sawdust floors and spittoons. "There you are," Hannah cried as they entered. "It is so good to see you up and about." The bustling zaftig of an ex-spy greeted Britte as if she were a long-lost sister, back from distant lands. All hugs and cheek-kisses—which was funny, watching the smaller woman stand on tippy toes to reach Britte's cheeks. "This way, this way. We have a table ready."

At eight o'clock on a Tuesday night, there were plenty of tables available. A couple occupied a booth near the front—a pair that Mahoney vaguely recognized as a local farmer and his wife. Bernie Castaneda, the letter carrier who delivered the Cottonmouth route, perched on a stool at the counter and made mooneyes at Gwendolyn, the burly waitress with red-hennaed hair and a pale, doughy face he had been courting for six months.

Gwendolyn was a regular citizen of Cottonmouth and if she had questions about the nature of her employers' occasional odd behavior, she kept them to herself. She was overpaid and under-worked, and she liked that situation way too much to stick her nose in where it didn't belong. As to how she felt about Bernie, the jury was still out, though Mahoney had a pool going for when she would cave into his awkward proposals for a date.

Asim waved from the kitchen as they passed. The cheerful little man wore an apron over his dress shirt and bow tie. Mahoney had asked him once why he didn't wear a Western string tie, and the Iranian had rolled his eyes and twitched a look toward his wife. Something else she had put her foot down over, apparently.

"The specials today," Hannah said after seating them at the last booth in the row. "Are lamb enchiladas with couscous and refried black beans, or goat fajitas. These come with a nice long-grain wild rice and *sangak* bread for the rolling up of the meat."

Mahoney flashed Britte an *I-told-you-so* look. Hannah placed menus in front of them and bustled off to get drinks.

Britte fluffed out her napkin one handed and placed it in her lap. "You people are obviously working to discourage business. Lamb enchiladas? A town named after a snake? I mean, come on."

"Hey, don't knock the enchiladas until you've thrown them up."

"How do you stand it?"

"I smother everything with hot sauce."

"No, I mean . . ." Britte twirled her free hand. "All this. Living here, away from everybody."

"Away from everybody is good, sometimes."

Hannah brought iced tea and water. "Sorry we have nothing stronger. No license." The Israeli woman said she'd be back in a bit to take their orders.

Britte turned away, hiding her scar from Mahoney. He was very aware of the window to his right. The fish in a fishbowl feeling was back, tickling his nerves. Darkness outside, light inside. Their reflection mirrored off the window, and he could see nothing beyond the glass. He wished the frilly curtain extended all the way to the top, covering the entire window and not just up to his shoulders.

"I see you dressed for the occasion," Britte said, startling Mahoney from his paranoia. "You even shaved."

"And I cleaned behind my ears." He had ironed his best short-sleeve button-down shirt, washed his newest jeans, and polished his cowboy boots.

The loose hem of his shirt covered the Sig in its Galco holster.

Hannah came back and took their orders: lamb enchiladas for Mahoney, and the most normal thing on the menu for Britte, a grilled chicken salad.

"You don't look so bad yourself," Mahoney said after Hannah departed. Britte wore a yellow blouse of a shimmery material—Mahoney guessed silk—and a pair of artfully knee-ripped jeans that probably cost more than the GDP of Belize. "Changing the subject adroitly—tell me about Milos Stankovic."

Britte flinched and seemed to draw back into herself.

"I mean, I know the basic facts," he said. "We did a background work up on him after the . . . after everything was over. But you know him, right?"

"Oh, yes," Britte said, studying her nails and pursing her lips. "Yes. I know him."

"I drove those two guys' phones down to the border and tossed them in the Rio Grande. The team has been on high alert since . . . the incident. They stood down only the day before yesterday. We haven't seen any new faces in town. Nothing out of the ordinary. It's like he didn't react at all to the disappearance of his men."

"Milos is . . ." Britte sipped her tea. "Unpredictable. One minute, he's all profit and loss. 'This is not making me any money,' is one of his favorite phrases when something isn't going right. Then the next minute, he's packing everybody onto a Gulfstream and flying to Greece because he has a craving for moussaka and *galaktoboureko* from his favorite Athens restaurant."

"Gala-what?"

"It's a dessert. One slice is twelve hours on the treadmill."

"You think he gave up?"

"If it cost him more to find out what happened than he expected to gain, he might." Britte winced. "The diamonds. I took those from him." With a bitter laugh, she touched the scar on her face. "I suppose they're gone now."

"Talk to Lofland," Mahoney said, and waited.

"I imagine Thomas and Kendrick wanted to recover the stones as much as they wanted to find me and Siobhan."

When Britte grew silent and appeared unwilling to say more, Mahoney prodded her with, "Why Siobhan? How was she mixed up in all this?"

"To keep me in line. She was a runaway, destined for the streets. Milos knew I would never let a girl that age come to harm. Not if I could help it. So he kept her locked up, just like me." The blond woman's eyes reddened, and she hunched over, as if struck in the belly. "But," she whispered. "I tried getting her out. I did."

Mahoney leaned over and touched her arm, gently, once. "Hey, I'm sorry. That was stupid of me. I shouldn't have brought it up."

"No." Britte sniffed and blotted her eyes with her napkin. "No. That's okay. I have to face it."

"I'm confused. Our research shows Milos is a big name in the diamond smuggling business. Why branch out? Into the sex stuff, I mean?"

"The money is only a sweetener. For Milos . . . I think Milos enjoys destroying innocence. He is abusive. Controlling. He wants to have power over women, and when he subjugates one, he . . . he gloats. It is all about power for him. He wears this necklace with a, you know, a thumb drive? Concealed in a silver pendant. On this thumb drive, he has all kinds of dirt on all kinds of people. Videos of them cheating on their wives, or . . . or doing things with . . . a prostitute. Or drugs. He brags about it."

The conversation lapsed as Mahoney allowed her words to settle in his mind. *What was your part in all this?* he wanted to say. The woman across from him carried a massive boulder of guilt around her neck. Her stunning beauty was marred by a cruel disfigurement, but her soul had clearly been shredded long before her face felt the jagged cut.

"Siobhan," Britte murmured. "That isn't even her name. It's the name Milos gave her. Told her it's her street name. Her real name is Shelly Ann Mott. She said she liked Siobhan so much better, and would I please call her that."

Mahoney struggled for something helpful to say that didn't sound banal or trite. Ended up with, "Hey, look. Asim's on his way over with the food. Whatever he puts in front of you, make a fuss over it. He's very sensitive about his cooking."

—

London Bridges pulled into the parking lot of Pineland Bank, on the opposite side of the highway and slightly offset from the target location. The bank was located at the edge of town, where there were more spaces than buildings. A single-story structure of pebbled concrete and glass, the bank sat alone, with open lots to either side. An alcove over the front door led to a vestibule, and inside the first door, the screen of an ATM glowed. He killed his lights but stayed in his car, waiting. A shadow detached from the bank's alcove and approached. In dark clothing, and carrying an MP5, Muhtadi Al-Din materialized at Bridges's window.

"Report," Bridges said.

"The man and woman are inside the restaurant. There are five others inside, including staff. Two men are covering the back, where there is one exit from the building. Three others are concealed close by, watching the front." White teeth gleamed. "They make it easy. The targets are seated next to the window."

Bridges twisted in his seat and assessed the target building. As the only building with lights on, the OK Cafe occupied the middle of a long, low, prefab building. Windows stretched across the front facing, and an awning jutted over the sidewalk. Batwing doors were painted on the glass entry, and a wagon wheel was propped near the entrance, next to a small cluster of stands offering free brochures.

"Cameras?"

"None at the target. Two outside the bank. Disabled." Muhtadi patted the silenced pistol in his belt.

"Any sign of counter-surveillance? Opposition?"

"Negative. These people are asleep."

Bridges climbed out of his car. At 200-plus centimeters, he towered over his lieutenant. The smaller man stepped back, an automatic response to a larger predator entering his space. Bridges popped the trunk and began gearing up. First, on went the tactical vest, followed by an ammo harness. He strapped a NOD—night optical device—over his head, but he left the goggles up and off. He then connected up a PRC-126 two-way radio with an earwig and throat mic, switched it on and verified he was on the team freq.

From his duffel, he removed an FN SCAR 17 automatic rifle, chambered in 5.56x45mm NATO. He seated a magazine and chambered a round. Set the selector to full auto.

Bridges keyed his mic. "Panther Six to all elements. Six will initiate action in five mikes. Blocking team, eliminate all squirters." Off net to Muhtadi he said, "Let's get closer."

—

Asim carried a fold-out stand in one hand and a food tray balanced on the other. Mahoney watched him dodge the farmer and his wife, who had paid their check at the counter and were on the way out the door. Steam wafted from the tray and Mahoney's stomach rumbled with anticipation.

"I must be hungry," he said to Britte. "That or I'm becoming immune to Asim's cooking."

"Here we are!" Asim snapped out the folding table and set the tray atop it. "My very best grilled chicken salad for the lady. And for you, Mahoney, the special of the day, lamb enchiladas. Although I don't know why I bother. You're just going to drown it in hot sauce."

"It's how I cauterize my taste buds."

Asim clutched his chest in dramatic agony. "Ah! An arrow. Straight to my heart."

From the register, Hannah called out, "I make him pay double for insulting you, my love."

"Don't mind him, Asim," Britte said. "This looks wonderful."

From outside, voices rang out, followed by a series of pops. Mahoney moved before his conscious brain identified the danger. He vaulted across the table and swept Britte's head away from the window with a cuff. Plates flew and hot food splashed his chest. The window shattered. Asim jerked in place.

"Down!" Mahoney screamed.

Glass rained and snaps of displaced air followed the trajectory of more rounds blowing through the window. Mahoney rolled to his left. He collapsed off the edge of the table in an uncontrolled fall, catching himself on his bad right arm. Pain lightning-bolted through the back of his brain. Rifle fire probed the space above him. Britte was huddled under the table, her back against the brick outer wall. Safe for the moment.

Hannah had disappeared. Gwendolyn stood frozen, a piece of pie suspended in one hand, as rounds chewed their way across the back wall. She was a heartbeat away from death. Roly-poly Bernie Castaneda, the cheerful letter carrier, vaulted the counter with an action-hero move and took the waitress to the floor.

"Stay down," Mahoney ordered Britte, and crawled to Asim.

The dapper little Iranian physicist had a round, red dot in the middle of his forehead. The back of his head was gone.

"Dammit!"

Blackness swirled around the edges of his vision. Mahoney crouched among a forest of table legs and seethed with raw emotion. It threatened to pull him into a whirlwind of rage. Demons screamed at him to get up, fight back. Charge straight in and kill and kill and kill until the killing was done.

Assess, Mahoney. Assess. Think before you act.

Hannah would be on the phone, calling for backup. The Committee had dusted off their quick reaction plan right after the meeting with Lofland. They had a phone tree ready for this type of situation. Mahoney racked his brain to remember who would be up and ready. Zee, of course. The big Russian would sulk if they left him out of a chance to shoot somebody. Hans was out. Complications from his leg injury meant he was sidelined. McCurry would be ready. The grumpy ex-SEAL was hell on wheels in any kind of fight. Then there was a Korean named Jeang-wu who could write his name in three languages with a submachine gun. Roxy would be out. Unless they wanted to wire the shooters' cars with plastic explosive, her skills wouldn't be needed. Abassi was good at sneaking around and Chan was their tech geek. Neither were fighters.

The indiscriminate firing had stopped.

Mahoney popped up in time to see a man in tac gear sweep through the front door, an MP5 at shoulder level. He paused at the entrance, half-concealed by the first booth in the row. The shooter's eyes tracked from right to left, giving Mahoney a half-second advantage.

The shot was twenty-five yards, well beyond his pistol-shooting skills, and his P365 was more of a pocket pistol than a distance shooter. Mahoney leveled his Sig across a tabletop, as if on a bench rest at a shooting range. He lined up the three-dots on center mass and squeezed . . .

Pop-pop-pop!

The gunman staggered, the post by his face spewed splinters, and glass shattered. He fell back. Down but not out, as the man's feet scrabbled away, pushing him out of sight behind the booth and toward the front door.

Hannah bobbed up from behind the counter and snapped off a double tap before ducking back down.

"Did you get him?" Mahoney yelled.

"No, he made it outside. Asim!? Are you all right?"

Mahoney's throat clenched and he met Britte's horrified

look. He ducked convulsively as more rounds pounded through the window.

"Asim!" Hannah howled. "Answer me! Mahoney, is Asim all right?"

"Hannah . . ." Mahoney choked on the rest of the sentence. Couldn't get it out past the block in his throat.

"What? What is it?" The Israeli woman tumbled over the counter, not as athletically as Bernie, but just as fast. She thumped to the floor gracelessly and scrambled on all fours through the maze of tables. Mahoney watched her face disintegrate when she caught sight of her husband. A banshee wail of pure grief tore out of her, as if ripped from her guts.

"Noooo!"

Mahoney caught the distraught woman as she crawled like a broken toy toward her husband. "Hannah! Hannah! Listen to me—"

"Get off me, Mahoney!" Hannah shrieked. "Damn you, get off me!"

"Hannah, stop. Listen. There's more than one guy. Has to be. I heard two different weapons. They're about to hit us and we need to be— Stop it and listen!" Mahoney wrestled Hannah to the ground, caught an elbow in the face for his effort. "We need a place to hide until the cavalry comes. You did call, right?"

Britte appeared by his side and wrapped her good arm around the older woman. She murmured words of comfort in Hannah's ear, too low for Mahoney to hear.

Hannah shuddered and her eyes snapped into focus. Mahoney had seen it before—had done it before, as a matter of fact. Boxed up the pain, strapped the lid down on it and tucked it away for later. Compartmentalize. Prioritize. Live to grieve later.

"Down the hall," she ordered. "Toward the bathrooms."

Directly across from the booth where they had been sitting,

a short hall led to an emergency exit. The bathrooms and office were located off that hall, as was a mop closet.

"Hannah," Mahoney said, as if to a delicate child, "they're probably waiting out back. We hit the exit, we're dead meat."

Hannah eviscerated him with a look. "Don't be an idiot, Mahoney. We're not going out back." She twisted toward the counter and shouted, "Bernie, Gwen, stay down! Go into the hall! Meet us there!"

Mahoney exchanged a look with Britte and offered her a one-shoulder shrug.

What the hell? We might as well do what she says.

Britte nodded.

"We're right behind you, Hannah."

18

Bridges cursed Muhtadi as he dragged the injured man away from the restaurant entrance. "This is your own fault. If you had not—"

"My fault! The old fool was yelling his head off!"

"The old people were not a threat," Bridges said through gritted teeth, even though the impulse to put down the couple as they came out of the restaurant had flashed through his mind as well. Muhtadi beat him to the trigger by a hair, shooting down the old man and woman the instant after the man challenged them. What had the old man been thinking? Facing two men with guns, and instead of running away, the old man had shouted at them. Now the man and woman were both dead, and the ambush had been sprung prematurely. Muhtadi had raced in to try and recapture the momentum and received a bullet in the shoulder for his effort.

Now the target was alerted and ready, although heavily outgunned. Bridges and his team retained the advantage, and the outcome was inevitable. The assault might be more difficult, that was all.

Bridges pulled Muhtadi behind a parked car and keyed his mic. "Panther Six to Panther Team. Blocking team, be ready. Assault team, on me."

Three men loped in from their positions around the front of the restaurant and gathered at the ready, surrounding Bridges and Muhtadi. Each took a knee, facing outward, rifles up and cheeks pressed against the stocks, scanning for threats. Bridges recognized Juma, Obike, and Saleem, which meant Ferar and Sayad were around back, holding down the rear.

"We must hit hard," Bridges told the men. "Hard and fast. Kill everything you see." He keyed his mic again. "Panther Six to Panther Five and Seven. We will drive them into your arms. Be ready."

Double clicks of breaking squelch answered him.

"Juma, take point," Bridges ordered. "Saleem, get the door. Muhtadi, cover our rear. Let's move. Quickly now."

The team sliced through the front door like a machete to the gut. Juma flowed in first, followed by Bridges and the rest of the team. The men fanned out, muzzles sweeping for threats. The odor of burning food came from the kitchen. Something left on the griddle too long, perhaps. Bridges snaked through the tables, using his peripheral vision to avoid tripping while keeping his eyes downrange for any threats.

Aside from the hiss of the grill, and the crackle of glass underfoot, there was no sound.

At a gesture, Saleem and Obike peeled off and slipped behind the counter. Bridges and Juma scouted the open seating area, checking under the booths and tables. They found one dead body, apparently that of the cook. Nothing else.

Saleem and Obike reappeared, having explored the kitchen. Saleem shook his head. "Nothing, boss."

That left the hallway in the rear corner. Signs indicated

the hall led to both the restrooms and an exit. Had the targets exited, the blocking team would have chewed them up, which meant they must be hiding in the toilets. Bridges signaled his men forward.

This would be over in moments.

Four minutes.

Four minutes from ending the call to McCurry and opening his garage door. In that four minutes, Zivon Zhivanevshkaya had strapped on Norwegian M77 combat boots, opened his gun safe and removed a Ruger M77 rifle chambered for .25-06—the rifle chosen because it already had a Trijicon REAP-IR night scope attached, the only rifle in his safe currently fitted with a night scope—and pocketed two boxes of 100-grain jacketed soft point cartridges. These actions ate up three minutes and thirty seconds.

He lost thirty-two seconds hunting for his keys.

The second hand swept across the clock ticking in his head. For others, time either compressed or accelerated with the onset of violence. Zivon had always been able to keep an uncanny track of time during an action. His former Spetsnaz colleagues had called him *Sekundomer*, Stopwatch, for his ability to know to the second how long they had been engaged in a firefight.

At the point his garage door lifted, Sekundomer's friends had been under attack for four minutes.

Four minutes was an eternity in a one-sided fight.

Zivon had heard the chatter of automatic weapons fire in the background of Hannah's call. She and Mahoney would have nothing but handguns to stop an unknown number of heavily armed assailants. Time was at a premium, and Zivon cursed his lack of readiness. They should have remained vigilant. They should not have shut down the observation posts. He had been caught in his sock feet, eating dinner in front of the TV when the attack came, not where he should be, which was perched in a high blind, with his Dragunov zeroed and his heart ticking over at a sniper's plodding pace. Dialed in. Breathing slow and steady.

Instead, he was behind the curve, diving into an unknown situation with only his bolt-action rifle to engage targets. Adrenaline and the headlong race to get on target was wrecking his heartbeat and raising his respiration, both conditions ruinous to the Zen of shooting.

Zivon slammed his van into gear and hit the gas before the overhead door was fully raised. The top of the cab clipped the door's trailing edge with a shriek of metal as the vehicle powered into the driveway. He lived one block behind his repair shop, which was at the opposite end of town from the OK Cafe. Call it twelve kilometers. He was already plotting angles. He considered and rejected attempting to scale any of the nearby buildings, such as the bank across the street from the diner. For one thing, he had no ladder in the van, and he could not recall if there was any external piping or fixtures that would allow easy access to the rooftops.

Zivon gunned his van around the turn onto 379, the top-heavy vehicle slewing hard right.

No, the best solution was to park one hundred meters from the restaurant and climb atop the van's roof. He drove what was commonly called a panel van, popular with repair men and kidnappers throughout the world. Sliding door on one side, double doors on the back. Cargo compartment with shelves for small parts and tools. Logo of his automotive repair shop on the sides. It would serve well as an impromptu shooting rest, giving him a small height advantage over the battlefield.

Assuming there was still a battle going on by the time he arrived.

Zivon jammed the gas pedal to the floor and the heavy van surged forward.

Five minutes.

—

Mahoney trailed behind, holding rear watch, as Hannah led the civilians down the narrow, wood-paneled hallway. The men's room was painted with a picture of a cowboy twirling a lasso, with the word *Pokes* stenciled under his boots, and the ladies room featured a fifties-era Doris Day lookalike in a short, checked skirt and white boots. Under her was the word *Gals*. Two more doors lay beyond the restrooms, one leading to the office and the other to a broom closet. Mahoney was expecting Hannah to enter the office, thinking she had a secret weapon hidden in there. Like maybe an M240 Bravo or an Apache gunship. An M1 Abrams would be nice.

To his surprise, Hannah passed all three doors and entered the last one on the left.

"The storage closet?" he asked. "Is that where you hid the arms locker?"

Barked commands snapped out from the front of the restaurant. They had seconds before they were caught like sausage in a grinder. The group bunched up around the door as Hannah rummaged in her apron and produced a ring of keys. When she opened the door, there was no arms locker. Mahoney saw . . . cleaning supplies.

"What the hell, Hannah? We gonna hold 'em off with mops? Maybe MacGyver up a bomb with toilet bowl cleanser?"

"No, Smarticus." Hannah shoved her way into the corner

of the room, where a metal ladder was bolted against the wall. "Roof access hatch is at the top of the ladder. Follow me."

Gwendolyn and Britte squeezed in behind Hannah. Bernie huddled close up behind them, holding his arms out to try and shield the women, while at the same time pressing them as far into the cramped quarters as possible. Mahoney had a thin sliver of cover between the letter carrier's butt and the door. He took a knee and braced his shooting hand against the frame.

The clatter of someone kicking over a mop bucket filled the room with a noise akin to a ball bearing in a bass drum. Hannah fired off a string of Hebrew curses. Mahoney winced. *So much for stealth.*

A face peeked around the corner. There and gone so fast, Mahoney had not taken up slack in the trigger before the target disappeared. He held his fire. With the rounds left in the pistol and his one extra magazine, Mahoney owned a total of eighteen 9mm cartridges. He intended to spend every last 130-grain chunk of copper-coated lead as if they were the hoarded dollar bills he once used to buy tokens at the arcade. With some righteous play, he once could stretch three bucks into an entire afternoon.

The gunman stuck an automatic rifle around the corner, holding it in one fist and firing blind.

"Jesus," Mahoney shouted. He powered back into Bernie's round ass, shoving himself away from the lead hurricane. Bullets fanned past Mahoney's head and hammered into the sheet rock in the back corner of the hall. The shooter lost control of his spray-and-pray attack and the muzzle reared up, rounds punching through the false ceiling.

Bernie fell forward with an "Oompf." Things tumbled from the shelves and Mahoney got a strong whiff of lemon-scented cleaner.

"Hannah! You might want to get a move on!"

"You might want to suck a bag of dicks!" Hannah was balanced on top of the ladder, one arm looped through a rung while she sorted through her key ring. A padlock secured the roof hatch.

Gwendolyn clung halfway up the ladder, directly below Hannah, and Britte huddled at the ladder's base. Bernie wrestled out of the mound of cleaning supplies and climbed upright. He favored Mahoney with a wounded look.

"Sorry, man. I have a lead allergy."

Mahoney stuck his pistol around the jamb and fired two blind shots of his own, abandoning his earlier resolution to conserve ammo in order to discourage the hitters from charging the hall. Someone yelled, though it sounded more in surprise than pain.

"Got it!" Hannah barked. The roof hatch clanged open and Hannah shimmied through the square hole. Gwendolyn raced after her. She was a big woman, and for a moment Mahoney thought she might get stuck in the hatch, which measured about three feet square. She breezed through like a champ, however, not even scraping the sides. Britte scrambled up the ladder, having no trouble monkeying up one handed.

"Come on, man," Bernie urged. "Time to go." He pounded after Britte and helped push her through the hatch while the others lifted from above.

Mahoney snapped off two more blind shots, then said, "Screw it," and emptied the magazine. He needed the attackers to be truly suppressed for the short time his back would be exposed. With no time for a mag change, Mahoney tripped the slide release and holstered his weapon. He lunged for the ladder, kicking aside chemicals and banging his shin on the same mop bucket that had snared Hannah. He grabbed the yellow bucket and flung the treacherous bastard at the door.

Barked commands came from the restaurant. The sound

of running feet pounded the hallway, registering despite the ringing in his ears.

Mahoney grabbed the ladder and launched himself up the rungs. Bernie's face was framed in the hatchway, hand extended to pull him out. A blast of shots chased him upward. Rounds blew concrete dust from the wall, zipping past his churning legs. A fiery burn slashed the outside of his left thigh. Another hot poker slashed the inside of his right thigh, way up high and too near his crotch for Mahoney not to panic. He flinched and teetered for a heart-stopping moment. Then he was flying upward. Bernie had him by the wrists and dead-lifted him straight up. It was an impressive feat of strength and Mahoney felt a spasm of gratitude, though his priority once Bernie set him on the roof was not to thank the man, but to clutch his jewels and make sure everything was still intact.

"Stop playing with yourself, Mahoney." Hannah flipped the hatch shut. There was no lock on this side, but they would at least be warned if anybody tried following them. "We're not in the woods yet."

"Out of," Mahoney corrected automatically.

A bullet chipped the roof parapet, and everyone dove for cover.

"Get away from the edge." Hannah waved a follow-me gesture and led everyone to the center of the roof. They clustered around an industrial vent with a mushroom-shaped cap that blew warm, greasy air. Mahoney started to make a joke about Asim's cooking smelling pretty rank when it hit him that the quiet little man was dead. *Lock it away. Live now, mourn later.*

Gwendolyn, who was not a shy woman to begin with, had recovered enough to find her voice. And it was loud. "WHAT IN JESUS'S NAME JUST HAPPENED?"

"Jehovah's Witness." Mahoney swapped his spent mag for a

fresh one. "They're looking for converts, and they're not taking no for an answer anymore."

"What do we do now?" Britte asked. She sat on the pebbled roof, cradling her arm. A fine sheen of sweat glazed her forehead, and her face glowed abnormally pale in the moonlight.

"Now? Now we wait for the QRF," Mahoney said.

"AND WHAT IN JESUS'S NAME IS THE QRF?" Gwendolyn appeared ready to chew bricks and shit concrete. Bernie put an arm around her and to Mahoney's amazement, the big woman allowed herself to be pulled into a hug.

"Don't worry, Gwen," Hannah soothed. "They can't get to us up here, and we have some friends on the way who'll take care of these *mamzers*."

"WHAT IN JESUS'S NAME IS A MAMZER?"

"Targets." Mahoney racked the slide on his Sig.

19

Bridges studied the ladder in the stockroom and considered all the ways this operation had turned into a giant cockup. His quarry had escaped to the roof. His men had no visual contact with them. One man was injured . . .

Sending men up the ladder would be stupid and wasteful. One person, perhaps two, were armed. They would easily shoot each man in the head the instant he popped up. They had a limited number of fragmentation grenades, but throwing them blind would be haphazard and unreliable. It might work, but . . .

As a tactical problem, this one could be solved. He had the tools. All he needed was time.

But they needed to get this done quickly. Research had shown there was no local law enforcement—police coverage was provided by the county sheriff's department. Response times would be slow, and his team could outgun one, or even two deputies. It might take upward of an hour for the sheriff's department to muster sufficient force to make life difficult. But involving law enforcement at all would bring a tangle of complications he did not desire, chief among them being the official reaction if any deputies were killed.

And there was the matter of the sniper. This individual remained unaccounted for, and that meant his team was exposed to a soldier's worst nightmare—an unseen enemy with a deadly accurate rifle. Bridges dearly wanted to resolve this standoff quickly, before any outside forces intervened.

A plan clicked into place.

Tapping Juma on the shoulder, Bridges held out his car keys and said, "In my trunk there is a five-gallon can of gasoline. The furniture in here is wood, the kitchen is full of grease. Burn everything. Start in this room. The fire will drive them off the building or kill them outright. Go!" Bridges turned to Obike and Saleem. "Go outside, one of you go left, one right. Find positions that cover each end of the building. Get under cover to prevent sniper fire. Understood? Move."

Bridges keyed his mic and relayed the plan to Muhtadi and the two men in back, Ferar and Sayad. Once he received acknowledgments, Bridges completed a more detailed survey of the storage room. He noted several cartridge cases scattered across the floor. This was encouraging, as it meant the targets had used up a good bit of ammunition, and it was unlikely they had a great supply to begin with.

Juma arrived with the gas can and Bridges left as the younger man began splashing the fuel in liberal doses around the stockroom.

Soon everything would burn, and his targets would be eliminated. All he had to do was hang tight and matters would be resolved.

Mahoney's legs hurt. Both of them. On outside of the left thigh, about halfway from knee to hip, a slash laid open his jeans. Inspection revealed the bullet had left a burned streak across the meat of his thigh. It leaked a bit of blood, but not much. The inside of his right thigh was more serious. The bullet had passed high enough to singe his testicle hairs. Had his tackle hung right instead of left, the future might have easily been deprived of a horde of little Mahoneys. The wound chafed when he walked, and tacky blood dribbled down his thigh.

Britte gasped when she saw him inspecting the leaking wound. "You're injured."

"Just a flesh wound, ma'am," he piped in a high-pitched voice.

"Mahoney!" Hannah snapped. She left Bernie and Gwendolyn and came over to him. "How bad is it? Are you functional?"

"Am I ever?"

Hannah, her mouth set in a grim line, tucked her pistol in the back of her pants. She whipped off her apron and twirled it into a roll. "Drop your pants."

Mahoney glanced at Britte. "No, I'm okay."

Hannah rolled her eyes. "Don't worry, no one will see your junk."

"No, seriously. I'm good."

"Mahoney, we don't have time for this. Drop your fucking pants."

With a last look at Britte, who wore an expression somewhere between amused and terrified, Mahoney turned his back to the blond woman and unbuckled his belt. Dropped his pants.

"SWEET JESUS," Gwendolyn shouted to the heavens, "You don't have no underwear on."

"Which they now know all the way to Kansas," Mahoney said, his face heating. Trapped on a roof with shooters on all sides, and he was embarrassed about his moon shining deep in the heart of Texas. At least his shirttail hung down and made it only a crescent moon.

Hannah dispassionately tied the rolled-up apron around his thigh. She cinched it tight enough to make him wince and tied a double knot. "There," she said. "Pull up your pants before Gwen has a heart attack."

"Check on Zee," Mahoney said as he jacked up his pants.

"Redbird," Hannah said into her phone, using Zivon's code name. "We're on the roof of the diner. Unknown number of assailants but assume three or more. Where are you? Uh-huh . . . Uh-huh . . . Copy that. Call me when you're in position." Hannah keyed off her phone and addressed the group. "One of our guardian angels has arrived. He's a sniper, and he's setting up about two hundred meters that way." She pointed east-northeast, the direction of 379 as it flowed in toward the center of town. "We just need to sit tight for a bit until the rest of our people show up."

"What people?" Bernie said. He knelt beside Gwendolyn, one arm over her shoulders. The waitress sat on the gritty rooftop, clutching the crucifix hanging from a chain around her neck. Britte sat against the vent hood, eyes bright, trying to watch everywhere at once, either from situational awareness or sheer terror.

Mahoney applied a little situational awareness of his own. The group was gathered in the middle of the OK Cafe roof. The restaurant anchored the center position of a strip mall. A calf-high parapet surrounded the rooftop like a castle's crenelated curtain wall. As long as they stayed low, they were relatively safe from shooters on the ground. The danger would come from the roof of the bank, across the highway. A shooter stationed there could make things interesting by keeping them pinned down with suppressive fire while other elements scaled the building and took them in the flank.

"Hey," Britte said from her position near the vent. "Does anybody else smell smoke?"

—

Mahoney had time to say, "What'd'ya mean, smoke?" before clouds of it billowed from the vent hood, shrouding Britte in a fog. The wail of an alarm kicked off in the restaurant below. Britte scooted across the roof on her butt, coughing and waving a hand in front of her face.

"Are we on fire?!" Gwendolyn cried.

Hannah's stiff lips quivered and her eye glittered. First her husband was killed, and now her place of business was being burned, subjecting Asim's body to further indignities. Mahoney moved to comfort her, but one look sheared him off.

"We need to get off this roof," Hannah said.

"Without getting shot," Bernie added.

"Preferably." Hannah looked to Mahoney. "We can use the awning to climb down—"

"They'll have the front covered."

"*If* we can use the awning to climb down, it'll be easier than dangling and dropping from the top."

"It's not the drop that hurts," Mahoney said. "It's getting shot on the way down." He broke off to goggle at Britte. "Where're you going?"

"It's me they want," Britte intoned in a dead voice. She was zombie-walking toward the street-side of the building. "This is my fault."

Mahoney bear-hugged her and pulled her back. "No. Stop it. Sacrificing yourself does nothing. I know how these guys work—once they get started, they won't stop for anything. We're in this together."

"But . . ." Britte's wounded eyes searched his. "Asim . . . he's dead because of me."

"He's dead because some assholes shot him."

Hannah put a hand on Britte's shoulder. "For once, I agree with Mahoney. One thing my husband taught me: Don't blame good people for the acts of the evil. It's one of the ways God tests our hearts. I don't blame you, Britte," she added with sincerity. "I blame the chickenshit cocksucker who pulled the trigger, and the bastard who sent him. Let's you and me survive this and we'll go punch that fucker's ticket to hell."

Britte's lips trembled through a weak smile. "I . . . I don't know . . ."

"I do know. Period. End of story."

"The all-wise Hannah has spoken," Mahoney intoned.

"Hold on." Hannah held up a finger and tucked her cell against her ear. "Talk to me. Uh-huh . . . Uh-huh . . . Copy that. Out." She looked at Mahoney and pointed east. "Redbird is two hundred meters that way, where the old car dealership used to be, right where Mayfield splits off from the highway."

"Got it."

"He's on top of his van, looking for targets. Kimchee and Fish are coming in from the opposite direction."

"Kimchee and Fish? Oh. Jeang-wu and McCurry. Ordinarily," Mahoney said, "I'd say we sit tight and wait for the cavalry, but . . ." He touched the back of his hand to the roof deck. "We may not have that much time. In ten minutes, maybe less, this place will be cooking."

"Agreed." Hannah cocked an eye at Mahoney and said, "I think you can let her go now."

"What? Oh. Sorry."

Britte favored him with a weak smile and gently pulled herself from his grasp. "I'm good."

"Listen up, everyone," Mahoney said. Bernie and Gwendolyn moved closer. "The roof's not that high. We can drop off the side, no problem. Might get a broken leg, sprain an ankle, but better than being roasted alive—"

"Amen to that," Gwendolyn said.

"Problem is, I suspect we're surrounded by shooters. We're totally exposed if we try and climb down. Now, we have some friends on the way. Ex-military guys. They're going to keep the bad guys busy, but we don't know how many are out there, or how much time we have."

"What's the plan?" Bernie asked. "How do we get down without getting killed?"

Mahoney checked with Hannah. "Suggestions?"

Hannah hitched her chin to the west. "We move to that side of the building. The fire will take some time jumping from the center building to the one next to it. What was it, a donut shop?"

"Yes," said Gwendolyn. "Closed two years ago."

"That'll buy us time," Mahoney said, "to get some support from, uh, Fish and Kimchee. Who came up with those names? Stupid names. Anyway, we get a flanking attack on that side going, and, ah, Redbird keeps them pinned from the east, then we can dangle-drop to the ground, using the building to shield off the guys in back and in front. Then we . . . y'know . . ." Mahoney ran across his palm with his fingers. "Scamper off to link up with Guppy and Cabbage-boy."

Hannah bobbed her head from side to side, lips pursed. "Yeah, okay. Let's do it. Everybody, start moving that way."

"Follow me." Mahoney duck-ran toward the western edge of the building, dodging HVAC units and vent pipes. He bellied down a few feet from the bulwark and motioned everyone else to stay put. He crawled until he reached the lip. Just one quick peek—

Muzzle flashes sparkled from the darkness and a bullet slapped the air near his head. One spalled off the parapet, spewing concrete dust and zinging off into the sky with a nasty whine. Mahoney flinched back under cover and the shots died out. He crawled back to the others.

"Well, so far this plan sucks."

"Alert, but nervous," Hannah said. "He should have waited until he had you zeroed."

"Yeah, what a dumbass," Mahoney scoffed. "Somebody should tell him."

Hannah was on her phone. "Redbird. Are you in contact with Fish? Cell phone, yeah, I know, it's ridiculous. I'll order some tactical radios from Amazon Prime. We'll wait. I'm sure it won't take long. Yes, I'm joking. Conference them in." The Israeli rolled her eyes and went silent for a couple of ten-counts, then spoke into the phone, relaying their current position and plan of egress. When she hung up, she reported to the group, "Redbird says the heat from the building is playing hell with his thermal optics. He's moving in closer on foot. Our other guys are moving in from the west. We just need to sit tight for a few more minutes."

The world shuddered as if thumped by the fist of God. A bone-deep detonation erupted from the rear of the restaurant. Flames belched through the roof. Bits of debris fountained into the air, followed by a cascade of sparks and flinders.

Gwendolyn threw her arms over her head and ducked. "WHAT IN JESUS'S NAME WAS THAT?!"

"Dammit. I forgot about the propane tanks," Hannah grumped. "They were chained up against the back wall. I told Asim that was a disaster waiting to happen."

Fire licked up the backside of the strip mall and roared into the sky, and choking clouds of smoke rolled over them. The heat was already uncomfortable, and Mahoney mentally cut his ten-minute estimate in half.

"Not to worry," he said. "We got two of the best in the business coming to lend us a hand. We'll be out of this in no time."

Britte regarded him with dull eyes that said she didn't care if she lived or died. Hannah's face reflected grim determination, as if this was her own personal Masada and she'd kill herself before giving anyone else the satisfaction. Bernie and Gwendolyn huddled together, eyes closed, and hands clasped. Their lips moved in a synchronous, near-silent recitation of the Lord's Prayer.

"Yep," he repeated. "No time at all."

20

Fifty-nine-year-old Billy McCurry pulled his Toyota 4Runner off the highway. The SUV roller-coastered through the bar ditch before he rolled it to a stop in a stand of trees. A bend in the road hid the OK Cafe from sight. It was two hundred meters away as the bullet flies, or twice that if he followed the road around the curve. McCurry climbed out and went around to the back of his vehicle.

A crotch rocket zoomed up and scorched to a stop next to his Toyota as he was opening the hatch. The rider wore black leather motorcycle gear, a jet-black helmet, and had an UMP45 submachine gun strapped across his back.

"Hey, Jeang-wu," McCurry said. "Glad you could make it."

The black helmet nodded once as the Korean operative killed his engine and settled the bike on its stand. Jeang-wu spoke about as often as the average tree, preferring to converse at six hundred rounds per minute on full cyclic.

McCurry proceeded to gear up: tactical vest, ammo harness, and an ATE bump helmet with attached NODs. Following that, he added his weapons of choice, a Springfield M1A SOCOM CQB chambered in 7.62mm. McCurry came from the bigger is better school of caliber, and so disdained anything in 5.56. ("When I hit it, I want it to die quick and not linger. I'm a humanitarian that way.") Around his waist, he strapped a Wilson Combat .45 ACP and an Ontario Mk III knife. Black oxide with a six-inch blade, the Mk III wasn't as sexy as the steel some of the team guys sported these days, but McCurry had carried his Mk III from Somalia to Afghanistan to Panama.

McCurry finished his load out and found Jeang-wu waiting with his helmet off and his UMP hooked to his chest plate. The younger man practically danced on his toes, obviously tired of waiting for McCurry to finish getting dressed.

He called Zee and reported their status. "Moving in from the west. Don't shoot us. Out." McCurry gestured in the direction of the cafe and said to Jeang-wu, "Through the woods?"

Nod.

"Lead the way."

Nod.

The Korean kicked off at a lope and McCurry followed. Or tried to. Instantly his knees howled in protest. Twenty-five years of jumping out of planes and fast-roping out of helos had compressed his spine, crunched his ankles, pounded his knees, and stretched his tendons to taffy. His joints had long since disintegrated to bone-on-bone, making running a grueling form of torture. *And people wonder why I'm grouchy.* The rifle in his hands felt as heavy as a car tire, and just as awkward.

Jeang-wu found a path between the pines and disappeared, black fading into black, silent as blood seeping from a wound. *Fucking kids.* McCurry remembered a time he could be that quiet. Appear like fog, kill like a cobra, and be gone before the body hit the ground. Now he ran like a spastic monkey and made as much noise as a washing machine full of nickels. *Stop whining and get your frogman on.*

And, slowly, he did. As he followed Jeang-wu into the trees, McCurry's creaky body transitioned from a rusty robot into something nearly akin to a warrior. He jogged into the darkness, his senses sputtering to life, muscle memory finding the groove. The aches and pains retreated. The weight of the rifle evaporated.

Mission focused. Combat ready.

And when I go home,
My mother she will say,
How ya earn your livin'
How ya earn your pay?
I reply as I point to my bars
I earn my livin' on a killin' squad.

"Hoo-yah, ah-hah," McCurry breathed aloud.

"Who's firing?" Bridges barked into his mic. "What position?"

The radio crackled with an excited, breathless voice, "It is Saleem! Ahh, side of the building! To the . . . to the west?"

Bridges nodded to himself, ignoring the breech of radio discipline. Saleem anchored the west, and Obike the east. Ferar and Sayad covered the back, leaving himself, Juma, and Muhtadi watching the front. He and Muhtadi had pulled back to the bank parking lot, and Juma, after setting fire to the restaurant, had withdrawn to the west side of the bank, almost directly across from the restaurant's front door. Since the first licks of fire had bloomed inside the diner, they had seen no movement on the roof.

An explosive boom punched out from the rear of the target building, and a fireball soared into the sky. Something volatile had obviously gone up with a bang. That was good. It would accelerate the fire and cut off options for the people they pursued.

"Panther Six to all, stand fast," Bridges ordered. "Panther Three, I am coming to you."

Saleem was the youngest member of the team, and excitable. He would need support. Bridges looked to Muhtadi, who had applied a field dressing to the wound in his shoulder. "Are you good?"

Muhtadi nodded, though sweat sheened his face.

Bridges looped wide, heading directly west from the bank toward an old, abandoned building. A barn maybe? Something that was collapsing in on itself from time.

Time. The press of time remained strong. Emergency response to the fire could arrive at any moment, and then they would have a team of firefighters and paramedics to deal with, on top of eliminating the woman and her companions.

Bridges cut across the highway. He was amazed he had seen no traffic so far. The night remained still, with only the crackling of flames and the buzz of insects providing any sound. To his right stood a cluster of pine trees, rendered in shades of green through the night optic device he wore. Ahead of him lay a broken field, in which Saleem lay concealed.

Bridges froze at motion to his right. Two men. Armed. Moving right to left across the field. In a few moments they would cross almost directly in front of him.

It took training and practice to fire accurately over open sights at targets illuminated by NODs. Bridges had both.

His thumb clicked the SCARs selector to automatic as he dropped to one knee. He shouldered the weapon and pressed his cheek to the stock. Bridges aimed at the nearest of the two skirmishers. Exhaled. Took up trigger slack.

Fired.

McCurry paused to mop sweat from his forehead with the back of his sleeve. He would take a knee and recon . . . if his damn knees didn't hurt so much. Instead, he stood at the edge of the pines and studied the approach to the strip mall. Jeang-wu ranged a few meters ahead and McCurry let him go. *Fucking kid. Needs to learn to slow down.* In McCurry's experience, he had seen more soldiers killed by impatience than IEDs. Mission success was a result of intel, planning, training, and then sudden, lethal execution.

McCurry studied the strip mall through his night vision optics.

A hundred meters of open field stretched between the tree line and the building, though the word "open" gave the wrong impression. Small mounds and thick tussocks of tall weeds broke up the landscape. A small platoon could be hunkered down in that mess, just waiting to fuck up Billy McCurry's day, and he wouldn't know it until he stepped on one of them.

Rifle fire cracked out. Jeang-wu and McCurry dropped. When nothing else happened for a full minute, McCurry lifted himself high enough to see over the broken field. He was looking directly at the strip mall when a bloom of light whited out his night vision device. A dull boom followed, and a fireball rolled up into the sky.

"Holy shit," he muttered under his breath. McCurry flipped up his NODs and blinked to clear his vision.

When he could see again, McCurry found Jeang-wu silhouetted by the glow of fire, ten meters ahead of him and already moving forward. *Fucking kid.*

McCurry scrambled up and drove himself forward. The situation had gone critical if the enemy was employing heavy munitions. No time for playing it safe, and he'd be damned if he would let a skinny brat outrun a goddamn US Navy frogman.

He put on a burst of speed and drew ahead of the smaller man, feet slamming into the uneven turf, crunching over broken bottles and other trash.

A hammerblow slammed him in the head and knocked him sideways. The world spun out from under him. McCurry kissed the dirt and lights pinwheeled behind his eyes. He recorded one image, like a snapshot from a tumbling camera: Jeang-wu crouching over him, hosing the darkness with streams of fire, the hard planes of his face cut with flashes of muzzle flare.

Fucking kid . . .

The first man dropped, and Bridges shifted fire to the second . . . only to fall prone as the second man reacted with uncanny speed. Rounds cracked overhead as Bridges tasted salty earth.

"Three," he panted into his mic. "There are enemies to your rear. Panther Four, move to support Three. And everyone! Watch the building!"

Saleem acknowledged and gunfire hammered out from his position. Obike radioed his own affirmative and said he was coming. Bridges crawled into the roadside drainage ditch, squishing through a puddle of stagnant water at the bottom. He bellied up under a small billboard with the words "God Does Not Believe in Atheists—Mayfield Road Baptist Church" with hours of worship in smaller script.

The second shooter had gone to ground. Bridges could make out nothing through the greenish glow—no movement, no man-shaped objects. His NODs had no thermal capability, so his vision was limited to enhanced starlight . . . well, enhanced firelight now. A quick check confirmed that fire consumed the center of the strip mall. The diner itself was nearly fully engulfed.

As he watched, the front glass blew out, and shards tinkled onto the sidewalk. No emergency sirens yet, which Bridges counted as a small blessing.

He clenched his teeth and growled curses. This situation had disintegrated into a barely contained disaster as quickly as water running through his fingers. The woman had managed to obtain professional support from somewhere. At least two shooters had fired back from inside the restaurant, and now two more had appeared from thin air to attack from the flank. Only Bridges's sweeping approach from the road had allowed him to ambush the flankers before they hit Saleem from the rear and prevented a total rout. Pure luck, nothing more.

Withdrawal was an option, though not one he considered viable. They were committed at this point. Pulling out would equate to total mission failure, which not only would mean a loss of profit, but suffering the disappointment of his mentor and friend, Onye Dawali. The army captain had done much for Bridges over the years, not the least of which was assisting his avoidance of punishment for so-called war crimes and his eventual resettlement to the United States. Also, Bridges would lose face. Retreat from a woman and her hired guards? Unacceptable. Once set on a task, London Bridges did not deviate, did not hesitate, and by the grace of Allah, did not run away.

"Panther Six to all units," he radioed. "Check in."

"Panther One," said Muhtadi. "On station, no movement."

"Panther Two and Seven. Same." This from Ferar and Sayed, the blocking team at the rear, followed by Saleem's harsh, breathless report. "Three, no further contact. Four has linked up and has eyes on the building . . . Reports no movement."

Juma, on the northeast side of the bank came next, "Panther Five, no movement,"

Bridges nodded silently. All was in hand, for the moment.

They need only wait, and let the fire take care of the woman and her bodyguards on the roof. They would either succumb to the flames or attempt to flee the building. If the latter, his Panthers would cut them down like so much wheat.

He settled the sights of his weapon on the last place he had seen the flankers. If one of them popped their head up, he would blow it off, ending that threat once and for all.

Patience. All he needed was patience, and this would soon be over.

21

Mahoney was losing patience.

The five of them sat with their backs against the parapet, spectators watching the OK Cafe go up in flames. Smoke billowed from all the vents and HVAC units, choking the air and competing with the oily stink of boiling tar. The close, hot, nasty atmosphere made it hard to breathe, and Mahoney's eyes watered with irritation. Sweat dripped off his chin and soaked his shirt. His *good* shirt.

"This is bullshit." Mahoney snapped out his cell phone and keyed the speed dial for Zivon. No answer. He tried Jeang-wu and McCurry, with the same results. Mahoney scrolled his contacts, searching the list for somebody helpful. He had no listing for Spy with Ladder Truck, or Armored Division.

"The shooting's stopped," Hannah said.

"I don't think that's a good sign," Mahoney muttered.

"What?"

"Hold on." Mahoney popped his head up for a second, using his hard, Irish noggin as bait. Sure enough, a heartbeat after ducking back down, a bullet cracked into the wall. "Nope. The forecast shows cloudy with a chance of lead."

Not that it mattered. They would have to risk it sooner rather than later. Already warmth was seeping up through the seat of his pants. If the smoke didn't choke them to death, the fire would cook them into blackened Cottonmouth corpses.

Zivon's caller ID appeared on his phone.

"Where in the Mother Russia are you?" Mahoney demanded upon answering.

"One hundred meters out. Top of fireworks building."

The "fireworks building" was more of a glorified trailer, a shed on wheels. Open four days a year, with lift up panels, one of the locals used the trailer to sell a veritable arsenal of Black Cats, blue whistlers, and exploding rockets to patriotic pyromaniacs from the surrounding county. It remained an empty eyesore the other 361 days a year.

"We're stuck on the roof, west side," Mahoney reported. "Three shooters over here. At least three. What's his name—Kimchee?—and Aquaman are engaged in a gun battle with the tangos, but at least one of these mutts has us trapped up here. We could sure use some long-range discouragement."

"I am copying. Two hostiles spotted behind building. Hiding at rail tracks."

"Can you take 'em out?"

"Mebbe. Is only tiny bit showing."

"Then what the fuck? Shoot the tiny bit, Long Ranger. Clear us a back door and we'll go out that way."

"There may be other."

"We're low on options up here, Zee. Have to risk it."

"Stend by."

One second passed, then two, then three. Mahoney heard the crack of a rifle shot in stereo, both from Zivon's position and the phone pressed to his ear. More silence. Then, "One down. Another moved and has taken cover."

"That'll have to do. Keep him pinned down, ZZ Top Shot. Over and out." Mahoney scooched around until he faced the others. "New plan. Our sniper has the guy out back zeroed in. If he sticks his head up, Red will make him dead. I say we take the initiative and get the hell off this roof. Who's with me?"

Hannah's dark eyes were focused on a distant shore, and she appeared to have disconnected from the Matrix. Mahoney left her alone for the moment and polled the others first.

Gwendolyn leaned into the letter carrier's comforting hug, her head on his shoulder. She nodded when Mahoney looked at her. "God's will be done."

"Let's do it," Bernie said with conviction. He appeared quite proud to have his arm around the woman of his dreams.

Mahoney winked at him. "You da man, Bern."

Britte gave him a weak thumbs-up. Smudged face. Bedraggled hair. Still stunning.

"Come on." Mahoney tapped Hannah on the knee. "Get a move on, Moshe."

He didn't look to see if she followed. He would come back and drag her if he had to, but for now his priority was to get the civilians out of immediate danger. And the danger was becoming more immediate by the minute.

Smoke fogged the roof, curling up over the edges and filtering up through every possible gap. Based on the heat and the volume of smoke, Mahoney guessed the fire had broken through into the empty donut shop below them. Either the explosion had taken out the demising wall, or the strip mall predated fire codes demanding at least a one-hour fire rating. Or, if Mahoney's East Texas experience was any judge, the fire marshal could easily have performed his inspection over beer and nachos with his cousin the contractor at El Casa de Payoff. In any case, it was well past time to unoccupy the burning building.

Mahoney reached the back of the mall and risked a quick glance at the ground below. The good news: No bullets sought him out from the darkness. Whoever was back there, Zee was doing a great job of keeping them pinned down.

But . . .

"Shit."

"What?" Britte joined him and looked for herself. "Oh, shit."

"Exactly."

Below them lay a forest of broken pallets and piles of crushed cartons. Threads of fire had already reached this ready-made bonfire and flames licked greedily through the tangle. Thick smoke boiled up, as if the mass breathed clouds of noxious gas into Mahoney's face. Dropping into the junk would not only risk being skewered by broken planks, it would also mean leaping directly into a Texas barbeque.

Mahoney sagged to his butt and sighed. "Frying pan, meet fire."

McCurry smelled gunpowder first. Then came the staccato rattle of a submachine gun firing short, controlled bursts. The combined sensory input acted as a tonic, the way the smell of caramel corn and the sound of ringing bells once ignited his heartbeat as a child attending the state fair.

Blackness receded. He lay on his back, staring up at the night sky. His helmet hung askew, blocking his view.

McCurry groaned. "My head hurts."

Jeang-wu glanced over from his prone position a few feet away. He said nothing, which surprised McCurry not at all. The Korean operative switched aim from a target to his left and focused directly forward, putting a burst downrange. McCurry rolled over onto his belly and scrabbled through the grass until he had his rifle back in his hands. Checked the muzzle for blockages and cycled the action. Once he was armed, McCurry fumbled with his helmet strap. The Kevlar pot was twisted sideways over his right eye.

"What's the situation?"

Jeang-wu signaled with his hands. *Two tangos at the twelve o'clock position. One tango, nine o'clock.*

"Hannah and our people? Are they still stuck on the roof?"

Nod.

McCurry finally undid the helmet straps and pulled the thing off his head. A quick inspection showed a long, shallow dent where a round had impacted the upper left side and sliced across the crown. The track indicated a glancing blow that failed to penetrate.

"Hah!" McCurry yelled at the darkness. "Should have used a bigger gun, asshole!"

Rounds homed in on his voice and dirt geysered up into his face. Jeang-wu spared him a dirty look and crabbed sideways, putting distance between them now that McCurry was operational again. McCurry showed him a hand signal of his own, one finger raised.

Okay, then.

He flipped down his NODs and examined the darkness toward the road. Whoever had shot him lay in that direction, threatening their flank. McCurry plotted his advance, determining the best course based on available cover to counter-flank the shooter.

Don't go away, dick-for-brains. I owe you one.

McCurry set out at a snail's pace. *How you earn your living; how you earn your pay? I drag my ass over the battleground, add your corpse to my burial mound.*

Mahoney slumped in defeat. They might have made it had everybody gone over the side right away, but in the long pause as Mahoney weighed the risk, flames had crawled through the forest of junk pallets below. He couldn't convince himself to jump into that mess, let alone try to talk the others into it. Mahoney's gift of gab had its limits and persuading people to drop feet first into a blaze of timber exceeded his personal bullshit quotient.

"What now?" Britte asked him. After her earlier attempt at self-sacrifice, she appeared to have recaptured some of her life essence. Reflected flames tinted her crystal eyes with orange sparks. A thin, gossamer trail of smoke swirled around her face like an exotic veil.

"Now?" Mahoney scratched the side of his head. "Now we're back to the bad people shooting us to Swiss cheese while we jump off a burning building."

"Oh. Right. Thanks for not sugarcoating it."

"That *was* . . ." Mahoney wheezed through a cough, "the sugarcoated version."

At least the damned bells inside his head had stopped ringing. Britte Thorpe seemed to have a dampening effect on his jangles—or maybe close proximity to a horrible death washed out the neural pathways. A clearing of the mind, so to speak. And it could be he was addicted to adrenaline and danger, making his nervous jingle bells a weird kind of withdrawal tremors that could only be sated by application of the appropriate amount of stimulus.

Mahoney broke out into another coughing fit, and he wasn't the only one. A round of teary, sweaty, nervous faces greeted him as Mahoney gathered the group back near the western edge. Smoke hung heavy in the air. The gritty tar under their feet had gone soft, and vicious heat radiated through his boots. His toes were beginning to toast.

Apparently, Gwendolyn was experiencing the same discomfort. "I'm telling you right now, I'm not staying up on this roof. It's time we get our butts out of here."

"Agreed," Mahoney said. "Hannah, give me your pistol. I'm going to lay down some suppressive fire while you get these people down. Umm . . . Bernie. Can you lower everyone as far down the side as you can manage without falling over? The shorter the drop, the better off they'll be."

"I can do that."

"Where's the fire department?" Gwendolyn said. "Why aren't they here yet?"

"I don't know," Mahoney lied. He didn't want to try explaining how all 911 calls from Cottonmouth were routed to a government call center in Virginia. Anything involving "special addresses" went straight to Lofland for approval before local first responders were called. Mahoney didn't want to picture the steam that was undoubtedly shooting out of Lofland's head at this moment.

"You're not taking my gun," Hannah said. "I can shoot as well as you. Probably better."

Mahoney matched the resolute little woman in a staring contest for a ten count and read the resolve etched on her face. "Okay, fine. No time to argue. Let's get moving—" His pocket vibrated and "Rule Brittania!" played as a ringtone. *What the hell now?* "Roxy! I'm kinda busy right now."

"Too right, mate. Looks like your arse is about cooked. Spot for me."

"What? Spot what?"

"Shot out!"

The sound of a hollow thump came through the phone. Seconds later a mild crack split the air. Mahoney risked a glance over the parapet and his jaw dropped. One hundred meters across the scrub field, a billowing cloud of white smoke spewed from an impact crater. The smoke expanded across the ragged terrain, hugging the ground as it thickened and spread.

Roxy's voice pulled him back to the phone. "Where'd it hit?"

"Roxy! You beautiful Brit! You have a mortar!?"

"A master of observation, you are. Now, what's the spot?"

"I mean, you. Have. A. MORTAR!"

"Yes, we've established that. Now," Roxy said, as if speaking to a small child with hyperactivity disorder, "I need to adjust so I can provide you some cover. Give us a spot, wouldya, luv?"

"Ahh," Mahoney chanced a second look. A bullet whip-cracked over his head. "Seventy . . . no, make it eighty meters longer. Like, closer to us, that is. Twenty meters farther to my, uhh, right."

"Mahoney, you're a terrible spotter. Stand by."

The next round impacted twenty feet away. A scream immediately followed the bang of the shell exploding. Mahoney popped his head up long enough to see a figure in black tactical clothing racing from the impact crater. Either the round had fallen close enough to scare the living daylights out of the attacker, or the man had been burned by the white phosphorus as it sprayed from the casing.

"That's good," Mahoney said into his phone. "Right there. Keep 'em coming." To the group surrounding him, Mahoney said, "Good news, folks. That scream you heard is the sound of artillery falling on somebody else. We'll have some cover laid down in no time."

"Fast would be good," Bernie said. He pointed to the center of the roof, which was in the process of collapsing into a raging inferno. Thick, choking smoke rolled over them, seemingly in competition with the WP smoke of Roxy's mortar rounds. It would be a race to see if Roxy could lay down enough concealment to protect them from incoming fire, or if the other kind of incoming fire would get there first.

Everyone was coughing and dripping with sweat.

"I feel like a brisket in the smoker," Bernie said.

"More like we have one foot in hell," Hannah said.

"Amen to that," Gwendolyn added, with feeling.

Another crack announced the arrival of a smoke round. Already the field was hazed by foggy clouds and lazy tendrils of mist. Visibility was down to inches in some places, though there were wide gaps in the coverage.

So be it. We can't wait any longer.

"Okay, people," Mahoney said. "I've had enough of the scenic view. Let's get the hell off this roof."

—

McCurry heard the first smoke round detonate and smothered a grin. *Welcome to the party, Roxy. Please don't drop one of those on my head.* Dropping mortar rounds into a six-hundred-acre field, threading them into a narrow gap between the besieged and their besiegers without hitting friendly troops . . . well, not many people had the skill. Roxy Clark made things go boom with the skill of a diamond cutter. McCurry dismissed the concern about eating a mortar round and got on with the job at hand, which was wasting the asshole who had made the mistake of shooting William Henry McCurry in the head. With that objective achieved, it would be on to servicing the remaining targets.

Ahead of him lay fifty yards of skanky ground, infested with patches of Johnson grass as tall as cornstalks, and junk left to rot by no-account mouth-breathers too lazy to haul something to a proper dump. A killing ground of broken cover and dubious concealment.

McCurry had paused behind a corroded, bullet-pocked washing machine, the appliance slouched to one side as if anxious to fall over. He surveyed his route with care. Getting caught in the killing ground would be . . . painful. Getting up from a bullet to the head twice in one night would be stretching even his superhuman power.

His best guess about where the future-dead-man had gone to ground was somewhere near a roadside billboard, about the size of a queen bed turned on its side and nailed to two sturdy posts. Between the posts, a riot of weeds concealed the base of the sign. A church sign, if he recalled correctly.

The stutter of Jeang-wu's sub-gun told McCurry the younger man was still in action, somewhere behind and to his right. A return volley probed the night. The rounds came nowhere close to McCurry, so he tuned them out.

Another smoke round landed. McCurry ignored it. But then somebody screamed. A figure ran across McCurry's field of vision, right to left, headed for the road and trailing streamers of smoke. *Heh. You no likey Mr. Mortar?*

A powerful voice barked out with the cadence of a sergeant tearing a strip off a grunt who was going shit-for-brains in the middle of a fight. McCurry would recognize that tone anywhere. The errant soldier slowed his run and dropped into the drainage ditch fifty meters to the east of the church sign. The soldier commenced a high-pitched yammering in the tone of someone miffed at the unfairness of the enemy daring to drop bombs on a nice guy like him, who was just trying to do his job. The sergeant voice snapped out again and the soldier fell silent. Sulking, no doubt.

Confirming his guess, the sergeant voice had emanated from the patch of tall grass under the church billboard, right where McCurry expected him to be. *Got you, you colostomy-sucking tick on a dead dog's ass.*

McCurry fingered the selector switch on his rifle and seriously considered hosing the grass under the sign with 7-dot-62. The problem with shooting at things unseen was that the chance of not getting a solid kill went way up. Also, firing would give away his position to all and sundry. Nope, this was a better job for a blade.

Heavy smoke belched into the sky from the mall, and Roxy's mortar barrage shrouded the field in white clouds. Orange light from the fire cast wavering shadows and rendered his NODs useless. McCurry tilted them out of the way. He shut out the aches and pains. Tuned out the noise. Blocked out all extraneous thought. Molded his body to the ground.

And inched into the killing ground.

22

London Bridges was not given to cursing. His father was a corporal in the British Army, stationed in Khartoum. When angry, the man had cursed fluently and often. And he was always angry. A mean and cruel man when sober, he turned vicious when drunk, with his face twisted into a mask of rage, foul language spewing freely from his lips. He inspired terror when London was a boy, which morphed into disgust as he grew. His father shrank into this little, petty rage-tyrant, a man whom in no way Bridges wished to emulate. So instead of vomiting his anger in a torrent of cursing, Bridges crushed it into a ball of energy deep inside him. Once released, that energy would fuel a cold and merciless destruction of his enemies. Only blood would quench the fire, not curses.

But his youngest crew member, Saleem, was testing his no-cursing resolve. The boy had seen little action in Darfur beyond the cleansing of a few villages, which involved not much more than the murder of unarmed peasants. He had never been under fire before, so his reaction to a smoke shell landing almost directly on top of him was somewhat understandable. Bridges, however, was not in a forgiving mood. This theoretically simple operation had turned into a giant conflagration. A massive fire would surely draw attention from the authorities—it was a miracle they hadn't already responded. And now Ferar was down, killed by sniper fire. Obike was engaged in a gun battle in a smoke-shrouded field. And Saleem was routed out of position by mortar fire . . .

Mortars! For the sake of Allah, they were using mortars!

And finally, to make things worse, it appeared the smoke shells would cover the targets' egress from the burning building. With Obike and Sayad pinned down by suppressive fire, Juma and Muhtadi covering the far sides, Saleem out of position, he and Bridges both unable to see the building for the smoke screen, the woman and Motel Guy would be able to drop from the roof and make their escape. Once gone, they would be difficult, if not impossible, to reacquire.

The anger boiled up from his belly like acid, and for the first time in years, Bridges felt like cursing. He keyed his mic instead. "Panther Six to all Panther elements. Move to the west side. Repeat, move to the west. Use all available cover to avoid the sniper. The targets are escaping in the smoke. Find them. Kill them."

A shadow moved in his peripheral vision, in a way no natural shadow would move. Bridges's instincts kicked in and he stilled any reaction, becoming motionless as stone. The shadow slid across broken ground and Bridges recognized it for what it was. A stalker, circling in from his right, sliding through the grass as quiet as moonlight. The man was good, his movements erratic, untimed, apparently disconnected, propelling his body from shadow to shadow as inexorably as a cobra.

He dismissed the mission from his mind. The target could wait. Bridges had to focus on slaying the stalker in the grass before he could assess whether to withdraw or continue the operation.

With infinite care, Bridges oozed away from his position,

sinking deeper into the darkness of the drainage ditch. The slimy, moldy wetness of the trench did not bother him. In truth, he embraced the muck, sliding into it as if he belonged, imitating a stealthy crocodile sinking into a jungle stream.

Waiting for his prey.

"Okay," Mahoney told Roxy over the phone. "That's good enough. Nobody can see shit through this."

"Right. Get on with you, then." Roxy disconnected before Mahoney could ask if she planned to drop any high explosive rounds to go with the smoke. He really hoped she did not.

The heat underfoot had become uncomfortable. Melting tar gummed the bottom of Mahoney's boots. "Okay, people, let's get off this roof. Bernie, same plan as before. Let's you and me lower everyone down as far as we can. Then you and I can go. Gwen, you're first."

"Hallelujah!" she cried, raising her hands to the sky. "Gawd, I was about to lose every bit of my Christian, right here and now." A crackly crash sounded as another section of roof collapsed. An entire HVAC unit disappeared into the fiery maw with it. "I'm sorry, Jesus! I didn't mean it!"

Heat bloomed in Mahoney's face, as though he stood in front of a blast furnace. Acrid smoke burned his lungs. All of them were choking and seized by powerful racking coughs. The entire center of the strip mall was engulfed, including all of the OK Cafe and a good section of the tenant space east of the diner—Mahoney couldn't remember the name of former business. On their side, at least half of the donut shop roof was gone, and more sagged in a wide circle around the licking flames. *Like the hungry maw of an open furnace.*

"Come on, Gwen. Time to go." Mahoney and Bernie braced themselves against the parapet. The waitress was neither small, nor agile, and sweat slicked her arms. Mahoney gripped one wrist and Bernie the other. Together, they helped her roll her body off the side until her legs dangled over the drop. Mahoney winked at her. "Okay then, the next part's gonna suck."

"Like it doesn't already! Praise Jesus, the Lord is my shepherd . . ."

At Mahoney's nod, he and Bernie allowed Gwendolyn to slip down. Already slick with sweat, Mahoney felt her wrist slip through his hand like it was greased with butter.

"Oh shit! Quick!"

Bernie obviously had the same problem. As one, they all but dropped Gwendolyn as far as their arms could stretch. The concrete parapet slammed Mahoney's tender ribs. He managed to hold on for a heartbeat, long enough to arrest Gwendolyn's fall and make it at least seem more like a controlled drop than an unchecked plummet.

The waitress slipped free of his grip. Bernie held for a twitch longer, then she dropped. Mahoney estimated they had given her a three-foot advantage on a fourteen-foot drop. Falling eleven feet was no picnic. Gwen screeched as she disappeared into the cloud of smoke. A thud and some un-Christian words signaled her landing.

Bernie cupped his hands around his mouth and yelled, "You okay?!"

"I'll live," came Gwendolyn's disembodied and very grumpy voice. "But I'm not happy with you, Devlin Mahoney."

"I understand," Mahoney said. "Watch out, because Britte's coming down next." He found the blond woman standing next to him. Her pale complexion had gone an impossible shade whiter. "I'll have to dangle you by one arm. No sense tearing up that shoulder more than we have to."

Mahoney wiped the sweat off and helped her up onto the ledge. Bernie guided Britte's feet over the side, then held her by the waist as she turned around and wiggled her legs into space. Sliding down, she paused to twist her slung arm free of the wall. Britte met his eyes before sliding free, her expression unreadable. She must have read the concern etched on his features, because she said, "It's okay. I've survived worse."

He nodded and lowered her. With Bernie bracing him around the waist, Mahoney was able to give Britte a full four feet of distance before he had to let her drop. She fell without a sound and Mahoney barely heard the impact when she struck the ground.

"I got her!" Gwendolyn called out.

Another three feet of roof sagged and fell away, as though eaten and swallowed up. Mahoney felt like the fire had grown to a living beast, and it was hungry for some Irish stew. He hated fire. The prison guards in Dubrava had burned him with cigarettes and the scars from that ordeal flared up whenever he stood too close to an open blaze. The scars were prickling like a dozen embers coming to life across his chest.

Hannah's voice startled him away from the tracks of his thoughts. "Quit daydreaming, Mahoney."

"Come on, Hannah," Mahoney told her. "You have no idea how long I've been waiting to drop you off a roof."

McCurry angled his advance to parallel the highway, putting the drainage ditch to his left and the church sign directly ahead of him. The fiery glow of the burning mall backlit the approach, rendering the scene in hard contrasts of black and orange. Panning his head like a satellite dish, McCurry scanned the next twenty meters with his peripheral vision, trying to pick up a tidbit of a human shape to give him a clue where Sergeant Dead Man had set up shop. The man had skills, for sure. He must have buried himself so deep in the weeds that the earthworms were feeling the pinch.

Is he even still there?

Now there was a thought. What if the guy had shifted and McCurry was sneaking up on an empty position? The temptation to go full-metal badass and empty a mag into the tangle of vegetation under the sign squeezed McCurry by the back of the neck. At twenty meters he could chop through the brush like a weed-eater and kill anything bigger than a chigger living in it. He had the SOCOM to his shoulder and his finger taking up slack before instinct pulled him up short. *Don't give away your position for free, and don't shoot what you can't see.* Good advice, but that wasn't what was holding him back. Both maxims could be broken if the situation warranted, as in laying down directed suppressive fire, or when probing fire was needed to flush out a hidden enemy. And if ever there was a need to flush out a hidden enemy, this was it.

But something in McCurry's battle-brain was throwing on the brakes. Twenty-five years of surviving the world's most brutal killing fields had honed his sixth sense to razor sharpness and his subconscious had picked up a detail he'd missed.

McCurry breathed in the smell of crushed grass and stinging smoke. A dandelion tickled his chin. Other than the crackle of flames, the night remained quiet. No traffic on the highway. Sooner or later, a citizen was going to come puttering along, see the bright, shiny fire, and stop to gawk. That would be bad for the citizen, assuming the bad guys were still around.

He oozed forward, willing his body into a motion so slow, a sloth would be a blur by comparison. The only sound he made was the coarse scratch of his ammo harness sliding over the ground, and even that was more felt than heard.

A rifle shot banged out, far away. McCurry noted it, then

dismissed it. He diverted all his attention to his senses, straining his eyes to pierce the ragged patches of blackness in front of him. Mosquitoes landed, bit, were ignored. Something in the strip mall collapsed with a crackle of timber, and sparks spiraled into the sky, fireflies in the smoke. McCurry inched forward. One foot. Two feet. Three.

Water exploded from the ditch to his left. Godzilla with a gun erupted out of the muck, spraying water and dripping weeds. The rifle's muzzle was swinging around. Two meters away. Even a blind man couldn't miss.

McCurry reacted before the creature had fully emerged. No time to get his own rifle into play. Instead, he rolled toward the threat, tumbling like a log at his attacker's feet, spoiling his aim and getting inside the man's engagement envelope before he could adjust. In the lifetime it took McCurry to get up close and personal, two distinct thoughts flashed through his mind—the first being *God made this one big.* The next was, *Take him out at the ankles. Get him on the ground and size won't matter.*

Splashing into the water, McCurry threw his whole body into the giant's shins.

And slammed to a complete stop. It was like rolling into a tree.

A rifle butt blasted into his side and drove a shock of pain from his hair to his toenails. McCurry lost all coherent motor response for a vital second.

The giant laughed and kicked the SOCOM out of McCurry's hands. The giant slung his own rifle and reached down. Enormous mitts gathered McCurry by the harness and lifted him like the sack of dead meat that he was.

"*This* is what I was worried about?" the giant said with humor in his tone. "And I thought you a threat." With his lilting accent, it sounded like he said, *I taught you a tret.*

McCurry fumbled for his sidearm and an eighty-pound asteroid hit him in the face. McCurry experienced a moment of flight before crashing to the ground. His pistol whirled away, and constellations spun in his head. He floated free through a galaxy of stars as every synapse and nerve ending shorted out from a massive overload. Once upon a time, in training, McCurry had slipped while fast-roping from a chopper, and had fallen ten meters to the ground, landing flat on his back. The stunning impact had blown his wind out, flared a colossal migraine to life, and left him paralyzed for twenty excruciating minutes.

That was nothing compared to the way he felt now. He shook his head at the blackness seeping in to steal his will.

Pain is temporary. Quitting lasts forever. C'mon, Billy, get in the fight.

And he would have, too, had not a size forty-seven boot stepped on his chest and pushed him back into the ground. McCurry slugged the man's calf with his balled fist. The leg didn't so much as budge.

The giant laughed again. "At least one of you will die tonight." The cold muzzle of a battle rifle pressed into his forehead. "This is for Ferar . . ."

23

Mahoney let go and Hannah dropped out of sight. Hebrew curses marked the end of her plunge. The thump of rifle fire pounded through the smoke and bullets cracked against the concrete. One of the women squawked, from injury or surprise, Mahoney couldn't say and didn't have time to ask. His back felt like a french fry under a heat lamp, and every breath drew as much smoke as oxygen. Timbers groaned and the footing became more treacherous as the roof shifted in deeply disturbing ways.

He clapped Bernie on the shoulder. "Grab my hands. You're next."

Sweat slicked the letter carrier's round face, tracking through the grime on his cheeks. "I'm heavier than you. You should go first."

"This is no time to throw your weight around."

"Huh?"

"Besides," Mahoney said through a cough. "I always wanted to drop a few pounds."

"You're . . . crazy, man," Bernie hacked out between coughs of his own.

"C'mon, dude. Time to go air mail."

The slight pitch of the roof deck gave way underfoot. The entire mass slammed down almost perpendicular, sloping into the fiery middle of the structure. What had been a mildly uncomfortable tilt instantly transformed into a steep slide, like an express ramp to the center of a volcano. Mahoney lost his balance, his arms pinwheeling. He caught a glimpse of Bernie's panicked face as the big man slid backward. Mahoney's stomach dropped and a moment of terror seized his heart. Burning to death was one of his greatest fears, and for a second, he was completely sure payment for all his sins had come due and the devil was calling to collect.

Mahoney's fingernails caught the parapet. A nail bent back and broke off. Despite the agony, he dug in and arrested his fall, though his feet slid out from under him. He hung suspended, fingers clamped on the edge of the concrete wall, and for a moment thought he might have made it. Then a great weight jerked at his legs and both feet were gripped together by a viselike bear hug. Mahoney glanced down and saw that Bernie had wrapped his arms around Mahoney's ankles, pulling him tight as a bowstring.

The big man's toes had to be toasting like marshmallows in the blazing fire, which roared inches away from his pedaling feet. Bernie screamed something incoherent. Mahoney ignored him because he had bigger problems. The added weight pulled at his fingertips, the concrete biting deep at the pads of his fingers. Tendons, muscles, and bones all screamed in pain. He had never been racked by the Spanish Inquisition, but this had to be what it felt like, and for added incentive, there was a short slide into a raging inferno if he slipped.

"Climb . . . up!" he shouted through gritted teeth.

"What?!"

"Climb! Up!"

Mahoney's arms quivered with strain. The rooftop took

some of his weight, as his belly and legs rested on hot, gritty tar, though there wasn't enough friction to stop his slide if his fingers slipped. Especially not with Bernie's weight added to the equation. For a brief and shameful second, he thought about kicking free of the letter carrier to save himself. He squashed the thought before it took root.

Bernie had finally grasped the concept of climbing. The death grip around his ankles loosened as the big man grabbed a wad of Mahoney's pant leg and pulled. A hysterical laugh almost bubbled out at the mental picture of his pants suddenly falling around his ankles, taking Bernie down for the ride. But his belt held. Hand over hand, Bernie climbed him like a tree. Mahoney dug his boot toes into the soft tar, which provided a little strain relief for his screaming fingers.

Smoke burned his eyes and bit his throat. He fought the urge to cough and lost. Great racking barks burst from his lungs and Mahoney scrabbled to keep his fingers and toes embedded in place. Bernie had him around the shoulders by then and had to pause for his own spasm of coughing.

The roof creaked and slipped. Not much. Maybe a quarter inch. But it was a warning. And Mahoney believed in listening to warnings.

"Go!" Mahoney rasped. "I . . . can't . . ."

Bernie got the message. The mass on Mahoney's back shifted. Pulled. Twisted. Dragged. And then the weight lifted. For a brief, shining moment, Mahoney thought it was over. Mission accomplished. All he had to do now was pull himself up, get a leg over, and drop down the other side. No problem.

With a lurch, the surface under Mahoney's belly fell free, the slope dropping out from under him. His body whacked the roof, then slid toward the heart of the volcano at his feet. Mahoney's fingers scrabbled, popped loose. He experienced a

shadows and flickering firelight. His search came up empty. Nothing moved. Likewise, no bullets flew into his face, so there was that. Where did the man go? Had he moved on to another target? Or was he even now sighting in on Obike's nose?

The voice from behind him sent electric shivers down his spine. "Hey, dude. Look, I'm really sorry about this, but you guys are starting to deeply and completely piss me off."

Obike twisted around. The man from the motel stood over him, a pistol leveled at his face. Words of protest formed in Obike's mind, but that's as far as they got.

A flash bloomed from the pistol—

—

Bridges stood over the fallen man as if he were a big game hunter posing for a picture. He pressed the SCAR's muzzle into the man's forehead and said, "At least one of you will die tonight. This is for Ferar." Bridges read the warrior's pride in his enemy's eyes. With coal-dark skin, hair spun from gray-steel wire, and a face lined by the souls of his dead comrades, the older man's defiance radiated from his entire body. *A pity*, Bridges thought as his finger took up slack on the trigger. *A grandfather of war should not die in a ditch.*

A bull elephant kicked Bridges in the chest, twice. He staggered back. Flashes bloomed in the darkness and more bullets clapped past his ears. Bridges stumbled and lost his footing, splashing into the drainage canal butt-first. He couldn't breathe, the punches to his sternum having shocked his lungs to stillness. Thoughts tangled in his head, but his body acted instinctively to put distance between himself and the shooter. Bridges propelled himself up the embankment and across the highway, scuttling more than running, uncaring of dignity or self-respect. Once he reached the far ditch, Bridges dropped into a prone position, only to find he had lost his weapon when the rounds had impacted his vest. His fingers wrapped around the grip of his pistol and pulled it free. Blackness fuzzed the edges of his vision as his lungs screamed for air. He managed tiny sips that held off the darkness until his diaphragm unclenched enough to work properly.

Across the road to Bridges's left, Saleem popped up on one knee and scattered a streamer of bullets across half the field. Bridges gasped a warning. Too late. The back of Saleem's head came apart and a bloody mist sprayed out behind him.

Bridges gulped air and tried to order his muddled thoughts.

Pistols cracked. Rifles boomed. Smoke drifted across the ground and billowed into the sky. Flames crackled ever higher, and finally, from a far distance away, the wail of sirens called their warning. The radio was filled with conflicting directions and shouted questions.

One by one, those voices went silent.

It was over. In his heart, Bridges knew it was time to go. To live to fight another day.

He dragged himself deeper into the darkness, feeling his muscles come back to life, the numbness leaving his chest. His heart ached, and not just from the hot pain of being shot. The men he was leaving behind had come from his native land. Men with whom he had fought and killed. Men he had trained. They were more than soldiers. They were brothers.

Not only did Bridges owe the people of this town for their deaths, but he was also tasting defeat for the first time in his life. It was bitter and acidic on his tongue.

Bridges slunk away into the night. Defeated, for now.

But he would be back.

Of that he was certain.

Mahoney found Hannah and Britte standing together, watching the fire hoses play over the blackened shell of the OK Cafe. Britte had her good arm around the older woman's shoulders and, wonder of wonders, Hannah appeared to be leaning in for comfort.

"We're clear," Mahoney said quietly. "Bernie and Gwendolyn are at the clinic. Lofland's with them, going over their NDAs. Billy and Jeang-wu are no worse for wear. Zivon cut his palm getting off the roof of the fireworks shed. The doc gave him a tetanus booster. Six KIA on the other side, but we think one got away. A really big sonofabitch, from what Billy says."

"London Bridges," Britte said.

Mahoney scrunched his face in confusion. "Huh?"

"London Bridges is his name. The big guy."

"Ah. Okay."

"This is all my fault," Britte said with a distant expression. "If I hadn't—"

"No," Hannah stated. "No. It's not."

"But if I—"

"No," Hannah affirmed with a tiny foot stomp. She pulled free and turned to face the taller woman. "One thing my husband taught me: Don't blame the innocent for the actions of evil. When I was young, I held all Palestinians responsible every time a crazy bastard blew up a bus of school kids or a market. I blamed all Muslims whenever a bunch of loons rained missiles down on us. But my husband lost his mother and father to the Iraqis, and his sister to an American drone strike. His Islamic uncle and cousin were killed by a Hamas suicide bomber, a fellow Muslim. He never blamed anyone but the evil bastard who pulled the trigger or the one who gave the order. In the case of his sister, he didn't even blame the American government who sent the drone, as she was apparently in the wrong place at the wrong time, collateral damage in a war without borders.

He blamed those who hate, and those who kill. He believed evil walks this earth, and it is up to us to do something about it. He chose the path of peace. I have always chosen a . . . more direct approach, when confronted by evil."

Mahoney kept his mouth shut, utterly convinced anything he had to say would come out wrong. After a long moment of silence while Hannah and Britte, women from very different backgrounds, stared into each other's eyes and formed a connection that Mahoney could feel click into place.

"I guess I forgot that," Hannah said at last. "I chose to hide as evil walked the earth. This is my punishment for turning a blind eye. God has reminded me that good people must act, or we allow evil to flourish."

Billy McCurry materialized at Mahoney's side. "Does that mean we get to go kill this asshole, Stankovic?"

"No," Mahoney said. He read the Old Testament glitter in Hannah's eyes, and it sent a cold hand sliding down his spine. "We're going to destroy him, salt the earth where he lived, and burn his memory from the universe."

PART 3

24

The *Siren Song* rocked at anchor a mile east-northeast of the entrance to Hatteras Inlet, North Carolina. At one hundred and eighty feet in length, the Benetti-built yacht dwarfed the fishing vessels and pleasure craft scooting through the inlet, standing to one side like a teacher herding students through a classroom door. With the sun an orange ball sitting on the horizon, most of the commercial fisherman were on the way back through the cut to off-load their catch, whereas the civilian boaters were heading out for a day on the water.

Having finished his morning swim—fifty laps around the *Siren Song*—Milos Stankovic lingered over his morning coffee. He had the sundeck to himself, with only the attentive steward, Roy, standing within signaling distance. As soon as Milos had received word of the botched attack at Cottonmouth, he had sent away his shipboard guests with a fabricated story of a malfunction in the *Siren*'s potable water pumping system. He wanted the ship free from curious eyes and ears when Dawali and Bridges arrived to deliver their report regarding this monumental fuckup. Not counting the special guest in the locked room below, the only two people on the *Siren* other than crew were the women in his cabin. Neither Burnadette, the Somali girl, nor Claudia, the Brazilian, had stirred from his bed this morning when he arose at 6:00 a.m., and Milos did not expect to see either of them until noon.

Onye Dawali had texted when he and Bridges arrived via charter at Billy Mitchell Airport thirty minutes earlier, which meant one of the boats crossing the gray-green choppy waters of the Cape Hatteras Inlet should be ferrying his men out to the *Siren* now. He couldn't wait to hear how Dawali would explain this latest catastrophe—six more men dead. Granted, they were contractors, but still . . . six. And nothing to show for it. Milos felt the anger working its way up through his torso, knotting the muscles in his back and squeezing his jaw shut with bear trap strength. He took several deep breaths and knocked back the dregs of his coffee. He set the empty cup down and waved Roy away when the man approached with the silver carafe.

The sat phone next to his plate rang and Milos rolled his eyes when he saw the caller ID. *Finally.*

When he answered, a female voice said, "Please hold for Senator Ruben."

This cockroach and his power games. Having his admin call to put me on hold. He needs reminding of who his friends are. Milos and the senator went way back, all the way to when Milos was moving up in the world and Ted Ruben was a governor from one of those New England states squeezed up into the corner of the country—Milos could never recall which one. Ruben found in Milos a partner willing to skirt campaign finance laws and invest his wealth in an up-and-coming politician. Also as the host of wild parties seasoned with snowy powder and filled with the kind of young women who were attracted to power—the kind of lifestyle the young governor had always envisioned for himself but was never able to quite attain without losing his position. In those early days, empty champagne bottles littered the deck like so much confetti—the forty-foot *Angel Face*, if he recalled correctly—and Milos had obliged the young governor with all the dope he could snort and access to pretty women, along with a secure environment to indulge himself, free of any surveillance devices. Except of course for the secret ones only Milos knew about.

Ruben had been seduced into a number of compromising positions, a secret Milos kept from him, waiting until the need arose to reveal his advantage. For now, the implied quid pro quo of his under-the-table campaign contributions was enough to ensure the senator scratch Milos's back when asked.

He kept the truly damning stuff on a thumb drive, hanging from a chain around his neck. Insurance for the future.

"Milos! How are you, buddy?" Senator Ruben's nasal tonality reminded Milos of old recordings of Roosevelt from World War II.

"Ted, so good of you to call. It has been too long since you've come for a visit."

"You can say that again. Why, I'm beginning to get a hankering for one of your special dinner parties."

"I will arrange something soon, I promise."

"Umm," Ruben crooned. "Sounds very tasty. Very tasty. I can't wait to sample some of your finest cooking."

"Ted, are you still on the Senate Intelligence Committee?"

"Yes, I am. Twelve years now. Hopefully another twelve, if the electorate keeps doing what it's supposed to."

"Tell me," Milos said, "have you ever heard of a place called Cottonmouth? It is in Texas." A pregnant silence followed, during which Milos received the distinct impression his "old friend" was deciding if he wanted to speak, or how much he wanted to reveal. Time to up the stakes. "I would not ask if it were not important. A recent problem there might put my . . . business . . . in danger."

"Ahh, I see." Ruben cleared his throat. "Let me . . . ahh . . . Look, Milos. Anything associated with . . . that place . . . is classified at the highest levels. Discussing anything about it could get me sent to prison for a good long while."

So could some of your FEC violations. Milos let the silence say it for him.

"Look, Milos, here's what I can tell you: Stay away from that place. Don't even mention the name of the town over the phone, in case our friends at the No Such Agency have a keyword filter for it. A lot of very dangerous people have been stashed there. You've heard of witness protection, right? Well, that place is like a witness protection commune, okay? For people you don't want to tangle with. People who were in, uh, government service at one time or another."

"Interesting . . ."

"No, Milos. Not interesting. Don't be interested at all. I'm serious, my friend. There are some powerful folks keeping an *eye*, if you know what I mean, on that town."

Surveillance, then. Perhaps even satellite coverage. If so, the government watchers had a ringside seat for the actions undertaken regarding Britte and the child. How much did Big Brother know about Milos Stankovic? It would be good to know the answer to that question.

"Have you heard anything else related to . . . that town?" Milos asked. "Anything that has perhaps turned an eye in my direction?"

"No . . ." Ruben drew out the word. "Nothing in any of the intelligence briefings, anyway. I would have called you if I'd heard anything like that. Why? What's your interest here?"

"I want to know everything. Everything there is to know about that town, get it to me."

"I—"

Milos hung up on the senator and fingered the William Henry Tellaro case containing his thumb drive hanging from his neck and wondered if it was time to jerk the senator's chain. Send him a snippet of video in the archive of recordings featuring the senator and his last "very tasty" treat. That would end this song and dance about "classified at the highest levels." He tossed the sat phone on the table and practically vaulted out of the chair. He crossed to the edge of the deck and leaned out, resting his elbows on the warm metal side rail. Milos hawked and spat into the sea, where his bullet of phlegm disappeared without a trace. He reflected how the remains of Ruben's last *treat* had looked sliding into the cold sea after his throat had been cut. The body had vanished under the waves much the same way as his spit.

The buzz of a boat motor grew louder, and Milos caught sight of a sport fisher with a flying bridge powering over the water on a beeline for the *Siren Song*. Dawali and Bridges, at last. He found himself clenching his jaw so hard, his teeth were aching. This was something his dentist had warned him about, telling Milos several of his molars were cracking from the strain. He should wear a night guard to bed, and practice meditation to relieve stress.

He inhaled for a count of four, exhaled for the same. Repeated the exercise until the tangy sea-salt air infused him with a semblance of calm.

Dawali and Bridges climbed the stern ladder to reach the *Siren Song* sundeck, where Milos had resumed his seat. He had mastered his anger, not discarding it, but tucking it away into a cupboard for easy access should the need arise. Emotions, Milos reasoned, were tools to be used for manipulation, and they should never be allowed to rule one's reason. Opening the cupboard and revealing a glimpse of his anger might be helpful for demonstrating the depth of his displeasure with the results delivered by his chief of security, but ranting and raving and throwing crockery would make him a caricature, a thing of ridicule to be despised, not a shrewd and capable superior.

Dawali and Bridges together were like a rapier paired with a broadsword. The blade-thin Dawali had finesse, skill. His victims were dead before they became aware of the knife through their heart. Bridges was a wrecking ball, and wherever he rolled, people died, and buildings collapsed. He required direction. Leadership. Obvious now, in hindsight, considering the monumental fuckup in Cottonmouth.

Though if what Ruben said was true, it may not have completely been their fault.

Dawali stopped a meter from the table and adopted a parade-ground stance, feet together, hands behind his back, his gaze fixed on the middle distance somewhere over Milos's head. The brute stood at his shoulder in a similar pose. Milos left them standing there, without an invitation to sit. The rising sun painted their faces with gold. Dawali was forced to squint, whereas Bridges acted as though his retinas were made of asbestos.

Milos counted to thirty and said, "We may have stepped on a hornet's nest." He went on to relay the information gathered from the phone call with Ruben. "It would seem our little Britte has found sanctuary with some very special people. How did she know where to run?"

"Sir," said Dawali, "we cannot rule out bad luck. Nothing in her background suggests she would have learned of such a place, and Kendrick observed her car in the mechanic's shop, as if in for repair."

"Coincidence or intent, it doesn't matter." Milos's jaw ached and he realized he was clenching it again. Relax. Breathe. Think like a businessman, not a thug. "Britte Thorpe has a great deal of firsthand knowledge that could be damaging if told to the authorities, which is why I ordered her recovered or silenced in the first place. But now, this. Is the risk worth the reward?"

"Sir," Dawali said with stiff formality. "We have lost many men to these people. To let that go unpunished—"

"Stop," Milos commanded. "I will not go to war over our injured pride. This town in Texas appears to have the protection of the government. We do not have the resources to fight the military might of the United States."

"What would you have us do?"

Milos picked up his coffee cup, realized it was empty and put it back down. He waved Roy over for a refill. While he waited on the steward to complete that task, Milos ruthlessly quelled any emotion from his thought processes. It really would be stupid to let anger or pride lead them into a war they couldn't win. Even if he recruited an army and razed Cottonmouth to the ground, there was no guarantee they would eliminate the loose end of Britte Thorpe, and he might very well bring down the entire weight of the US justice system upon his head. Transportation of conflict diamonds required discretion, as did the myriad uses to which he invested his proceeds. The eighty karats of FL and IF stones stolen by Britt had stung him badly, as they had been paid for and the money placed in escrow. Those funds had been earmarked for his clients in the Sudan, and unless he recovered the diamonds, that expectation would not be met—a situation that made Stankovic very uncomfortable.

Milos directed a question to Dawali, who remained at parade rest. "Have your cameras been discovered?"

Dawali looked to the giant beside him. Bridges shook his head.

"You can maintain surveillance on the motel."

A nod from Bridges.

"Mmm." Milos tapped his front teeth with a thumbnail. *What is the risk? What is my exposure?* There were so many cut-outs between himself and the men who ran his operation, Britte would have no way of leading law enforcement to any direct evidence of illegal activity. She could testify that she had smuggled diamonds on his behalf, and with a bag full of diamonds, she might be able to convince the authorities to take action. But would she? Sixty quality stones would bring between two and four hundred thousand on the underground market, and Britte knew enough, she could move them for a good price.

His mind ran in circles. Would she sell the diamonds and use the money to hide herself and the girl? Or would she trade her testimony for immunity?

Milos remained uneasy. He wasn't comfortable with the idea of a light being shined on him or his operation. Discretion made it easier to operate and allowed him to enjoy the company of celebrities and world leaders. Coming under investigation would render him toxic to the self-absorbed, inflated egos carried by the coterie that guzzled at his trough.

No. Milos would never see the inside of a prison—one whiff of handcuffs and evidence of his poison pill would reach the Ted Rubens of the world. Once those merry gentlemen (and one lady) saw samples of his secret recordings, to be released upon his incarceration, they would insure intervention within the appropriate agencies.

Still . . . a little distance wouldn't hurt. Maybe it was time to take the *Siren Song* on a sea voyage. Stock up the wine cellar and make for a tropical port while this matter sorted itself out. Britte struck him as someone too fearful to be an avenging angel. Likely she wanted to find a deep, dark hole—and Milos could thing of nowhere deeper and darker than Texas—and pull the blankets over her head. In the meantime . . .

"Here is what you will do," Milos said to Dawali. "We need to act with intelligence. Maintain discreet surveillance of this little town. If you spot Britte, and the opportunity arises to kill her cleanly, then do so. Otherwise take no action."

"No action!" Dawali stiffened and swelled with anger. "But what about—"

Milos slashed a hand through the air. "I don't care about your contractors. You had your chance and you failed. Now it is time to let the dust settle and see if any sleeping giants have been awoken. We need to pull back and not allow Britte Thorpe to hurt us with anything she might know. If she goes to testify, or comes out of hiding for any reason, you will get another chance. Until then, pull the file on Britte. I seem to recall something about a sister, back in Frostbit, Minnesota, or whatever little shit town she came from. I want to know everything about this girl: where she lives, where she goes to school, what she eats for breakfast." Milos stood and rewrapped his robe around himself. "Now . . . Sit. Have some breakfast, drink some coffee. Roy will see to your needs."

Dawali appeared ready to argue, and even the stoic Bridges seemed perturbed.

Milos made a placating gesture.

"Patience, Dawali. Let me work my contacts and gather intelligence. We have rushed in and gotten our nose bloodied. Now is the time to step back and plan our next move very carefully."

With that, he left the men to their breakfast and went below for a nap.

25

Hannah, Zivon, Billy McCurry, Chan, and Roxy arrived by separate transportation, while Mahoney rode with Britte in her Lexus. The ride to the meeting was quiet, broken only by the quiet flutter of Mahoney's shuffles.

In the days since the attack, he and Britte had spent long hours going over the details of Stankovic's operation. When the debriefing finished each day, she disappeared into Mahoney's apartment, very firmly closing and locking the door behind her. When she wasn't locked in her room, she was holed up with Hannah. Mahoney remained stranded in Room One, spending long hours with his cards to keep the jangles at bay.

To avoid Big Brother, the Committee gathered forty miles from Cottonmouth. The Snodgrass Convenience Store & Deli sold gas, beer, wine, tobacco, lotto tickets, and packaged junk food in one section. In the other section, they operated a fast-food restaurant that specialized in hot dogs with a side of ptomaine relish, and hamburgers made from frozen and compressed patties of non-USDA beef. Today's special was tamales smothered in chili con carne and sprinkled with chopped onions. The dining area contained three Formica booths with bench seats and three round tables with mismatched chairs. Zivon pushed together two of the tables and arranged eight chairs around the double-circle. They only needed seven, but Mahoney guessed Zee's OCD prevented going with an odd number. At 2:00 p.m. on a Tuesday, they had the place to themselves.

When coffee was poured, or soft drinks filled at the dispenser, Mahoney kicked off the discussion with a question. "What's the most important element to any operation?"

"Weapons," Zivon said.

"Intel," Hannah stated.

"Electronics," Chan said.

"Donuts," McCurry muttered while eyeballing the pastry case.

Mahoney raised an eyebrow with the expression of a teacher disappointed in his students. When he met Britte's eye, the blond woman said, "Money."

"Bingo." Mahoney winked. They had choreographed this presentation prior to the meeting. "Funds. Any operation requires funding, and lots of it. Once you have funding, then you get equipment, weapons, intel, and yes, even donuts. In our current situation, we have no infrastructure . . . or, to be more accurate, the infrastructure we have may well be compromised. Our home base is under a government microscope—"

"You fart and the NSA knows what you had for dinner," McCurry added.

"Crude, but accurate. This operation is strictly off the books. Which reminds me . . ." With a meaningful look at the faces around him, Mahoney gathered everyone's attention. "I'm going to say this again. Anything we do, operationally, is not sanctioned by our host government. Lofland absolutely cannot find out about this. If you participate in any way, and we get caught, it could cost you your retirement in our lovely little village. I'm going to say it again: Anyone who does not wish to be a party to this, um, endeavor, leave now. This is volunteer only. But"—he stabbed his index finger into the table—"if you stay, you're in for the duration. No backing out once we go operational."

"This we have done already," Zivon said. "We are all in."

"True that," added McCurry.

When her turn came, Hannah confirmed her commitment to the cause. Chan and Roxy signaled their agreement.

Mahoney signaled to Britte. "Tell us about Stankovic's operation."

Britte took a deep breath. "Milos generates a ton of cash from prostitution, which he launders through his legitimate businesses, including a chain of clubs . . ."

Mahoney had heard it already, so he tuned out and studied Britte Thorpe as she spoke. She wore a simple dress, belted at the waist, with spaghetti strap shoulders and a hem that reached midthigh. She had defied doctor's orders and removed the sling, though she cradled her left arm and used it as little as possible. On the drive over, Mahoney's unfailing gift of gab had dried up completely and not one single conversational gambit other than, "Humid today, huh?" came to mind. His eyes kept drifting to catch glimpses of his passenger. He marveled at the way sunlight streaming through the windshield lit up the fine hairs on her bare arms, or the play of muscles under the velvet skin of her legs.

He heard the Irish lilt of his paternal grandfather in his head. "*Jaysus, Mahoney. Yeh got it bad, doncha, boyo.*"

". . . and guys drop off bags of cash," Britte was saying. "The money is funneled into the clubs as revenue. I have no idea what day or time these drops are made. I imagine it would depend on the location of the club, and how many porters Stankovic uses for the distribution."

Britte took a deep breath and Mahoney forced his eyes to stay on the road. A fine bead of sweat trickled down his ribs.

Since she had arrived, Mahoney had plenty of opportunity to observe Britte Thorpe in a variety of situations and conditions. Somehow—and he couldn't figure out how—she had gotten under his skin in a way no woman had managed in the last ten years. His hard-won exterior shell of indifference had been breached. A virus had mutated and overcome his immunity to infatuation. Symptoms were sure to follow, including fever, chills, and a tendency to write ludicrous poetry.

"What do you think, Mahoney?" Hannah said, snapping him out of his thoughts.

Mahoney scratched his head and scrambled to catch up to the conversation. "Uh . . . yeah . . . That's the situation we have."

Hannah rolled her eyes. "And what's your plan?"

"I'm glad you asked, Hannah-banana. You're gonna love this."

Britte sat with her hands in her lap, feeling very much like the dunce of the class, accidentally assigned to the smart kids' table for a group exercise. The former spies and operators gathered in the convenience store exuded a powerful air of competence and deadly purpose. Except for Mahoney, of course, who exhibited nothing but a manic-depressive edginess coupled with a self-appointed role as class clown. When Britte met his eyes, the motel owner flashed a lopsided grin that Britte might have found charming, had she been in a mood to be charmed. With his black hair flopping across his forehead, his five o'clock shadow darkening his jawline, and his thrift store clothes, Devlin Mahoney appeared incapable of anything more onerous than tying his shoes. Had she not seen him in action—like in the diner, where he had flown across the table and knocked her to the ground before the first shard of broken glass had hit the table—she would have mentally pigeonholed him as an escaped mental patient. In her old life, Britte would not have hired Devlin Mahoney to wipe the mud from her shoes. And yet, three times now he had overcome enormous odds to save her life. Over the past few days, Britte had felt her worldview shifting under her feet, and it was leaving her stomach unsettled and her nerves scraped raw.

"Before we get into this," Mahoney was saying. "We need to keep in mind one teeny, tiny detail. Retaliation."

"No shit." McCurry cradled a fresh cup of coffee. Number four if Britte's count was right. "Two times this guy has come after Ms. Thorpe, and both times his boys have had their asses handed to them on our best china." He nodded gravely at Hannah. "Not meaning to make light of our casualties."

"No, you're right," Hannah agreed. "Stankovic can't be happy that he has lost eleven operators. While we go on the attack, we must defend our own goal. Britte, how do you think he will react?"

Britte experienced the same jittery dread she felt when the teacher would call on her to solve a math problem. Then she remembered she and Hannah had already covered this topic in their private conversations. *I've already told her what I thought. Why is she asking me this in front of everyone else?* "I . . . ahh . . . At this point . . ." The faces around the tables regarded her with serious attention. No one smirked. No one hinted amusement at the dumb blond girl squirming at the front of the class. "Milos, I don't believe, will cut his losses. Not anymore. I thought at first, he might, since the return on his investment—that's how he would see it—has not been acceptable. His chief of security, Onye Dawali, has a huge number of contacts in the mercenary community, and ties to his old friends from the Sudan, which is where he recruited London Bridges. Thomas was an ex-mercenary as well, I think."

McCurry leaned back, fingers interlaced behind his head. "So how does a cat like Stankovic get hooked up with a former Sudanese Army captain in the first place?"

Britte shrugged. "I don't know. Dawali was there when I first met Milos."

"We should notify our community," Zee said. His rumble caught Britte by surprise. He dwarfed everyone at the table, yet he somehow managed to fade into the background. A big, Russian Cheshire Cat. "Warn of danger."

"Excuse me, please." This from Chan, the diminutive electronics expert. "Based on the cameras we discovered, the opposition appeared to be focused only on the motel. This would seem to be the logical place to expect the next attack."

"I should shut the place down," said Mahoney. "Clear everybody out. They find nothing, they have nothing to blow up."

"Awww," said the British woman. Roxy? She pouted her lower lip, which was tinted with an eye-watering shade of chartreuse lipstick.

Britte watched Mahoney's hands as he shuffled the ever-present deck of cards. Everyone else treated the habit like background noise, but it was beginning to scratch Britte's last nerve. Mahoney dealt out three hands of five-card draw poker: a full house, a low-ball straight, and his own hand, four aces. He smiled to himself and gathered up the cards.

Hannah said something that Britte didn't catch, as her attention was focused on a memory from earlier in the week. Britte had looked out the window and seen Mahoney, with his shirt off, skimming the pool. As a physical specimen, he was unremarkable. Wiry muscles and good abs, maybe, but nothing of heroic proportions. What had caught her eye was the number of white marks contrasting with the tan flesh of his chest and back. It had come as a shock when she realized the marks were scar tissue. Circular dots the size of a pencil eraser. Streaks like knife cuts. Or whip marks. His body resembled a map from the state of Pain.

"What's his story?" she'd asked Hannah.

"Not mine to tell," the Israeli woman had replied, then relented enough to say, "He worked undercover for the DIA."

"The Drug Enforcement Agency?"

"No, the D-I-A. Defense Intelligence Agency."

Britte remembered the conversation as Mahoney shuffled and cut. The cards moved in a blur, whisking together in complicated patterns. She could almost see it, the undercover operative hiding inside Mahoney's easy-going manner. He had a way of disarming people with his lopsided grin and goofy patter. Britte found herself dropping her guard whenever he was around, forgetting her face, forgetting her past, and experiencing an odd spectrum of emotions, from bemusement to exasperation at his manic behavior. She felt comfortable, like she was able to take the mask off and be herself. Although she wasn't exactly sure who that self was, or how she should act.

Hannah admitted privately that she had a hard time staying mad at Mahoney, and Britte suspected the Israeli woman could nourish a grudge until the sun expanded to consume the Earth a billion years in the future. It amazed Britte that Hannah seemed to harbor no ill will toward her over her role in Milos's organization, nor did she blame her for Asim's death. Their sessions had been more like two old friends chatting over tea, though Hannah led the conversation and probed every dark corner of Britte's memory, wheedling out tidbits she hadn't even realized she possessed. The older woman had been compassionate, yet persistent, empathetic when Britte related a particularly painful event, yet unrelenting at ripping the scabs off long-festering wounds. The pus and bile had poured out of Britte's soul, clearing away dead flesh and leaving nothing but new, pink skin behind. While Mahoney's debriefings had been all business, she and Hannah had talked like two old friends, or perhaps more like a patient and her therapist.

She couldn't help but contrast her present company with the associates from her past. Here she sat among serious and gifted people. Warriors, spies, and patriots. Very different from the self-satisfied and petulant dilettantes circling Milos like blowflies around a rotting corpse. Though that wasn't really a good metaphor. Milos may have had a rotten core, but on the surface, he was cool, urbane, and sophisticated. His clients and sycophants were cut from the same thin cloth: silky-smooth, expensive, and beautiful, yet fragile and prone to break at the slightest stress. Knock-off humans, whose poor workmanship was revealed only when tested by adversity.

She tried to imagine Billy McCurry mingling with the celebrities and politicians at a party on the yacht. Or, good God, Mahoney! More than one rich brat would probably be thrown overboard before the night was through. Britte found herself smiling, the scar tugging at her lips, clenching the left side of her face in its ever-present tension. When she looked up, she discovered Mahoney watching her. He winked and favored her with a lopsided grin of his own. She forced herself to meet his stare head-on, and not try to hide her disfigurement. Warmth crept up her neck, but she held her head high.

None of the residents of Cottonmouth seemed to give her ruined face more than a passing look. Even Mahoney, whom she suspected of bearing a small torch for her, acted as though she was a normal person, valued more for her contribution to the team than for her physical assets. They all treated her like . . . like an equal.

Without thinking about it, Britte reached out and plucked Mahoney's deck from his surprised fingers. "Stop shuffling and pay attention," she told him. "Chan is explaining what he needs to make your cockeyed plan work."

"Thank you," Zivon said. "Was going to shoot him soon, he did not stop."

Mahoney put on the hurt expression of a scolded puppy. "Just for that, I'm suspending all room service at the motel."

"You don't have room service," Britte said.

"I'm going to start room service, then suspend it."

Britte smiled again, feeling the pull of her scar and for the first time in her memory, decided not to care what she looked like. The grin wouldn't leave her face.

26

Ravi Malik parked under the portico of the club, allowing Javier Bustamante to lever himself out of the air-conditioned vehicle into the muggy Orlando, Florida, morning.

A casual tourist could easily mistake the Millionaires Club on South Orange Blossom Trail as a high-end steakhouse, or a swanky nightclub. Grecian columns adorned the fascia and supported a portico for valet parking attendants in red jackets. Palm trees complemented the landscaping, and at night the building was lit by exotic swathes of color. Neither nightclub nor steakhouse, the Millionaires Club catered to a primarily male audience in the mood to watch beautiful women wearing nothing but a G-string and garters dance to hip-grinding beats. One of the high-class places, in Javier's opinion, unlike the stale-beer-smelling joints they visited on their daily route.

The club featured four stages and numerous private lounges, leather furniture and brass appointments. The drinks weren't watered down, and the shelves behind the various bars reflected a refined choice of alcoholic beverages, from single malts to craft beers. The dancers, as uniformly gorgeous as good health, great genetics, and surgical enhancement could make them, came from all walks of life, though more than a few of them were college girls collecting tips for tuition. The women did not, as a rule, turn tricks, and if they did, it wasn't on the premises, as such behavior would find them thrown out of the club and barred from employment at any similar establishment owned by Prestige Enterprises, the front company which owned over a hundred such clubs across the United States.

Prestige Enterprises was a wholly owned subsidiary of Diamond Entertainment, which was a shell company acting as an umbrella for a dozen business entities operating in various sectors of the sexually oriented business vertical. The majority shareholder of Diamond Entertainment was MS Ventures, a venture capital firm registered in Delaware, though existing only on paper, the articles of incorporation kept by an attorney's office in Tallahassee, Florida. The sole shareholder, and president, of MS Ventures was Milos Stankovic.

At 10:00 a.m. on a Monday morning in May, the parking lot of the Millionaires Club lay vacant under the bright Florida sun. Inside, the place was deserted but for the cleaning crew, the manager, and a dancer who'd come in to pick up a paycheck. Javier Bustamante shot the shit with the woman while the manager finished counting the drop. The woman turned out to be a housewife from Kissimmee who danced part-time with her hubby's blessing. He kept trying to steer the conversation to a place where he could reasonably ask for a private dance, but so far she had deflected his every attempt.

"Here you go." The manager handed Bustamante a receipt. The manager would slide the cash into the club's books as revenue, thereby cleaning the source: a string of hookers who worked the Orlando resort and convention scene.

Bustamante snapped a frustrated goodbye at the dancer and

headed for the exit. Already he dreaded leaving the cool interior of the club and facing the dreaded spring sunlight. The winter had been mild, and the spring unseasonably hot and wet, which was saying something for Orlando. He sucked in his gut and pushed through the club's doors. The bright white daylight hit him in the face like an open-handed slap. Bustamante dropped his Ray-Bans over his eyes and lumbered toward the gray Chevy SUV parked under the portico.

Humidity saturated the air, turning any outdoor activity into a sweat bath, especially for someone as heavy as Javier Bustamante. As a native of San Juan, Puerto Rico, Bustamante felt it was very unfair that he was apparently unable to get accustomed to the oppressive swelter of central Florida. At 320 pounds, he crushed most scales, and though the bulk of his weight was in gym-enhanced muscle, the extra flab he carried around the middle acted like a heating pad. It wasn't his fault he had a slow metabolism.

Ravi Malik, Bustamante's driver, waited in the car with the engine—and most importantly, the air conditioner—running. Bustamante popped the rear hatch and sighed when the chilly air rolled out and caressed his face. He sat the empty duffel next to six full bags waiting for delivery to other clubs. This was their first stop of the day, and they had two more before for lunch. The accumulated wealth in the back of the SUV edged close to six figures, more than he earned in a year. He wasn't lucky enough, or handsome enough, and didn't have connections enough, to hit the big time, like Stankovic. Some guys were born with a silver spoon and others had it shoved up their ass.

"Hey," Bustamante said to the back of Ravi's head. "Why don't we try that new Cuban place for lunch? Zaza, or something like that. Up in Altamonte?"

Ravi turned around and said, "Lunch may have to wait," though it wasn't Ravi. The man had a pistol pointed across the backseat and centered on Bustamante's forehead. Another chunk of cold iron pressed up against Bustamante's temple and a rough voice said in his ear, "That delay may be permanent if you give me any shit. I'm in a bad fucking mood today."

"He really is," said the driver. "And dude, I've put up with his grumpy ass all week. I have to tell you, traveling with Groucho Barks there is like peeing on a bear to wake him up. You should do exactly what he says."

Bustamante raised his hands and said, "Man, y'all really don't wanna do this. You know whose money this is?"

"Yep," said the voice next to his ear. "And it's ours now."

The voice belonged to a guy about fifty or sixty years old, wearing shorts and a Technicolor shirt. The dude may have been old, but he made quick work of zip-tying Bustamante's wrists and ankles together, gagging him with a golf ball stuffed in his mouth and tied in place with a bandanna. The geezer dragged him around to the curb on the driver's side of the car and dropped him next to Malik, who was in a similar condition. A moment later, the Chevy's door thunked closed and the car drove away, leaving the stink of burned gas behind.

Sweat was already beading Bustamante's forehead, but not from the heat this time. He had a call to make and he didn't look forward to doing it. Dawali wasn't known as a patient or forgiving boss, and even though there hadn't been much Bustamante could do to prevent the robbery, somehow he knew he would be sprayed by the blowback.

Bustamante stewed in his own sweat and shook his head. It just wasn't fair.

Giancarlo Barberi, fifth-generation Italian American, was not now, nor had he ever been, a member of the Mafia. None of his relatives admitted to knowing anybody from the families, and none of Barberi's careful inquiries had resulted in an invitation to join that exclusive club. This didn't stop him from dreaming. He dressed the part, talked the part, and acted the part of a made man. One day, he was sure, a true mafioso would recognize his talent, like one of those stars who gets discovered at a coffee shop in Hollywood, and take Barberi under his wing. A recurring fantasy was that Barberi would pull his piece in defense of a big-league hitter from the Marazanos or Lucianos, maybe ice a few cops, at great danger to himself, and the grateful gangster would induct Barberi in a solemn ceremony over Chianti and lasagna in a candlelit back room.

Until that day came, Barberi bided his time with small-time gigs. For now, the best he could do was be a bag man for a bunch of pimps with cribs in every pisshole from Queens to Newark . . . and there were a lot of pissholes in those zip codes.

Barberi and his partner, Jaime Rosa—also not Mafia—made the rounds twice a week—three times during Christmas and the Super Bowl—in a forest-green Land Rover. They collected cash in gym bags from pimps and whorehouses and ferried it to a counting house in back of a Queens laundromat. Of course, he and Rosa skimmed enough of the take to wear nice suits, eat in mid-tier Manhattan steakhouses, and hire a better class of girlfriend than the goombahs from his old neighborhood. A thin slice of graft was expected.

Rosa, who was behind the wheel as they inched toward the tollbooths near the Newark Airport, kept glancing in the rearview mirror. It was starting to get on Barberi's nerves.

"What the fuck, Rosie? You lose something back there?"

"I think we being follow."

Barberi glanced back over his shoulder at the mass of cars jockeying for position behind them. "Being *follow*? Damn right, we being *follow*. Half of fuckin' Jersey is *follow* us." One thing Barberi never tired of was making fun of Rosa's broken English.

"No," said Rosa, hunched up to the wheel like he needed a booster seat. Fucking twerp was all of five four. "Is one car. Ah, black Ford . . . Effusion?"

"Fusion, you mean?" Barberi looked again and saw about six black cars. One or two were Fords. "Yer whacked. They ain't nobody back there."

Rosa shrugged. "Black Fusion is behine us, lass two stop."

Barberi shifted in his seat. A tiny squeeze of adrenaline jiggered his heart. Were they really being followed? By who? The Feds, maybe? All the Feds drove domestic crap—Fords, Chevys, Dodges—in plain brown wrappers, so it could be them. But why come after him and Rosa? *Followin' the money, dummy.* Barberi had only a vague idea of the criminal enterprise who paid him to do pickups—they weren't part of the Five Families was all he knew—however, the Feds would sniff after their bags of money harder than a junkie needing a fix.

Alternately, if it wasn't the Feds or the cops, it could be another crew scoping them out for a hijacking. Barberi touched the pistol in his shoulder holster. He carried a Baretta, because it was made in Italy, with two spare mags of 9mm. He figured he had enough firepower to discourage anybody dumb enough to try that little stunt. *I'll fuck 'em up good, and that's a promise.*

"Which one?" Barberi asked, squinting through the grimy rear window.

"No see now. Is behine big truck."

"All right, then," Barberi said at last, settling back into his seat. "Keep your eyes peeled."

Rosa favored him with a disrespectful look that said, *Duh*, but in Spanish.

They fought through midday traffic along 78, crossing Newark Bay, then struggling past Liberty Park before reaching the Holland Tunnel into Manhattan. From there it was a slog across lower Manhattan to reach the Williamsburg Bridge, which was of course backed up due to construction.

"I tol' you," Barberi said, "you should'a taken the southern way and gone across the Verrazzano."

This kicked off a continuing argument about routes and traffic that helped pass the time. As die-hard New Yorkers, Rosa and Barberi believed with equal fervor they knew the fastest, least congested routes through and around the Tri-State area. Neither one would deign to consult Google Maps for directions.

It was after four by the time they pulled off the LIE at Springfield in Queens. Slate-gray clouds socked in the sky, and spitting rain dotted the windshield. Gusty winds buffeted the Land Rover and blew trash along the gutters. Rosa navigated the side streets with one eye on the mirror.

"Any sign of 'em?" Barberi asked for the tenth time.

"No," came Rosa's tenth reply.

"I tol' you you were whacked."

Rosa breathed out through his flared nostrils and said nothing.

The EZ Clean Laundromat was the second business in a row of shops at 73rd and Bell. Modern laundromats used reloadable payment cards to pay for services. Not at the EZ Clean shop. Six of their two dozen wheezing, sluggish Speed Queens ate quarters like slot machines and ruined as many clothes as they cleaned. The other eighteen units were out of order. For the rare, brave patron who dared the wrath of the Clothes Monsters, an attendant grudgingly made change from behind a Plexiglass window. Under the desk at his knees, an HK MP5 submachine gun rested in quick-release brackets, right next to a panic button that would signal the team in the backroom of a raid by cops or crooks—which history had proven were not always different sets of people.

Rosa turned the SUV into the alley behind the row of stores. Crud-encrusted red-brick commercial buildings lined both sides of the alley, along with a collection of dumpsters, electric meters, and piping. Rosa pulled up with the rear deck, level with door number two, which looked like any other door of beat-up, rusted metal, but instead was a solid-core reinforced steel beast of a door, with inch-thick deadbolt bars that locked into a steel frame. A high-definition surveillance camera tracked their every movement, whirling silently on its oiled gimbal. Inside, the take from ten teams like Barberi and Rosa was sorted, weighed, and stacked for transportation to the next stop on its journey to the boss's pockets.

Barberi piled out and stretched while Rosa went to push the buzzer. It felt good to get out of the car after a long day. *My back hurts, my butt hurts, and I gotta whiz like a racehorse.*

A black Ford Fusion screeched into the alley and squawked to a stop a few feet from the Land Rover's rear hatch. A cold wash of panic flushed through Barberi's body. He froze. Forgot about the pistol in his shoulder holster. Forgot about warning Rosa of the danger.

He goggled when a skinny little woman in ragged purple jeans and a pink leather jacket popped out of the passenger side of the Ford. The woman's pure-white hair stuck up from her head in a forest of icicles. She had a nose ring and raccoon makeup around her eyes. A giant white guy with a flattop haircut exited the Ford from the driver's side. Barberi didn't have time to absorb any more details as the woman tossed a green ball at his face.

"Here ya go, luv. Catch," said the woman. Something

plinked and twirled away from the green ball as it flew through the air. Barberi caught the object by instinct and instantly recognized it from a million war movies and TV shows. Not a ball. A fucking grenade.

Barberi screamed and tried to do three things at once—throw the grenade, run away, and dive under the car. He ended up in a tangle on the wet, garbage-stinking concrete of the alley with the grenade stuck somewhere near his groin. Barberi clenched his eyes and waited for the bang.

A second ticked by. Then another. And another.

Nothing happened.

A cold circle of metal pressed into his neck. "Don't worry, ducks," the woman said. "That one was a dud. Be a doll now and put your hands behind your back. I hate guns and I don't want to have to shoot you with this one."

Within a minute, Barberi's hands and feet were zip-tied, and the big man had hauled him and Rosa to sit up against the far wall. Barberi was sitting in a puddle, which was fine with him as he could use the wetness to cover the other puddle soaking his crotch. If Rosa noticed the dark blotch on his slacks, Barberi would never hear the end of it.

"They will not open door." The man had a heavy accent. Russian, maybe?

The little Brit bounced on her toes and clapped her hands like a teenager getting a pony for Christmas. "Ooooh, thank you, God."

The woman rushed to the trunk of the Ford and rummaged around. Meanwhile, the Russian popped the Land Rover's hatch and lifted out four bags of cash, two in each hand. Barberi watched, his jaw hanging loose, as the Russian transferred the bags to the Ford while the woman carried some junk over to the laundromat's steel back door. No, not the door. The brick next to the door.

"Are you trying to break in?!" Barberi shouted. He looked at Rosa. "They're trying to break in."

Duh, said Rosa's expression. In Spanish.

Inside the counting room, two worker bees handled the money, and two guards hung out with fully automatic weapons for just this eventuality, not counting the guy up front with his MP5. Right now, one of the guards would have pushed the silent alarm and backup would be en route from . . . wherever backup came. Barberi didn't know how long they had until reinforcements arrived, and in four o'clock traffic that could be minutes or hours. Too bad he didn't know the starting point, so he could figure the best route.

The Brit scuttled back to the Ford and pulled her companion down. "Fire in the hole," she yelled.

A tremendous thud clapped Barberi's ears. Smoke and dust billowed out from the back wall across the alley and rolled over him and Rosa. They were protected from the blast by the Land Rover, although a few pebbles and bits of shrapnel arced over the car's roof and pattered down. Barberi ducked and avoided any stray debris. Rosa wasn't quite so lucky and caught a chunk of rock in the forehead. He cursed in Spanish and Barberi knew enough of that language to understand somebody's mother enjoyed sex with a variety of barn animals.

"Sorry, guys," the spiky-haired woman called out as she rushed into the smoke. She held two more grenades. Barberi suspected these were real, and his suspicion was proved correct when twin bangs lit up the smoke. The Russian followed her. He now carried a sub-gun of his own. Gunfire rattled out. One burst. Then another.

Voices yelled back and forth. One British accent. One Russian.

Then quiet.

A man, passing by the mouth of the alley in jogging sweats, took one look at the commotion and hurried away, eyes very much focused forward.

Barberi sat in his wet puddle as the pair came out of the smoke, carrying shrink-wrapped bundles of cash. They loaded the Ford until the car squatted on its rear like a low-rider. The operation took all of five minutes. The couple jumped in the car and drove away. The Brit tossed off a jaunty two-finger salute and Barberi found himself hitching his chin in reaction.

"I been thinking," he said after a long pause. "Maybe a life of crime's not for me. Whaddaya think about maybe driving a taxi?"

27

Mahoney and McCurry joined the team at an empty CNC machine shop with a For Lease sign in the window. The shop squatted on one of the approach vectors to Atlanta's Hartsfield International Airport, on top of a potholed asphalt parking lot surrounded by a forest of weeds, some tall enough to qualify as trees. A Delta jet thundered over close enough Mahoney could gauge the treadwear on the landing gear. For a July day in Atlanta, the temperature was pretty mild, and the humidity wasn't too bad. Of course, it was nothing compared to the humidity of Cottonmouth, where gills were required six days out of seven.

Hannah and Britte waited inside a Lincoln SUV with black tinted windows and sparkly-chrome fixtures. A draft of cool air puffed out when the driver's window powered down, revealing Hannah's dyspeptic scowl.

"Hey, Hannah," Mahoney said. "Nice ride."

"Have you heard from Abassi? He's late."

Mahoney checked his watch. "By six minutes."

"You finished the last of the deposits?"

"Yes, ma'am."

It had taken sixteen days for the two action teams to scope out and plan the takedown of Stankovic's cash crews. Both hits had gone down on the seventeenth day of the operation. Roxy and Zivon hit the jackpot when they followed the Manhattan couriers back to the countinghouse. Their score netted over three hundred thousand, whereas Mahoney and McCurry had picked up a paltry ninety-eight thousand, six hundred. This sent McCurry into a snit.

For the next two weeks, all eight of them had taken the cash and converted it to money orders and cashier's checks, in four and five thousand dollar amounts spread across six states. No more than one transaction per institution, and always in an odd amount. Almost forty transactions per person. The next layer required a DBA filing in the State of Georgia for a business called Peach Blossom CNC and Metal Shop, a sole proprietorship owned by Mavis Goldstein—a clean alias belonging to Hannah. There had been a logjam at first regarding whose fake ID would be used, as no one wanted to admit to having, let alone burning, one of their carefully constructed false identities. When not provided by the ID shop of one's native clandestine service, legends required a ton of work to create and maintain. Hannah had given in after Mahoney suggested they build one from scratch.

After receiving the appropriate documentation, the next step was to open numerous bank accounts for Peach Blossom, each started with a single cashier's check. Once opened, the team started making regular deposits, keeping the daily amount small enough to escape notice of anti–money laundering software that filtered for higher-value transactions and looked for patterns of unusual activity.

Mahoney leaned on the windowsill to get his face closer to the cool air. "You know, even with all our subterfuge, it's only a matter of time before the banks start filing SARs." For any aggregated transactions over twenty-five thousand dollars, or single transactions of five thousand dollars or more, or really in any case where they suspected money laundering, US banks had thirty days to file an SAR—Suspicious Activity Report—with FinCEN, the Financial Crimes Enforcement Network of the US Treasury Department.

Hannah rolled her eyes. "Not this again."

"I'm just saying—"

"Look," Hannah grumped. "We all know you're a financial genius, but we don't have time for fancy-schmancy schemes."

"Wait, what?" Britte's brow creased. "Mahoney's a financial genius?"

"Don't let the clothes fool you," Mahoney said in a Groucho Marx voice. "I'm really a billionaire, living an eccentric lifestyle."

Hannah snorted. "Mahoney was undercover as a banker, a money man for arms dealers. At the cessation of hostilities in Bosnia, there were, like, a million-billion guns laying around. The jihadis were getting their hands on them. Remember the shooting in Paris? The big one? The guns came from Serbia. Mahoney flew around on a Learjet and hobnobbed with all these low-lifes, until . . ." Hannah trailed off and dropped her eyes.

"Until what?" Britte asked.

"Until the opportunity to open a fabulous resort in East Texas opened up," Mahoney said. "I have to say, the reality didn't match the brochure."

"Here's Abassi," Hannah said. She seemed relieved to change the subject, signaling an apology to Mahoney with her eyes. Mahoney patted her arm and smiled. *All good.*

The former Libyan spy pulled up in a red Mustang. Another rental car driven by Chan, with Roxy riding shotgun, followed the Mustang into the lot. Abassi climbed out and held up a ring with a set of dangling keys. "The lease is signed," he said.

Zivon fought his way clear of the passenger side of the Mustang. It looked like a magic trick, someone that big getting out of a sports car.

Mahoney and the others followed Abassi to their new base of operations. Abassi unlocked the door and led them on a tour.

"Here is the reception area and office." He flicked a switch and the overheads flickered on. "Ah, good, the services have been turned on. There are six offices down this hall," he continued, turning on lights as he went, and pausing to adjust the thermostat. A moment later, a *thunk* sounded and air started wafting from the vents. "This last room is a network closet with extra cooling service. And through this door at the end of the hall is the break room, with full kitchen set up. Past that is the shop. Come, let me show you." Abassi went through the last door and everyone tagged along. The cavernous space had high ceilings and a concrete floor. It was bare of any equipment and swept clean. A faint tang of steel and oil scented the air. Abassi waved a hand like a game show host showing off a prize. "It is big enough to hold a dozen vehicles, a weapons locker, and any other equipment we might need. The restroom facilities for men and women are through those doors. There are showers in each one." He pointed to a pair of marked doors against the side wall of the shop.

"And the IT stuff?" Hannah asked.

"Mr. Chan will be pleased to know we have fiber to the curb here, and I have signed up for T2 service to begin Monday. I have placed orders for all the items on his shopping list, which I expect to begin arriving tomorrow."

Chan smiled and bowed slightly.

"Way cool," Mahoney said. "Everyone stake your claim to a space. We'll order in some cots and blankets for when we have to stay here. Zivon, you're on weps. Get us the gear we need and find a way to secure it. Someone will be here twenty-four seven, depending on mission needs. Britte, Roxy, you're on shopping detail. Get us set up with food and toiletries. Don't forget the toilet paper."

"Brilliant," Roxy chimed in. "Get me some C-4, Zee. We should def have some C-4."

"One can never have enough plastique," Mahoney said.

"Not half, mate."

"Hannah," Mahoney said. "You get the reception area. Use that motherly look of yours to charm any visitors."

"I'll mother you," Hannah fired back.

Mahoney sighed as if burdened with the fate of nations, then rallied with a visible effort. "Okay everyone, we're off to a good start. We have way more money than we planned for, and Abassi did a fabulous job on our base of operations. We stung the bear, but make no mistake, the four hundred we stole was a tiny little needle compared to what we're going to do next."

Mahoney looked over at Britte, and for the first time in a while, saw a natural, unforced smile on her face.

—

Background conversation echoed in the Peach Blossom's open shop floor. The team gathered in the shop, sitting in a ring of chairs arranged in front of a dry-erase board on an easel, upon which Abassi finished drawing the last bit of a diagram detailing the connecting entities of Stankovic's empire. There was a scraping of chairs and clearing of throats as Abassi turned to address the assembly. Nervous sweat trickled down his back—it had been a long time since he'd been on an operation, and the pressure was like an old-but-crabby friend.

The past few weeks' activity had awoken something inside Abdul Abassi.

Ever since he had escaped the fall of the Libyan Arab Jamahiriya in August of 2011 and defected to the West, thus ending his career as an asset for the CIA, Abassi's soul had withered like an olive tree deprived of water. He had lacked purpose. Direction. Usefulness. Abassi had survived thirty years inside Qaddafi's Byzantine snake pit of a government, rising to the post of deputy finance minister, a task akin to juggling swords while blindfolded. Then in 1988, he realized he had played an unsuspecting role in diverting funds for an operation conducted by Abdelbaset Ali Ahmed al-Megrahi and Al-Amin Khalifa Fhimah to place a bomb in the hold of Pan Am Flight 103, which resulted in 259 deaths. The action disgusted Abassi and led him to seek out a case officer within the CIA and offer his services. He then began walking a greasy tightrope over a shark-filled pool. The constant danger had been like a drug. So intoxicating, the withdrawal had taken years of sweat-soaked nights and a diversion to online gaming to fill the empty hours. He had resigned himself to a slow and toxic death.

And then Devlin Mahoney had pulled him aside after the attack on the cafe. "Abdul, you're the best I've ever seen at following the money. We need to develop a briefing package on Stankovic's operation. Can you do it?"

Abassi had nearly wept.

He canvassed his audience, from Mahoney on his far left, to Hannah on his far right. All of them watched him with complete concentration, though in Mahoney's case that included fiddling with a deck of cards.

"This," he began, "is a very simple chart of Milos Stankovic's legitimate business holdings."

"If that's simplified," Mahoney said, "I'd hate to see complex."

"Da," said Zivon. "I, as well."

"I make even more simple. Here are key entities." Abassi pointed to four boxes in the diagram, one after the other.

"Starstruck Media; Ultimate Fantasies, LLC; Diamond Entertainment Group; and Bohemian Productions."

"Ha!" Mahoney said. "Bohemian Productions. I'll bet that translates to 'dirty movies.'"

"Yes, exactly," Abassi affirmed. "Bohemian is heavy into adult films. The appetite for full-length adult films is not what it once was, but there is still a market. Plus, they provide clips and short videos for so-called 'tubes.' These are the websites devoted to free and to paid viewing of erotic, ah, material."

"Ew." Roxy made a face. "Porn."

"Graphic, I assume," Hannah said.

"Very."

"The internet can be an ugly place," McCurry said. "Way different than sneaking a peek at your dad's *Playboy*. But without access to bank records, we are not able to follow the money—"

"We can fix that," Mahoney said, "now that we know who the players are."

"Exactly." Abassi pointed to the box labeled Diamond Entertainment. "My suggestion is to start here. Each of these four companies will accumulate revenue from their subsidiaries, but I sense Diamond Entertainment is the, ah, jewel of the collection."

"We should target all of them," Hannah said. "I don't want to pinprick this bastard—I want to cut his nuts off and feed them to him, raw and unsalted."

Abassi tipped a slight bow toward the former Mossad operative. "Of course. Once we know how the funds flow from these entities to Stankovic's pocket, we can, ah . . ." Abassi slashed a thumb across his throat and vocalized a cutting sound. "*Shrrrikkk*."

"And with that visual aid in mind," Mahoney said, "let's get to work on following the money, for sure. Cutting throats and nuts and all other body parts is great for the main course, but I have an idea for an appetizer I think you'll really like . . ."

28

Todd Mason left his office in Walnut Creek, California, a little after 9:00 p.m. with a goal in mind: a stop at Asia Palace for sushi, then a quiet evening at home. A simple goal, maybe, but with a master's in computer science from Rice, and a job as a senior web developer for Whiteboard Designs, Todd hated the label of computer geek and worked hard to stay off the stereotypical lanes in which his colleagues traveled. He avoided video games, had no knowledge of Dungeons and Dragons, did not attend comic book conventions, and owned a modest two-bedroom townhome six miles from his office. He lived alone, no family, no pets, and occupied most of his evenings the way he spent his days: writing code.

The parking lot of the modest office complex off Civic Drive was mostly deserted. The sodium lights were just flickering on as early evening draped the lot in deep shadows, turning the few cars parked there into dark bulks outlined with silvery reflections. Though located too far inland to receive much benefit from the Bay breeze, the air in Walnut Creek this May evening felt surprisingly soft and cool. Traffic hummed from nearby

Interstate 680. Todd breathed deeply and spent a moment savoring the night. It would be a great evening for a stroll with a girl. If he had a girl. Knew a girl. And could walk more than two blocks without his asthma acting up.

Being an introvert and socially awkward was the one trope Todd could not seem to escape. His beanbag body, Harry Potter eyeglasses, and indifference toward shaving put him down two strikes and a foul ball in the dating game, whereas his stratospheric IQ and tendency to speak in calculus made it nearly impossible to dive into the mainstream and swim with the regular fish. These traits, plus his deep love of immersing himself in code for ninety hours per week, meant that Todd had accepted he would remain single for the foreseeable future.

Todd snorted at the irony. The single biggest client of Whiteboard Designs happened to be Starstruck Media, who operated the largest accumulation of "free" and paid pornographic websites on the internet. Their top-grossing site, Pornstar.net, received over seventy billion hits per year, and Starstruck operated over two hundred sites with content ranging from photo galleries to live webcams to scat video collections. In aggregate hits, Starstruck pages took second place only to sites like Amazon, Google, and Facebook.

At first, the content with which he worked had fascinated Todd. In his first few weeks on the job, he had become immune to the ways humans could connect their parts. His one sexual encounter had been a hasty, sweaty, and contorted coupling in the backseat of his Prius at the age of nineteen, so he had been ill-prepared to write search engine optimization code for popular search terms. The photo and video sites required constant updating of media, acquired from adult content providers, along with affiliate marketing links to providers of sex toys, adult video games, and fake Viagra. It had been an eye-popping introduction to a world Todd never knew existed.

Now, after four years on the job, he rarely noticed the content. The mechanics of site optimization and traffic analysis were much more interesting than the methodology of human fluid exchange.

Todd reached for the door handle on his BMW M5—he had come a long way from his college Prius, though the fancy car had done nothing for his sex life—when a high-pitched cry shocked him nerveless.

"Help!" a woman's voice rang out, accompanied by the clatter of high heels on concrete. "Please help me!"

Todd spun to see a for-real supermodel in a handkerchief skirt and midriff blouse rushing toward him. Her blond hair was tousled from her fist dangled a small clutch bag by a strap in her fist as she ran. The woman resembled a patron of the kind of high-end nightclub in which Todd would never feel comfortable, no matter how much money he had in his bank account, or what kind of car he drove.

She rushed up to him and Todd was taken aback when he noticed that a vicious scar disfigured her cheek. He revised his assessment from a night club refugee to streetwalker, though he had to admit he had never seen a hooker with a body like a princess from the Planet of the Amazons. For a crazy moment, Todd was sure this was no damsel in distress, but rather a female mugger who would bash his head in with her purse and take his wallet while he lay senseless on the ground.

The stunning woman crushed his lapels and the scent of exotic perfume filled Todd's senses. Crystal eyes beseeched him. "Help me, please!" Even the woman's breath smelled nice.

"W-What is it?" Todd managed, despite the nervous fear clogging his throat. "What's wrong?"

"My boyfriend," she gasped, throwing a frightened look over her shoulder.

Todd's stomach twisted. The mental picture of the kind of man who would date a woman like this leaped into his mind: the size of an asteroid with the temperament of a rabid bear.

"Please," cried the woman. "Can you get me out of here? I jumped out of his car and ran, but he's crazy mad and I'm scared!"

"I . . . uh . . ." Todd's brain tried to pull itself together, but the woman pressed up against him, shocking him like live voltage. "I don't, ah . . ."

"I think I hear him coming!" She twisted around to look behind her and she put an arm around his waist. Rational thought abandoned him.

"Get in!"

His hands shook when he opened the door. The supermodel rushed around to the passenger side and dove in as soon as Todd hit the unlock button. Wiggling into the seat did amazing things to the tiny skirt. Amazing because Todd found the sight more erotic than the thousands—millions—of images and videos he had seen on the websites he managed.

The moisture in Todd's throat had evaporated. His tongue felt like a dry block scraping around in a sandpaper mouth. He fired up the BMW and squealed rubber getting out of the parking space. Todd aimed the car at the curb cut to Civic Drive and powered the sportscar into a skidding turn to the south. He drove for six blocks before the tightness in his chest started to ease. It was six more blocks before he could breathe without wheezing.

"Whe—" Todd cleared his throat and tried again. "Where would you like to go?"

"I . . . I don't have anywhere." The woman studied her hands in her lap. "I was living with my boyfriend."

"Do you have any friends you can stay with?"

"Tyson knows all my friends. He'll find me if I stay there."

The silence in the car deepened. Heat crept up Todd's neck. Carnal desire fought with chivalry. He was proud of himself when chivalry won. "I can get you a motel room."

"That's very kind of you." She placed a hand on his forearm. His skin tingled under her touch. "But . . . I feel so alone right now. Do you . . . do you mind if I stay at your place? Just for the night."

Todd rolled to a stoplight and took the opportunity to study the apparition he found, against all probability, sitting in his car next to him. Pale eyes under dark brows regarded him with such fervent, abject need, his cynical, jaded heart melted into a gooey puddle.

"What's your name?" he asked.

"Nikki," said the woman in a tiny voice. She dropped her eyes. "Nikki Larsen."

"I'm Todd. I have a spare room you can have for the night." Again, he was proud of his chivalry. Who wouldn't help a person in need, said his conscience. And maybe . . . No. Best not to think of any maybes. Disappointment lay at the end of that road.

Though when Nikki cried, "Oh, thank you," and hugged him around the neck, pressing into his side, *maybe* jumped back up onto the table and refused to be put down.

—

Mahoney, Chan, and Zivon waited in the car. Todd Mason's two-story townhouse occupied one corner of a fourplex in an upscale community. Cedar shingles lapped up the sides of the angular structure, and two big garage doors faced the street. A square balcony jutted out over the garage. To the left of the driveway, a path led around the side to a gated, fenced-in porch.

"That's our signal," Mahoney said when Britte came to the gate and waved the all clear.

"Obviously," Zee stated ponderously.

Mahoney and the others followed Britte along the stone path to the open front door. Interior light spilled onto a walkway bordered by red yucca and aloe plants, along with some other greenery Mahoney couldn't identify. Inside, Mahoney discovered a well-furnished, open-plan living area with two sofas, a glass coffee table, and thick pile rugs over hardwood floors.

On one sofa, the chubby Todd Mason reclined. His glasses were askew, and he snored gently. Two glasses of melting ice sat atop the coffee table, dripping condensation onto stone coasters.

"Well done, Team Britte," Mahoney said, pulling on nitrile gloves. "You're a natural."

"That doesn't make me feel better." Britte rubbed her temples. Her shoulders slumped. "He seems like a nice guy."

"Don't worry, he won't remember a thing. You write him a nice note about what a tiger he was in bed, and Zivon and I will stage the scene so he believes he rocked your world."

Zivon handed Chan the sleeping man's keycard, dangling from a lanyard. The key would access Whiteboard Designs's office doors. Without apparent effort, he hoisted Mason up on his shoulder as if lugging a sack of potatoes. "Where bedroom?"

"I don't know," Mahoney said. "Where the bed is, I suppose. Try the stairs."

"Will he get in trouble?" Britte bit her lip and watched Zivon tromp toward the stairs.

Mahoney gripped Britte by the upper arms and looked her in the eye. "I'm not going to blow purple pixie dust up your skirt—"

"Good," she said, tugging at her hem. "Not much skirt there anyway."

"We're moving against some very bad people here," Mahoney answered. "It's possible some good people are going to get squished in the treads as we roll on to victory. Look, if we do this right, they won't even know Toddles here was snookered." Or so he hoped. After Chan worked his wizardry, all hell would break loose down at Whiteboard Designs and all up the Milos Stankovic chain of command. If Todd was dumber than his bio suggested, he might report the close encounter with a blond bombshell to his bosses, whereupon they would easily put two and two together. Mahoney felt a strange impulse toward honesty and heard the truth coming out of his mouth without warning. "So, okay, he could get fired, all right? But I think that's the worst that could happen. Seriously."

He turned away, strangely disturbed by the concern in her eyes. *What? Are you jealous?* he asked himself.

Chan had set up a laptop and a card reader. He was busy flipping through a chain of blank plastic cards linked together on a lanyard. Like credit cards, some of these blanks had embedded chips, or magnetic strips, or both. Todd Mason's keycard rested on the reader plate, which in turn was attached via Ethernet cable to a laptop computer. Chan found the card he wanted and replaced Mason's card on the reader with his selection. He diddled with the laptop for a minute, then favored Mahoney with a slight nod.

"It is done."

"Great," Mahoney clapped his gloved hands. "Time for Phase Two. Britte, would you like to drive Mr. Chan back to Whiteboard for a little nighttime skulduggery? Chan will install his Man-in-the-Middle devices on their servers, Zee and I will finish setting the scene, and we'll meet back up at the motel."

"Sure," she said. The prospect of some real spy work seemed to brighten her mood.

"Oh, and don't forget to write that note for Todd. Use your imagination. We want to leave him with some good fake memories."

"Before he gets fired, you mean."

Mahoney winked at Britte and flared his hands in a gesture that encompassed her slinky dress. "Some fates are worth a firing."

29

Six days on the job and already Jay'nelle Morrison wanted to kill her boss. That was some kind of record. Normally she lasted a whole month before the urge to murder set in.

"Call the internet provider," Toby Richards told her for the third time, like she didn't understand him the first two times. She didn't expect much from a guy named Toby, and Toby fell below even her low bar of hope. The name, Toby, should have been her first clue not to take the job. Stupid uptight suburban name, with a stupid uptight suburban attitude, all condescension, like she was too dumb to know to call the internet provider with the internet being down and all.

Six days as office manager—which amounted to glorified receptionist, truth be told—at Diamond Entertainment, and Jay'nelle was ready to quit. Throw her damn computer right in Toby Richards's fat, uptight lap and get the hell out of this place before she did something she would regret even more.

"Yes," she told him with as much patience as she could muster. "I have called the internet provider. They say they don't have any trouble in our area."

"What about the building supervisor? Did you call maintenance?" Toby Richards, operations manager of Diamond Entertainment, looked like he wanted to pull his combed-over hair right out his head. He was red-faced, sweating, and his tie hung like a noose around his neck. Sixteen people worked at Diamond, including accountants, bookkeepers, and operations people, and none of them could access the internet, which was for all intents and purposes a crisis of biblical proportions at Diamond Entertainment. Nobody able to check they Facebook and whatnot. Hella day.

"The building people pretend they don't know nothing about nothing."

"And the internet provider. Did you talk to a supervisor, or just listen to the recording?"

"I talked to a real, live person," Jay'nelle said. "They checked and told me they don't show no outage in our area. I asked for a service technician, and they said between one and four p.m. on Friday."

"That's three days from now!" Toby stuck out his hand. "Give me the number. I'll call them."

"Okay. You're the boss." Jay'nelle wrote down the number on a Post-it Note and handed it to her uptight boss, though Lord only knew for how long he would stay her boss.

Toby stormed away and slammed his office door. Jay'nelle was about to settle back into a spreadsheet—which didn't need no internet to work, thank God—when the front door opened, and two men walked in. They wore yellow hard hats and yellow vests with shiny strips, and a phone company logo on the chest. One was a lanky white guy, the other was Asian.

"Can I help you?"

"Yes, ma'am," said the white guy. He had black hair and the bluest eyes Jay'nelle had ever seen. He was kinda hot if you liked men of the scruffy white-boy persuasion, of which Jay'nelle wasn't completely opposed to. "I wanted to find out, have you all been having trouble with your internet?"

"Have we? Oh, hell yeah. My boss, he's on the phone with the internet people, but they said they don't know about no outage."

"Probably true," said the man. When he leaned on her counter, his vest fell open and revealed a name tag sewed on his shirt that read Mark. "We think it's a trunk line issue with this office building. We've been chasing it all morning, from the third floor on down. There's a glitch in the DHCP transfer to the SFTP server, which is part of the T1 backhaul protocol. Every time we get close, I swear, the damn glitch jumps somewhere else. Like there's gremlins eating the wires."

He grinned and Jay'nelle sat a little straighter in her chair. "Well, your gremlin sure been causing us some problems."

"I'll bet. I think we have it trapped here in your suite. Do you have a network room? Someplace with a bunch of routers, maybe . . . ?"

"Yes, we do. Do you need to get in there?"

Mark grinned again, the kind of smile Jay'nelle's mother had always warned her about, but Jay'nelle found utterly charming.

"I thought you'd never ask," he said.

—

Britte's head snapped up as she caught herself falling asleep in her chair. She blinked. Yawned. Checked her watch. It was after midnight, meaning they had been at it for nine hours straight. No wonder she was tired.

Mahoney and Chan remained huddled together behind the desk, Chan typing and clicking, Mahoney directing the action like a mischievous elf, or the devil sitting on Chan's shoulder.

The office where they worked was one of the larger ones in the Peach Blossom building. Though bare and undecorated, the space could be any office in any business in the world, complete with cushioned executive chairs, a wood veneer table, and a desk so new, the tags were still adhered to it. The roar of jets overhead vibrated the windows with such regularity, she no longer heard it. Empty coffee mugs adorned every surface, or left brown rings behind, and a demolished tray of sandwiches lay covered in crumbs and crusts on the conference table.

Britte stood and stretched, reaching her hands toward the ceiling and standing on her toes. In her tank top and shorts, she must have made quite a show, for Mahoney raked her with his eyes, then twitched away as though he'd been caught peeping. Britte smiled to herself and held the stretch a moment longer, seeing if she could make him look back. He kept his eyes resolutely on the monitor, though he seemed to lose his train of thought and stumble through the next sentence. Mahoney's record as a perfect gentleman now extended to three months. In that time, he had treated her like one of the gang, not once making a pass or even hinting at an innuendo. She very much appreciated his restraint, as hooking up was the last thing she wanted or needed. Or was it? Perversely, the more he ignored her, the more she found herself trying to get his attention.

"Okay, Chan." The stubble on Mahoney's chin rasped when he scratched it. "Let's blast an email to all vendors. No, make it everyone on the contact lists for every company. Start with, Dear Boot-licking Fart-smellers . . ."

Britte rolled her eyes. She had to admit, Mahoney seemed to have the kind of diabolical mind required to wreak havoc on Milos's life. She had long since lost track of all the mayhem he was causing, but the gist of it sounded delightfully horrible.

Had it been anyone but Milos, she would have broken down and begged for mercy on their behalf.

Instead, she asked, "How much more can you do?"

Mahoney opened his mouth to answer, then shut it with a frown. "Hmm. Good question. We're down to harassment at this point, really." He consulted a printed sheet labeled GOALS with a long list of bullet points. Most lines were crossed through with black Sharpie, some were checked, and others circled. "I think," he added through a yawn, "we should be close to wrapping up. What do you think, Chan?"

The computer expert man rubbed his eyes and stifled a yawn of his own. "Yes. I would agree. Phase Two is almost complete."

The operation was going better than anyone wanted to admit. All of Chan's covert, off-the-shelf Ethernet interception devices they had planted on the targeted networks had performed flawlessly, delivering every secret to be found on every one of Milos's shell companies and web developers. The passwords had been the proverbial keys to the kingdom, leading to bank accounts, authorization codes, and website domains. After two weeks of data collection, Abassi had created complex charts and produced what Mahoney called "strike packages." The team—including Britte, much to her surprise—had pored over these and developed an action plan, which is what the three of them had kicked off early that morning . . . yesterday morning now.

"Phase Two will be a body blow," Mahoney had said, "but it won't knock him out. Stankovic will run for home base, his compound in Florida. He'll hunker down and try to regroup. That's where we'll hit him. Britte, I need you to draw a diagram of that place, inside and out . . ."

Things were about to get real.

"I'm going out for some air," she said.

Mahoney grunted and went back to composing his "fart smeller" email.

Britte left the office and headed for the front door, stretching and twisting as she went. Her injured shoulder gave her a warning twinge, which she ignored. She stepped out into the warm Atlanta night, breathing deeply the mingled scent of pines and jet exhaust, and reflecting on how far she had come in a little over a year. In her former life, she had been a shallow, vain, materialistic bitch. She had danced the all the tunes in every abused woman's playlist. *Down deep he really loves me. It's my fault he's hurting me.* And on and on until he ripped her face open with a broken bottle and Britte Thorpe—no, Bridgett Knudsen—woke up to reality. She had been a possession, to be used and discarded when the best-by date expired. A broken toy tossed aside by a petulant child. Britte considered it a rebirth of sorts, as she had discovered within herself a well of courage she hadn't known existed. Also, a well of deviousness, as she had begun to plan her escape. When Britte bolted captivity with Siobhan, she had drained every drop of her newfound bravery. But she did it. She broke free. Only to suffer another loss when Siobhan was injured—a blow that threatened to rip the soul from her body and leave her a husk.

Mahoney, more than anyone, had brought her back from the brink. She marveled at how he insisted on including her in the planning of every operation, giving her more and more responsibility. More challenges. Never once treating her like an object, or an empty-headed adornment. Hannah had been kind, of course, but Britte had never felt completely comfortable with the older woman, despite their long talks. Not with Asim's death hanging between them. Mahoney spoke to her like a person, not a possession.

Britte smiled as she strolled the perimeter of the shop

building, remembering when she had dressed for the Todd Mason operation, the way Mahoney kept looking at anything except her. The guy was interested all right, though he kept it in check better than most men she had known. She could almost smell the hormones in his sweat, no matter how hard he tried to hide his attraction.

And therein lay the foundation of another change inside her. At first, Britte had held the motel manager in near contempt, as if her former attitude toward the hoi polloi had reemerged and possessed her judgment. Then came the trial by fire, not once, but twice, followed by months of working together as part of a team, where she saw his genius for covert operations firsthand, and came to appreciate that he was a damaged man trying to fit in with a world that essentially frightened him. Something had happened to Mahoney. Something bad. It had scarred his psyche and taken a chunk out of his soul. That, at least, was something to which Britte could relate. She was broken, as well, and like Mahoney, had been reassembled poorly and put back into service with parts that didn't quite mesh.

Britte paused in her aimless ramble around the parking lot. Her heart was thumping hard, but not from exercise. There was another task she had been putting off and had yet to find the courage for. She plucked her cell phone from her back pocket. This was one of several burners Abassi had purchased at a local Walmart. Britte dialed a number from memory.

"Hello?"

Britte's heart triple-timed and her throat went dry at the same time her eyes welled with tears. "Ella?" she squeaked. "It's me. Bridget."

"OH MY GOD!" shrieked her sister's voice. "Where have you been? I thought you were dead! You haven't called in so long! What's going on? Where are you? How are you? Are you okay?"

Britte laughed at the flood of questions. "Slow down, Ella. I'm okay. A little battered, but I'll live."

"What happened to Milos? Are you guys still together? I hope not. That guy is no good for you, Bridget."

"Oh, Ella," Britte said through a sob. "So much has happened since we spoke. Sit down and I'll tell you all about it. First, the good news: I've met this really weird guy. You would like him . . ."

Milos Stankovic grew bored with ship life and took the runabout into San Pedro, on the coast of Belize, to stretch his legs. He dined at his favorite San Pedro establishment, a cozy French restaurant located on Barrier Reef Drive. With heavy purple curtains and velvet furniture mixed with modern appointments, the place gave off the kind of eclectic vibe that suited his whimsy. The black mussels in capers and white wine were excellent, and the filet mignon practically melted away at the touch of his fork. Stankovic whetted his appetite with a Lagavulin 18, neat, and paired the steak with a bottle of Louis Latour Château Corton Grancey Grand Cru 2015, a hearty Pinot Noir. He finished off the meal with a tart Key lime pie and a snifter of exquisite Louis XIII cognac.

This being Belize, the bill, when it came, was surprisingly modest.

Stankovic handed over his black Amex card and settled back to savor the last few drops in his snifter. The first inkling of a problem arrived in the form of a very nervous waiter and an obsequious manager appearing at his table. The manager presented him with the folio containing his credit card.

"My sincerest apologies, monsieur. There appears to be

a difficulty with processing this instrument. Perhaps another form of . . . ?"

Heat sprang up under Stankovic's collar and his jaw tightened. "Run it again."

"I would assure monsieur, we have attempted several times."

"This is ridiculous." Stankovic thumbed through his wallet, knowing he had no other payment method available but searching anyway. His skin heated and a film of sweat broke out on his forehead. "I have no other cards. I have never needed any."

The manager raised a supercilious eyebrow. "Perhaps monsieur would like to contact the issuer. I'm sure this is nothing but a clerical error."

"Of course," Stankovic muttered through teeth clamped shut tighter than a bear trap. He pulled out his phone . . . only to discover he had no service. "I . . . I . . . uh . . ."

The manager snapped his fingers and the waiter bustled off to find a cordless phone. Stankovic dialed the 800 number on the card and keyed his way through the phone tree to finally reach a live operator. What he heard sent his heart thundering and fire racing up his neck.

"What do you mean," he repeated, "this account has been closed? I did not close it! How can it be closed!?"

The night grew progressively worse. Stankovic escaped the restaurant only after reaching the captain of the *Siren Song*, who sent a sailor over to the mainland with petty cash to settle the bill. Once he had returned to the ship, he used the ship's sat phone to call his business manager, Gabriel Serrano.

Serrano practically screamed into Stankovic's ear once they were connected. "My God! You haven't heard? It's a disaster! A total fucking disaster!"

"Slow down," Stankovic commanded. The calm in his tone came from years of managing his emotions in a crisis. The anger torching his belly remained hidden, but for the thumping of the veins in his neck. "Start from the beginning and tell me everything."

"Okay. Small shit first . . . okay? Okay. Listen. Every single website we own—every single website—has been . . . diverted."

"What do you mean, diverted?"

"Just that. Every single URL is redirected to somewhere else. Like a site with unicorns and rainbows. Nobody, and I mean nobody, is getting to our sites. They're all being, like I said, redirected. Little Johnny wants to jerk off to a video of Alice in a three-way, he gets Alice in Wonderland instead." The tinkling of ice cubes carried through the phone and Stankovic pictured Serrano pacing in his den, highball glass in hand.

"So have our web people fix it."

"We can't! We've been hacked at the domain level, and someone has locked us out of our own control panels."

Stankovic pinched the bridge of his nose and tried to order his thoughts. "This does not explain my credit card, or my cell phone."

"No. That's the bad part . . ." The heavy whistling of Serrano's breath came through the sat phone earpiece, as did the ice tinkle and the sound of swallowing. Stankovic stood and began some pacing of his own, walking the rear deck of the *Siren Song* under a blanket of stars. The sat phone grew hot and damp against his ear. His head felt like an overinflated balloon.

"Spit it out," he prompted when the silence had gone on longer than he could endure.

"Milos . . . Milos, I don't know how to tell you this . . ."

"Just say it!"

"The bank accounts for every business entity, all your personal accounts . . . even the Cayman accounts, have been drained." Serrano's voice proceeded in mechanical fashion, a robot reporting a meteor on a collision course with Earth. "The passwords have been changed, and in some cases the accounts closed. All of your subscription accounts—phone, lease vehicles, and so on—were provided through one of the intermediary companies, either Diamond or Starstruck. All those company-paid accounts have been shut down. Everything. Hell, they even fucking closed your Netflix account. For the past eight hours, you have been under attack. A premeditated, determined, and very sophisticated attack."

Stankovic found himself perched on a deck chair. All the pressure inside him had drained out through the floor, leaving behind an empty husk. Queasiness roiled his stomach and that, coupled with the motion of the ship, threatened to expel his very fine dinner all over the pristine deck.

"*Attack*," he managed to say. "Who? The FBI?"

"No," Serrano stated with certainty. "Not the Feds. If it was law enforcement, they would have just frozen the accounts and raided your offices with a dozen agents and seized all your files. Besides, I just got off the phone with Dawali. His personal cell, not the company cell. He's been running down some leads on the two robberies—the ones where somebody took down the courier and the countinghouse—and he believes those hits are connected to this somehow. All part of a larger scheme."

Stankovic noted the change in pronoun. It was no longer "our" operation under attack, it was "your" businesses. Your livelihood. Like a rat, Serrano was trying to jump off the ship before it sank.

"No," the rat continued, "these guys act like enemies. Like they have a personal axe to grind."

At the word "enemies," realization crystallized in Stankovic's mind.

Britte. Britte Thorpe and the people of that strange little town in Texas. They're behind this. I made a huge mistake. I calculated the expense and decided further action wasn't cost-justified. I tried to treat it as a business matter, instead of what it was. I should have burned that town to the ground, damn the consequences. Should have killed and kept killing until Britte Thorpe was gone and all the threats eliminated once and for all. Dawali tried to tell me, but I was being penny-wise and pound-foolish. And look at what that's cost me.

"Start the recovery," he said to Serrano. "Get us back in business. Open new shell companies in different locations. Consider everything we currently own as contaminated, and if we touch it, we'll bring the virus into our bodies. We still have cash rolling in, so open new accounts and get those funds deposited. I need cash, and I need it now. I don't care how you clean the money, just do it. Do not rest until it is *done*." Stankovic clicked off without waiting for a reply. He dismissed the business concerns and relegated those to the back of his mind.

The time for business was over.

Now it is time for war.

30

Milos flew commercial from Belize to Miami, using Serrano's credit card to book travel. From there he flew to Tallahassee, where Dawali and one of his men picked him up in a black SUV. Dawali's thin, pocked face appeared haggard, with heavy, red-rimmed eyes. His normally immaculate suit was rumpled, as if slept in, and a coffee stain blotted the white shirt he wore under the navy suit coat.

The second man acted as valet and driver, taking Milos's overnight bag and placing it in the trunk while Milos and Dawali climbed into the backseat. The instant they were in motion, Dawali removed a thick folder from a case by his feet and showed it to his boss.

"From Ted Ruben," he said. "An executive recap of the Cottonmouth operation." He handed a second file to Milos. "Devlin Mahoney. The motel manager."

Milos opened it and found a headshot photo clipped to the inside jacket. The face captured there showed a dark-haired youth with a military haircut and a finely chiseled face. He exuded a jaunty attitude, despite the institutional nature of the photograph. An ever-so-slightly crooked tilt to the lips, and wrinkles at the corners of his eyes.

"Summarize for me," Milos said.

"Mahoney, Devlin, age thirty-two," Dawali reported. "Joined the Army at eighteen after an undistinguished record in school, though he did win several state-sponsored trophies in a variety of martial arts competitions. Made corporal in the 82nd Airborne Division and saw action in Afghanistan. Again, nothing of note in his service record. Seconded to the Defense Intelligence Agency and assigned on a classified mission, presumably in Bosnia or Serbia."

"Why presumably?"

"The operation's name has been redacted from the file, as is any reference to the nature of the op, or the objective. However, the file indicates Mahoney was incarcerated on espionage charges, and served two years in Dubrava Prison in Kosovo. He was tortured there. Quite extensively, from the medical report in the file. Three years ago, Mahoney was released in a prisoner exchange, received medical treatment for his injuries, and was relocated to the Cottonmouth . . . ah, location . . . for evaluation and observation."

"No connection to Britte Thorpe?"

Dawali shook his head. "None that I can find, sir."

Milos watched the lush countryside south of Tallahassee rushing past the tinted windows. A tension headache twisted a tight knot behind his eyes, and he had to force his jaw to unclench. "Explain this Cottonmouth situation to me."

"It is a site for a DHS operation to . . ." Dawali opened the file in his lap and read from it. "Ahh . . . to co-locate deactivated intelligence and military assets in order to facilitate the protection, observation, and settlement of said assets . . ." He closed the file and looked up. "In plain language, it is a dumping ground for ex-spies."

"Wonderful." Milos pinched the bridge of his nose. "Absolutely wonderful. What does the senator have to say?"

"He has notified his people at Homeland to investigate their attacks on your business interests. There is a note from Senator Ruben directing your attention to a section of the file. I have marked it for you. As part of the exchange for protection and anonymity, the residents must not operate against any US citizen or break any state or federal law. Which means . . ."

"Which means, what they have done to me is unsanctioned."

"Exactly." Dawali held up a cautionary finger. "If these people are behind the disruption of our operations, they are doing so illegally."

"Who else would it be?" His tone left no doubt he meant the question rhetorically. He stared out the window and spoke his thoughts aloud. "First, Britte runs there—on purpose or by accident, it does not matter. Then Kendrick kills one of the residents and assaults the people harboring Britte and the girl. Then Bridges attacks the town in force, destroying buildings and harming more of these . . . these ex-spies, I suppose. And now they have escalated. I can see it all clearly now. My mistake was in acting without information and planning without understanding the nature of the woman's allies."

"How could you have known? How could anyone have known?"

"We need to bring this matter to a close." Milos massaged his cheeks, eyes closed. "We cannot afford to raise the ire of the federal authorities—there is only so much our friends in high places can cover up."

"But what do these people want?"

"An excellent question. Retaliation? Protection for the woman?" Milos waved as if batting a fly. "We need leverage, because right now they have all the momentum. Has Bridges accomplished his mission up north?"

"As of this morning." Dawali consulted his wristwatch. "The team will drive all night. They should be arriving at the compound tomorrow afternoon."

"And you've taken care of the security situation?"

"Of course. I have placed twenty-four extra men on guard at the compound, for a total force of nearly thirty soldiers. All ex-Sudanese Special Forces, and well-known to me, personally, and under the direct command of Bridges. We have enough weapons and ammunition to hold off a battalion."

"Remember, these Cottonmouth people are not fools, Onye. They have defeated everything we have thrown at them."

Dawali squeezed his mouth into an offended pinch. "They are old, broken-down spies, not soldiers in their prime. We were caught by surprise before, and on their home ground. If these fools attempt a direct assault on us, they will be chewed to pieces by my men. Besides . . . I have prepared a few surprises for any unexpected guests."

Milos studied his security chief's shark-tooth grin. The man could look positively demonic at times. "You sound as those you hope they try a frontal assault."

"Oh, I do," Dawali assured him. "I very much hope they do."

Six people crowded the machine shop's breakroom. Hannah, Chan, and Roxy sat at the table, while McCurry rested against the counter, arms folded as if guarding the coffee pot. Britte squeezed herself into the back corner of the room, behind Hannah; and Mahoney stood on the opposite side of the room, next to a white dry-erase board on the wall. A laptop computer on the table allowed Abassi, Zivon, and Jeang-wu to conference in electronically, without their webcams turned on. They appeared in a grid of small squares, each denoting a man's initials.

Once everyone was more or less settled, Mahoney took a deep breath and dove in. "Phase Two is essentially complete. We have choked the target's web traffic until it resembles O'Hare in a snowstorm. We made the news with that one, all those porn sites going down. Productivity skyrocketed. Internet bandwidth across the world increased. All the bank accounts of all the business entities we can reach have been sucked dry. We have closed accounts and reset passwords and forwarded reams of incriminating documentation on the major players in the target's organization to local law enforcement. In summary, I'd say we have poked Stankovic in the eye with a blunt stick."

"And we didn't kill hardly anybody," Roxy said with a pouty schoolgirl expression.

"Better luck next time," McCurry growled.

"But," Mahoney continued, "all of this is nothing but a wrist slap to a guy like Stankovic. He has assets and cash that we'll never be able to reach, even if we doubled or tripled the operational teams. It would be like each of us running into a burning house carrying one cup of water at a time. His prostitution operation alone nets enough hidden cash to keep him in caviar and biscuits for years to come."

"Caviar and wot?" Roxy turned to Hannah with a frown.

Hannah ignored her and said to Mahoney, "The point was to get his attention, not kill him. We did that, right?"

"Zivon had the business manager, Serrano, under surveillance." Mahoney nodded to the laptop. "What do you say, Zee? Did we get his attention?"

"Da," came the reply after a short delay. "Man was walking

around in little circle. Drinking whiskey. Talking on phone. Very upset. Very agititted."

"Agitated," Mahoney corrected.

"Da. All day he do this. Back and forth. Wear hole in carpet. More on phone than I hef ever seen."

"Thanks, Zee. Sounds like Serrano's madder than a lemon picker with a paper cut. Stankovic has to realize he's under attack, so the most logical move would be to head back to his home base, gather his lieutenants, and plan a counterattack."

"And when they all get together," Roxy said, "we blow the shit out of them. Nuke 'em from orbit, right?"

"If we only had a nuke . . ." McCurry mumbled.

"No," Hannah said. "No frontal assault. Any kind of direct action needs to be on our ground, not his, and carefully staged to manage force disparity."

"So we offer him a deal," Mahoney said.

"So we offer him a deal," Hannah echoed. "We draw the spider out of his hole . . ."

McCurry's lips thinned in a predatory smile. "Then we take out his guards and stomp him flat."

"None of you are stomping anything," a deep voice boomed from the doorway, which was then filled with the presence of their minder, Lofland. "I'm the only one going to do any stomping, and I'm starting right here."

The shock that rippled around the table could have been measured on the Richter scale. Mahoney was surprised the dishes didn't rattle out of the cupboards and he had to check the impulse to dive under the table. Lofland stood at the door to the breakroom, hands on hips, surveying the group like a high school principal busting a bunch of truants.

"Ah hell," Mahoney said. "Who left the front door open?"

"In fact," Lofland said, "all of you are going back to

Cottonmouth, forthwith. This illegal operation is terminated, and you'll be damn lucky if your contracts aren't terminated right along with it."

—

"Give us the room," Mahoney said, and no one doubted to whom he was speaking.

Chan and Roxy scraped their chairs back and filed out past Lofland, who stepped aside at the last second. Roxy patted his cheek on the way by, which earned her a glare. She giggled and waggled her fingers in goodbye. McCurry unfolded from the counter and marched out without a word, although the expression on his face spoke in loud tones of disgust mixed with anger. Britte started to move but Hannah stopped her with a gesture.

Mahoney adopted an at ease posture and stayed right where he was.

Lofland closed the door and took up a rigid stance, arms crossed, and waited.

"We have cause," Mahoney said.

"He killed Asim," Hannah said in wire-tight voice.

"*Somebody* killed Asim," Lofland snapped back. "You don't know it was Stankovic."

"I—"

"You *think* it was Stankovic," Lofland rode over Hannah's objection. "You have some *coincidental evidence* to support that theory. And I will go so far as to say, the *probability* of his guilt approaches the ninety-fifth percentile. But vigilante justice based on conjecture is not how we settle grievances, no matter how upsetting they are."

"And what were we supposed to do?" Mahoney steamed,

his face turning hot. “Call the *police*? They killed one of ours, Lofland. And they put Siobhan in a coma.”

“You were supposed to call me! Or have you forgotten that little rule?”

“And what would that accomplish? You would have buried it, right?”

“No, I would not have buried it. I would have done exactly what I’m going to do now, which is go through channels—”

“Channels, my ass!” Hannah exploded from her seat and planted her fists on the table. “That is such . . . such *shtuyot b’mitz*! Nonsense! My *ba’al* is dead. Dead, Lofland. Asim was killed by this man, Stankovic. And what would your channels do about that?”

Lofland stood firm, weathering Storm Hannah like a lighthouse in a gale. “You know what would happen if your little scheme went balls up and your face was plastered on CNN? Or Zivon’s? Or Jeang-wu’s? Iran, Israel, Russia, and North Korea would be all up in our ass for harboring you people.”

Mahoney pulled a face. “Here we see the camouflaging adaptation of a GS-16 bureaucrat wrapping himself in protective red tape.”

“Not to mention we’d be hip deep in hit teams infiltrating Cottonmouth to kill you people,” Lofland continued, sending Mahoney a withering glare. “We would be stomping on assassins like cockroaches, to borrow your analogy. And what if you drop this guy? What then? Law enforcement gonna just shrug and say, oh well, another bad guy dead, so what, let’s go get a donut? Or will the media ignore a juicy story about the King of Smut getting blown away? No. You’ll have people poking this thing for months. Hannah, I’m sorry for your loss, but we have protocols to follow. The local FBI office—”

“Oh, fuck you, Lofland,” Hannah snapped. “I’ve heard enough.”

She grabbed her bag off the seat next to her and marched the long way around the table to avoid passing next to Lofland on the way out. Mahoney squeezed himself against the whiteboard as she stormed past.

"We're not finished here, Moshe," Lofland called to her retreating back.

"Oh, yes we are," echoed Hannah's reply as she disappeared down the hall.

There was a moment of suspended silence, then Mahoney said, "Handled that like a pro, Leland."

"Shut up, Mahoney." Lofland's eyes targeted him like twin muzzles. "What are you still doing here? Get your crazy ass out of my sight and start packing bags. You need to be back at the Cottonmouth Motor Court, forthwith."

"Why? Tourist season doesn't start for another fifty years. Does the Room Three toilet need plunging again? Wait, don't tell me. We got a one-star Yelp review."

"If this operation isn't shut down, packed up, and your sorry ass is not back there in forty-eight hours, I'm kicking you out of Cottonmouth."

"Oh no!" Mahoney clutched his chest. "You're killing me."

"No, I'm not. But that option remains on the table."

"So, seriously, man. What's the deal with Stankovic? What's your *channel* plan to deal with him?"

"Why do you care? Asim wasn't *your* ball."

"*Ba'al*," corrected Mahoney. "You have to put in the glottal stop. Husband in Hebrew. I may not have an interest in Stankovic, although Asim was my friend." He flicked a look at Britte. "And Siobhan had a life to live before she got involved in this. Now what would happen to her, even if she comes out of her coma? Some things are just the right things to do. An old lady falls down and you help her up. You pick up a wallet full of cash off the sidewalk, you find the owner and give him his money back."

"Somehow, I think your motives aren't quite so altruistic." Lofland cast a meaningful look at Britte. "You're helpless when it comes to a pretty . . . ah, pretty woman." Lofland grimaced and added. "No offense, Ms. Thorpe."

Britte waved it off as if batting a gnat away from her face. The intensity in her crystal eyes could shatter glass. "Do you know the things Milos has done?" Britte added. "Do you understand the lives he has ruined? Forget the prostitution for a minute. The sale of conflict diamonds funds genocide in Africa. It's why they're called Blood Diamonds!"

Lofland shifted and looked uncomfortable for the first time since he had entered the room. "It . . . Yes, I understand. But that isn't my responsibility. We have protocols for dealing with this type of . . . situation . . . and for Mahoney and the . . . the other residents of Cottonmouth to get together for this kind of mission is a severe violation of several laws, breaks their contracts, and puts national security at risk. I'm not kidding when I say the governments of many foreign countries would pay dearly to find some of the people we have stashed there."

"But—"

"But nothing," Lofland snapped. "I'm done with this conversation. Ms. Thorpe, when you signed your nondisclosure agreements, I offered you a very nice incentive to drive away from Cottonmouth and never look back. Instead, you chose to remain behind—"

"They tried to kill me!" Britte's cheeks had turned bright red. "Again!"

Lofland steamrolled over her anger with implacable government pedantry. "You chose to remain behind with this gang of misfits. As a consequence, I no longer have any obligation to assist you with relocation. You may go wherever you wish and do whatever you want, as long as you do not speak of these matters or these people to anyone. And I mean anyone. One whisper from you and I'll have you in federal prison before you finish the next sentence. As for you, Mahoney, you and the Scooby Gang will pack up this operation and be back in Cottonmouth in forty-eight hours. Stay far, far away from Stankovic and keep your hands off his organization."

Mahoney cocked an eyebrow. "And if I don't?"

"Then I will consider your contract terminated. You will be on your own. No more government paycheck, no more hiding you from the rest of the world, no more rehab."

"No more motel?"

"No motel."

"Wow." Mahoney sighed. "You slept through Motivational Management 101, didn't you?"

Lofland shook his head and left the breakroom, throwing a final statement over his shoulder on the way out. "Forty-eight hours, Mahoney. Or all of you are out on your asses."

31

Mahoney carried two cold bottles of beer outside and found Britte leaning against the shop's pebbled-concrete wall, a phone tucked against her ear. Night bugs sang while moths clotted under the parking lot lights in aerial dogfights. Light from downtown Atlanta yellowed the underbelly of the low clouds to the north.

Mahoney hadn't heard a jet thunder overhead in some time, and when he checked his watch, he was surprised to find that it was just past 2 a.m. Britte had gone outside a little over an hour earlier.

"Hey," Britte said to her phone, "call me when you get this, okay? Love you. Take care. Bye."

"Your sister again?" Mahoney said.

Britte nodded. "She hasn't answered her cell in a while."

"She's in college, right? So probably has it switched off . . . studying or whatever."

"Hmm."

"You should be careful out here," Mahoney said, "I'm pretty sure Roxy planted mines around the perimeter." He handed her a bottle. "Cheers. All the gear is packed, and all the kiddies have gone to bed, dreams of mayhem dying in their heads. As Zee put it . . ." Mahoney tried on a thick Russian accent and said, "'I am not heppy.'"

Britte managed a weak smile. "So, it's over?"

"One more chore, but it's an easy one."

"Huh. What's that?"

"We've siphoned off a little over fourteen million dollars from Mr. Stankovic—"

"What?!" Britte choked and coughed out a sputter of beer, which she tried to catch in her palm. "I had no idea he had that much."

"Well, he *did*. Now we have it and I'm thinking we should donate a really big chunk of it to charity. I was thinking of the National Center for Missing and Exploited Children, but really, it should be your choice."

Britte's eyes clouded as if she might cry, but she blinked them clear. "Thank you, Devlin. I think that's a great idea."

Mahoney joined her with his back to the wall and they shared the silence of the night. They spoke little, and then only of trivial things. He slapped a mosquito. Mahoney became very aware of the woman's breathing.

"Tell me about your sister," he said. "What's she like?"

"Ella? Well, she looks a lot like me."

"Jeez, there's two of you?"

Britte's lips twitched up in a half-smile. "Except she inherited the brains and ambition to go with the looks. She's a junior at Minnesota State. Majoring in Biochemistry."

As he looked at Britte, Mahoney was struck again by how she had managed to untangle the taut strings of emotional barbed wire wrapping her psyche since Siobhan's injury. The girl had yet to regain consciousness. The pain of regret was still there, surfacing at odd moments, grief subsumed by anger, which had fueled a powerful work ethic. Britte had pitched in with her whole being, taking on every dirty job, doing all the scut work required for the operation without a single complaint.

"I hadn't spoken to her in months. Ella. Not since . . . before . . ." She brushed the scar on her cheek with light fingers. "I didn't have the courage to admit what he'd done to me. She warned me about him, and I didn't listen."

"Where are your parents in all this?"

"They disapproved of my life choices early on. When I moved in with Milos, Mama fretted and Daddy went all stoic and granite-faced. They wanted me to come back home, but the place seemed so . . . small." Britte twisted her lips in a rueful smile. "Ella was the good daughter. Good grades, perfect attendance. She asked to come with me once. Take a cruise on the yacht, meet all the glittery people I kept name-dropping to her. Mama and Daddy nearly had a fit."

"You never told me how you . . . how that came about," Mahoney said. He left the comment hang there, an open invitation more than a question.

"Milos," she said in a distant voice, her eyes fixed on the horizon. "At first, he was awesome. Caring. Considerate. A powerful man with powerful friends and he wanted little Bridgette Knudsen to be a part of all that. Then came the occasional swat if I did something that displeased him. The swats turned to . . . something worse. But then he would apologize and shower me with gifts, all contrite . . . Stop me if you've heard this before."

The choppy flow of words ground to a halt, and Mahoney waited, sensing there was more to come.

When Britte started again, her voice came rough. "Then came one smack too many and I tried to leave him. He flew into a rage and smashed a champagne bottle on the deck rail. The next thing I knew, I was on the ground, bleeding. My face was torn. Milos refused to get me a doctor. Just threw me a towel and said to go clean up. I wanted to die, Mahoney. If I had the means, I would have done it, right then and there."

"I know."

"Onye stitched up the cut. Crudely. Without painkillers. Then he took me and locked me in a room next to the security team's quarters. And there I stayed, for weeks. A damaged and broken tool that no longer had a use. Or so I thought. About a month later, Milos told me to get back to work. A shipment of stones was waiting in Surat, and I needed to get on a plane that night.

"'What if I said no?' I asked him." A sad smile crossed Britte's face. "And that's when he brought Siobhan into the room. Told me what would happen to her if I refused."

"After a while, they let me wander the grounds. I knew I had to get her away. Siobhan and me both. One of my guards was sweet on me. His name was Victor and I convinced him that I would be his 'forever girl' if we could just get away. He was dim. Gullible. I planned everything, including a raid on the diamond vault. Victor got us out, and then I ditched him as soon as I could and took Siobhan and ran. Until my car broke down." She floated a weak smile his way and added, "You know the rest of the story."

Mahoney let out a shaky breath. "Come here."

She folded into his arms, and he held her as the racking sobs shook her body. He patted her back and murmured soothing words. Britte was nearly as tall as he, and her chin rested on his shoulder. Her hair tickled his nose. He held her not like a lover, but as a friend. It came to him with a strange sense of the world shifting, that somewhere along the way, he had ceased thinking of her as a Miss America knocked off the stage and needing only a turn of circumstances to resume her place in a universe beyond the mundane world in which he lived. She was no goddess, fallen to earth, temporarily lost among mere mortals. Britte Thorpe was a real person, as alone and desperately lonely as the rest of them. As broken and in need of a purpose as the castaways living in Cottonmouth.

His heart ached for her, not from pity as it once had, but as one damaged human recognizing another.

"I'm sorry, Britte. We tried. We both tried."

"Bridgette," she whispered into his ear. "My name is Bridgette Knudsen."

Britte woke to bright daylight filtered in through metal blinds.

Four of the Peach Blossom's offices had been converted to sleeping quarters, with two cots, sheets, pillows, and blankets. Pretty bare-bones compared to the luxury she had once enjoyed. She shared a room with Roxy, while Chan and Abassi took another. Mahoney's roommate was Zivon, who was currently in Tallahassee, watching the lawyer, Serrano. Or more likely on the road back to Texas by now.

Which was how she found herself in a room alone with Devlin Mahoney, both of them tangled like creeper vines in one cot. Fully dressed, much to her surprise. They had slept together. Actually slept. For a time, she had thought, *This is it. This is when he takes payment for saving me.*

But Mahoney had just held her. Not tried for a kiss or a cheap feel. Snuggled with her, stroking her back like she was a fractious cat who needed soothing. Not far from the truth, actually.

She was tucked into his shoulder, their thighs twined. His breath sawed in and out, not a snore, but a deep, contented sleepy sound. She lifted her head a bit and watched his eyeballs move behind closed lids. Smelled the slightly stale odor of his breath and found it didn't bother her. His lips were dry, but a tiny bit of dampness trailed from the corner of his mouth, and Britte found it oddly adorable. An urge to kiss him tickled through her.

She had thought that particular response burned out of her forever after the way Milos treated her.

Britte had lost her virginity at fifteen to a college freshman in an upstairs bedroom at a friend's house—though "lost" was the wrong word. More like gave it away, and glad to be rid of it. The experience had been brief, painful, and sticky. Two more attempts in the following three years had not improved her outlook on sex.

Sexual intimacy was a means to an end, a gratification of a physical need, nothing more. Like scratching an itch. There had been no love, even with Milos. What she had thought was love had been infatuation, at best. Young Brigette Knudsen, so fresh off the farm she smelled of hay and cow patties, had been dazzled and besotted by the handsome, wealthy tycoon on his yacht, with his celebrity friends and never-ending supply of delights for the senses. She had made her bed willingly enough. Jumped into it eagerly, in fact. Shamelessly traded her body for mindless, narcissistic pleasure, shedding her strict Lutheran upbringing like a stifling, heavy coat. Gratification without commitment.

Mahoney snorted in his sleep, smacked his lips, and squirmed against her. He tightened his grip, holding her tightly, as if he never wanted to let go. Warmth returned to Britte in a flush, and along with it came a stab of fear. Fear? What was she afraid of?

Britte propped her head on an elbow and studied Mahoney's face. It was an ordinary one, though cut with strong lines. Well-chiseled. A perpetual five o'clock shadow darkened his cheeks. But all in all, nothing special. She wondered what made him so different than the men she had known before.

Because I might . . . have feelings . . . for him, said a tiny voice from a hidden corner of her mind.

As if hearing her thoughts, Mahoney's intensely blue eyes popped open at that moment, spooking her so much that she gasped aloud.

"Good morning," he mumbled.

"Uh, yeah. Good morning to you, too."

"You weren't watching me sleep, were you? 'Cuz that would be creepy."

"Nope. Nuh-uh. Of course not." Britte started the process of squirming free of the tangle of body parts and blankets and sheets. "Just about to wake you so I could get up."

"Yeah, good idea."

Their eyes locked from a foot apart. Something passed between them, a hidden message that Britte couldn't quite decipher. He was a trained spy, he could make his face show any emotion he wanted, so what were his eyes telling her now? Was that fear she saw? What was *he* afraid of? Was he repulsed by her face? Her past? Did he want to have sex with her? And did she want him to?

After a long, charged moment, Mahoney blinked and threw out a lopsided grin. He made himself busy getting out of bed, looking at everything but her. He chuckled and said, "Prepare yourself to endure taunts and catcalls. Coming out of the same room like this . . . everybody's gonna pull a muscle jumping to a conclusion. I think there's bagels and stuff in the kitchen. From yesterday. I'm going to get something to eat." He raked fingers through his black hair, straightened his shirt, scanned the room as if he'd forgotten something, and all but ran to the door. "Yeah, well. See you in a bit."

Britte stared at the closed door, feeling . . . what? Disappointed? Relieved? Sad? Happy?

Yes. All of that and more.

Britte sank back into the cot and breathed in Mahoney's scent from the pillow. She found herself smiling, surprised to find she was actually excited to see what the day might bring. And that there was someone with whom she wanted to share the experience. There was no rush to see what happened.

Without the threat of Milos looming over her, she was free to do what she wanted with her life. Maybe it was time for her to close the book on her past. Forge a new life as Bridgette Knudsen instead of Britte Thorpe. She could take her government cash out and the money she and Victor had stolen from Milos and take a road trip up to Minnesota. It would be great to see Ella again. Or head west and see the Pacific Ocean. In all her travels with Milos, they had never made it to the West Coast, which was always something of a bucket list thing for her. She could watch the sunset off Malibu Pier, maybe, or surf the risers off the San Diego coast.

The thing with Mahoney would sort itself out, one way or another. Whatever she decided to do, at least there was time and space to do it now. All the time in the world.

Britte rolled over and hugged the pillow against her chest. She allowed a smile to break out across her face.

32

Mahoney sat in the receptionist's chair behind the Peach Blossom shop's front desk and swiveled in slow arcs, his vision panning the parking lot, but his thoughts were focused inward. Bright Georgia sun baked the asphalt and glittered painful shards of brilliant reflections from the few cars parked out front. A cup of breakroom coffee cooled on the desk, untouched, in a stained enamel mug with an industrial logo. The muffled sound of voices mumbled through the drywall behind his head. Britte laughed, a low, throaty sound that knocked Mahoney's thoughts off track, spinning them in a new direction.

Britte. It didn't take much to nudge his thoughts back to her. They had talked through the night about nothing. He couldn't recall a single topic of relevance, and yet there had been no uncomfortable pauses, or forced conversational gambits. Everything had flowed as smoothly as rain sluicing down a drainpipe until pink touched the eastern sky. She had followed him back to his room without a word being said. By some unspoken consent, they had transitioned from two people talking to two people holding each other, with no awkward moments. No bullshit should-I-or-shouldn't-I make a pass. Not even a strained silence provoked by the sexual overtones implicit in being in bed together. They had stretched out next to each other, her head tucked into his shoulder.

Fully clothed. Together. In bed. And then they had gone to sleep. No kissing. No roaming hands. It was just . . .

Weird.

But pretty amazing.

"Hey there."

As if his thoughts had conjured her, Britte appeared in the lobby. She wore the same tan shorts as last night, though she had changed into a buttery-yellow, sleeveless, button-up blouse that hung down low enough it could almost be a dress. She nudged Mahoney's chair out of the way, giving herself room to hop up onto the reception desk. Britte tucked a ribbon of loose hair behind her ear and dangled her feet like a kid on a swing set.

"You have knobby knees," Mahoney said.

"And you have the entire Black Forest growing up in your nostrils."

"I know. But I'm still charming and lovable."

"As a yeast infection." Britte rolled her eyes.

Mahoney grinned and rocked in his chair, fingers interlaced behind his head. Britte retreated into silence. She glanced away, checking out the walls, ceiling, and carpet. She worried at her bottom lip with her perfectly white, perfectly straight teeth.

"What's the matter?" Mahoney asked.

Britte sighed after a long pause and said, "What are we doing? I mean, no wait—" She stuck out her palm to forestall Mahoney's quick comeback. "I mean, we're done, right? You're going back to the motel. No more Milos."

"It looks that way." Mahoney cocked his head. "You don't sound disappointed."

"I'm not. Strange to say it. I mean, I was pissed yesterday, don't get me wrong. And I still loathe the bastard. He deserves everything we've done, and he should be staked out naked on an anthill, but . . ."

"But maybe it's time to move on and let fate or karma decide what to do with Milos?"

"Exactly." Britte drew in a deep breath and cleared it out in a long whoosh. "Time to move on. Close the book on the past. All that cliché stuff."

"If it's any comfort, I think this has gone beyond you now. Hannah is out for blood, and she wants Old Stinky's hide nailed to the door. She's been stomping around here like a teenager who had their phone taken away."

"What's she going to do?"

Mahoney shrugged one shoulder. "Probably lay low for a while. Hey, listen, okay? We're not the cops, and this ain't a spy show on TV. We're not going to put together some clever caper where the lead actor pulls off a latex mask and produces a tape of the bad guy's full confession, which he conveniently monologued into a recorder. I mean, we've all seen how guys like Stankovic skirt the law or use their influence to skate away. Dude's got a fucking ship, right? One whiff of the law, and he gets on his boat and sails off to Tahiti." Mahoney scrubbed his hands over his face. "Look, I took an oath, okay? Protect and defend the Constitution of the United States, which I have done my entire adult life. I broke that oath. I was also raised Catholic, so you can imagine how many Hail Marys I'll need for drop-kicking the Big Kahuna Commandment and waxing Mr. Stankovic." He leaned forward and lightly clapped his palms on Britte's thighs. "But I'm okay with it. And you know why? . . . This guy's a bug. He's the leftovers from an egg-smelling fart. He's a poisonous snake and he needs stomping in an industrial press. So, I'm okay with violating my oath, breaking federal and state laws, and disappointing my dear, sainted Ma, should she find out—and God help me that she does not. Though come to think on it, she'd probably be okay with it. But no. I'm good. And so is Hannah. But one day, and I suspect sooner rather than later, Mr. Stankovic will wake up with a bullet hole in his forehead and Asim's name carved into his chest."

"Wow. Some speech."

"I know, right," Mahoney said. "I should have ended it with a bigger finish. We won't go gently into that good night! Win one for the Gipper! Yay!"

Britte slid off the desk in a sinuous motion. She took half step closer and the scent of her body wash—apples and cinnamon—kicked Mahoney's heart into overdrive. He stood to meet her, his hands finding their way onto her hips as her arms snaked around his shoulders. The world paused as they drifted closer, as tentative as two kids at a high school dance. Britte's neck flushed red, and a vein beat in her throat so hard, Mahoney could see it fluttering under her skin. He touched his lips to her neck where it emerged from the collar of her blouse, brushing against the silken warmth of her skin and tasting the pulse thundering there. Britte shivered and pulled him into a kiss. She clutched him as a drowning woman clings to a life preserver, feverishly hot, her breasts heaving against his chest and her panting breaths fluttering against his lips.

All of Mahoney's cherished cynicism, his carefully cultivated disdain for emotional commitment, and his love 'em or leave 'em attitude, crumbled to dust and was blown away by the heat of his need for this woman. Somehow, at some point, Britte Thorpe, or Bridgette Knudsen, or whatever she called herself, had smashed his shields, undermined his defensive walls, and pierced his invulnerability. She was his Kryptonite.

She stiffened and pushed away, hands against his chest.

"Mahoney, wait . . . wait . . ." Britte shuddered through a few deep breaths, her eyes downcast. "Wait."

"What is it?" he asked quietly. "What's wrong?"

"I'm not sure," Britte said. She sounded close to tears. "I don't think I'm ready for this."

Mahoney took a shaky breath of his own. He had not a clue what to say, and he sensed anything he did say would be wrong, so he chose the option his ma always preached, which was to keep his trap shut.

Britte slumped against his chest and her words came muffled by his shoulder. "I'm sorry, but I don't think I'm ready."

Mahoney patted her back. "No, don't be sorry. Never be sorry. That wasn't your fault."

He held her and said nothing else for long minutes, both of them listening to the roar of jets overhead.

"What are you thinking?" she said at last, her lips moving against his shoulder as she spoke.

"Oh no," he said in mock horror. "Not the dreaded 'What are you thinking?' question. Jay-sus, woman, haven't you learned never to ask a man that question? I was thinking about the Mets' chances for a pennant. I was thinking about the advantages of commercial weed killer over natural vinegar. I was thinking about how to do a perfect faro shuffle. I was thinking I have an itch behind my left nut and how could I scratch it without looking uncouth."

"Since when has uncouth bothered you?"

"Yeah, good point. Hold on, let me scratch a minute." Mahoney took Britte by the upper arms and held her so he could look into her eyes. He wiped all traces of goofiness from his expression so she would see how seriously he meant what he said next. "You want to know the truth here? The truth is that

I want to kill that fucking asshole who hurt you, then raise him up from the dead and kill him again. That's what I'm thinking."

"Oh." Britte blinked and a tiny smile touched her lips. "Is that all? I thought you wanted *me*."

Britte stood, forehead to forehead with Mahoney, and fought the panicked flutter of her heart. A cascade of emotions tumbled through her, flaring to life and dying, faster than she could sort them out. Fear, of course. Fear of making another mistake. Joining that fear was the terror of perhaps finding real affection for the first time in her life, and then potentially blowing it because she couldn't shake her past fear that she would lose Mahoney—because the only way she had ever known how to relate to a man was by fucking him.

And then he goes and tells her how much he cares for her, though not with the false promises of affection she'd heard so many times before, but with the solid conviction of his anger at her tormentors. She felt his determination. She sensed the bedrock of his conviction through the steadiness of his gaze, the sincerity with which he laced his words. If there was one thing Britte could do, it was read men, and her reading of Mahoney showed her he didn't want to own her. He didn't want to just fuck. He wanted to heal her. He wanted to protect her. He might even—and this was the hardest to believe—he might even want to love her.

And that scared her more than anything.

Britte jumped when his thumb touched her cheek, caressing the thick, waxy scar tissue there. He traced it gently, and she shivered. He moved, and his lips brushed it. Britte could hardly breathe. Mahoney trailed tiny kisses along its length, from her eyebrow to the corner of her lips. They stood together, chest to chest, nuzzling each other like a pair of timid deer. His fingers traced patterns across her back, gentle paths that left tingling, pebbled trails where they touched. Her throat had gone dry. She lifted her chin a fraction and his lips met hers, feather-light, like the silken brush of a rose petal.

"There's no rush," Mahoney whispered against her lips. "We have all the time in the world to see if this is right."

"I think it's right," she whispered back. "I'm just . . ."

"Scared?"

"Mm-hmm."

"Yeah, me too."

She pulled back and blinked in confusion. "Scared? What are you scared of?"

"Algebra," he quipped, then grew serious. "I haven't let anyone get close," he said, trying and failing to add a disarming smile. "Not since . . ."

"Since?"

"Since they put me in Dubrava. It's a prison. In Kosovo."

"I know," she said. "Hannah mentioned something about that, so I looked it up. You were tortured there, I'm guessing."

"You may have noticed," Mahoney rocked a hand in a seesaw gesture, "I'm a little not right in the head. Though many would argue that started way before Kosovo."

Britte pulled him close. Rested her chin on his shoulder. "Oh, Mahoney. Are we two fucked-up people, or what?"

A trilling from her back pocket acted like a high-voltage wire jabbed between them. Britte fumbled for her phone at the same time as trying to disentangle from Mahoney, and as a result dropped the device to the carpeted floor. It thunked and skidded under the desk. The trilling continued as she crawled after the thing. When she finally got her hands on it, she read the display.

"It's my sister," she said and swiped to answer. "Ella! What's up?"

A man's voice answered. "Hello, Britte, darling. Long time, no talk."

Milos.

All the air went out of Britte, and a wave of blackness crashed against her mind. She fought to stay upright. Mahoney's eyes bracketed with concern.

"What . . ." She tried to swallow and spoke again. "What have you done with my sister?"

"She's safe. For now," Milos's silky voice sounded very self-satisfied. Mahoney leaned in and she tilted the phone so he could hear. "Your people have attacked my business and, although I admit you may have had provocation, I simply can't allow that to stand. You have cost me quite a bit, little flower, and I intend to get restitution. One way or another."

"What do you want?" Mahoney asked.

"Is this one of Britte's new friends? Devlin Mahoney, perhaps?"

"I repeat," Mahoney said. "What do you want?"

"I want what any businessman would want in such a situation."

"What's that?"

"I want to make a deal."

33

"Jay-sus and Mary," Mahoney muttered under his breath when he opened the third full-size Halliburton case and found it packed with ammunition in a variety of styles, from .223 NATO up to cigar-sized .50-caliber rounds, all of it packed into mil-spec boxes in olive drab and neatly stenciled with its contents. "How much ordnance did you buy, Roxy?"

The first two cases he'd tried contained explosives, detonators, and electronic doohickies that did things to make other things go boom at the right time and place. Seven cases remained unopened.

Someone, probably Hannah, had switched off the shop's air conditioner and Mahoney didn't dare roll up the overhead doors on the off chance that a mail carrier or dog walker would happen by as he was unpacking an M4 at just the wrong moment. In Texas, nobody would bat an eye, but this was near the airport in Atlanta, so Mahoney wanted to play it safe. Sweat soaked his T-shirt and dripped from his forehead.

All the equipment, from Chan's computer gear to Roxy's munitions, along with the team's personal luggage, was staged near the shop's roll-up doors. McCurry and Roxy had gone to rent a truck to haul it all back to Texas, while Hannah had buggered off to God knew where. Britte had been nearly catatonic with worry, so Mahoney stuck a bottle of water in her hand and sent her to lie down.

Now he wished he had brought her along to help him find where Roxy had packed the fucking gear he wanted.

"There you are, my lovelies," he said on the fourth case, lifting out a British-made SA80 battle rifle. The weapon was similar to a bullpup configuration, in that its magazine stuck down from behind the trigger grip. It also featured a vertical handle extending downward from the foregrip. Sadly, it was a pain in the ass to fire left-handed due to the spray of brass from the ejection port, so Mahoney reluctantly set it aside and pulled out a Heckler & Koch 416. The HK 416 was based on a standard M4 design and operated much the same, although with fewer jams at critical moments.

Mahoney cleared the weapon and propped it next to him, then went digging for spare magazines. He was head down in the case when sharp heel taps announced the arrival of Hannah. Mahoney read the tempo of the tapping as Angry Woman Incoming. His shoulders slumped. *Maybe if I keep my head down, she won't see me.*

"What are you doing?" Hannah barked from directly behind him.

"Right this second? Looking in this crate for a place to hide."

"Mahoney! Look at me."

With the air of a condemned man, Mahoney straightened, picked up the HK, and closed the lid on the Halliburton case. With a long-suffering sigh he plunked down on the case and rested the rifle across his knees.

Hannah faced him, hands on hips, wearing a pantsuit and

an expression of annoyance. "Britte told me about her sister," she said. "And she told me you had some *narish* idea to get her back."

"If *narish* means courageous and heroic, then yes."

"It means stupid."

"Then it's not me."

Hannah gestured at the rifle. "What are you planning to do? Rambo your way in, all by yourself, and extract the girl?"

"Seriously, Hannah . . ." Mahoney scrubbed his face with the hem of his T-shirt, not that it helped. "I didn't see a whole bunch of options available. Lofland has laid down the law and put everybody on notice. No way I can ask you guys to risk your lives over this. Like you said, a frontal assault is suicide."

"Kidnapping is a federal crime. We could get Lofland back here—"

"Shit, Hannah," Mahoney snapped. "When did you become a Lofland fan? You know how he is—he moves with the speed of a frozen turtle. It'll take hours to convince him we're not bullshitting for the sake of continuing our operation against Stankovic. Assuming we can make that case on just Britte's word, then he'll have to start cranking the rusty gears of the FBI, which would undoubtedly involve the Tallahassee field office. The same office that already dropped the ball on Stankovic and may just be in his pocket. The man gave us a deadline, Hannah. Money back by midnight, or he disappears the girl to the slave trade. That's less than twelve hours from now. And we don't have his money, remember? We gave it all away. So, there's no negotiating."

"Dammit!" Hannah stomped her foot. "Britte is one of ours, now. She's family. There's no way we're taking the pass on this operation."

Mahoney blinked in surprise.

"Don't look at me like that," Hannah growled. "You need

to get busy. Come up with a real plan, not this . . . this John Wayne bullshit."

The shop's interior door creaked open and Britte entered the cavernous space. Her eyes were red from crying, and she had a tissue twisted through her fingers. She stopped next to Hannah and the older woman reached up to pull Britte closer, a motherly gesture of comfort that should have been awkward, given the difference in height, but Hannah somehow made it look natural and easy.

"Don't you worry, *liebling*," Hannah soothed. "I'm here now, so there's no need to worry about the ding-a-ling doing something stupid."

Mahoney straightened. "Hey!"

"Shut up, Mahoney," Hannah all but snarled. "What did I tell you? Get to planning something. I'll call Jeang-wu. Get him on the first thing burning to Atlanta. Then I'll call the rest of the team and get everybody back here. After that, Britte and I will start unpacking all this junk."

Mahoney's heart jumped into second gear. He couldn't help the loopy grin that crept onto his face.

Hannah's eyes narrowed into a predatory look that gave Mahoney a chill. "Let's kill this sonofabitch."

34

Britte imagined she could feel the wooden dock under her feet vibrating in tune with the thundering of her heart. She swallowed repeatedly, trying to force the tennis ball in her throat to go down, and fought to control the tremors shivering through her body.

I'm going back played on a closed-loop soundtrack in her head, disrupting coherent thought.

The dock projected into a river channel, a quarter mile from the Gulf of Mexico, one of hundreds of similar little inlets scattered along the Gulf Coast. Sixty or seventy some odd miles southeast of Tallahassee, and accessible by a private drive off a two-lane backroad highway, the dock existed to allow Milos and his people to ferry to and from his island home. It was lit up at intervals with well-tended security lights suspended on poles.

"I really, really don't think you should go," Mahoney said. They stood together on the dock in a patch of darkness between pools of yellow light, close enough she could feel the warmth of Mahoney's shoulder. "You know you don't have to."

"So you've said." Britte was proud to hear her voice come

out strong, without the shakiness she felt inside. "But it's my sister we're talking about."

Unseen creatures chirped and croaked and buzzed, and from a distance, the sound of rollers crashing on the coast provided the pleasant soundtrack of a Florida night. A crescent moon hung in the eastern sky amid a blanket of stars. The steady ocean breeze helped with the temperature, though humidity saturated the air. Britte's blouse stuck to her back and sweat soaked her underarms. Though how much of that was panic-induced and how much was due to humidity was debatable.

The hum of a boat engine rose in volume, coming from the sea. A giant hand squeezed Britte's chest and she had trouble breathing.

I'm going back.

"Here they come," Mahoney said. "Again, I think it's a bad idea for you to be there. It gives Milos one more chip in a stacked game."

"Shut up, Mahoney."

He let out a long-suffering sigh. "I get that a lot."

A boat appeared out of the darkness, pushing a white bow wave in front of it. Milos employed a number of small vessels to ferry between the dock and the island. The one approaching the dock was a sleek ski boat, big enough to seat six comfortably, and eight in a pinch. The ship's pilot motored in close, then swung the prow out in a curve and cut the motor back to idle, using momentum to push the side of the boat against the pier. Another man, slender as a lizard, looped a line over a bollard and whipped a quick knot to secure it. As it drifted into the light, Britte saw that the second man was Dawali. Her knees jellied and she fought the urge to collapse into a quivering puddle.

He climbed the ladder to the dock and approached with his teeth gleaming in a predatory smile. Britte's feet seemed rooted to the dock. She wasn't moving, even though the voice in her head was screaming at her to run.

"Ah, Miss Britte," he said in his lilting accent, somehow sounding unctuous and threatening at the same time. "I have missed you very much."

Britte's throat had gone chalk-dry and she labored to draw a breath.

Insane. She had been insane to think she could face these people again. No way could she go back there. What if Hannah's plan failed? What if Mahoney was killed and she was captured?

But then Ella's face appeared in her mind, and it allowed her to regain a measure of her composure. When she spoke, the words came out raspy, but steady. "Burn in hell, Onye."

"Hi!" Mahoney said, stepping between her and Dawali with his hand stuck out for a shake. Dawali accepted the grip, obviously taken aback by the flamboyant greeting. "I'm Devlin Mahoney, and if I'm not mistaken, you must be Onye Dawali. What a night, right? I have to say, this is a real treat for me. I never thought I would get to meet a syphilis survivor. Or did you get that face by standing too close to an IED?"

The surprised look on Dawali's face had begun to transition to anger when Mahoney twisted the hand he was vigorously pumping. Dawali's arm pretzeled, Mahoney shifted his weight, swiveled his hips, and Dawali took flight. He hit the water with a slap and a splash. Droplets pattered the deck and rained on Britte's toes.

"Oh, dude!" Mahoney cried in what sounded like real horror. "I'm so sorry, man. I'm such a klutz. My ma always said, 'Devlin Mahoney, if you could just get through a whole day without knocking something over, I'd go to heaven a happy woman.' Here, take my hand. No? Okay. At least let me help you up the ladder."

"Get the fuck away from me," Dawali snarled. He climbed

onto the pier, water sluicing off in sheets. A pistol appeared in Dawali's hand—at least it did for an instant, then Mahoney magicked it away, dropped the thing holding the bullets and snapped something so another bullet spun glittering away.

"Uh, uh, uh." Mahoney waggled a finger at the guy in the boat, who had brought out a wicked little machine gun. "You shoot us, your boss doesn't get his money. Behave yourself. Okay, Onye? Don't make me resort to violence—it gives me heartburn like you wouldn't believe."

For a moment, Britte was sure Onye would unleash the rage clearly boiling under his skin. To her surprise, he mastered himself and gestured at the man in the boat to lower his weapon. He held his arms out and looked down at his soaked clothing, then back up to Mahoney. The malice burning behind his eyes promised a future filled with pain for both of them. Britte shuddered.

"All right, Mr. Mahoney. All right. You are correct in that Mr. Milos wishes you alive. Please get in the boat." With a wave of his dripping arm, Onye bowed them to the ladder like an obsequious maître d' in a fancy restaurant.

Mahoney turned to Britte, the lines of his face etched into a look of concern. "Last chance. Please stay here."

Britte clenched her jaw and filled her lungs with soupy air. "What is that saying about getting back on the horse?"

"Um, use a ladder?"

"These men don't own me. They hurt me, but they don't get to control me." Britte unglued a foot from the dock and took a step forward. Then another one. And just like that, she was walking to the ladder. Every bit of her shook from fear, but she was moving forward.

I'm going back. Fuck them. I'm going back.

—

They drove up from the island's boathouse in a golf cart that undoubtedly cost more than Panama. Mahoney rode up front with the driver, who was the same guy that had piloted the boat. Mahoney asked his name, being polite, but all he got in return was a grunt and glare, which forever named the man Grunt as far as Mahoney was concerned. The damp little security snake rode in back with Britte, right behind Mahoney, causing his neck to itch and the opening symphony of bells to ring inside his head.

He checked over his shoulder and winked at Britte. Poor girl looked like she might throw up at any second. Ever since seeing Dawali, fear had radiated off her in waves so strong, Mahoney worried about catching a sunburn. Dunking the smug little swizzle-stick had been very satisfying. Stupid. But satisfying.

Mahoney got his first look at the house when the cart zoomed through a pair of wrought iron gates that opened automatically via some hidden control. Probably remote operated by a guy in a camera room.

"Jay-sus," he said. "Château Stankovic looks like the Smithsonian fucked a French poodle."

Nobody laughed. *Tough crowd.*

Beyond the gates, the golf cart whispered over a marble-tiled driveway that opened out to a parking circle in front of the main doors. Mahoney leaned over to check again, and sure enough, the path was laid with marble, and the tiles were polished as bright and shiny as his ma's kitchen floor. Grass as neat and tight as Astroturf bordered the drive for a few feet on either side, then gave way to flower beds filled with exotic blooms, whose perfume infused the air. The occasional palm tree rattled its fronds in the steady ocean breeze. Beyond the vegetation, an eight-foot wall surrounded the property, and cleverly hidden fixtures bathed large swathes of the landscape with light. He couldn't see them in the dark, but based on Britte's description, high-definition cameras covered every approach. Without the lighting, the cameras could switch to infrared, but Mahoney thought it was a mistake to leave some sections in shadow. The contrast between lighted areas and dark patches would play hell with the cameras' processors as they tried to figure out which mode to use.

Or so he assumed. Hell, he was five years behind the technology curve, and a lot could change in that length of time. *I should ask Chan, next time I see him.*

He clocked four security guys in dark sports coats, fashionably armed with MP5s, patrolling the grounds. When Britte escaped, there had been four guards, total. Unless every guy was on patrol, and you didn't count Dawali and Grunt . . .

Shit. They added more people.

Grunt drove the cart counterclockwise around the circle and glided to a stop under the château's portico.

"We're hereeee!" Mahoney piped. "Everybody out of the cart and please form an orderly line at the ticket window. As you can see, the Château de Smuggler is vaguely French Provincial. More like a double-stacked box with two wings of gray Lego blocks embracing the circular drive. Skinny trees accent the windows of the evil lair, laid out in a fascist row along the front. The glass entry adds the air of a warm and inviting place to abandon all hope and skip to your death."

Grunt led them through the front doors and into a foyer bigger than Mahoney's apartment. *A low bar, but still* . . . An overly ornate chandelier sparkled overhead, casting prismatic beams onto the brilliant white marble floor.

"Must be tough getting the blood out of these tiles," Mahoney said.

Although Dawali had patted them down before getting in the boat, another security guy in an ill-fitting sport coat wanded them with a handheld metal detector, then did it again with an RF detector. The guard, who had the brow ridge of a Cro-Magnon, shook his misshapen head to confirm they were clean, then moved outside to stand on the porch.

"This way," Dawali commanded.

Mahoney forced back a smile when Dawali's damp shoes squeaked as he walked. The security chief led the way up three wide steps to an intersection with hallways branching off right and left. Directly ahead, through a pair of open doors, a grand Cinderella ballroom glittered with subdued lights and a hardwood floor. Dawali turned left at the top of the stairs.

Mahoney frowned. "We're not going to the ball?"

Britte kept pace with Mahoney, though she walked with the stiff-legged gait of a zombie, and presented a waxy, sweat-sheened face to the world. She was clearly terrified, though Mahoney had to give her credit—she was marching forward into what must have been her worst nightmare. Bravery wasn't the absence of fear, it was doing the job despite the fear, and for that alone, Britte Thorpe deserved all the likes.

He slipped his hand into hers and gave it a quick squeeze and was rewarded with the flicker of an uneven smile.

Dawali stopped at the first door on the left, knocked twice, and entered without waiting for a response. Mahoney and Britte followed, trailed by Grunt. They entered a wood-paneled office as generic as a lawyer's conference room. Mahoney dismissed the surroundings to focus on the man sitting with one butt cheek up on the desk.

Milos Stankovic cupped a crystal glass of what Mahoney suspected was sparkling water because of the bubbles and the dead lime floating in it. Stankovic regarded his visitors as if they were his slightly naughty kids who had done something wrong but funny, and he was trying to control his laughter before punishing them. He wore a silky gold shirt with an open collar. A platinum chain hung around his neck, and suspended from it was a rectangular charm, carved with intricate designs. European-style jeans and loafers with no socks completed the look. Mahoney hated a man who wore loafers without socks.

I bet his feet stink.

"You must be Milos," Mahoney said. "I've heard so little about you. Have you got that skin condition under control?"

"Britte," Milos said. "So good of you to come."

"Fuck you, Milos. Where's my sister?"

Stankovic scanned the soggy Dawali and his lip curled. "What happened to you?"

"I . . . fell in the water." Dawali stepped forward and handed Stankovic a tin can the size of a cigarette pack. "This is all he had on him."

Stankovic opened the tin and shook the contents. "Playing cards?" He dropped the cards into a palm and thumbed through them. "What were you planning to do with these, Mahoney? A game of solitaire?"

"Nah, I use 'em for physical therapy." Mahoney held up his hands. "My fingers were broken not too long back."

"Of course. You were tortured in Dubrava, yes?"

"Nice! I like how you showed me you have the juice to get my file while acting all solicitous." Mahoney tipped his head in appreciation for the point. "Score one for the criminal mastermind."

Stankovic's eyelids twitched. He replaced the cards in their case and tossed it back to Mahoney, then circled behind the desk and took a seat. He gestured to the guest chairs. "Please. Sit."

As Mahoney settled, he studied the man across the desk. Milos Stankovic was reportedly of Polish birth, but he could easily have passed as a Greek god. Shoulders wide enough to buttress an overpass filled out a shirt so fine and shiny, it was probably made with golden fleece sheared from the winged ram Chrysomallos, and hand-carried to the tailor by Jason himself. Dark chest hair teased the open collar of the shirt, which framed a chin carved from blue granite. Liquid brown eyes looked down upon the world from the slope of a sharp nose, and his white teeth gleamed from a wide, expressive mouth. His hair lay in loose black curls and looked silky soft.

"Britte was always my favorite. She could take a punch like Mike Tyson, and then apologize for it. I taught her everything she knows about sex."

Mahoney twisted his emotional dial from Hate to Hyperactive Loathing. He could feel Britte shivering like a drawn bowstring, held too long and too tight. "And who taught you? Your mom or your dad?" He picked up his card tin and dropped the cards into his hand, then placed the tin bottom up on the desk in front of him. He riffled through a couple of quick shuffles. "Okay then, now that the unpleasantries are dispensed with, let's get down to business."

"The business is simple." Stankovic spread his hands, palms up. "Return my money, fix my websites, and I will return Ella to you, unharmed. Failure to do so in"—he glanced at the multi-dial chronometer on his wrist—"three hours will result in the young lady experiencing a life much like her sister did toward the end of her stay here."

Mahoney checked his own watch, a Timex on a plastic band. "Okay then. First off, let's see her. Proof of life before we get to second base."

Stankovic nodded at Dawali, who departed without a word. Grunt remained behind, a stoic presence behind Mahoney's left shoulder. Mahoney craned around and checked Grunt's position. Grunt looked back. Mahoney turned to Stankovic, who remained quiet, a half-expectant look on his face.

"Here's a counterproposal," Mahoney said into the silence. "Assuming the girl's in good condition. Unharmed, as you say . . ." Mahoney raised an eyebrow and Stankovic rolled a hand for him to continue. "I propose a wager. The stakes are Britte and Ella, and all the money."

Britte spun to face him. He didn't have to look to see the outrage on her face.

Stankovic smirked. "And how do you propose we settle this wager?"

Mahoney grinned and spread his hands, spraying the cards in a whickering cascade from left to right and back again. "What say we cut the cards? One hand, winner take all."

35

"What say we cut the cards? One hand, winner take all."

"What the fuck is he doing?" McCurry muttered. "Did I hear that right?"

Zivon, crouched beside him at the base of the wall surrounding Stankovic's château, merely shrugged and said, "Is Mahoney," as if saying, *What did you expect?*

Jeang-wu, on a knee and watching the rear, said nothing.

The tiny transmitter Chan had built into the false bottom of Mahoney's card case had been activated when the cards were removed from the tin. It operated via cellular communication rather than RF, with a SIM card that picked up the best carrier signal for Stankovic's island, giving it significantly more range than a similarly sized radio frequency device.

"*No, thank you,*" said a man's voice, presumably Stankovic.

"*By the way, I'm super impressed with the security here,*" Mahoney said. "*I counted, like, what? Four guys on the grounds, plus Grunt here, and Dunkin' Dawali.*"

"We have taken . . . certain precautions. Knowing what we do about the company you keep."

"Ah, shit," McCurry whispered. "That tears it. We got no idea how many hostiles we're going up against."

Zivon grunted. "This matters how?"

"Yeah, okay," McCurry admitted after a minute's worth of scowling consideration. "But it sucks."

The big Russian rose from his crouch and shook out a rope with a padded grappling hook, which he lofted over the top of the twelve-foot wall. It landed with a muted clatter. Zivon hauled back on the rope until it went tight, then tested it with his weight. Satisfied the hook was well-seated, Zivon climbed the wall like a spider, easy as a walk in the park. He disappeared into the darkness above, then the rope went slack.

McCurry tapped Jeang-wu and pointed to the rope. The Korean nodded and scampered up with all the effort of a spider climbing a drain. McCurry cursed under his breath. He had deliberately held off until last so the other guys wouldn't see him trying to get up a piddly little twelve-foot wall. Back in the day, he could have scaled it with one arm in a sling and carrying ninety pounds of gear. But now . . . ? He had a torn rotator cuff in one shoulder, arthritis everywhere, bursitis, tendinitis, and old-itis. Shinnying up a rope with any kind of speed was out of the question. He just hoped to God he didn't embarrass himself and fall off.

The instant McCurry clamped his hands on and lifted one foot up, the pain in his shoulders shot up a little warning flare of the agony to come.

C'mon, now. Hand over hand, one foot in front of the other. Pain can be conquered. And up!

"Aw, Jesusfuckingwhorebitchbastard," he hissed. Eyes screwed shut, teeth clenched, and beads of sweat, or maybe blood, popping out on his forehead, McCurry pulled and . . . stepped. Pulled . . . and stepped. Pulled . . . and . . . stepped.

Had to pause to catch his breath. Knives of pure fire had pierced both shoulders and his arms trembled worse than they had the first week of BUD/S. A quick look told him he had gone less than halfway up the wall. *Ah, hell. I ain't gonna make it.*

And then the rope moved under his hands, scrolling upward. McCurry moved his feet to keep up and, in an instant, arrived at the top of the wall. Where Zivon waited, sitting astride the top. He reached out a hand and hauled McCurry up as easy as landing a fish, then finished gathering the rope.

Jeang-wu crouched nearby, a silent gargoyle with a submachine gun.

"No time to do the lollygagging," the Russian grumbled. "We hef timetable. And we are six minutes behind schedule."

"I would have," McCurry said between pants, "been up in a second."

"Da," Zivon said blandly. "I see this." He tossed the rope down to dangle on the inside of the wall. "Come on. Show is about to start. And Roxy will not wait."

Jeang-wu vanished in a black-clad scramble. Zivon paused with the rope in his hands and looked at McCurry.

"Do not be worry," the Russian intoned. "Down is much easier than up. Hold rope, let go. Is simple."

"Get out of my sight before I shoot you myself."

From the depth of the forest, someone shouted. An instant later, the staccato rattle of full-auto rifle fire shredded the night. Zivon slithered off the wall and disappeared into the forest below. More weapons opened up. McCurry estimated at least five hostiles closing in on their position.

"Shit, that tears it." McCurry keyed the mic at his throat. "Roxy, go! Blow the gates."

"It's too soon!"

"I don't care," McCurry snarled. "Blow the fucking gates."

He fast-roped off the wall, hitting the ground hard enough to buckle his already-sore knees. McCurry stifled a curse as a bullet chipped the wall next to his head.

Sorry, Mahoney, but you're on your own for now.

—

Mahoney riffled the cards again and calculated the odds. For the moment, he had only two opponents to account for, with one returning any moment. Now would be the optimal time to make a move, before Dawali returned and added a third tango to the force disparity equation. This was one of the scenarios he had gone over with Britte beforehand, so if he gave the code phrase, she *should* react as they planned. Although with an amateur you could never tell. A sidelong glance to his right revealed that Britte was chalk white and rigid as a statue. Would she even hear him if he triggered the plan? Or was she so frozen in fear and worry that she would be slow to react, leaving his back exposed while he had his hands full?

One thing was for sure: Dawali would be back in seconds and Mahoney needed control of the situation before he showed up.

"Okay then," Mahoney said. "How about five-card draw, jacks and deuces wild?"

"I don't think so—"

Mahoney snapped the first card off the deck and whipped it at Stankovic's face.

Made of heavy stock and resin-coated, the cards in Mahoney's deck were great for party tricks, and Mahoney could stick one in a wine cork at ten paces when he was on his game. Even so, it was impossible to do serious damage to the human body with a thrown playing card. Such a lightweight piece of paper could not be accelerated enough to make up for its negligible mass, so it couldn't hit a human body hard enough to inflict anything more than a paper cut.

However, humans have long been programmed at a survival level to protect their eyes. If a spinning disk zips through the air, straight for your eyes, you flinch. Every single time.

Stankovic bucked back in his chair, hand flying up. The card bounced off his cheek.

"Go, Britte!" Mahoney spun out of seat and shot two more cards at Grunt. The guard was made of sterner stuff than his boss. He barely flinched.

But barely was good enough. The flinch interrupted the smooth draw of the pistol in his waistband, costing Grunt precious moments before he could bring the gun into play.

The chair was too heavy to lift, so Mahoney kicked it into Grunt's waist. Grunt lurched back with an *Oof!* and Mahoney scrambled for clear space. He drove a side kick to Grunt's knee. Something cracked and the guard squawked, leg buckling.

Grunt's pistol appeared in his hand and Mahoney had to give the man credit for sticking with it. He pistoned the same heel, delivering shots to Grunt's thigh, midsection, and gun hand. Like climbing a ladder with one foot. The pistol spun away.

With a roar, Grunt launched into Mahoney's waist in a pro-level open-field tackle. Mahoney's feet left the ground and his back slammed into a bookshelf. Books and knickknacks tumbled over his shoulders. He doubled his fists and slammed his elbows into the back of Grunt's neck. The grip around his middle loosened slightly, so Mahoney did it again. Then once more for good measure.

Grunt staggered out of the clench and threw an uppercut to Mahoney's ribs. The punch was weak, fluttery, and

Grunt's eyes appeared to be wobbling. Mahoney stamped a heel onto the man's instep and pushed him back, giving himself room for a punt to the balls. Grunt's eyes crossed and he fell to his knees.

"Here," Mahoney gasped, "take in a good book." He slammed a thick, leather-bound volume down on the man's head. Grunt teetered and fell over.

—

Britte wasn't sure she would ever get used to the feeling of her heart slamming so hard in her chest that she felt like an over-pressured boiler about to explode. The first time she experienced it was when she escaped from Milos, with Siobhan in tow, piling into the boat driven by Victor Catano. From that point on, there had been a sequence of high-octane events, during which she had been sure she would die of a heart attack if her terror lasted one minute longer.

Mahoney and Milos were speaking. Background noise. She could barely focus over the hammering inside her skull. The words came as if from the end of a distant tunnel, echoing so much the meaning was lost.

Waiting for Mahoney's cue went far beyond that last minute before her heart should have exploded, and then some. At the signal, she would somehow have to occupy Milos long enough for Mahoney to take care of the guard.

How?

"Jump on him like a trampoline," had been Mahoney's suggestion. Billy McCurry had offered a more practical approach, showing her some moves that would incapacitate the man. Good in theory, but with the reality of having to come to grips with the man who once dominated her, controlled her, beat her, and had slashed her face with a broken bottle, all of those techniques had vanished from her memory.

"*Okay then*," Mahoney said. "*How about five-card draw, jacks and deuces wild?*"

"*I don't think—*"

Britte heard the words. Repeated them back in her head.

Jacks and deuces wild.

Wasn't that the—?

Mahoney flicked his wrist. A playing card flew from his fingers.

He whirled into action. "Go, Britte!"

Except she couldn't. She was frozen in place. The back of her tongue buzzed with a taste of copper. Muscles locked. Brain blank.

Milos recovered from his startlement at having a playing card strike him in the face. A very familiar expression of anger replaced his comic look of surprise. He pushed back from the desk, tight jawed, with nostrils flaring.

Britte's insides went hollow and loose. She had seen that darkening thunderstorm presaging the violence that lay beneath Milos Stankovic's skin once too often.

Get up, get up, get up!

Her legs refused to move. Her hands were locked on the arms of the chair. The next few minutes flashed forward as though she were clairvoyant and could see the car wreck coming without being to stop it. First would come the open-handed slap that would snap her head to the side and leave her cheek burning. Following that would come the body punches . . .

Mahoney struggled with the guard. He might or might not win that fight. If she failed to control Milos, keep his assistance away from his thug, Mahoney would definitely lose. And losing meant losing everything. Losing Ella.

No.

Milos was steps away. A second, maybe less, and he would be around the desk.

Britte launched herself upright and tottered into Milos on jellied legs. "No, Milos," she croaked through a dry throat. "Stop."

Milos picked her up and threw her sideways across the desk. Her back slammed into the blotter, sending pens and paperclips flying. Then he was on her, his hands wrapping around her throat.

"You filthy bitch!" His face contorted, lips drawn back in a snarl. His thumbs clamped into her windpipe, cutting off her air.

Desperately her hands scrabbled, scratching his forearms, flailing at his face.

Milos leered, spittle dripping from his lips. "Die, you whore!"

Her vision tunneled, lungs burning for air.

She bumped an object with scrabbling fingers, fumbled for it, then gripped it, recognizing it by touch. A crystal paperweight. The size of a baseball. Waterford, if she recalled correctly.

She swung, left-handed, putting all her waning strength into the blow.

Milos blinked in shock in the split-second before the paperweight connected with the side of his head. Too late, he swung his arms up to block, perhaps stunned that docile little Britte would ever do him any harm. The thud of solid contact shivered up Britte's arm and Milos twisted away, crying out and wrapping his arms around his head.

Britte dragged in air through her raw throat. She couldn't stop, though. Milos was stunned, not down. In the next second, he would be on her. Through the darkness surrounding her vision, Britte managed to see the top of his head.

Something inside her caught fire.

She let the flames take her.

Britte!

In their mission planning, Mahoney had covered this situation. *If it's Milos and one or two other guys, your job is to keep Milos from stabbing me in the back while I take out the heavies. I'll give you the code phrase about jacks and deuces wild if I think it's time to act.* Britte had nodded that she understood, but there was a lot of rough road between understanding and action. Mahoney had no way of knowing if she would charge into battle or freeze up and leave Stankovic to commit all kinds of mayhem. It was one of *many* weak points in their plan.

It turned out he'd worried for nothing.

Britte stood behind the desk, chest heaving, hair in a tangle. She clutched a blood-smeared crystal paperweight in one hand. Mahoney raced around the desk and found her standing over the recumbent body of Milos Stankovic. The porn king's finely chiseled face was a ruined mess of torn flesh and broken teeth.

"Is he dead?" Britte asked in a shaky voice.

Bloody snot bubbled from Stankovic's nose, and one hand slid up his chest with the slow, aimless motion of something run over on the highway.

"No," Mahoney said.

Britte tensed and cocked the paperweight up next to her ear. "Then let me—"

"No, no, no." Mahoney muscled into the enraged woman and held her back. "No time for this. Quick, help me move Grunt."

"Who?"

"Grunt, the guard."

"Move him?"

"So Dawali doesn't see him when he gets back with Ella. Help me straighten this shit up."

The windows rattled in their frames, and a dull boom shook the house.

Mahoney groaned. "Dammit, why doesn't anybody listen?" He picked up the card tin and yelled into the microphone. "Too soon, Roxy!" To Britte, he said, "Never mind. Dawali is sure to have heard that. We need to get to him before he decides to . . ."

Britte was already running for the door.

Mahoney scooped Grunt's pistol off the floor and ran to catch up.

Then stopped. He about-faced, stepped over to Grunt and fired point-blank into his forehead. Walked to Milos Stankovic. The man's eyes were blinking myopically from a mask of bloody flesh. He seemed to focus on Mahoney. Then focus on the bore of the pistol.

"This is for Asim," Mahoney said, and shot Stankovic through the bridge of the nose. "May God and Hannah forgive me."

Hannah and Roxy bellied down by the root ball of a nearly horizontal palm tree. Fronds brushed the ground, though the trunk seemingly refused to give in to gravity, and the tree clung to life by a toehold sunk into the sandy soil. They had dug into the sand next to the overhanging clump of shaggy roots, angled uphill, with their toes almost touching the beach, three hundred meters from the gates of Stankovic's compound. Gates that now sagged apart, one flat on the ground, the other clinging to the wall, leaning drunkenly outward and twisted by the force of the explosion.

"My husband used to watch a movie," Hannah said, too loudly. Her ears were still ringing. "About Butch Cassidy and the Sundance Kid. Used to drive me crazy, this movie, he watched it so many times. A hundred times he must have watched it. No matter, though, he always, always laughed at the scene where they blow up a train, and Robert Redford says to the other guy, 'Think you used enough dynamite there, Butch?'"

Roxy gave her a blank look. "What's your point, luv?"

Hannah rolled her eyes and returned her focus to the night sight mounted on the SA80 battle rifle. Smoke blurred the scene through the scope, greenish fog against a green-dappled background. "No movement," she reported.

Far into the night, and somewhere off to her left, the percussive beat of automatic weapons rapped in counterpoint to the high-pitched acapella whine in her ears. McCurry and the boys were deep in the shit over there, judging by the sound of things. The guard force had to assume the blast meant an assault on the front gates. If God was good, some of the guards would move to cover the open front, relieving the pressure on McCurry's team. If their luck held, the guards would dig in, preparing for an assault which Hannah had no intention of initiating. She was a fifty-year-old widow, and she had no desire to Rambo around the woods at night with a half-mad Brit for company. Getting Stankovic in her sights was one thing, but this scheme left her with few options to reach that endgame. For now.

"What are you doing?" Hannah whispered.

Roxy had occupied herself with setting out various push-button devices that looked much like garage door openers, arranging them in front of her in some sequence only she could decipher.

"McCurry and I left some prezzies behind after we wired the gates." Roxy's teeth glittered in the starlight. "For when company calls."

"Of course you did, Butch."

Movement in her scope drew her attention. A green soldier appeared by the gate, there and gone in an instant. Then another dashed through the opening and dived into the brush. The first one jumped back up and pelted through the gap, moving diagonally opposite the first. Both had passed through her sight picture so fast, Hannah was forced to hold her fire rather than give away her position for nothing.

"Fiddle-faddle," she breathed. "These guys are too aggressive for their own good."

Roxy bumped hips with Hannah as she squirmed. "Ooh," she groaned softly. "Please, please, please."

Hannah flashed her an alarmed look. She couldn't see Roxy's eyes behind the night optics, but by every bit of body language, breathing, and scent on the air, it was obvious that the crazy bitch was more than a little turned on.

If I live through this night, I swear I'm going to kill Mahoney for getting me into this.

Two more guards zig-zagged through the gate at a run. If they kept coming like this, then Mahoney's life appeared to be safe from her, at least. She was a good shot, and well-trained, but she had never been a commando, and the odds were tipping way out of her favor.

Hannah settled her cheek into the stock of the SA80. Her lips pinched into a thin line, and she scanned the undergrowth where the first man had gone to ground. This might well be her last dance, but she was at peace with that. Dying only meant she would be rejoined with Asim.

And that would not be a bad thing.

"Okay, Roxy," she murmured. "Time to show the boys how it's done."

36

Mahoney bailed out into the hall. Based on Britte's sketches, the door at the end of the hall to his left led to the master suite, which filled most of the entire east wing's lower floor. To his right, the corridor stretched the length of the house, terminating at a staircase to the second floor. There were five staterooms on the second floor, and two storage rooms. One of the storage rooms had an external lock, which had puzzled Britte when she first came to the mansion, though she had dismissed the mystery soon enough. In hindsight, the purpose of a locked room seemed obvious.

Another staircase, wider and grander, peeled off from the foyer near the middle of the house. When he exited the study, Mahoney was standing practically at the foot of the grand staircase, its carpeted treads rising to the left.

Britte had vanished, though her footsteps thundered above, followed closely by shouts of anger.

Mahoney grabbed the newel post and slung himself up the stairs.

McCurry touched his cheek and his fingers came away sticky with blood. Either a bullet or a splinter had grazed him at one point during the fight, though he couldn't remember it happening. He was breathing hard but moving well. Adrenaline provided lubricant for his rusty joints, and endorphins blocked the pain. Or maybe it was the other way around. Hell, he was never any good at that science shit.

The firefight on the eastern side of the property had been short, sharp, and intense. Neither side appeared to have done any lasting damage, despite the high concentration of lead in the air. Within minutes, the opposing force had collapsed back toward the house in an orderly withdrawal, seemingly conceding the ground with only token resistance.

"Zivon," McCurry whispered into his throat mic. "How many you think?"

The Russian came back after a considered pause. "*Ten. Fifteen. Maybe more.*"

"Shit."

"Da."

"Let's get closer. Jeang-wu, wide right. Zee, up the middle. I got wide left."

Double clicks of breaking squelch acknowledged his transmission.

Lights from the château glowed through the trees, guiding McCurry toward the objective. Tropical vegetation tickled his nose with strange pollen, forcing him to pinch his nostrils shut to keep from sneezing. The island was a little over a mile in width, and two miles in length, so the sea breeze carried the tang of salt. Perfume from night-blooming flowers rode with it, as did the faint whiff of burned gunpowder. He belly-crawled up to the tree line for his first look at the target house and discovered his route had taken him to the rear of the property.

Every window in the house glowed, casting yellow across the one hundred yards of open ground. Manicured like a golf course, the grass sloped up in a gentle swell to an edged flowerbed. The bed seemed to circle the house, except at the rear, where a low, decorative wall enclosed the patio. Security lights directed high-intensity beams over the grounds in long, oval washes of white light.

According to Britte's sketch, a pool big enough to hold a nuclear submarine covered most of the patio, overlooked by a second-floor balcony and surrounded by outdoor furniture. McCurry checked off the features and found the intel had been accurate for once.

The security lighting flooded the open ground, as bright as a ball field.

"*McCurry,*" Zivon's voice crackled in his ear. "*Note the firing positions. Up against the landscaping.*"

The what?!

McCurry shaded his eyes from the glare and focused on the flower beds. Now that he was looking for them, the emplacements became obvious. Someone had gotten real busy and prepared the château for an invasion. Spaced at regular intervals all along the perimeter, sandbag-reinforced positions had been dug into the grounds. Two positions he could see, and by extrapolation that meant another six he couldn't. The dark metal tubes of heavy machine guns protruded through a gap in each sandbagged wall. And every barrel panned in short arcs, seeking targets. Meaning every position held at least one soldier and probably more.

There were not four or five guards on the property.

"There's a whole goddamned army," McCurry muttered in awe.

The château's ballroom was a vast space, which could be configured to accommodate anything from raves to state dinners, hedonistic bacchanals or Victorian waltzes. A glass ceiling arched high overhead, and crystal chandeliers glittered with hundreds of diamond droplets when lit. Brazilian walnut covered a floor as wide as a gymnasium. White-paneled walls enclosed three sides, leaving the back wall an expanse of windows overlooking the patio.

At the moment, the room was empty but for a single, straight-backed chair.

London Bridges waited patiently, well back and to one side of the room, out of direct line of sight from the windows. He held a tablet device used to control the lighting throughout the house. For the moment, he left the lights on, though the time was coming when he would shut them off. His radio earpiece crackled with crosstalk from the sergeants overseeing the deployment of their men. They were competent soldiers, so Bridges left them to their job. The explosion at the gate had come as a bit of a surprise, but the floating squad had reacted quickly and reported no assault force approaching. Bridges suspected the explosion was a distraction, meant to confuse—and to diffuse—the defender's attention.

He had read the file provided by Mr. Milos's tame senator. The Cottonmouth people could field nothing more than a half dozen warriors, if that, and many of those were well past their prime.

But . . . somehow, they had beaten him during the attack at the town. He had dreamed of a second match, and wanted it, very badly. The one he wanted more than the others was named McCurry. A goat-fucking SEAL. Bridges wanted to spit. The Americans glamorized these SEALs—TV programs, movies, books . . . it was a fetish with them.

He'd had McCurry under his foot, muzzle to forehead, only to be forced away at the last second.

When Bridges had learned the motel guy Mahoney and the woman, Thorpe, were coming to negotiate, he had been disappointed. A negotiated settlement would leave him without the revenge he sought. The loss of his team galled him, and he wanted to rain death and fire upon the people who had done it. So, he had hoped negotiations would fail and guns would answer. And Allah be praised, so it had happened.

Now McCurry was coming. He could feel it. Somewhere, out in the darkness, one of America's best approached, an old wolf about to learn the meaning of fear and taste defeat again. London Bridges was better than any SEAL. He had proved it once, and he would do so again. All he had to do was wait.

Bridges had carefully left him a path forward. If McCurry recognized the opportunity and seized upon it, if he took the bait, it would lead him right to where Bridges waited.

This time there would be no last-second reprieve.

This time, the SEAL would die.

Hannah lost count of the number of guards who had ducked through the ruined gate. More than ten but less than a battalion was her best guess. The guards hopscotched across the broken ground, one group setting up a firing position to support the next group as they probed outward. A calm, professional, and military-proficient operation.

"It's like a clown car, init?" Roxy confided in a low voice, full of awe. "They just keep coming out."

"Except we're the clowns," Hannah murmured back. She stayed glued to her night sights, targeting a cluster of trees at one hundred meters. She considered this her virtual line in the sand. The first skirmisher across that line would get a bellyful of

5.56mm, and from there she would service as many targets as she could before return fire drove her down. After that . . . well, it was in God's hands.

There weren't supposed to be this many guards. Britte said Stankovic kept no more than six on the island. Given the recent escalation in tension, Hannah had expected they might double up, and maybe go as high as twelve. But *this*? Hannah had completely underestimated the enemy's response to a potential assault by a few old soldiers and ex-spies. She found it ironic that a lack of intel had left her ass swinging in the breeze, seeing as how she was in the intel business. Professionally speaking, it was pretty embarrassing.

This was all Mahoney's fault, of that she was sure.

A flicker of movement in her scope caught her attention. They were getting close now. Maybe seconds away.

"I think it's time," Hannah said, "to say hello."

At the word *time*, Roxy pressed a button on one of her remotes. Before "hello" left Hannah's lips, the sky lit up with a volcano of light and the ground between the gate and the tree line erupted in a cloud of dense, dirty smoke. Grit and vegetation fountained into the air, along with bits of enemy soldiers, and rained down through the trees in a storm of pattering droplets. The explosion thumped through the earth and jolted Hannah, and the flash whited out her scope.

Hannah cursed and squinted her eyes shut. "Fucking warn me next time!"

"Sorry!" Roxy cried, sounding not very sorry at all.

Screams of the wounded echoed through the trees, and confused shouts filled the air. Someone let off a burst of automatic weapon fire that came nowhere close to Hannah and Roxy's position. Hannah kept her finger off the trigger and blinked hard to wipe away the purple spots dancing in her vision. Just as her sight was coming back, Roxy triggered another device. A second pressure wave blew through the palm trees. Bits of debris plunked down around them, and something made a squishy splat sound when it hit.

"Fire in the hole!" Roxy shouted.

"A bit late, don't you think?"

"I mean for this one!"

For the third time, fire and thunder ripped the undergrowth, and this time Hannah distinctly saw the figure of a man tumbling through the air, backlit by the explosion. More screams threaded through the foliage.

"Here they come," Hannah said as figures coalesced through her night scope. "Any more prezzies I should know about?"

"No," Roxy said, sounding infinitely saddened. "That's the lot."

"Oh, goodie." Hannah sighted and fired. The man in her crosshairs dropped. Immediately, return fire chewed into the palm tree's root ball, showering her with dirt. "Best get to shooting, then!"

"I can't!" Roxy yelled over the din. "I don't have a gun! I hate guns, y'know?"

Hannah spared her a shocked look, then returned to firing back at the stirred-up nest of hornets coming their way. Based on the rate of fire, eight or ten soldiers remained alive and were committed to throwing everything they had at Hannah and Roxy. Rounds chewed up sand and blew grit into her eyes, and more whapped into their sheltering palm tree or whip-cracked overhead.

Eight or eight hundred, the final tally didn't matter. It was more than Hannah could take on her own. All they had to do was keep her pinned down with suppressive fire while flankers approached from the sides. They could drop a grenade on her or blast her position with small arms fire and she would never be able to prevent it.

"Of all the people to get stuck with," Hannah fumed. "I get the pyro who hates guns."

Running away seemed like a good option, except the boat they came in on was a kilometer to the east, tucked up under a screen of palm fronds, and a rocky protrusion across the beach cut them off from it. Hannah had no objection to getting wet and would happily swim around the finger of rocks . . . and had she thought of it ten minutes go, it might have worked. At this point, however, if they tried to disengage, they would be shot in the back before they made it to the water.

More bullets zipped in, forcing Hannah to turtle into the sand. Roxy squirmed beside her, arms crossed over her head. The enemy had them zeroed now, one bunch pinning them down while another leap-frogged ahead. Fire and maneuver. Maneuver and fire. Classic infantry tactics.

"Shite!" Roxy flinched and grabbed her forearm. Blood welled out in a thin line.

Hannah poked the SA80 up and fired blindly, in the worst kind of spray-and-pray possible. Hot brass pattered around her ears. The bolt clunked open as the last round blew from the barrel. Hannah scrambled to change magazines while her lower body wormed deeper into the sand. Incoming fire battered their position like sleet driven in a storm. Hannah gritted her teeth and popped the rifle's bolt loose to chamber a round. Calm descended and her muscles unclenched. Background noise faded. Time dilated to the extent she fancied seeing individual copper-jacketed pellets streaking past.

In a minute, maybe two, it would all be over.

Hannah smiled with crooked lips.

Okay, Asim, honey. See you soon.

37

Between the house and the forest, the regular manicured grounds stretched flat as a golfing green. With one exception. At the very rear, from the patio to the tree line, a rose garden broke up the terrain like a Victorian maze. It was a no-man's-land of black vines and dappled shadows.

"I see a gap in the coverage back here," McCurry said into his mic. "A blind spot for the gun emplacements that I can use to infiltrate the main house."

"*Is trap*," came Zivon's laconic reply.

"I know it's a trap!" McCurry hissed. "Get your big Commie ass back here and provide me some cover while I spring it. Break-break. Jeang-wu, keep everybody's attention focused out front. Cause a ruckus. But don't get shot."

Click-click.

"And stop jamming the freq with so much chatter," McCurry said to himself as he eyeballed his approach.

Presently, the counterpoint beat of heavy machine guns versus a lighter battle rifle opened up from the front of the house. In back, however . . .

No movement or sound, and more importantly, no machine gun fire, came from the sandbagged emplacements that overlooked the rear garden. A suspiciously dark and well-concealed alley through landscaping led to a marble-tiled outdoor sitting area and a paradise-sized pool. From there, exterior furniture, balcony support columns, and potted ferns would provide excellent cover as he made his way to the château's back doors, which glowed with an inviting golden light. With a little bit of stealth, and a heaping of luck, McCurry could infil the château in under ten minutes.

No time like the present. Except he hesitated. Gift horses often came with a bellyful of Greeks, or in this case a landmine all set to blow body parts off the handsome and heroic Billy McCurry. Nobody with half a brain left open the back door unless they had a nasty surprise planned for the luckless bastard who skipped down the yellow brick road without a care in the world.

But what choice did he have? The plan called for getting Mahoney and the civilians out of the château. And now, penetrating the house to outflank the machine gun nests was imperative to that objective. McCurry didn't see a better way in.

"*On station.*" Zivon's voice crackling in his ear made him jump. "*At your five o'clock, fifty meters back.*"

"Roger that," McCurry radioed back. "On my way. Don't shoot my ass."

"Hard to miss but will try."

"Everybody wants to be a comedian," McCurry said to himself without keying the mic. "Mahoney, I blame you for this."

Mahoney vaulted up the stairs three at a time and arrived at the second-floor landing. An open door to his right revealed a bedroom. To his left, a long hall ran the length of the château's upper floor. Mahoney turned that way in time to see Dawali dragging a blond girl, presumably Ella, into a room at the far end of the hall. The girl kicked her feet and fought the arm around her neck without much apparent effect. Britte Thorpe appeared at the far landing and rushed after her sister.

Expecting to hear a gunshot, Mahoney pounded down the corridor. He slowed at the last second and laid his back against the wall next to the open door. Voices were raised in shouts and at first Mahoney couldn't decipher who was saying what—it was a jumble of shouted commands, demands, and counter-demands.

Mahoney spun around the doorframe, following his weapon's sights.

Britte faced away from him, confronting Dawali, who had a gun pointed at her. The girl, Ella, a younger carbon copy of her sister, clutched at the security chief's other arm, which was still wrapped around her neck. Her face was bright red and shiny from fear or exertion, or both. They were in an enormous bedroom, and Dawali was backed up against a king-sized bed that featured a Laura Ashley duvet and fluffy throw pillows.

Dawali focused over Britte's shoulder when Mahoney swung inside. Dawali's gun swiveled, and he fired. The bang of the shot clapped Mahoney's ears and splinters of door molding peppered his cheek. Britte flinched and then dived away.

Mahoney flung himself back out of the room and rolled to the side. More rounds popped through the drywall.

"Wait!" Mahoney yelled. "Wait, Dawali! Don't shoot! I have a deal for you!"

Miraculously, Dawali held his fire. "What is this deal?"

"Hey, man, listen okay?" Mahoney gathered himself to a knee. "Your boss is dead, okay? You're the head of the organization now. All of Stankovic's money is yours. I have twelve million dollars in an account, ready to transfer to your name. All we want is the girl and safe passage out of here, and it's all yours, man."

No reply came right away, which Mahoney considered a good sign. He stood and eased up against the far wall, holding the pistol in a two-handed grip. If the security man said *no deal*, he would have to go in shooting, which wasn't his strong suit. One stray round . . . well, he really, really hoped it would not come down to his skill with a pistol.

Where the fuck is Zivon when you need him?

"Whadaya say, man?" Mahoney edged his back along the wall, expanding the slice of room he could see from the hallway. "This ain't your fight, Dawali. All we wanted was for Stankovic to back off. We could call it a day right now, go have a beer, and reach a mutually agreeable solution. Act like adults, in other words."

Of course, the mutually agreeable solution would leave Dawali dead, as Mahoney no longer had Stankovic's millions. As soon as Dawali realized he was bluffing, it would come to guns anyway, but Mahoney hoped to at least have the Knudsen sisters out of danger before that happened.

"Okay if I come in?" Mahoney said. "So we don't have to talk through a wall?" *And so I can at least aim before I try and shoot you?*

"Come ahead," Dawali called out. "Throw your gun through first though."

"Ahh, no. No can do. Then you shoot all of us, and it's game over for Team Mahoney."

"If I shoot you, I don't get the money."

Mahoney stifled the urge to groan. Fucker was too smart for his own good. "Okay, I'll tell you what: I'll tuck my piece away and show you my hands."

"I'll kill this girl!" Dawali shouted. He sounded like he

might be edging toward unhinged. "Then this woman, here."

"If you hurt the women," Mahoney said, "you definitely get nothing. Look, I'm coming in, okay. Hands are bare, see?" He tucked the pistol in his waistband and showed his hands at the door. "Look. I'm unarmed, okay?"

Mahoney dragged in a deep breath and reentered the bedroom, finding the scene much as before, except now Britte crouched like a tiger, her legs coiled under her, and fingernails clawed into the carpet. Dawali's gun muzzle was firmly pressed into Ella's scalp. Mahoney met the girl's eyes and saw a spark of her sister's grit in the clenched jaw and steely look in her eyes.

In contrast, Dawali appeared almost feverishly angry. He had the look of a man trying to deal with customer service at the cable company, which was to say, ready to chew steel and spit staples. Mahoney had time to wonder what had made the man this angry. Was it loyalty to Stankovic? Or was there a deeper motivation of which Mahoney was unaware? Either way, Mahoney decided he needed to reassess his assumptions and proceed with great caution, as Onye Dawali looked like a man on the brink of pushing the big red button and letting the fallout cover the earth in ash.

"Okay, then," Mahoney said. "We're all cool now. Let's make a deal."

Then the lights went out.

McCurry reached the château's back entrance without being blown up.

Instead of easing his suspicions, this only served to make him more skeptical of what awaited on the other side of the

French doors. Leaving an unguarded gap in your rear was like leaving your quarterback unprotected on his blindside. It just wasn't done. Unless, of course, you wanted a large, angry man to fuck up your day. McCurry examined the prospect of crossing the last six feet of stone tile and entering the building itself. Which is when the lights went out.

"Oh, just peachy," he growled.

Detail and depth were lost using his NODs, so McCurry left them up. Before the lights had gone out, McCurry had noted an open space on the far side, which corresponded to Britte Thorpe's drawing of a ballroom in the center-rear of the château.

"*One down*," crackled Zivon's voice in his ear.

The roar of a heavy machine gun blasted out and McCurry hit the deck. Nothing impacted near him, and McCurry realized a second later that the gunfire was headed outbound from the position to his right-rear quadrant.

"Repositioning."

Zivon must have dropped a soldier manning a machine gun nest with a long-range shot, then gotten kicked in the face by return fire, forcing him to relocate positions.

"Serves you right," McCurry grumped to himself. "Scaring the shit outta me like that."

Using the rattle of the machine gun as cover for noise, McCurry slithered across the tile and reached up to test the door.

Unlocked.

"Hmph," he muttered. "Ready or not, here I come." Into his mic he added, "Making entry."

McCurry slid inside the darkened ballroom, opening the door just enough to slip through and closing it behind him. He flipped down his NODs and scanned the interior. The space had the echoey feeling of an empty gymnasium. No furniture to speak of. Just some high-back chairs lined up against the side walls. McCurry put his back against the closed door and sidled to his right, laterally along the rear-facing windows. The NODs over his eyes rendered the interior in high-contrast greens and blacks.

There came a thunk, and light bloomed around him. McCurry's goggles whited out and shafts of pure blue pain seared his eyes. He flinched for a crucial half second and what felt like God's angry backhand slammed him in the chest plate. McCurry bounced off the window and fell in a heap.

His wind was gone. His lungs refused to function. McCurry rolled onto his back. He had the presence of mind to whip the NODs free and try to blink his vision back from the purple world behind his eyes.

"*Stay down*," Zivon said in his ear.

Stay down? Who the fuck is he kidding? I couldn't get up if I wanted.

Glass cracked over his head and splinters flaked his cheeks.

"Missed. Target retreated to the hall. Repositioning."

The heavy MG rumbled again, hammering the night. A second position opened up a can of fury. McCurry felt as much as heard the gunfire. And he felt the burning lance of a round through the chest. The vest failed to stop the bullet, meaning it was either armor-piercing or from a high-powered rifle round fired at close range. It felt like an elephant had stepped on his sternum. McCurry's vision came back about the same time as his lungs remembered how to inflate. Breathing hurt. He stayed on his butt for a ten count, fighting the blackness seeping into his vision. He drew shallow sips of air, ignoring the flaring pain from his ribcage.

"Who was it?" he wheezed into the radio. "Who shot me? How many?"

"*One only. Big man*," said Zivon. The sound came back

choppy, as if the sniper were on the move. "*Big, big, man.*"

"Oh. Him. Of course." He winced and felt warm wetness squish inside his vest. "Come on," he told himself. "How do you earn your pay? Sittin' on your ass? I don't think so."

McCurry trembled off the floor, motored into a stumbling stagger, and headed for the doors on the far side of the room.

38

Zivon's first indication of skirmishers in the forest, enfolding his position, came when he ran full tilt into an enemy soldier. They collided with a burst of grunts and the clatter of tac vests banging together. Zivon reacted first. He chopped the butt of his Dragunov SVD rifle into the man's face. It was a solid strike to the cheek, and something cracked. The man stumbled back, producing a gargling sound from his broken face. Zivon twisted at the waist, stuck the rifle's muzzle into the man's throat, and pulled the trigger. Flame stabbed through the soldier's neck and spiked a full ten centimeters beyond, lighting up a spray of gore. The smell of burned meat and gunpowder blew back with the wet droplets of blood that splattered Zivon's face.

Shouts followed the echo of the Dragunov's report, and Zivon was forced to dodge incoming fire from several directions. He ducked and weaved between the trees, knee-high sawgrass scraping at his pants. Probing machine gun fire had driven him farther and farther away from the château, and steadily degraded his ability to support McCurry's incursion. Now, he found himself being chased against the compound wall by a team of enemy soldiers.

Rounds clipped the grass by his knees, or crack-whined past his ears. They had to be using either thermal or light-enhancing technology, as the incoming fire was remarkably accurate. Zivon considered himself very lucky not to have taken at least one—

A hammerblow slugged him in the shoulder blade and Zivon crashed to the ground in a tumbling heap. Even in his shock, he cradled the Dragunov to avoid damaging the optics or digging the muzzle into the dirt, though he was only partially successful as both he and the rifle took a severe battering. He rolled until his back slammed into the base of a palm tree. Zivon gasped for breath as a sheet of pure agony bloomed through his right shoulder and flushed a wave of numbness all the way to his fingertips.

He had no time to gather himself. A hornet-like sting bit his ear as a round slapped into the bark next to his head. Dirt fountained up as more rounds plowed into the ground by his feet. Zivon squirreled around the base of the tree trunk, putting it between him and the oncoming fire team. He fumbled the Dragunov into position, praying it would operate safely when he pulled the trigger—*if* he could pull the trigger. He flexed his right hand and willed feeling back into it.

Zivon snugged his eye against the Hensoldt sight with its attached IVR-900 thermal optic device. The ghost-white image of a man instantly appeared, ducking and weaving through the foliage. The range was under fifty meters, so there was no need to offset for wind, though he held low to compensate for the ballistic arc of the 9.3 x 64mm Brenneke cartridge. Zivon centered the crosshairs and fired.

The enemy soldier seemed to vault backward, feet flying over his head.

Zivon wasted no time on the fallen man. He panned right, then left. A flash of white flickered in his scope, but by the time he shifted aim, the image disappeared, the soldier having dropped into the sawgrass below his line of sight. Zivon wicked sweat from his face with a shirt sleeve and took a second to key his mic.

"Zee to McCurry. Fully engaged with enemy force. Sixteen minutes into mission. You're on your own. Break. Jeang-wu, could use support at the rear."

The radio crackled to life, magnifying the staccato bursts of full auto hammering in the distance. "*Busy,*" came the terse reply.

"*Sounds like you're on your own, too,*" McCurry radioed. He wheezed heavily when he spoke. "*This has turned into one big shitshow. I blame Mahoney.*"

"Copy that," Zivon replied with a sigh.

The palm tree he sheltered behind shivered with impacting rounds. The enemy team was using good discipline, approaching with a classic bounding overwatch technique, denying Zivon time to set up and aim without the pressure of incoming fire. He had minutes before he would be flanked and overrun. His vest had taken the hit to his back, which mitigated the damage somewhat, but something back there grated and flamed his nerves with raw pain whenever he moved. With this injury, retreating to the wall and attempting to climb over it was out of the question. Fighting was the only option, though dying seemed the only likely outcome.

The long gun would be a hindrance at close range, so Zivon slipped this pistol from his thigh holster.

"McCurry?" he radioed.

Click-click. McCurry broke squelch twice rather than reply out loud.

"You see Mahoney, tell him I'll see him in hell."

A pause, then . . .

Click-click.

The lights went out and the stalemate in the bedroom threatened to go nuclear in a heartbeat.

Ella screamed.

Britte yelled something unintelligible.

Dawali bellowed, "I'll kill her! I'll kill her!"

"Calm down!" Mahoney added to the cacophony. "Everybody stay calm!"

"Stop moving!" Dawali shouted.

"Ella!" Britte countered.

Mahoney slid to his right, gun back in his hands, tracking the action by sound. Scuffling from the direction he'd last seen Dawali. Harsh words spat in a foreign language.

"Britte," Mahoney yelled desperately. "Stay put! Dawali, it's cool, man. Stay cool."

Muzzle flash followed by the percussive report of a gunshot. A bullet burned past Mahoney's ear, close enough he could taste the copper jacket. The afterimage bloomed in his retinas and faded slowly.

"Stop shooting, Dawali! You kill us, you get nothing!"

"Stop moving!" the security chief screamed back. "I'll kill this bitch, I swear. Arrr! Bitch! You fucking bit me?!"

Another shot cracked out. Britte shrieked, "NO!"

The thud of a meaty collision sounded as bodies slammed together.

Mahoney cursed and dropped his pistol. He plunged toward the silhouette of tangling figures, vaguely backlit by the thin light filtering through the windows. Dawali's gun thumped, the sound muted by point-blank impact with a human body. A feminine grunt of pain registered on Mahoney's senses in the split-second before he crashed into the scrum. With sick dread, he fought to separate one set of thrashing limbs from the other. His groping hands found a woman's torso, and he shoved and twisted her—he guessed it was Ella—to the side and discovered Dawali by virtue of the weapon that went off next to his cheek. A blistering strip of hot metal burned his ear, and the concussive blast rocked his brain as if he'd taken a line drive to the head. Mahoney powered through the disorientation, fighting with an instinct powered by pure, gut-wrenching terror.

He struggled with Dawali, grasping his gun hand by a miracle of divine intervention, and bulldozed the smaller man backward. They tumbled onto the bed in a tangle of sweating, cursing, twisting, thrashing muscle, bone, and atavistic animal intensity. Mahoney's head rang with an orchestral crescendo of crashing cymbals and the clamoring of all the bells from all the churches in the world. Dawali hit him. He understood this, accepted it, and ignored the pain. It meant nothing. Either Ella or Britte had taken a bullet. He knew that in his marrow. Nothing else mattered.

Mahoney gripped Dawali's throat with his right hand and shoved his thumb into the ridged larynx. Dawali thrashed under him and pounded his fist into Mahoney's face, over and over. Mahoney squirmed up Dawali's bucking torso, riding him like a rodeo horse. He twisted sideways and pinned the man's right wrist with his knee, freeing his other hand to clamp Dawali's throat. Dawali scrabbled and scratched with his flailing left hand, at least until Mahoney pinned it down with his other knee.

It was over then. All but the dying.

Ugly, squawking noises blurted from Dawali's mouth. He twitched and shivered. The stench of voided bowels saturated the air. With a final shudder, he went still. Mahoney held on for another ten count, then forced his aching hands to relax.

"Britte," he croaked. "Britte? You okay?"

"Help me," cried another voice.

Ella.

Mahoney shook his head like a wounded bull. He had trouble focusing, and squeezed his eyes shut to try and silence the clamor inside his head.

"Help me," Ella cried again. "I think she's dead! There's so much blood!"

"You see Mahoney, tell him I'll see him in hell."

McCurry double clicked a response, holding back the comment that judging by the blood soaking his waistband, he would likely be in hell before either Zivon or that asshole Mahoney. Plus, he didn't have the breath to reply.

He staggered out of the ballroom and swept his weapon in a shaky arc across an open reception area. Entry doors lay directly ahead. A grand staircase rose immediately to his right, leading upward, and halls branched off, left and right. McCurry recalled from Britte's drawing that one way led to a master suite, and the other to a dining room, kitchen, and whatnot.

The high-pitched tenor of an upset woman's voice echoed from upstairs.

McCurry looked at the stairs and groaned. A wave of blackness swept over his consciousness, and he fought back the urge to stop and rest for a moment. Sitting down would lead to passing out and passing out would lead to death. The ache in his chest had subsided to a steady, unrelenting pressure, as if a giant had him in a bear hug and wouldn't let go. He wanted to cough, but the mere thought of the racking pain that would cause forced him to control the impulse.

His BUD/S instructors had liked to torment him with pithy phrases like "Pain is weakness leaving the body." Well, McCurry had a new one for them: *Pain is blood leaving the body*. And a lot of it was leaving his body at that moment. He found himself on his hands and knees. Bright red droplets fell from his lips and splatted on the glistening marble floor.

Upstairs, a woman screamed.

"Have to get up there," McCurry said to himself.

The staircase might as well have been Mount Everest, but it wasn't like he had much choice. He didn't have the strength to stand, so instead he stayed on the floor and crawled.

"How do you earn your pay," McCurry mumbled. "One step at a time . . . Oh, sweet Jesus this hurts . . ."

He collapsed and—

Mahoney dug for Dawali's cell phone and fumbled through activating the flashlight feature. Following its narrow cone of brightness, Mahoney found Ella crouched over Britte's prone body. The younger girl's hair hung in a shroud around her face as she pressed both hands into the center of a blotchy red stain on her sister's midsection. Britte writhed and her legs made crawling motions as if trying to plow trenches with her heels.

"Ah, hell no," Mahoney groaned. He retrieved a pillow from the bed and stripped off the pillowcase. Rushing to Britte's side, he knelt across from her sister. "Hold the light. Let me see."

Ella's saucer-eyes blinked at him from inches away. Mahoney's gut flip-flopped when he saw Britte's face reflected from a younger set of features.

"Who're you?" the girl asked.

"A friend of your sister's." Mahoney plucked at the buttons on Britte's blouse, then gave up and ripped it open. Blood welled from a blue-tinged hole a few inches above her belly button. Britte uttered a guttural growl, and she clamped a hand on Mahoney's bicep, squeezing it with shocking strength. Mahoney glanced up and caught her eye for a quick second. Pain blanched her features. "What is it with you and getting shot?" he quipped in a light tone. "You some kind of bullet magnet, or what?"

"We . . . have to quit . . . meeting like this," she panted out through gritted teeth.

The lights flickered back on, and Mahoney almost wished they hadn't. Blood squeezed out from the hole in Britte's belly with every shaky breath. Mahoney folded the pillowcase into a square pad and laid it over the hole. To Ella, he said, "Hold this firmly in place. I need to check for an exit wound."

He reached under Britte's back and slid his hand over her smooth skin.

"Getting . . . a . . . cheap feel . . . Mahoney?" Britte twitched a crooked smile.

"Not how I pictured this moment."

Ella bit her lip and a tear trailed down her cheek. "Is she going to be all right?"

Mahoney bit back a heated *how the fuck should I know* and tried for calm confidence instead. It was hard to hear himself think with the noise in his head. "Sure. We'll get her to a hospital in a few minutes. Just as soon as my friends get here to extract us."

"Your friends aren't coming," rumbled a deep voice from the doorway. "They are all dead, or soon will be."

Mahoney froze like a mouse before an owl when he looked up. The absolute largest man he had ever seen loomed over them, the tactical M-14 in his mitts so small in comparison, it appeared to have been made by Mattel.

"London . . ." Britte husked out in a wet voice. "No . . ."

"This is London Bridges?" Mahoney said. "I always pictured it smaller."

39

Bridges propped his rifle next to the door and said, "Now you're going to tell me where the diamonds are."

Before Mahoney could pop off a witty rejoinder, the behemoth slid a mile-long blade of shining steel from a sheathe at his hip. The thing was the size of Excalibur and yet looked no bigger than a steak knife in Bridges's paw.

"Jay-sus, what botched lab experiment created you?" Mahoney spotted his pistol laying on the carpet by the big man's feet. The giant noted the direction of his enemy's gaze and kicked the piece to one side. It scooted under a bureau and disappeared. Mahoney had a vague recollection of Dawali's pistol falling off the side of the bed, which meant it might as well be on Pluto for all the good it would do him. He didn't need a pistol, anyway, with this guy. He needed a shoulder-launched cruise missile.

Mahoney levered himself upright and mocked the giant's accent when he said, "And if I doan wan' to tell you where is de diamonds?"

"First, I cut the old bitch's throat," Bridges snarled. "Then I start on the young one's fingers."

"Why is it always the women with you evil henchmen assholes, huh?" Mahoney crabbed sideways as he spoke, trying to edge out away from Ella and Britte to give himself room to fight.

Room to fight. Now, there was a laugh. The bedroom spread over more square footage than one of Mahoney's hotel rooms, all in, but that didn't make it big enough for a fight with a Titan. Mahoney practiced a blend of martial arts combining jujitsu, judo, Krav Maga, and junkyard ass-whooping, all of which required room to operate against a much bigger opponent.

"Why don't you pick on somebody your own size? Like the Empire State Building?"

Bridges snarled and moved, his open hand reaching for Ella. With his long arms, it wasn't much of a reach. Mahoney skipped forward one hop and snapped out a side heel kick at Bridges's kneecap. The giant saw it coming and lifted his leg, catching most of the force of Mahoney's kick on his calf. Bridges swiped down with the knife and Mahoney danced away.

Danced all of two steps away. There wasn't room for much else.

Mahoney bounced back in tight as the knife swept past and hammered a fist into Bridges' solar plexus. It was a textbook strike, delivered with a twist of the hips for power and aimed to drive his knuckles all the way through the big man's torso and snap Bridges's spine. Reality diverged from textbook when Mahoney felt the shock of striking a leather-coated rock vibrate up his arm. Bridges grunted a tiny bit, then grinned. The knife whipped up and froze, a molecule short of Mahoney's left eyeball.

"Are we through playing around?" Bridges said from behind his mouthful of yellow teeth.

"Drop the knife!" yelled a squeaky tenor.

All the attention in the room shifted to Ella, who stood

beside the bed, Dawali's pistol shaking at the end of her extended arms.

Zivon whirled right, fired his pistol. Spun left, fired again. Two double taps and two soldiers dropped, though Zivon didn't bother watching them fall. Whatever he aimed at, he hit, and whatever he hit, died. Sunrise, sunset. It was inevitable. Problem was, the SVD was no good for close quarters combat in a heavy forest—sight lines were limited and there was a good chance he would snag the barrel on a bush or a limb during a critical moment. Problem two, he only had one magazine for the pistol, a nice Walther PPQ in .45 ACP caliber, with a twelve-round capacity. Four rounds had been expended, leaving him with eight. Problem three, more than eight enemy soldiers surrounded him, collapsing the pocket as if tightening a noose around his neck.

And now they had him zeroed. Nowhere left to run. Or hide.

Zivon dropped a knee to the sandy soil at the base of a whiskery palm. His breathing was even. Calm. Heart rate mildly elevated but dropping as he focused on it. He was at peace with the concept of death. The afterlife held no terror for him as, despite his *babushka*'s attempts to scare religion into him, fear of hell and damnation had never taken root.

He breathed the night air. The ocean breeze cooled the sweat on his body. A crescent moon had risen over the treetops, favoring the world below with its silver light. Men moved in the darkness. Zivon closed his eyes and tuned his ears to the soft scrape of cloth on foliage, the thinnest crunch of sand underfoot . . .

It wouldn't be long before the enemy worked up the nerve for a final rush. For Zivon, that would be the end.

No, he was not afraid to die.

However, Zivon thought as he waited for the final rush, *I plan to take as much company with me as I can possibly manage.*

"What do we do?" Roxy screamed.

Hannah ignored the voice in her ear and keyed the mic at her throat. "Jeang-wu, come in. Zivon. McCurry, come in. One of you fuckers answer me!"

The enemy had drawn tighter around their very tiny little safe space under the tipped-over palm. Both she and Roxy had been grazed more than once by rounds that came too close for comfort or prickled by splinters chopped from the bark of the tree under which they sheltered. Hannah had been unable to raise a single one of her commandos on the radio, leaving her with the suspicion they were dead or otherwise incapacitated.

And running for the ocean was out of the question as well. Any movement up or away from their hiding spot would result in a withering rush of incoming fire, as the puncture through her upper bicep could attest. They were out of room and out of options. As soon as the enemy figured out her ammo was all but gone, they would head in to finish the job.

Hannah reached over and grabbed Roxy's hand. She locked eyes with the Brit and said, "Do you know how to pray?"

One second, Mahoney was standing in front of Bridges with a knife next to his eyeball, and the next he was flying through the air. Bridges had struck faster than a cottonmouth's strike, picking him up with his free hand and slinging him into the wall like a toy. Mahoney's head slammed hard enough to crack the plaster. He slid down onto his butt, his feet next to Britte's head. To say his bell was rung would be severely underestimating the size and power of the *bong* bouncing around between his ears.

"Do you think you can shoot me, little girl?" Bridges stepped over Britte and approached Ella, who was shaking like a scarecrow in a hard wind. He walked up until the muzzle was buried in his chest. "When I took you from your dorm room, you screamed and wet yourself, you were so scared. You begged me not to hurt you, did you not? You cried and cried. *Please don't hurt me, please don't hurt me.*" Bridges spoke in a soothing murmur, his tone at odds with the sneering words. He crept closer and Ella remained frozen, apparently hypnotized by the approaching giant. "And now you have the power of vengeance at your hands. But can you use it? Can you take a life, my little dove?"

Mahoney shook off the cobwebs and put his hands flat on the floor to push himself upright. When he noticed Britte, his insides turned over. Her face had gone slack, and he couldn't tell whether she was breathing or not. One delicate hand rested on the red-soaked pillowcase on her belly, and the other lay limply on the floor, palm up. Rage boiled up from his stomach, and with it, all the fuel he needed to get up. Off the floor. And beat the everlasting shit out of London Bridges and any other of Milos Stankovic's goons left in the building. All he had to do was reach across the spark gap induced by the blow to his head. Seize the anger. Use the fuel.

His vision tunneled out as the bonging sound crescendoed inside his skull.

Not now. Mahoney squeezed his eyes shut and begged every spiritual being who might be in range, from God to Allah to Casper the Friendly Ghost. *Please. Not now. Let me be okay for the next ten minutes and then you can have whatever else of me you want.*

When Mahoney blinked again, Bridges stood over him, Dawali's pistol dangling from his hand. At some point, while Mahoney fought the ringing in his head, Bridges had clearly disarmed Ella and returned, no doubt to finish what he'd started. And there wasn't shit Mahoney could do about it. His hands felt like wooden blocks attached to his arms, and his legs acted like they didn't want any part of anything going at that particular moment.

Bridges crouched down in front of Mahoney and peered at him with concern. "Are you okay, man? Your mouth is moving, but no words are coming out."

"Now that's a first."

Mahoney's head flopped in the direction of the new voice.

"I don't believe I've ever seen Mahoney when he wasn't talking," said Billy McCurry, who was propped with one shoulder against the doorframe. Wetness glistened in a sheet from his chest and down both legs.

That's blood.

"You're blee'ing," Mahoney slurred.

"You should be dead, Navy SEAL," Bridges said, standing up.

"Right on both counts," McCurry said agreeably. Then he raised the rifle in his hands and fire bloomed from the muzzle.

Bridges staggered. He took a step back. But McCurry wasn't finished. He held the HK 416 against his hip and walked a line of bullets from Bridges's crotch to his neck, reseated the weapon and did it again. He kept that pattern going until the bolt locked open and a thin stream of smoke rose from the barrel.

London Bridges fell. He toppled backward and collapsed on top of the corpse of his pal, Onye Dawali. *May they both rest in hell, amen and forever.* Mahoney tried crossing himself and thought it came off pretty well.

"Hoorah," McCurry said. And fell over as well, straight-legged and stiff, like a redwood falling in the forest.

Hannah aimed and fired as the first group of soldiers bounced up and rushed her position. One dropped. Another spun away, and the remaining three went to ground less than twenty meters away. A second group popped up on her left flank and Hannah shifted to squeeze off her last two rounds. She hit nothing, but that group dropped as well.

Then the first bunch was up and running.

"I got nothing left," Hannah admitted.

"Well . . . fuck," Roxy said.

They shared a smile and Hannah said, "It's been real, sweetheart."

"Real shitty, you—"

A sound like the world's largest sheet being ripped in half filled the world with its vibration. A glowing line of fire lanced from the sky and ripped through the oncoming squad like they were paper dolls. Men vanished in pink mists and those who weren't hit directly died from a mere touch of the wrath streaming from the heavens. The streak moved laterally and churned through the position taken by the second squad. Hannah couldn't see the results, but she could picture them well enough.

Over the ringing in her ears came the thumping cadence of rotors. A flight of three helicopters thundered overhead, and more streaks of fire leaped from their sides, burning into the jungle and leaving behind sundered palms and chopped vegetation. A fourth chopper banked over the beach, washing sand into Hannah's eyes and forcing her to cover her face.

The helicopter settled and a single figure disembarked.

Hannah blinked away the grit and her jaw dropped.

Lumbering bearlike through the powdery, blowing sand, a portly man in ill-fitting black tactical loadout skirted the fallen palm and came to stand in front of their tiny redoubt.

Leland Lofland put his hands on his hips and glared. “What fucking part of ‘we’re handling this through channels’ did you not get?”

EPILOGUE

Perla, the day maid, pushed her cart into the lobby and fixed Mahoney with the evil eye. "We have a rat."

"A cat?" Mahoney leaned on the front desk and cupped his ear like he was hard of hearing. "No, we don't have a cat."

"A rat. Room sixteen."

"A rat? Are you sure? Maybe it's a mouse."

"A big rat." She held her hands a foot apart. "This big."

"Maybe a possum. Or a cute, little, furry raccoon. We could name him. Make him a mascot for the motel."

"You need to kill him, Señor Mahoney. I won't clean with a rat."

"Kill him?" Mahoney drew back with a frown. "That seems pretty drastic. What would PETA say? We should trap him and release him in the wild. Besides, are you sure it was a rat?"

"I from Juárez. I know rat."

The door jingled and Mahoney shifted his face into guest check-in mode. The glass doors swung open, and a blond woman entered. The sunlight haloed her cornsilk hair. She was tall, with a swimmer's broad shoulders, and she glided across the floor in a hip-rolling stride that set off a tactical nuclear device in Mahoney's chest. The woman's face was in shadow until she reached the desk and Mahoney waited until he could see the scar bisecting her cheek before he felt the vice around his chest ease a notch.

"Hey," he said.

"Hey back," said Britte Thorpe. Her skin was an almost translucent white, drawn so tightly over her bones, Mahoney thought a small bit of pressure might split the surface. She'd lost weight, too, which gave her an emaciated, half-starved look.

"You're okay then?" he said, almost a whisper.

"I'm okay."

"Lofland said you were, but that bastard lies about what he ate for breakfast."

"He's been very . . . kind."

"He'd better be," Mahoney said. "I'll have his ass fired if not."

Britte laughed, then her expression turned serious. "How is . . . everyone. Siobhan?"

"Siobhan's gonna make it." Mahoney grinned. "Believe it or not, Hannah volunteered to help her with her recovery. Nurse Hannah. Imagine that."

Britte nodded. Her eyes watered and her breath shuddered out. Mahoney anticipated tears at any moment, so he added, "Zivon came out with a wound in his shoulder, but he's tough. He's back to work arranging his screw drawer by size and color. McCurry was touch and go for a while, but I think he'll make it. He looks like death on toast. Hannah and Roxy are good." Mahoney examined his fingernails and added in a small voice, "Jeang-wu showed up without a scratch. He took out about six guys on his own." Mahoney tried on a fixed smile. "And how's your sister? All good?"

"Uh-huh." And suddenly it was Britte's turn to look away.

The warm feeling in Mahoney's belly turned cold. "She's home. With Mama and Daddy. I'm headed there next. Taking it slow and easy, I should be there in a few days."

"Ah."

"Yes. Unless . . ."

Mahoney remained mute for an awkward moment, then his brain engaged. "Perhaps you would like an all-expenses-paid stay at our palatial resort, the fabulous and lovely Cottonmouth Motor Court?"

"It has rat," said Perla, who had finished putting away her cart and was untying the apron from around her waist. "I come back tomorrow. Please. No rat."

Mahoney leaned close and confided to Britte. "It's a raccoon," he whispered. "Don't tell her."

Britte sniffed and swiped the back of her hand across her eyes. "I can stay?"

Mahoney waited for a beat and said, "Well, I could use a new maid. One who doesn't mistake raccoons for rats."

"I heard that!" Perla called out as the door swung closed behind her.

"For the longest time," Britte said in a musing tone, "I belonged to someone else. I was beholden to a man for my identity. For my safety and livelihood, and for everything. Now. It's different. Now I've found value . . . in myself. Do you understand?"

"Yes. I do. Better than you might imagine." He straightened and edged back from the counter. "Well. What do you know about catching raccoons?"

Britte's fluttering smile lasted a second and was gone. Tears tracked her cheeks. "Thank you, Devlin. Thank you for giving me back my life."

"All part of our one-star service, ma'am."

Britte leaned her elbows on the counter, and Mahoney's

mouth dried. His heart fluttered. He did not, for a change, hear a single bell.

"Hey," Britte said. "How did you avoid Lofland's wrath? He refused to say a word except that everyone had gone back to their lives here in Cottonmouth. After all those threats, I thought for sure he would kick everyone out."

"Eh." Mahoney hooked a necklace out from under his collar with his thumb. The chain was platinum, and from the end of it dangled a thick charm in the shape of a coffin. Intricate designs covered the surface. "I now have friends in low places."

Britte's eyes glittered, and she bared her teeth in a wolfish smile. "Tell me you're not doing anything . . . *illegal* to the degenerates in those files. That would be against the Cottonmouth rules."

"Who, me?" Mahoney propped his elbows on the counter and leaned in close. He pitched his voice low and winked. "I would never put a plan in motion to disgrace a US Senator with leaked video footage of him engaged in carnal knowledge outside of marriage."

"Of course you wouldn't."

"Not only would that be against the rules, but Lofland would have a USDA-approved cow. If he found out."

Britte laughed. She caught the back of his head and pulled him into a kiss. When she drew back after a long moment, she stared him deep in his eyes. "So. Tell me. Have you got any vacancies?"

"Hmm, let's see." Mahoney made a show of tapping away at his computer. "Yes, ma'am, our freshly cleaned Raccoon Suite is suddenly available. How long will you be staying?"

Britte's lips curled in a wicked smile. "We'll see, Mahoney. We'll see."